QUEEN OF THE GANGSTERS

STORIES BY MARGIE HARRIS

VOLUME ONE
BROADWALK EMPIRE

edited by
David Bischoff
&
John Locke

Off-Trail Publications
Elkhorn, California

DEDICATION
For our friend Bill Trojan (1948-2011)

SPECIAL ACKNOWLEDGEMENT
To Rob Preston, for pointing the way

Front cover line art by W.C. Brigham from
Gangster Stories, July 1931

QUEEN OF THE GANGSTERS
Volume One: Broadwalk Empire
By Margie Harris

Copyright © 2011, Off-Trail Publications
ISBN 978-1-935031-18-5

OFF-TRAIL PUBLICATIONS
Elkhorn, California

Printed in the United States of America
First printing: December 2011

CONTENTS

— — § — —

Breakfast in Gangland
By David Bischoff

IT'S HARD TO COMPREHEND TODAY how bitter a pill was the American Depression of the 1930s.

After the stock market crashed, and the banks failed, after the jobs were lost and the homes were lost, after the breadlines and the dust bowl, the average American wasn't just angry and broke.

The average American was angry and bored.

I can well remember reading Russell Baker's autobiography *Growing Up* in which he described a Depression-era Baltimore in which people had nothing to do but sit around, smoke cheap cigarettes, drink cheap coffee and talk.

There was the radio, of course, but radios were expensive, so if you didn't have one you had to listen to someone else's. Movies were cheap too, but you couldn't go to the movies every day. And books from the library? Dull as dishwater floating with spud scraps.

Enter the pulp fiction magazines.

Behind garish, colorful colors, these inexpensive magazines not only entertained—but they provided a catharsis for the resentment simmering in the population.

One of the many reasons that pulp magazines are rare these days and highly collectable, is that each copy was probably read by many, many people. Read, perhaps, to shreds. Maybe that's the reason that so many of the '30s gangster pulps are so hard to find now.

Inside were stories not just of blazing action, like the western pulps and the hero pulps. Inside titles such as *Gangster Stories*, *The Underworld*, and *Mobs* were sewage systems of human fury.

One of the best writers of these stories just happened to be a woman. Her name was Margie Harris.

In an era when the women of crime fiction, like Agatha Christie and Ngaio Marsh, tended to prefer polite murders like poisoning, or at least murders offstage, Margie Harris was slamming her typewriter like a machine gun, mowing down good guys and bad guys alike with all sorts of guns, then knifing them and blowing them up—often with metaphysical commentary on the destinations of their damned souls.

Such brash bromides must have been balm for the embattled in that era. After a Margie Harris story, maybe a reader found that life looked just a bit brighter in the real world.

In any case, as we look back at the stories themselves, Margie Harris also turns out to be a kind of Robert E. Howard of these gangster stories, with a literary tang to her talk. If the plots here aren't profound, we nonetheless find all kinds of interesting language and attitudes and color.

In short, these stories have added value experienced in the Twenty-First Century.

Through the work of Margie Harris we peer not down at, but out of the stench of gasoline fumes from sleek Packards barreling down city streets; out of the taste of illegal hooch; out of the thrill of hot jazz blasting over beautiful clothing purchased by racketeering, hijacking, extortion, gambling, prostitution—heck, we glory in the sin of any crime that flips a nickel.

In "Cougar Kitty," Harris shows her claws—and her ease with the gangster patois of the era. Sex and violence ooze from the Argyle Club in Seattle, where Cougar Kitty has taken up residence as hostess at midnight, which "was merely breakfast time in Gangland." But is Kate Dever the moll on the lam from New York—or a Valkyrie in velvet pumps, with a stiletto and an agenda?

James Cagney in all his Celtic ferociousness could not have matched the white heat of "The Night Before Hell's" Spud McGrahan. Spud's been framed. Spud's going to fry in the electric chair for the murder of a cop. But when the real killer, vicious wop Tony Sintonetti, kidnaps the police commissioner's daughter Aileen, Spud shows his true mick cop colors like a berserker on the blood fields of Kilcullen.

With "Hellcat Buys a Stack" we find two veterans of World War I with a bond of loyalty and friendship. When Stanley Chambers is killed, Reginald Kiley—"Hellcat"—tears apart New York City with a shocking viciousness and gat-fire galore.

Rough stuff!

Reading "The Raspberry," you have to wonder if Donald E. Westlake had a pile of gangster pulps off to his side when he wrote the classic Parker novels of the '60s under the name Richard Stark. This is unforgettable high velocity gang warfare. And dollars to donuts you'll never be able to eat raspberry pie again without thinking of that Mills bomb at the end.

The cops in these stories aren't the other side of crime's coin—but they are pretty rough and ruthless. Take Police Captain McGrehan. Got a problem with mean Irish cops? Tough taters, boyo. "While Choppers Roared" is a kettle of corned beef and cabbage you'll need to wash back with a pint of the brown stuff, fer sure. And stock up on Alka Seltzer! Or is that the sound of Tommy guns?

Fans of *Boardwalk Empire* should check out "Angel from Hell." Angel Refkuski is very reminiscent of the killer played by Jack Huston, with half his face gone. Only Angel likes to kill with a gun which shoots nitric acid. A little bit too outrageous even for HBO.

Did you know that "twist" is a '30s gangland term for "girlfriend"? In "Understudy from Hell" Lota Remsden—the Black Moll—is a hard boiled twist. When Lota's guy goes out "on the hot end of a slug," Lota's in charge of his mob. Only there's more twist than one in this tale.

Finally, to round out this grim package, we have "Twisted Vengeance," a story that starts off with a gal named Beulah Allen getting run over by gangster Monk Diller, head of a White Slave ring. But a witness to the killing named "Gimpy" has a surprise for Monk and his henchman in an ending similar to what *Little Caesar* might have looked like if Sam Peckinpah had directed.

Whew! Heady, nasty stuff.

Take one swig at a time and let it settle a bit before you lift the flask again.

Who Was Margie Harris?
By John Locke

THE ORIGINAL VERSION OF THIS PROFILE was written for the Off-Trail collection, *City of Numbered Men: The Best of Prison Stories* (2010), which included Harris' "Big House Boomerang." Readers uniformly agreed that it was the jewel of the collection. Becoming acquainted with Harris and her fiction at that time was part of the reason that this jewel box of Harris stories came into being. We'd like to say that there's been an explosion of Margie Harris scholarship in the last two years and that we can now paint in the missing elements of her tantalizingly thin biography—but such is not the case. Despite an international search effort featuring automatronic bloodhounds parachuted from black helicopters into time machines, only a little new information on Harris' life has surfaced.

Margie Harris was the unlikeliest of gang pulp authors, a woman whose prose was as tough as it comes. Her first known fiction appearance was the novelette "Death's Trapeze" in the May 1930 *Gangster Stories*. For several years, she appeared exclusively in Hersey gang pulps, *Mobs*, *Racketeer Stories*, *Gangland Stories*, *Complete Gang Novel Magazine*, and *Prison Stories*. She eventually provided Hersey with thirty-one stories, most of them long novelettes. Most of her stories featured male protagonists, in the custom of those magazines. Occasionally she used female protagonists, as in, for example, "Cougar Kitty" in this collection.

Through the remainder of the decade, she branched out to other publishers. There were more gang stories—to Spencer's *Gang World*, Carwood's *The Underworld Detective*—but that genre was all but dead. She began appearing in detective pulps like *New Detective*, *Ten Detective Aces*, *Super-Detective*, *Clues*, *The Feds*, etc. When Winford attempted to revive gang pulps in the latter part of the decade, Harris had a brief return to glory in *Double-Action Gang Magazine* and *Ten Story Gang*. Her last known published stories appear in 1939.

Judging strictly from her publishing record, several things stand out. She seems to have been drawn to the pulps by Hersey's gang magazines, as no prior published fiction is known. Their emergence may have given her the "I could do just as well" inspiration to try her hand. She also seems to have come to the field fully formed. She entered writing longer, well-plotted stories; and her prose is more polished than much of the hackwork in the gang pulps.

Harris was, early on, a mystery to Hersey and his readers. The March 1931 *Gangster Stories* included this query: "Is she really a girl, or is she baldheaded and a smoker of corncob pipes like Aunt Patience of the newspapers? Who is she and where does she get her inside dope on Mobs and Molls?" Hersey's response:

> Honest—we haven't an idea ourselves what Margie Harris looks like. We've never seen her. She (?) sends her yarns all the way from Texas. Maybe she's really a cowboy gone wrong; maybe she is he, and has lammed from some burg or some rap. As you say, she certainly (or he certainly) knows plenty about mobs and molls! We gave up long ago. Maybe you can turn dick for us.

Hersey got on the ball and prompted Harris to fill in her background, which led to the following remarkable letter in the June 1931 *Gangster*. It remains the best source of information about her.

> *Dear Ed:*
> A biographical sketch of Margie Harris?
> Scram, Baby; whaddyuh think I am, a canary—yelpin' on myself?
> I got your slant, though, somebody's maybe asked "Who's this frail who cracks wise from the inside?"
> Just another twist, sisters and brothers—maybe, but look out for my lipstick. You know some of the sugar Molls carry one for their own use, one for "the other jane"—and that one has cyanide in it. So look out for my lipstick, too.
> How did I get that way? Maybe newspaper work; maybe just associates. I never got a dirty deal from a "digger" or a gambler in my life. I've had plenty from the other kind.
> I've known some great guys. I interviewed Tiger Jake Seidenwand after he'd done four years "solitary" in San Quentin. I wrote a Sunday Mag. series on Sontag and Evans, the California bandits; Morel, their waiter-partner used to be my pal. I met Charlie Becker at the Sausalito ferry the day he got out of San Quentin after the Crocker National Bank forgery. The Bankers' Association hired him at $500 a month as a bad-check expert—and to make him be good.
> In Chicago, I "palled" with Jim Colosimo and his wife, Dale Winter, before somebody shot Jim out from inside his shirt. Mossy Enright, Ike Bloom—Wise Guy of the South Side—Dion O'Bannion; I knew 'em all. And on the other side, Maclay Hoyne, the Chi. district attorney. Ike Bloom taught me how to "stack" Canfield solitaire and how to run up the big mitt in poker.
> I've flitted from Coast to Coast—border to border, and across. I know Tia Juana, Mexicali, Juarez, Laredo, Reynosa and Matamoras like a country boy knows the way to town. Maybe I know more mokkers and lollygows than senators, more frails than Vanderbilts—but I like 'em.

And it's nice to write yarns for you inquiring ones—and the rest, too. I'm not going to tell you whether what I write saves my life by providing food, or what I don't write saves my life because I'm trusted. Two guesses. You can have 'em both.

Somebody asked if I ever wore a badge. Witness declines to state at advice of attorneys. Anyway, I haven't one now, and nobody has my fingerprints.

I know a slue of coppers too. Some of 'em I've liked; others, not so good. Among these is the New Orleans dick who said: "Quit writing them crook yarns, girlie; whyn't you try goin' straight?"

Maybe your mother and sister wouldn't like me—but I could show sister how to build a Mickey Finn.

Anyway, I try to be regular. I never turned up a pal in my life. A crippled grifter can take me for my back hair, but when they get a hypocritical reformer on the rack, I'll trample a lot of folks to get in and give the wheel one good twist on my own account.

I'm not "nice," nor am I "awful." But I'll bet four seeds I know a better story than YOU for I've made Broadway George laugh and he's the undertaker's assistant who told the first Pat-and-Mike story.

Anyway, thanks for being interested.

                                                         Margie Harris.

The letter dovetails neatly with our deductions. Her journalism background and acquaintance with criminals and underworld figures made her a natural candidate for the gang pulps. Some possible experience in law enforcement may have given her additional perspective. It's hard to tell from the letter, though, whether she's being cagey from sincere motives, or simply to create a mystique for her readers.

Apart from the scattered travels she alludes to, her discoverable background breaks into two periods, California and Chicago. The names which she assumes are familiar to readers of the '30s, are not so well-known today. But pinning down their records gives an idea of when she may have lived in their respective areas.

From the California period, San Quentin prisoner Tiger Jake Seidenwand appears to be the notorious murderer, Jacob Oppenheimer, also known as the "man-tiger," "the human tiger," or "the prison tiger." Serving a fifty-year sentence, he was moved from Folsom to San Quentin in 1898. After attacking prison guards, his sentence was upgraded to solitary confinement for life. He was confined to a cell above San Quentin's jute mill, which figures so prominently in "Big House Boomerang." By 1911, Oppenheimer was back at Folsom, where he was executed in 1913. Harris' interview would have to have been sometime between 1903 and 1911. Seidenwand and Oppenheimer aren't remotely similar names, but that doesn't preclude a memory error on

Harris' part. At any rate, no Jake Seidenwand could be found.

John Sontag and Christopher Evans were two railway robbers of the San Joaquin Valley who faced off against law enforcement in a bloody battle on June 11, 1893. Sontag died as a result of the wounds received. Evans recovered from his own wounds and received a life sentence. "Morel" was Edward Morrell who busted Evans out of the Visalia jail after the trial. Evans was recaptured and eventually released in 1911. He died in 1917. Morrell served sixteen years of a life sentence in Folsom and San Quentin, resided in solitary confinement near Jake Oppenheimer, published a book about Oppenheimer in 1912, and went on the lecture circuit to talk of his experiences from the point of view of a prison reformer. He died in Los Angeles in 1946. Harris' Sunday articles sound more like a retrospective than firsthand reporting.

Charles Becker, the "King of Forgers," was released from San Quentin on September 28, 1903 after serving four-and-one-half years.

From the Chicago period, Vittorio "Big Jim" Colosimo was the boss of Chicago's Levee district. Dale Winter started out in Chicago as a singer in Colosimo's Café. Big Jim divorced his wife and married the beautiful Dale. A week after returning from the honeymoon, on May 11, 1920, Big Jim was murdered in his restaurant, a crime that was never solved. Dale became a stage actress.

Maurice E. "Mossy" Enright, the labor czar of Chicago, was murdered on February 3, 1920. Isaac "Ike" Gitelson Bloom was a power in Chicago Democratic politics; he died December 15, 1930. Dion O'Bannion, known as the "King of the Beer Runners," was shot to death in his Chicago florist's shop on November 10, 1924. Maclay Hoyne served as Cook County State's Attorney for two terms, 1912-20; he died October 1, 1939.

"Broadway George" couldn't be identified.

No journalist, male or female, could be discovered to thread the California and Chicago periods. Complicating the search, bylines were not commonly given to news articles in those days.

If Harris was a journalist in California right after the turn of the century, and we also assume she was young at that time, a birth date around 1880 makes a plausible estimate. Given that, she would have been about fifty when she started appearing in the gang pulps.

Her fiction publishing record is fairly consistent throughout the '30s, but slows down slightly in 1938-39. She'd made a handful of appearances in Standard's *Thrilling Detective* and *Popular Detective*. Her last known published story was "Problem for a Ranger," an eighteen-pager in the December 1939 *Popular Detective*.

As noted by Hersey, Harris' earliest known whereabouts during this period were in Texas. In 1932, Hersey sold off his magazine assets to another outfit, which published under several imprints, including the Artvision Publishing Company. They continued *Gangster Stories* as *Greater Gangster Stories*. Harris continued as a featured author, providing another nine sagas. Artvision also started a true-crime magazine, *American Detective*. Harris was a contributor here as well (as was another *Gangster* notable, Anatole Feldman). She provided at least seven articles; the earliest known in the October 1934 issue; the latest in October 1937. All seven involve crimes set in Texas. Three were set in Houston; three others were set in Orange, Dallas, and Milburn, ranging from one hundred to two hundred and fifty miles from Houston. "Problem for a Ranger" takes for its setting a fictional Texas town near the Mexican border. We conclude that Harris lived in Texas for the entirety of her pulp-writing career, probably in the vicinity of Houston.

Evidence of her whereabouts before or after the '30s, other than her letter, has not surfaced. It's very likely that "Margie Harris" was a penname; and that further information on her life awaits discovery of her actual name.

Stories by
Margie Harris

"Cougar Kitty"

A mystery night club queen, with a look of death in her eyes and a little black book filled with names . . . a steadily shorter list!

SEATTLE, QUEEN CITY OF THE NORTHWEST, gleaming like a great, white jewel on rising ground overlooking Elliott Bay, is a city beautiful. There roses bloom the year around. There men and women live and love and die, far from the tenements and slums of the great Eastern cities.

But in Seattle lies hidden one canker spot. It is the district below Yesler Way, which is the sole blot on the city's fair escutcheon. There is to be found the last remaining trace of those other days when lumberjacks from the woods and miners from Alaska came whooping forth with gold-filled hands, demanding of Life those things of which they had been deprived.

"Below Yesler" is evil, and of all the evil things within its purlieus, none is more depraved, more terrible in the minds of the decent and law-abiding than the underworld cabaret and speakeasy operated for nearly two decades by "Scar" Argyle. There gathered waterfront thugs, gangsters, racketeers, gunmen.

Most fearsome of all, to the uninitiated, was its proprietor. His face was thoroughly repulsive. A great red seam led from the stiff hair above his left temple and down across the bridge of his nose. It ended at the right jawbone after creasing the cheek deeply. In healing it had drawn the flesh so that the mouth seemed cast in a permanent sneer. The right eye was so affected that half of the lower eyelid turned down, gleaming redly.

That was Scar's reminder that he once had double-crossed "Nigger George," a piano player. True, Scar had seen to it that there was an early funeral in George's personal social circle, but the razor slash had put a permanent end to whatever was delightful, either in countenance or disposition, of Argyle. Now he was a leering, gross mountain of fat. For hours he would sit, seemingly without movement, his piggish black eyes searching, always searching for new methods of vile profit.

On a bright afternoon in March, Scar sat cursing his luck, his failing patronage and most of all the police of his precinct. Their increasing demands for graft and favors bade fair to turn his once prosperous business into a losing venture.

Only that day he had received a shipment of liquor and had paid his "delivery charge" to the policeman on the beat without demur. Later he had sent to the precinct captain the usual weekly payment for protection. Now, within the last four hours, four sergeants had slipped in to see him.

One had compelled him to buy four tickets for a police ball. The next had asked for two quarts of prime liquor "for the lieutenant." Number Three asked for a couple of drinks and then borrowed five dollars.

The fourth brought the crowning blow. With him came a stranger—a supposed friend. Scar had been bullied into cashing a twenty dollar check for this man. He tore it up after they left. Too many such had bounced back from his bank. Truly the lot of an underworld cabaret owner was trouble filled.

The side door bell rang as Scar cogitated on his woes, and the doorman turned to say:

"Lady to see youse, Scar. Good looker!"

"Hell, let her in!" Scar almost spat the words. "Probably a hen cop with another touch; they're all that have overlooked me this week."

His eyes brightened, however, as a modishly gowned, athletic appearing girl stepped through the door and looked unconcernedly about her. Few such had been there since the days of the gold rush. When her eyes encountered his, Scar beckoned. She walked to the table and took a place opposite him.

"Pat Jennings told me to see you," she said confidentially. "My name is Kate Dever. I'm on the lam from New York—witness in a gang killing, which means a year in the sticks for me. Jennings says you need a hostess to pep up your game; I need a job. Also I know my stuff, Big Boy, and the jack

I can make for you will be nobody's business. I'll have to do it in my own way, though; no buttinskys."

As Argyle stared suspiciously at her, the girl dropped her coat from her shoulders and removed a close-fitting hat. Scar's eyes lighted as a throat and shoulders a Diana might have envied, were revealed. He grunted in renewed admiration as the dim lights outlined a beautiful, resolute face and a frame of dark-red hair, well kept and bobbed in the latest mode.

"Hell, kid," Scar burst forth breathlessly. "Sure! You're fixed fer life."

The tone, the gleam in his eyes, made his meaning all too clear. Kate Dever did not seek to evade his burning glance.

"Yes?" she queried coldly. "You wouldn't kid a little girl, would you, Scar? You think you want me? Then come and take me."

The man lurched to his feet with a speed surprising in one of his bulk and clawed at her in an awkward attempt to draw her into his arms. One hand fixed itself on her shoulder. Before he could do more, she sprang up, thrusting with both hands against his chest.

Scar stumbled backward a step and the girl slipped out from behind the table. In her hand, seemingly juggled out of thin air, was a gleaming Spanish dagger, needle-pointed and with a blade almost paper thin. Scar eyed the knife; noted that it was held in the thrusting position—and that the point was aimed directly at his stomach. His arms dropped to his side in token of surrender.

"What th' hell do you think—?" he began thickly.

Kate, smiling now, resumed her seat.

"Oh, sit down, stupid," she said quietly. "Sit down and buy me a drink. You had to learn it some time—and right at first is the best time. Remember this hereafter. I'm no man's woman. Any man who puts his hands on me gets hurt. I know how to take care of myself morning, noon and night—also vacations. Now how about the job?"

Scar had signaled for a waiter, who brought whiskey. Scar gulped down a huge portion. Kate poured a few drops in a glass with ginger ale and tossed it off.

"My first and last drink in your place," she said. "If I work here I'm served tea for whiskey, distilled water for gin and sparkling cider instead of what you call champagne. And Lord help the waiter who brings me anything else!"

Here was a new type to Scar. A beautiful woman who dared to come to his own joint and flout him when the odds were all his way, would be an asset. He visioned the returning trade when the word went out through the underworld that the Argyle Club had a new hostess who could not be "made."

"You've got the job," he said decisively. "Seventy-five a week and a piece of the profits over the first thousand. That's about what I'm doin' now."

"Big-hearted Scar!" Kate mocked him. "Hundred a week, five per cent of the gross—and I start tonight."

About to protest, Scar thought better of it and extended his hand for the underworld shake of acceptance. Instead, Kate turned sidewise, circled his arm with her left, caught the knuckles of his fist with her right and bent the member downward. Scar grinned. It was the gangster method of making the sucker loosen up from whatever he held.

"Know your grapes, don't you?" he chuckled. "Well, I've loosened for a yard and five per cent a week, so be here at eight. Wanna little advance?"

Kate opened her purse and smiled. A wad of yellow-backed bills had been thrust in there loosely.

"No, thanks," she replied sweetly. "A nice old gentleman on the train attended to that for you. Somehow he got off at the next station; the conductor put him off. He tried to get into my berth."

"Onto all the games, hey?" Scar queried. "Now, what's your deal?"

"What are you using?" she countered, looking about at the small stage and the orchestra stand.

"Pretty fair nigger string band, six dancin' girls who double as drink grafters and cigarette girls, an' a good boy hoofer. You sing, kid?"

"Nor dance," Kate replied. "I work from the floor; out where the money jingles and the saps need encouraging. Leave it to me, Big Fellow, and don't mind later on if I make some changes."

Scar nodded perplexedly.

"It's O.K. by me, girlie," he replied, "but leave Little Laura on th' job if you can. She's a good little guy—kinda fond of me. And by the way, kid, what's your moniker? Got one?"

Kate looked him squarely in the eye and said:

"They call me 'Cougar Kitty'—better let that spread around a little."

"She mountain lion, huh?" Scar mused. "Damn if they ain't right."

Midnight in Scar's cabaret was merely breakfast time in Gangland.

Kate, resplendent in a gold sequin gown which cast forth points of light in every direction as she moved, sat chatting with Scar at a table near the orchestra. With them, snuggled close against the proprietor's bulk, was the cigarette girl, Little Laura. She was a big-eyed, wistful child woman of the clinging type, but except when she looked at Scar, there was a hard little glitter in her eyes.

Scar had said she was "kinda fond" of him. Strangely enough, Kate reflected, there seemed reason for the statement. Between the big-eyed girl and the gross flesh-mountain of villainy there existed some bond. When he spoke to the girl, Scar's tone was gentle and as nearly affable as it could be. Laura was serious in her talk with him and actually seemed to enjoy his elephantine pawings.

The grapevine telegraph of the underworld had carried the news of Scar's new attraction. Already the tables had filled with a swaggering crew of gangsters, sleek haired, gorgeously dressed young gunmen, and here and there older men—cold of eye, and each seemingly determined to sit so as to face the door.

Many brought their molls and, because a thug's standing is measured by the appearance of his woman, they made a brave showing of costly garments and gleaming jewels. Only those older men, the square jawed poachers in the Land of Rackets, were alone. They hunted among the ranks of the hostesses and entertainers.

Presently Kate caught Scar's eye and nodded. He had his orders and when he lumbered to his feet and stopped the music, everyone became quiet.

Scar was about to make a speech! Usually he contented himself with howling, profane comments from his chair by the orchestra.

"Listen, guys and molls," he rumbled. "Seattle ain't so big as Noo York, but she's just as lively, and when it comes to givin' you the best in ent'tainment, Scar Argyle's the boy to do it. From now on, the Argyle Club's the live spot here. And I now takes pleasure in int'ducin' to you Miss Kate Dever—knowed mostly as 'Cougar Kitty,' our new hostess."

Kate, self-possessed as her namesake in the home nest, walked to a place beside him and smiled brightly. Prolonged hand-clapping and a few cheers greeted her.

"I am glad to be here," she said, "and I want one and all of you for my best pals. Scar Argyle has given me the right to do what I please for your entertainment. The word hereafter is 'Go as far as you like, as fast as you like, so long as you keep fairly quiet—and so long as you don't get fresh with the new hostess.' "

New applause burst forth and Kate nodded to the orchestra. Instantly a mad, jazzing dance number flared forth. Some derisive laughs had greeted Kate's reference to herself and some of the bolder of the young cannons left their tables to gather around her.

Scar was watching, fascinated. Kate dismissed the pleas of dance partners one by one, until Speedball Kane, a leader among the gunmen and handsome in a wild, boyish fashion, clasped her about the waist. He fell into a dance step and tugged. The smile never left her face.

Suddenly her hands came up apparently to hold him off, but instead they caught both of his shoulders firmly. At the same moment she stepped forward with the speed of a striking reptile. She thrust her toe back of his left heel, then pushed him backward with all her surprising strength.

Though he was a rough-and-tumble fighter trained on the docks, Speedball had not expected the reverse back-heel from a handsomely gowned night hostess. The backward thrust was too powerful, the fulcrum supplied by her foot too far below his center of balance to be resisted.

The gangster crashed to the floor on his shoulders. A split-second later his head collided with the maple with a resounding thump. A roar of laughter followed. It stilled a few seconds later when the young tough failed to rise. Two of his friends moved toward him.

"Leave him there," Kate commanded coldly. "I want him to come to there so he'll realize that he's to keep his hands off me in future. I'm no better than he is—but I'm as good—and when I want a man's hands on me, I'll ask him to put them there."

Speedball stirred, blinked, dragged himself to his knees. Then his glance swept upward and encountered the gleeful eyes of Cougar Kitty. He shook his head and looked about. On every hand he saw the awe-stricken eyes of his friends. Instantly a dull red suffused his face. He gathered his muscles for a leap at the mocking girl before him.

"Damn you—" he began. Then the words choked in his throat and his eyes went wide with surprise.

Kate's right hand was extended toward him. A dull ring of blued steel peeped out between her second and third fingers; the whole hand was tightening on something within her palm. Too well Speed knew what that meant.

For Cougar Kitty was holding in her plump, beringed hand one of the dwarfed, vicious little plunger guns of Gangland. It was a mere ring of metal extending out of a firing chamber, back of which was a trip plunger which released the pin against a solitary bullet of heavy caliber.

Speed could be forgiven for pausing. The one-inch barrel was trained directly on his forehead. A child could not miss at that distance. The crook teetered on his feet uncertainly. Then a girl's voice cut the silence:

"Slap the broad down, Speed," it said. "Don't spoil a good notion."

Kate smiled bleakly and waved Speed back to his place. Then came a muffled roar and gray smoke curled from between her fingers.

She had fired the weapon into the floor as the best means of squaring Speedball against later accusations of cowardice. Everyone leaped up; all had some question to ask.

Kate held the still smoking weapon above her head.

"Sorry, boys and girls," she said. "I hate to pull off rough stuff on our first evening together—but I had him covered—plenty. I had to let you know I meant it when I said: 'Don't get fresh with the new hostess.' All right? Well, let's play again."

She motioned to the goggling bandsmen to continue playing. Then, under cover of the opening notes, she walked straight to where Speedball was struggling into his light overcoat. He felt alone, disgraced in the eyes of the other gangsters and their molls. The red of shame colored his face, but about his mouth was the deadly white line which marks the killing rage in man.

Everyone was watching openly. Kate moved as one who has decided on a definite course. Speed jerked his coat into place and clapped his hat down over his eyes. She was at his side now, hand extended.

"Sit down, Speed," she said in a tone intended for his ears alone. "If you go out now, you'll leave these others laughing. Be nice and I'll make it all jake for us both. Now shake hands like a sport and tell me it's all right—even if you did start it."

Speed took her hand, shook it heartily and grinned. Too well he knew it was his only course. Unless there was more to add to the story, Gangland would be yelping taunts at him for months to come. Maybe, he reflected, he could turn the tables on this wise broad from New York if he was crafty.

"I'm game; speak your piece," he half whispered. "But don't figure to start nothin' more."

"Be your age," she replied. "Now, listen, Speed, I'm starting a new racket here and I need at least one friend on whom I can depend. You made me tangle with you before your friends, but I didn't ask you to. Now, we can be the best of friends, and at the same time I'll show you how to get yourself some good out of it.

"I've heard about you. They call you 'Speedball' because you drive the stickups and hijackers away so far and so fast, they have to wait ten minutes before they start to make an alibi. What?"

Such tribute to his unerring efficiency at the wheel of a getaway car caused the young gangster to flush happily. Maybe here was a woman worth hanging about after.

"No," Kate went on as though reading his thoughts, "you don't mean any more to me than any other man, but if you wish, I'll let you be my Number One Pal. We'll play around together and sometimes you can take me home—as far as the door.

"What I want of you is to keep them off my back if things get rough— nothing more. If the others see us palling around together we'll be accused of having fallen for one another. Now, say it. Want to play, or will you put on the funny hat and coat and go out and get yourself laughed at? First and last chance, boy."

"Sure, Kitty, I'll play," he answered, "just to square myself."

"Speedball and I are all made up 'n' everything," Kate announced to the watching crowd. "And now I want you all to walk past here in line and shake hands with us both. Then we'll all be the best kind of pals. Scar will buy a drink for the house, and I'll show you the latest New York racket."

She was exerting herself now, putting into her simple little speech and almost childish plan of personal contact with each, all of the hard won personality she possessed. She let her eyes flicker toward Scar. He sat there, a contented mountain of evil, literally drooling over the manner in which she was earning the attention of his patrons.

The idea struck the gangsters and their molls favorably. There was an instant rush to get into line. Speed fell into place beside Kate as the orchestra struck up a slow drag march. The head of the line moved forward. Kate had a bright smile, a word, a nod for each. One plump patron found himself being prodded in the ribs. Another laughed when Kate flicked his tie from under his vest. One pretty girl simpered when Kate whispered: "Gosh, kid! I'm jealous of you—you're so darn lovely."

Scar came to his feet as the last of the line passed and bellowed for the drinks. Kate held up her hand for silence.

"Wait, please," she said. "Will the tall gentleman in dinner clothes, the one at the last table—you, handsome—; the girl with the black hair and the red dress; the man who left his hair at home but wore a horseshoe pin in his tie—and you, Mister Red Necktie—all please come forward?"

The four responded somewhat sheepishly.

"I want you to search my new pal, Speedball," Kate said smilingly. "I think he's turned dip. Look in his left, outside pocket."

Speedball did not wait to be searched. He felt in the pocket himself and gaspingly brought forth a watch, attached to which was a fine chain and gold key; a gold mesh coin purse wrapped in a handkerchief, a diamond stickpin and a thin, but costly, cigarette case.

The crowd roared with laughter at Speed's consternation. No other group could appreciate better what had happened. None had even a remote suspicion of the youth. He was a known gunman and gangster, and as such, he looked down on the dip as dips in turn look down on doormat thieves.

Kate waited until there was a measure of silence.

"That's one of the New York night club tricks," Kate laughed as she restored the property to its owners. They get you all hot and bothered over something that's happening and then the waiters and house dips put the vacuum to you. One man swore somebody'd stolen his underwear while he waited to kiss a toe dancer whose number he'd drawn in a lottery!"

"What a dame," someone croaked admiringly. "She's oke for me," another chimed in. For minutes the place buzzed with admiration for Kate's deftness. Scar bought for the house. The two losers of property would not be outdone in generosity and the girl in red, whose coin purse was restored, argued her boy friend into loosening up as well.

It was daylight when the last patron left. That was Speedball, who had waited for Kate. She dismissed him with a shake of her head.

"See you tonight, pal," she said. "And wear your rod."

When Scar counted up, he found a take for the night of $900.

Cougar Kitty was an established institution in Seattle's underworld.

As she walked to the corner of First Avenue to catch a cab, Kate noticed one of the waiters slipping from door to door behind her. As she entered the taxi, she saw him sprint forward and flag down another.

"Drive around for half an hour," she told the driver. He nodded joyously at such luck at the beginning of his day's work. Kate, sitting in the center of the rear seat, used her compact mirror to watch the street behind her. She was not mistaken, the other car was dawdling along half a block behind her.

"Keep ahead and when you get a chance pretend to try to lose a cab that's following us," Kate told the driver, putting a folded bill into his hand. "Then when you get a chance, make him pass you and cut him off at the curb. I want to talk to his passenger."

The driver looked at the bill and smiled knowingly. "I'll have him in two blocks," he said.

At the next corner he slipped along the right hand curb until traffic changed for east-and-west travel. Then he meshed his gears and swung right up the hill to Second Avenue, going at a furious pace in low gear.

At First Avenue he turned south again and stopped with a shrieking of brakes just past the building line. In a few moments the other cab charged up the hill and turned right also.

"Get him!" Kate commanded. Her driver swung wide from the curb, ran even with the other cab and forced it slowly but surely against the curbing despite the other driver's shrill curses and the sounds of his horn.

A policeman ran up. "Here!" he demanded. "What's goin' on?"

Kate opened the cab door and smiled at the officer.

"The man in the other cab has been following me all over town," she said, "and I wish to prefer a charge against him, if you please, officer."

The policeman dragged the luckless waiter from the cab by his collar.

"Tell me about it," he demanded of Kate.

"He works at Scar Argyle's," she replied. "I was there for awhile and when I left this fellow got in another cab and followed me."

But great was the power of Scar in policedom.

"I wouldn't do that, lady," the officer replied. "You go on about your business and I'll keep this baby here. If you have him pinched, you got to go to court."

"All right, officer—and thanks," Kate said as her cab moved off.

It was late afternoon when Kate emerged from her tiny apartment in a huge building on the shores of Lake Union to go abroad again in a taxicab.

Her first stop was at the office of *The Hour*, greatest of the city's newspapers. Largess properly distributed to a reception clerk and office boy bought her way into the paper's morgue of photographs and clippings.

A chubby, partly deaf statistician was in charge. His sole desire seemed to be to prevent any intrusion into his domain. A five dollar bill again wrought wonders and soon Kate was deep in a huge envelope of clippings out of the "H" file.

When she departed, the attendant also dumped out the clippings and studied them.

"Humph!" he grunted. "Now I wonder?"

From the newspaper office she drove to a tall building given over to plastic surgeons, beauticians and hair dressers. One of the latter "touched up" the roots of her dark-red hair. A dermatologist on the floor above injected a white liquid under her skin at the temple, massaged it, and said:

"Lay a good cold-cream base under the powder. When you are ready I will radium-peel your face and we'll hide that scar entirely."

"Thanks, doctor," she replied. "But I'm a busy girl now."

Dinner at one of the better cafés, a picture show afterward and then Kate took a cab to the Argyle Club where she found a deferential corps of barmen and waiters ready to extend her a grinning welcome. Also she found the place well filled. Her name and fame had spread rapidly among the cannons and molls of South of Yesler.

Scar too waved a warm welcome. She walked to his side in response to a beckoning finger.

"Where you livin', kid?" he demanded. "It's a police regulation, you know." He produced a soiled memorandum book and a stub of pencil expectantly.

"Find out like you tried to this morning," Kate jeered, but she softened the taunt with an amused smile.

"That's a bet!" Scar replied. "Think I can't, huh?" He was in nowise disconcerted.

"Not by using a waiter for a gumshoe, anyway," Kate replied, seating herself at his table. "What did it cost you to get him loose?"

"Crook of me finger," Scar jeered in turn. "The bulls don't want none of my boys."

"Right, Scar. Now tell me, how did you like my stuff last night? Shall I keep it up?"

"That's what I hired you for." Scar was becoming wary now.

"Then we'll have a novelty night once each week, beginning tonight. You know what I mean? Funny light flashes, contests with everybody doing goofy things like they do at highbrow parties? Get everybody into it and the losers have to buy. Get the idea?"

"The dump's yours from now to closin' time. Take it apart if you want to."

Kate rose, smoothed down her skirt, and said casually.

"By the way, I ordered a regular stage electrician to be here at 11 o'clock to handle the lights. He's bringing a dimmer; the rest we'll do with the master switch."

"Bring two," said Scar grandly, "or three—if he's triplets. Keep on getting in the jack and you can hire the devil himself."

"No need, Scar old thing," Kate laughed. "He's here already—and wearing your union suit."

Scar grunted happily, the nearest to a laugh of which he was capable.

"Wrong," he said. "Mine's two-piece."

Meanwhile Kate was going from table to table, welcoming the friends of the night before and newcomers, attracted by the news of the tiger-girl hostess at the Argyle Club.

The bleak-faced victim of the pocket-picking episode of the previous night was back at his usual table in a corner across from the orchestra and not more than three feet distant from Scar's customary seat. As Kate stopped before him, he stared at her searchingly.

"Did I ever see you before?" he asked suddenly.

"Surely you did," she laughed. "I'm King Tut's daughter. Remember how you used to hold my hand under the purple Egyptian skies—or what have you?"

"Can the jokes," the man snapped. "I'm serious."

"Oh-h-h!" Kate said derisively, "so, Mister Kinney, racketeer-in-chief and Big Fixer mustn't be kidded by a night club hostess."

"Drop it!" the man snarled. "Forget that name here. It's 'Hanson' now. What the— Say, did you know me in Detroit?" With the question he snatched at her wrist, his fingers pinching deep into her flesh.

The girl did not reply, nor did she wince. Instead she leaned slightly forward, bringing her sneering, ice hard glance on a level with his own.

"All right, Kinney-Hanson," she said, and there was a deadly chill in her tones. "Don't move that other hand. I can get you before you ever could touch your gun—and believe me, it'll be one big pleasure to do it."

Hanson's hard eyes searched hers angrily. The smile clung to her lips but he recognized the basilisk expression of the natural killer seeking the slightest excuse to slay. Yet he held to her wrist, trying to probe her mind—to find some reason for such bitter hatred from the mere touch of his hand.

"Let go!" Kate rapped the words out venomously. "I said last night that nobody is permitted to touch me. If I let you get away with it, then I'm sunk here." Then, in a louder tone for the benefit of those nearby, she said airily:

"Unhand me, vill-yun—and when are you going to buy a drink?"

Hanson's steely fingers relaxed. He gestured to a seat across the table.

"You're a nice, pleasant little thing," he said sarcastically, "but tell me what you want to drink—and all about Detroit."

"Champagne," Kate replied with a disarming smile. "Detroit? No, I don't know much about things there. A girl friend of mine was married to a boy named Wilbur Bealey—'Wib the Gun,' they called him. He was mixed up in a booze running gang, and soon after I left there he was killed. Someone said his own gang finished him."

"Know him pretty well?" Hanson demanded.

"Oh, in a way," Kate replied nonchalantly. "Daisy, his wife, was an old sidekick of mine, but Wib was away most of the time when I was visiting her."

"Who else did you know there?" Hanson continued.

"Let me see—why, you were there! I saw you out at a Grosse Pointe roadhouse the night Merrill Orrum, the criminal lawyer, was killed."

Hanson's eyes were pinpoint lights of green now, but his poker face did not change. Quietly he produced a cigarette and lighted it. Kate noted that the hand which held the ornate gold lighter did not tremble.

He let a thin cloud of smoke drift from his mouth and Kate felt his eyes studying her critically. Her expression was bored, a trifle uninterested.

"Ah yes, Merrill Orrum," he said musingly. "I'd forgotten his name. And by the way"—he almost hissed the words—"how does it happen that you, a stranger, remember it? That was a whole year ago."

"Oh, I don't know," she shrugged her shoulders as though tired of the subject. "Probably it was because it was an unusual name and the papers said they—the other mobsmen—called him 'Mary Lorum' for a nickname, sort of a pun name. Things like that stick in one's mind, don't you think so?"

"Not so you'd notice it," Hanson replied quickly. "You haven't told me all of it. Damn it, you remind me of someone—"

"Some dizzy blonde from over the river in Windsor probably," Kate suggested teasingly. Hanson's eyes narrowed to mere slits.

"Blonde!" he said explosively. "What do you know about a blonde in Detroit?"

Kate laughed merrily.

"Listen, Big Boy," she replied, "What I know about all Detroit blondes is plenty. Did poor, little Hansy-Hanson get all mixed up with a fuzzy yellow-head?"

Hanson flared up again at the derisive note in her voice.

"Hell with her!" he growled. "I fixed her up good and plenty; don't worry. But it's you I'm wondering about. What're you holding out on me?"

"What would you give to know?"

"Nothing or a lot; I don't know which. I've got a hunch about you, Miss Cougar Kitty whatsyourname, and the first thing you know I'll be calling the turn on you. Don't figure me for a dumbbell."

"Do your prettiest, Big Boy," she replied as she rose. "And if you guess right—you'll have something coming to you. I said—'you'll have something coming to you'!"

She accented each of the drawled words. Hanson caught a note of menace in her voice; frowned as he watched her retreating form and sought for the answer to the riddle.

He motioned to Scar to come over.

"Where'd you get that damned twist?" he said in a low tone. "She just called the turn on me in Detroit—cracked about 'Wib the Gun,' and that lousy mouthpiece, Orrum."

Scar grinned knowingly.

"She's a wise head," he husked. "Doin' all right here and maybe'll stand a little watchin'. If she gets flossy she'll go for a ride—but I ain't worryin' none about her. Don't you, neither."

Further conversation ended with the entrance of Speedball Kane.

"Whoopee!" Kate sang out. "Solomon in all his glory! Lookit the boy friend!"

Speed was attired in his first dinner clothes. His broad shoulders filled the pinch waisted coat perfectly. He had been shaved, pomaded and massaged into the condition of pink shininess which in Gangland is accepted as perfection.

It is true that he hitched once at the harness of his shoulder holster, but in Argyle Club circles that meant no more than button-fiddling meant in the higher walks of life.

"Everybody give the dressed-up boy friend a hand!" Kate demanded. The guests obliged. "Boy friend and I will buy a drink now." She continued. There was more applause. Kate drew Speed to a place near the orchestra.

"Speed is to be associate master of ceremonies tonight," she continued. "So I told him to bring his rod. His job is to see that everybody does just what I tell them to. We're going to raise hell tonight and put a chunk under it, but we can't do it unless everybody helps. The first number will be a button busting contest, with Scar Argyle leading off."

"Huh?" Scar grunted in amazement. "Run your own damn show."

"Burn him down, Speed, if he don't mind," Kate laughed. "Oh come on, chief, it's easy. Draw a big breath, lean against the inside of the old vest and see what happens. Snap into it, dearie, take a big breath and do your stuff."

Scar's mind dealt largely in cash-register terms. Kate had said the loser would buy the drinks. Very well, then, the idea was for him not to lose.

Slowly he inflated his huge chest. His cheeks began to purple as he set his muscles and began to expand. Quickly the vast mountain of fat and muscle pressed outward. An audible "pop" followed and a button tinkled on a glass table top across the room.

"One!" cheered Kate. As she spoke there were three other "pops." "Two, three, four!" she counted. "Don't anybody wisecrack. If Scar laughs now he'll undress himself." The final button held but tore its way through the buttonhole.

"Fine!" Kate exclaimed. "Four buttons and one buttonhole. Now, who's next?"

Several of the gunmen patrons went into a huddle. Presently 'Shanty' Boles turned and said:

"Us four's buyin' for th' house, Kitty. Name it an' we pays. Dat's cheaper'n buyin' new vests!"

"Lovely!" Kate responded. "Did someone tell me Shanty wasn't bright?"

As the round of drinks was being served, the electrician touched Kate's arm and told her the dimmer was connected.

"Don't test it," she ordered, "just follow up the orders I gave you. Everybody out now," she demanded, turning to the patrons. "There's another surprise for you. We start off with a march around the room. When the lights go out, drop your partner and take the girl ahead of you for a partner. That leaves an extra man and he goes to the end of the line.

"When the orchestra stops playing, everybody buys a drink for the girl with him. Remember now—no cheating or hitting in the clinches."

The orchestra struck up a jazz march and the patrons, hard-boiled thieves and killers playing a "kid" game for the first time in their lives, began to parade about the room. Kate nodded and the electrician pulled the main switch. Stygian darkness followed.

"One, two, three, four, five, six!" Kate counted slowly. "Lights on!"

As they flared forth everyone went into shrieks of laughter. From a recess back of the stage where Kate had concealed her, an immense negro girl had emerged, taking a place silently beside Scar. She had been well coached for, as the light came on, she leaned confidingly toward the proprietor and snuggled her head against his shoulder.

Scar leaped up, glaring ferociously at Kate while the patrons vented jeers and catcalls. Kate raised her hand and said:

"The house buys on that one, gang—and Scar ought to be thankful that we didn't see her coming in with him."

The negress, grinning happily, waddled out. Kate patted Scar's shoulder and whispered:

"We've got to give 'em stunts, Scar—and we can't kid the money customers all of the time."

The evening was off to an auspicious start. Stunt followed stunt in rapid succession. The lights, on dimmers now, went up and down the range of their power; again they flashed like lightning's play. They would go out and come on again, occasionally disclosing grim gunmen and their molls engaged in the softer process of "necking." This brought jeers and another round of drinks.

Kate kept it going at fever heat. Between dances she had the girls balancing on beer barrels laid on their sides, or trying to step through the "U" made by their arms and a broom handle. It was a real novelty to the socially starved tough boys and girls and through it all Scar sat and listened happily to the tinkle of the cash registers.

Here and there heads not hard enough to resist the kick of Scar's raw liquor, had succumbed. Shanty Boles and his moll slept side by side, their heads pillowed on the table before them. Someone had taken a lipstick and painted Shanty's nose a violent crimson.

Through it all, Hanson sat sipping his liquor, smoking innumerable cigarettes—but always watching Kate narrowly. He seemed to enjoy chatting with one of the chorus girls—Gladys King—whom he had chosen for his companion of the evening.

Once, as the lights came back on, Kate saw him slip a heavy automatic back under his arm. He was taking no chances of an attack in the dark. She slipped to Speed's side and asked:

"What's the matter with Hanson? He's out with the gat every time the lights go down."

"He'd better," Speed whispered. "He's a wholesale junkie. There's a gang back east gunnin' for him, and some of the big boys here figure to spot him if they can get him right. He's nudgin' in on their racket."

As they talked, a clock outside chimed the hour of four. Thereafter, Kate kept a close check on the face of her watch.

Fifteen minutes later she snapped into action. First she nodded to the orchestra with a signal for a mad jazz number, calling to the electrician, "Use your own judgment, Johnny."

With this she stepped over beside Scar and Little Laura. It seemed to Scar that her fingers, pressing on his shoulder, were unduly heavy. Thus she stood while the electrician ran the gamut of his light changes. Scar still could feel the weight of her fingers on his shoulder when the lights went completely out.

There followed a moment of silence, punctuated by minor squeals of fright and laughter. Suddenly someone grunted as though in pain.

A gun roared heavily in the blackness. A girl's screaming moan sounded as a body struck the floor. The music had been silenced with the sound of the shot.

Out of the babel of sound came Kate's clear voice: "Lights—quick," she commanded.

As they came on the horrified merrymakers saw Gladys King squirming on the floor, blood flowing from a wound high up on her right shoulder. Scar leaped up and barked angrily:

"Shut up your damn noise—want the bulls in here?"

Kate knelt beside the injured girl. A cool-headed waiter brought water and Kate began bathing the girl's forehead.

"What was it, dear?" she asked tenderly. "What happened?"

"He—he—shot me!" Gladys replied. She pointed weakly at Hanson.

From the others there came a growl of anger. Gladys was a favorite. Then followed a concerted rush to the table where Hanson sat, apparently unperturbed. His eyes were half closed. But as the foremost of the gang reached him his body seemed to sag. Then he toppled and his chin struck the table with a thud.

The color had drained from the flesh in his neck. Right at the edge of the hair a single drop of blood stood for a second. It rolled down inside the dead man's collar and another welled slowly in its place.

Hanson unquestionably was dead. Too many present knew the marks of the coming of the Dread One. An unerring hand had struck once at the base of the brain, severing the spinal cord.

Scar glared around the room ferociously. A mighty anger shook his frame. Hanson, as an individual, meant nothing to him. As a racketeer, head of a junk-running organization of no mean proportions, his murder spelled trouble.

"Who done this?" Scar roared. "Get up on your damned hind legs and have the guts to say so—" A stream of horrible profanity welled and bubbled from his lips.

Kate whispered something to Speed under cover of the noise. The gangster moved quickly to Scar's side. He talked rapidly in an undertone. At first the proprietor shook his head impatiently. Speed continued talking until silenced with a gesture.

"Listen, guns and molls," Scar said after a moment of thought. "This here thing ain't goin' to do us any good. Now, we're all-right guys here tonight; there ain't a rat or snitch in the joint. Hanson's croaked. Nobody knows who done it, but me and Speedy figgers it will be a good idee for him to be found somewhere else. What say?"

"Take the blankety-blank out and dump him in the bay," someone growled. "That's the ticket—out in the streets some'rs," another said. Scar and Shanty Boles turned to the gruesome task of dressing the corpse in overcoat, gloves and soft gray hat.

"Whose car are you going to use?" Kate asked quietly. Then before anyone answered, she suggested: "Better steal one, Speed, and leave him in it out in the residence district. And while we're about it, poke a gun in his ribs hard. The blood will settle there and the dicks will think his kidnappers did it."

"Damn smart," Scar applauded. "Go ahead, Speed. Find a likely lookin' bus and shoot her in the alley. I'll have a lookout waitin'."

Thus it was arranged. Hanson's body, with a gangster on each side of it, was loaded into a stolen limousine, Speed at the wheel. Larry Michaels, his buddy, followed in another car. Within thirty minutes all were back at the Argyle Club.

Scar closed soon afterward. Kitty, en route home, made certain she was not being followed. When she had disrobed and made her night toilet, she unfastened a secret compartment in a suitcase and brought to light a small memorandum book.

Then she drew a heavy black line through the first of three names inscribed on its fly-leaf.

The name was "Lester Kinney."

Seattle morning newspapers had good reason for first-page streamer lines that morning.

Henry Wilson, a milkman, discovered Hanson's body, rigid behind the steering wheel and with the gloved hands in driving posture. It was in a shining limousine, standing before one of the beautiful homes in the exclusive Queen Anne Hill district.

Wilson notified the police and detectives made several startling discoveries. The first was a footprint in the mud of the gutter where apparently someone had stood beside the car. Plaster casts were made, but later the sleuths were chagrined to find it matched perfectly to the milkman's brogans.

Next came the news that the limousine had been stolen from a patron of the Elk's Club. Atop of this came the medical examiner's announcement that Hanson's death had been brought about by someone thoroughly skilled in surgery.

Then the discoloration on the side of the body was discovered. As Kate had predicted, the detectives seized on this as proof that someone had jammed a gun against the victim's side, had kidnapped him and taken him for a ride.

"Gawd, kid!" Scar said to Kate when she entered the club that night, "you sure saved ol' Scar's bacon with quick thinkin' last night. Hereafter they's another five per cent in the cut fer you."

"Thanks, Scar," Kate said listlessly. "Who do you think did it?"

Scar ruminated for a time, then said in a low voice:

"If you hadn't stood with your hand on my shoulder all the time the lights was out, I'd have said, 'Mebbe you!' I seen you and Hanson glarin' at one another, an' I copped you two watchin' each other all evenin'. But I ain't answerin' any questions—nor askin' any. I know where you was every second."

"Who was against him in the dope game here?" Kate asked after a brief pause, during which she studied Scar's face attentively.

"Mugs Dietrich," Scar replied. "He was the big junkie until Hanson showed up nine-ten months ago. Hanson nudged in on the alky racket, but as soon as he'd built up a gang, he hijacked a trunkful of dope, coming from Kansas City to Mugs.

"They was better'n fifty thousand dollars worth in it. Hanson sent for Mugs, covered him with a rod and they talked turkey. When Mugs left, he had half the dope and Hanson had half the town. That's how Hanson worked. Since then, he's been edgin' in on Mugs and four-five boys on both sides has been croaked. Mugs got sore last week and cracked that Hanson better come smokin' next time they met. That's why the dicks is figgerin' last night's job as a gang-spottin'."

"Who is Hanson's Man Friday—his next in command?" Kate asked.

"A guy twicet as hard as Hanson ever wanted to be. They call him Sugarface Mallon. He's the reason I didn't want anybody to know Hanson was croaked here. This pritty boy came from the East with Hanson, and after the first week none of our gunnies wanted any of Sugarface's game. He throws hot lead faster 'n easier than anybody I ever did see—and some of the best of 'em has come through that door there."

Thrill-seeking and curiosity brought back all of the crowd of the night before and yet others who had heard of the live-wire Cougar Kitty. It was by that title she was known in Gangland now; few could have told her last name.

But it was an apathetic crowd. Even Kate's flaming personality could not evoke a real response, except from the newcomers. The shadow of tragedy still lingered over the place.

The bar patronage was holding up well, however. Some of the patrons seemed anxious to drink themselves insensible in the shortest possible space of time. These were succeeding admirably. Such failed to witness the new situation which unfolded itself suddenly.

During an interval when the orchestra was silent, the doorbell pealed shrilly. When the doorman swung the steel-faced portal open, two well-dressed men stepped into the room. Both stood looking the crowd over coldly.

One, the taller, might have posed for magazine collar advertisements. Nature had given him a trig slenderness, height, a handsome face and a certain air of real gentility. His companion was shorter, dark and glowering, seemingly dissipated and he had a hangdog air. As he turned it was apparent that one of his ears was badly cauliflowered. Both had one thing in common. Their air was purposeful and either could be depended on to do what was needful, no matter what the circumstances.

Scar started to struggle to his feet, but sank back at a signal from Kate. Straight to the pair she went, eyes shining, teeth flashing in a smile of welcome.

"Greetings, Mr. Sugarface Mallon," she called from the middle of the floor. "Come on in, both of you. The water's wet—and we haven't any."

Mallon eyed her with evident admiration, yet curiously. His companion scowled darkly and whispered something. Sugarface stepped forward and took Kate's outstretched hand.

"A stranger in town, yet she calls my name," he said suavely. "Who am I—to be so honored?"

"Tell you later," Kate said in a low tone. "Play up now."

Now Scar came lumbering forward. Mallon gave him a cold nod; his companion struck the owner's outstretched hand aside. Scar turned and waddled back to his chair.

Two of the waiters removed a somnolent drunk from one of the tables, brought a third chair and Kate, Mallon and the other man sat down. Kate and Mallon faced each other across the table; the other's back was to the dance floor.

"This is Kid Sharkey," Mallon said, pointing to his companion. "He's with me always—now that Hanson's dead."

"Oh yes," Kate said nonchalantly, "I read of it in the papers. You were his associate, weren't you—both here and in the East?"

Mallon's eyes probed hers ominously, curiously, for a moment.

"See here," he said as though in sudden decision. "They tell me you're a wise head; anyway you look it, and I'm going to lay 'em right out before you. There is a whisper that Hanson was done in right in this room. It is a whisper that hasn't reached the police, however. One of my boys heard a girl stew talking about it and came to me with the story.

"Now get me right; I'm not caring one half-witted damn about Hanson being rubbed out. Probably it saved me the trouble. He was a bad one and would knock me off in a minute, but he knew I could let him draw and then kill him. For the last six months when we talked he sat with his hands folded over his most recent meal. I'd warned him to.

"But I'm head of the gang now. I'm taking over where he left off. If it was one of Muggsy's gang that croaked him, then I know where to watch. If it was done here, then there's a new enemy for me to go gunning after.

"What would you do in my place?"

He fairly hissed the last words.

"I'd buy a drink!" Kate said nonchalantly. "Waiter!"

A red surge of color leaped to Mallon's pale face.

"Damn it!" he snarled. "Answer me, you rotten—"

Kate's hand—the right one—slipped over the edge of the table. With the index finger of the left Kate pointed casually toward it. Mallon's eyes dropped; visioned the deadly steel muzzle of the little plunger-gun between her fingers. Kid Sharkey gasped. For the fraction of a second the weapon turned on him, then flashed back to Sugarface.

"Rotten—what—?" she demanded. "Say anything that's in your system—and if I don't like it, then it's my turn to say or do something—you fool. Say it!" she demanded coldly. Now she was Cougar Kitty indeed.

Speedball Kane, who had lost no item of the byplay from a distance, came slipping to the table. His body was poised on the balls of his feet. The right hand was under his left lapel.

Kate sensed, rather than saw him.

"My affair," she said over her shoulder. "Don't interfere unless things get hot—and if they do, then burn Kid Sharkey down and burn him fast."

"Baby," Speed said with deep conviction. "He's afire now."

"What a broad!" It was Kid Sharkey's unwilling tribute as he realized just how hot things had become.

Mallon it was who broke the tension.

"Stand off all around," he said putting his hands before him on the table. "I'm apologizing—not because of the palm-gun, but because they taught me as a kid not to call girls bad names."

The deadly muzzle slipped out of sight beneath the table. Mallon had a dubious impression that it still covered his stomach.

"Right," Kate snapped. "Now what do you want to know?"

"Was Hanson fixed up here? That's all."

"He was not," she replied steadily. "He left here about two."

"Alone?"

"Alone. I think he had a telephone call." Then, before Mallon could stop her, she called over her shoulder, "Oh, Scar!" When he lumbered over, she asked:

"Hanson left last night about two, didn't he—alone?"

"Uh-huh, about then," Scar said easily. "I got th' idee somebody was waitin' for him—or did he get a 'phone call?"

"Thanks!" Mallon said carelessly after a moment's close scrutiny of the scarred, evil countenance before him.

"S'all right," Scar rumbled. "Let's us have a drink."

"Why not?" the younger man replied lightly. "Kid, you go along and see about the trucks. I'll be at the hangout later."

Sharkey started to protest, then rose and lurched from the place. His last glance at Kate was one of reverent worship. Kid Sharkey had seen his first real gun-moll.

Mallon rose as Kate did and accompanied her to the table adjoining Scar's lookout chair, unwittingly dropping into the seat where his chief's body had been but a few hours before.

Suddenly Kate felt his eyes on her and turned about to surprise the same searching, calculating expression she had encountered in Hanson's eyes. She smiled, blandly, seated herself across from him and said:

"Want to tell an inquisitive girl something, Mr. Mallon?"

"What?" he demanded. She paused before replying, holding his glance by sheer willpower for a moment.

"How is it that a man of your class, who could be anything he set out to be, is in the booze and dope game?" she said at last.

"Just naturally bad, I guess," he replied, but Kate saw she had scored her first victory in her fight to draw his interest to her personally.

From then until the moment later when Mallon, now warmed by a number of drinks, began paying her elaborate compliments, Kate used her every art to let glances and half spoken sentences show him that she was not indifferent to him. At last, while the electrician had dimmed the lights to almost out, he leaned across the table and whispered:

"I'm waiting for you tonight, baby—and every other night, if you say so."

Kate did not answer, contenting herself with letting her hand touch his for a moment in a quick, firm pressure. Then she excused herself and turned to the other patrons. The crowd was thinning out now. Several of the more intoxicated still slumbered in their chairs.

Not more than fifteen couples were on the dance floor when Kate stopped the music with a wave of her hand and said:

"Not enough pep, gang. We're closing soon now, and let's make it all hot 'n everything in the meantime. Make it snappy now, for Speed and I have a surprise for you pretty soon."

The orchestra swung into a mad jazz number, quickening the cadence until the dancers' feet literally were flying. Kate called Little Laura to her away from Scar's side, and whispered something. The girl laughed and took a chair at a vacant table.

Kate caught the electrician's eye and nodded, holding up a silver chime whistle as a signal. He nodded and began a furious succession of light changes. They flickered up, then dimmed down to mere red-brown shapes within the globes. On again—and the electrician snapped the main switch off and on rapidly, giving the effect of lightning flashes. Once Kate caught

Mallon's eyes and tossed him an airy kiss from her fingertips. Scar, sitting three feet distant from him, scowled wonderingly.

Occasionally couples would barge together on the dance floor, the girls screaming curses or ribald commands. Kate's eyes narrowed calculatingly watching the unconscious distribution of the couples about the floor.

Suddenly she sounded a musical trill from the whistle. The music rose to a shrill crescendo of noise as the electrician pulled the main switch and threw the entire club into darkness.

But over the music, the shouts of laughter and the scrape of feet, there sounded ten clearly spaced blasts of Kate's whistle as though she was marking time for the next stunt.

Three sharp blasts followed one another in rapid succession. The lights flared on and the music ceased in the middle of a bar.

For an instant there was a grave-like silence; then gasps of surprise—here and there a nervous titter from one of the molls.

There was reason. Midway down the room, clear of the dancers and at a point where every person in the room was under her eye stood Cougar Kitty, in each hand a thirty-eight automatic. Flanking her, four at each side, stood the club's eight waiters. Now they were masked with handkerchiefs tied across their noses to conceal mouths and chins. Each carried two snub-nose, small caliber automatics! These were trained on the dancing group and the orchestra.

Kitty's guns covered Mallon and Scar.

"Up with them," she demanded dramatically. "Drag me down a star and let me look at it. This is a stick-up and I don't mean perhaps."

Mallon and Scar laughed happily, admiringly.

"Some twist, that one," Scar said out of the corner of his twisted mouth. "Who else'd think of a stunt like that?"

With the words the tension broke. The waiters snapped the handkerchiefs from their faces, broke the seeming automatics and disclosed that they were cigarette guns, made in the shape of pistols. These were distributed to the dancers as they crowded about the smiling hostess.

Kate, meanwhile, stood toying with the weapons hanging loosely at her side. She looked anxiously about for Speedball. He was at one of the tables, retying a shoelace. He looked up at her and grinned.

It was Scar, master of the double-cross and personification of vileness, who was the first to sense the tenseness which had descended on the room.

As he dropped his hands to the chair arms, ready to derrick his great body to a standing position, Kate whirled and leveled both guns.

"Down!" she snapped savagely. "Up with them—both of you—you're in on this too, Mallon. "Quick—fingers together behind your heads."

The muzzles of both guns jumped in unison. With the roar came a splintering crash as the missiles flew past the heads of the two men and buried themselves in the wall behind them.

There was no question now of obedience. Mallon, white, silent but watchful as a snake, cradled the back of his head in his hands. Scar was slower and his gross face was splotched and purple as he too withdrew his hands from his holster.

The girl's tense figure, alone in the center of the floor as she held two redoubtable gunmen helpless, appealed to their sense of the dramatic. They were breathless with suspense when at last she broke silence to say in a lifeless monotone:

"Listen everybody—I'm going to tell you about a couple of damned, lousy skunks—the two sitting there, and another I got last night—Hanson.

"In a little while, I'm going out of here. It is up to you—you boys and girls who, like me, have had to fight for yourselves—it's up to you whether I go out of here—or whether I don't! But I'm going to take Skunk Mallon and Skunk Argyle with me! It'll be the hot seat for them! And I've nothing on you!

"I'm a slum kid from Brooklyn. My dad was a drunk; mother was a decent woman. I had two brothers, Wilbur and Merrill. Our family name was Orrum. Merrill, the older brother, was a good kid. He made me go to school just as he did. The other was weak, a sneak thief at twelve and an ex-con at twenty. They called him 'Wib the Gun.'"

Scar's arms jerked at the words and the girl's finger tightened for an instant on the trigger of the weapon in her right hand.

"Means something to you, doesn't it, Skunk Argyle?" she taunted. "Wib was the lad you and Hanson and Mallon, jobbed into killing his own brother that night in Detroit—the lad Mallon and Hanson killed later to stop his mouth."

Someone in the crowd grated out a curse. She continued her story.

"Merrill had worked his way through law school and had taken up criminal practice. In a few years he was known as the best crook mouthpiece in Detroit. I was his helper—his private investigator.

"But Merrill fell out with Hanson and Mallon, and also with Scar who was the big money back of their booze and dope running. They got poor Wib drunk one night and planted him out to kill a Federal dick near a roadhouse. They decoyed Merrill to the spot and let Wib kill his own brother.

"When he found out what he'd done, he went into hiding. It took me days to find him and when I got there he was croaking. He had just enough strength to tell me the story and to let me know that Mallon had run him down and shot him to silence him.

"I went crazy then. When I found where Hanson was planted out I went there one night and got into the house. I hoped to get him as he slept. But Sugarface Mallon was on the prowl and got me before I could shoot.

"He tied me up. He didn't call Hanson. He just gagged me—and for that night I was his prisoner. Figure that for yourselves.

"The next morning he threw me down the front steps. He'd finished wrecking the Orrum family. Nice boy—Skunk Mallon—isn't he?"

"Hanson and Mallon disappeared," she continued, and now she was tumbling the words forth with machine-gun speed. "But I found they were here, working with Scar Argyle on a new dope underground.

"My hair was gold-yellow. I dyed it red. My figure was slight. I ate sweets, drank heavy cream, stuffed like a Strasbourg goose until I had gained twenty pounds. I went to Chicago and then New York to establish a new identity, but always I kept track of the three skunks.

"You know most of the rest of it. I came here and tricked Scar into giving me work. Last night I stood beside Scar, pressing my fingers into his fat shoulder until the lights went out. Then I got Hanson in the neck with a thin, knife. I was back beside Scar when the lights went on again. He thought he had felt my hand on his shoulder all of the time."

She paused for a quick glance about the tables, flashed her eyes toward the doorway where waiters and barmen were grouped.

But even that brief second of respite was enough for Sugarface. As she turned back his right hand was flitting under his coat lapel, fingers clawing for the gun butt nestling there.

Cougar Kitty's left gun jerked twice and a horrible oath spat from Scar's lips as two black holes appeared, one above the other, in Mallon's smooth, white forehead. He teetered for a moment in his chair, then fell sideways across Scar's feet.

The death threat in the girl's eyes as they flickered to Scar nerved the gross man to action. He threw himself, wedged as he was in his great chair, sideways to the floor. His hand flashed with incredible speed to the butt of his gun.

Cougar Kitty, her eyes pinpoints of blazing hate, waited as the thick fingers grasped the weapon, started to raise it.

Crash! Crash! Crash!

Her gun spoke thrice in rapid succession. A jet of blood leaped from Scar's lips as the first bullet smashed against his set teeth.

The second smashed through the center of the scar under the victim's right eye and ploughed into the brain.

The third struck squarely between the eyes—a small, purple edged perforation which wrote the final period on the life-tale of Scar Argyle.

For a moment Cougar Kitty stood silent, staring at the two unmoving bodies on the floor. "Killing was too good for them!"

Then with a gesture of finality she let the guns crash to the floor. Turning, her hands outstretched toward the silent group of grim-faced onlookers, she whispered:

"And now—the verdict. Getaway—or?"

Tense eyes stared back into hers. Still no word was spoken.

Suddenly, as though an invisible wedge was driving into the group, they began to fall back.

White lipped, staring unseeingly before her, Kitty passed the grimly watchful cannons and molls who lined her pathway.

The Night Before Hell

And Old Molly said: "And you'll never come back—it's your last night, Spud, so make it a big one! And take Old Moll's blessing with you—down into hell!"

BARNEY KANE, TRAFFIC COP, never knew that the coughing fit which attacked him that cold night, doubling him over and leaving him weak and gasping for breath, really saved his life. But for the sudden seizure, Barney would have followed his hunch to stop the black, low-swung roadster that whizzed down the street with only hood and parking lights showing.

That is to say, Barney would have tried. Yet at the first glimpse of the officer on fixed post, Spud McGrahan's right hand snatched at the butt of the heavy automatic on the seat beside him, bringing the blunt muzzle up to the level of the opening in the windshield.

Spud wasn't having any interference from police that night, at least not without protest. That afternoon he had been convicted of first degree murder and on the morrow was scheduled to hear a sentence to "fry" in the Big Chair. Now, aided by judicious spreading of many "grand" in money, the use of high political pressure, and a sudden, flaming exhibition of his own insane temper, he was free of the county jail. There would be flaring headlines in the newspapers in the morning.

When he passed Barney Kane's post he was but a few blocks distant from the hideout, and the members of his own gang, who were to aid in the raid he was planning on the warehouse headquarters of Tony Sintonetti's rival gang of alky runners and high jackers.

Three months before, at the head of his own gorillas, Spud had rocketed forth with machine guns, sawed-off shotguns and rods, on the same errand. Tony and his crew sat tight and a lovely brannigan was in progress when a precinct police captain came into the line of fire. A second later he lay dead with a bullet in his brain.

Tony's agile mind worked faster than that of the more stolid Spud, with the result that evidence was placed in the hands of police showing that the bullet came from the ranks of the attackers. At the trial, experts declared that it showed marks of the rifling of Spud's personal rod and the inevitable conviction followed.

Spud's black eyebrows came together in a wolfish scowl when he saw the bulky form of the cop at the crossing, but relaxed when he realized the coughing fit had saved him. Stepping on the gas, he was two blocks away and turning into a side street before Kane quit gasping and resumed his watch for the escaped killer.

The word was out by radio, telephone and police prowl cars that Spud, during those few brief moments when the jail lights had winked out, had slipped through the mysteriously unlocked doors of his cell and the cell block—to say nothing of the front portal with its great magnetic clamps.

One and only one of the keepers had encountered Spud in the darkness. This one, Under Turnkey Bell, flashed a light in Spud's face and grappled with him.

Spud flamed into silent action. There was a muffled grunting and straining, a low groan of agony; the sound of a body pitching to the stone flooring. Spud stole silently forward. Behind him lay the turnkey, his face a bloodless mask, his head sagging in ghastly fashion on its dislocated neck.

A pasty faced youth, sitting at the wheel of the black roadster slipped out and faded into the darkness with a muttered word as Spud came up out of the shadows. On the seat beside him he found a dark overcoat, slouch hat and automatic with extra clips.

Three blocks from Barney Kane's corner, Spud twisted the wheel and entered an alleyway. Halfway down the block he stopped, backed into a garage and heard the doors close silently after him. Stilling the engine he sat quiet, listening intently. Soon feet scuffed on the concrete flooring and he heard a rasping whisper.

"O.K., Spud. Took you a hell of a while to get here."

Spud's nerves went taut at the words. Silently he swung the well oiled door open; tested his weight on the running board. There was no telltale creaking. Gun in hand he slipped down and stood clear, waiting. The footsteps came nearer, someone collided with the open door. Instantly Spud lashed out and downward with the butt of the rod.

In the stillness the rasp of metal on bone resounded sickeningly. Something heavy, metallic, fell to the floor at Spud's feet as he reached out and caught the unconscious form. His blow had fallen true. The man was helpless.

A derisive, malicious grin curved Spud's lips. The police had set a trap for him and he had slipped through its jaws. This man, whose form he still held upright, was twice the size of Kid Lally who had been assigned to await him in the garage and give him the office if all was well at the hideout.

The breath came from his victim's lips in bubbling gasps. But there was another sound. Something had touched an empty oilcan back there in the corner.

Another cop lurked there; maybe more! Knowledge of the trap had come when the watcher in the darkness had said "Spud." The agreed code word for that night of nights was "Blackie." That was why he had swung his automatic; now he knew that the other lurker in the corner must be an enemy too.

Instinct brought him about, the prisoner still in his arms; gun raised on a level with his hip. The form in his arms jerked spasmodically twice—to the tune of a double roar of shots which smashed the silence, tearing his ear drums like blasts from a field gun.

Back of the flashes he made out the dim outlines of another bulky form. His own weapon spoke twice. The man in the corner screamed in agony; let his gun fall. Then the empty oilcan went spinning from under a falling body.

Spud dropped the shielding form which had stopped the lead intended for him. Grimly his mind flashed over the events of the last hour. Three men were dead or dying and he was on but the first lap of his race to Tony Sintonetti's warehouse. True, one of them carried slugs from police guns in his chest, but the death would be charged to his account just the same.

Stepping lightly over the prostrate form, he started on hands and knees for the rear of the garage. His questing fingers found the hatless head of the second victim, flitted across the forehead and to the eyes. These were closed. No danger there.

As he knelt, blows crashed against the garage doors; hands fumbled at the push handles. These were strangers, unaware that the doors were held inside by a bar which lifted electrically when a key was inserted in the lock. The newcomers cursed and crashed against the doors.

At the same second Spud sensed a movement near him. That was it!

There was a third watcher in the darkness! That would mean the opposite rear corner. He could see the plan now. One man to impersonate Kid Lally and get close enough to grapple with him, the other two to attack from the rear.

"Morgan—Williams! Open up. Captain Larkin speaking." The command came from outside the door.

Spud, his ear but a few inches above the floor, sensed the rub of leather against leather—the song of the shoe—as the third man shifted his weight from one foot to the other. Again he heard it—and again. The ambusher was stealing to the door to admit the others. Spud counted five, raised to his feet and slipped to the tool closet in the rear wall.

His groping left hand encountered the edge of the boards, slipped about and thrust downward quietly on a spike from which depended an oil-stained coverall suit.

In other and equally dangerous days Spud had sensed the need for a getaway if attacked in the garage. Aided by a mechanical expert he had installed a pivot door, on ball bearings, which seemed a part of the wall and which swung with pressure on the spike.

Spud stepped silently into the outer darkness, found the rusty hook which served as a handle; let the door swing shut behind him. The slightest of clicks came from within. Probably it would go unnoticed in the hammering from in front.

Before him Spud could see the black loom of a three-story building dimly outlined in the glow from distant street lamps. The yard about him was a pit of blackness. There might be more of his enemies hidden there. Surely the police would have a guard outside in the rear.

Twenty feet of turf lay between the silent spectre which was Spud and the safety within. Spud owned this house as well as the one fronting the same sector on the street behind him.

His tenant and pensioner there was Old Molly Pearson, one time queen of the dips, now a rheumatic, poison-tongued old ex-convict. Molly was waiting there for him, unless the plan had gone awry—ready to open the narrow window which gave access to the basement.

Spud slipped to the ground at full length, putting objects about him against the background of the city's lights reflected in the sky. There was the outline of the garage, a clothes prop set against the line, the top of the fence.

Foot by foot the fugitive's eyes searched all about him. Somewhere near at hand an arc light guttered and flared up. For a second the shape of a hat showed beside the fence, then disappeared as the owner crouched down.

There was a watcher there; someone probably dangerous as a cobra. At the first sound rods would flame and the place would be surrounded. Spud rolled over carefully twice in the direction of the house. Then he lay quiet, listening. For a moment the uproar outside the garage was stilled.

In the quiet, Spud sensed a singular whistling sound. His head jerked up as he centered all of his faculties in his ears. Again the sound came—a sibilant note like the sound made by blowing gently between two sheets of paper.

Spud relaxed, came to his knees, his gun covering the man before him. Pressing his tongue against the roof of his mouth he made a clucking sound twice. It was the warning signal of his gang.

The soft whistling sound stopped. Spud clucked twice again. The sounds were duplicated from the darkness. Feet moved silently in the grass. A form stole forward.

"Here, Smoky," Spud whispered. "All safe?"

"Ye-ah! Molly's waitin' at de win'ow fer youse. Beat it."

Spud arose and slipped through the blackness to the rear wall of the dwelling. Smoky remained hidden in the shadows, on watch. Spud's knee struck against the spigot of an outside water pipe. From within came a torrent of muttered curses. Despite the danger, he smiled grimly. Old Molly certainly knew all of the words.

He could picture her wrinkled, hate distorted old face, twisted now with anxiety for his safety while she swore at him for his carelessness.

Hands outstretched, he found the casement, felt within. The window was open. A claw like hand caught at his foot in the signal of safety. A second later he stood within, the click of the window latch sounding in his ears.

Old Molly preceded him through the familiar door and the area at the bottom of the kitchen steps. She opened a door on her left, thrust him inside and then turned on the lights. The room was one of three cubicles along the side of the basement, each opening into the other. At the end was a flight of steps to a concealed door under the front steps which gave access to the sidewalk.

"Thought they'd got you," Molly hissed through her toothless gums. "Sent Smoky out t' watch. How'd you find him?"

"Heard his breath whistling through that hole in his teeth," Spud answered briefly. "Close, Molly, eh?"

"Too damned close," the dame sputtered. "They'll be searchin' here any minute. Here's money, a rod—a police gun at that—an' they's another car waitin' across the street, headed east. Get the hell outta here before the cops start searchin' the houses."

Spud turned for a second to stare into her watery old eyes.

Whatever of loyalty exists as between crooks, that in full measure Old Molly gave to Spud. She was a vicious old wolf of the underworld who thought of him only as her adopted cub. No threat, no promise, no brutal third degree ever could unseal her lips of words harmful to her black browed benefactor. His was the only kindness she had known in years. When they turned her out of the Big House after her last long jolt, it was Spud who had sent her money and a ticket, Spud who provided her wages and a home for the rest of her life.

"Get the word out to the boys," Spud said after a moment of tense thought. "Tell them to scatter; the plan's off. I'm going after Tony—but I'm going alone."

There were tears in Old Molly's eyes—real tears.

"And you'll never come back," she said with the conviction of a witch at her cauldron. "It's your last night, Spud. I feel it. So make it a big one—and take Old Moll's blessing with you—down into hell."

Spud drew his slouch hat down over his eyes, patted the rods in his outside pockets as he stood in the shadows under the front steps. The thought came to his mind that Old Molly had said one was a police gun. Queer old girl, that. There'd be a kick in it for her to send him out on his last, flashing, flaming lone wolf raid with a rod once dedicated to the cause of law and order.

Another thing she had just said was coming clear in his mind. "Old Moll's blessing will go down to hell with you." He shrugged, mentally. It was hell for him, one way or another. Better go out to the tune of hot lead than fry in the hot seat. This way he'd make damned sure of having company, Tony and his white-toothed smile, and Sara—the flashing eyed moll, once his own "heart" and now, with typical Syrian faithlessness, doubled with Tony. The wop had cleaned up thoroughly on his Celtic enemy.

Spud shook his head to clear it for the work at hand. Street lights flashed on silvered metal on the breast of a figure standing at the next corner. Another cop. Spud drew back into the shadows and reconnoitered to the right. Nobody in sight there. Turning, he watched as a burst of firing sounded from the alleyway. They were riddling the garage with sawed off shotguns, certain that he still lay hidden in the darkness.

The officer at the corner broke into a run, passed out of sight with the first crashing volley. Now was Spud's chance. Calmly, unhurriedly, he stepped up on the sidewalk, crossed the street to the curtained touring car waiting there. There were no lights showing, but the motor was running silently.

He approached the machine from the rear; stood waiting, gun in hand, while he struck the tonneau a smart blow with his left fist.

The springs creaked as someone moved inside. The left front door swung open an inch and a voice said "Blackie!"—the right code word. Spud stole to the door and slid in, gun against the side of the occupant.

"It's Red," the other said. "Nix on the cannon. Where to, Spud?"

"Slide out, Red," was the reply. "This is a high lonely."

"Hell, you say. Old Moll said for me to go wit' youse—all de way. You drive. I gotta scatter-gun here wot wants t' spit."

"Out!" commanded Spud, dully.

"Nuts! Pull your party, Spud. Me an' cough and spit'll do our prowl outside. Goin' after Tony? He ain't at de warehouse no more. Him 'n Sadie's floppin' in a new dump over Kerrigan's."

Mechanically Spud jazzed the motor and let in the clutch. He forgot his orders to Red. Under him was a powerful car. For a few minutes yet the streets would be open. Kerrigan's! Another count against Tony.

It was Spud's dough that had staked the ex-confidence man to the Kerrigan club—ground floor cafe, closing early; second floor cabaret with a two o'clock police order against it; third floor split between gambling rooms and a comfortably furnished apartment at the front.

"Tony take that over too?" he asked heavily.

"Uh-huh. Him 'n his guns went in there the second night after you was arrested. Tony's two-thirds owner now. We didn't tell you about it. You had enough to worry about in jail."

Spud's heavy shoulders slumped. The night was passing. Before long some wise dick would remember about the Kerrigan Club and they'd be there too. Tony, safe on that third floor, could thumb his nose at him. But was he safe, even with his gunnies scattered about in the cabaret and gambling room?

Had Tony learned the secret of the attic yet? The trap in the bathroom ceiling in the dark corner over the flush tank? What was it the jail chaplain had been jabbering about last Sunday? The words re-formed themselves in his mind:

"Man's evil deeds come from below; vengeance from above."

Spud grunted derisively. Tony should have been there for the jail service to get himself a tip. It would be a help to him tonight, for there lay the only path the fugitive could follow with any certainty of coming to grips with his enemy.

Keeping to the darker side streets he drove rapidly crosstown. Once, crossing a main traveled artery, he brought his car to a halt within six feet of a corner cop as the red traffic light blinked on.

Red shifted in his seat. Spud heard the clatter of metal against metal as he brought the blunt-ended scatter-gun up inside the front curtain. Green supplanted red, and the car surged forward without the policeman giving them more than a casual glance.

Now two blocks more and he would reach his objective. At the alleyway back of the club he turned in sharply. For a brief moment he flashed the full strength of his headlights down the dark tunnel. There was no movement. He cut off the lights, waited for a moment for his eyes to readjust themselves to the darkness, then crawled ahead silently in second gear until he had passed the rear of the club building.

Above him loomed a four-story brick structure, once devoted to varying lines of business but now used as a storehouse for the adjacent paper box manufactory. Leaning out he looked upward, then went into reverse for a few feet, and drove ahead. The side curtains scraped against a projection on the back of the building.

"Wat de hell, Spud?" It was a hoarse whisper from Red.

"Going in from the top. I can reach the fire escape from the top of the car, get inside here and then into the club from the side."

"Kin I go wit' youse?"

"No, Red. My party—and mine only. Pull down to the next corner, park the car and plant somewhere in the dark. If the bulls come, ramble. If not, wait until you're sure I'm not coming."

Spud's hand caught at Red's shoulder, slid down to his hand, pressed it.

"See you in hell, kid," he said evenly, and was gone.

The car swayed with his weight as he stepped from fender to hood and thence to the top. The ancient fire escape creaked as his hands hooked about its edge; drew him up.

One word came down out of the darkness. It was "Lam!"

Red slid under the wheel and spun the car out of the alleyway.

Up two of the iron ladders went Spud, to crash against a window sash on the third floor. No need for caution here. The place was unoccupied. Even the watchman from the next building never entered at night.

Inside he found himself in a room surrounded with immense slatted packing cases. A lane led to the central hallway. Down this Spud made his way to a room extending across the front. It was dark in there; boxes were piled almost ceiling high around the walls. At his left was a splinter of light showing between the piled cases.

In a moment he slid two of the boxes down and into the center of the room, disclosing the window he sought. He looked out. The attic window of the club was at least seven feet distant and fully a yard higher then where he stood. For a moment the sense of defeat was strong within him. How to cross that black gulf, climb to the higher level, and then cling there while he forced the other window?

Maybe he'd have to go back to the street and take his chance of shooting his way through the ranks of Tony's rodmen after all.

As he stood, perplexed, a scuffling sound came from the rooms across the gap. Then a woman's scream, high and piercing, rang out. Another started—ended in a gurgle.

Spud raised his eyebrows satirically. Sara, perhaps? Sara not having such a pleasant time with her new sugar daddy after all? And a hell of a lot it concerned him!

Another scream sounded, this time accompanied by the crash of breaking glass. Then a moan, the sound of a falling body.

Spud was all interest now. Too well he knew the soft-bodied Sara. She lacked the nerve to continue screaming after a preliminary choking. And the voice was too high, too terror stricken to be hers.

Well, it mattered little. If she kept Tony busy enough with her tantrums, it would be easier for Spud to force an entrance through that attic window. But how?

He lit a match; looked about him. The way was provided.

Braced against a corner of the room was a twelve-foot plank. Instantly Spud sensed its use. It was kept there to use on the stairs when sliding the light but bulky boxes of finished stock down to the loading platform.

In a trice Spud had the window open and was bracing his huge muscles against the weight of the plank. It was an awkward load; one impossible for another lacking his enormous strength. Up and out he swung the makeshift bridge, bracing his knees between a packing case and the windowsill.

Now the end of the plank was opposite the sill of the other window, but still a yard distant in the air.

It seemed that his great muscles must tear under the strain as he let the end of the heavy strip of wood sink until it rested at last on the opposite sill. Tentatively he thrust forward. The plank moved an inch—another—stopped. Spud moved a packing case forward against the inner end of the bridge, blocked another behind it. Then he twisted another lengthwise and jammed it against the wall forming an anchor to prevent the plank's slipping under his weight.

His overcoat and hat were tossed in a corner. One gun he thrust into his trousers band. The other he jammed into a holster improvised when he unbuttoned vest and shirt top and pushed the weapon down next to his skin. The blued steel was cold, uncomfortable—but the rod was at hand ready for instant use.

Lying on his stomach he edged forward on the steep plank. Its surface was smooth, as glass from the constant rubbing of heavy loads as they were slid from floor to floor. Spud gripped the sides with his knees, crossed his toes, Indian fashion, as a secondary brace; reached up with his hands and pulled his body ahead a distance of more than a foot.

He was over the dark passageway now, forty-five feet up from the ground, but mercifully hidden by the shadows. Another thrusting lift followed—and another. Sounds from within the club building came to him plainly now. There was the clatter of glassware, sounds of music from the cabaret—an occasional burst of laughter. The gambling rooms, below him and to the left, seemed soundless. Business probably was not good.

His eyes swung to the right, toward the front. From his perch above he could see that the rooms were brilliantly lighted. One of the windows was open a few inches from the top.

Somewhere someone opened a door and the inrushing air moved the pull curtain out with a snap but the fraction of a second. But in that split second Spud had made out the form of a girl, bound and gagged, lying on the floor of the room.

He closed his eyes to hold the picture. She was a young girl, blonde—of the athletic type. Spud's impression was of a girl still in her teens, the sort one would see driving a sports roadster near the better golf clubs. More of Tony's dirty stuff, he mused, thinking back to the screams he had heard, the shrieks he at first had credited to Sara.

Well, that was something else again. His task for the moment was to reach that tiny attic window, get it open and plant himself safely within. He smiled bitterly at the thought of Spud seeking even a temporary sanctuary under the roof of his greatest enemy.

Yet with the thought came another. Why not? He could afford to stay hidden there indefinitely until hunger and thirst drove him out, should he find himself unable to come to grips with Tony that night. No other place in the city could offer him such security while the hue and cry was on.

Again he thrust with his legs, drawing himself upward with his arms. The window was just past the tips of his out-stretched fingers. Wriggling forward and upward he felt about the sash. The four panes were intact. Loosening one hand, clinging tight with the other, he pushed upward but without result. Again he mustered his strength and tried to shove the window clear. It was immovable.

Panting from the exertion he rested for a moment—then caught madly out for the side of the window opening. There had been a dull sound of movement in the warehouse room behind him; the plank had shifted. His groping fingers told him that it held by not more than an inch.

It was easy to picture what had happened. His shifting weight on the plank had brought more and greater pressure against the wedged boxes until one had shifted sufficiently to allow the plank to slip back.

Moving carefully, he raised his hands to the sides of the window casing, seeking sufficient leverage so he might pull the plank ahead another inch or so with his leg muscles.

The right hand touched the window frame instead of the casing, then slid over to the side and stopped. He thrust forward the index finger of his left hand, felt about there unbelievingly.

Instinct already had told what he would find. The window instead of opening vertically slid from left to right! Working his left hand forward he slid the sash back another three inches, reached through and hooked his arm over the sill.

Now the right. The window stuck, slid back with what seemed to him to be a deafening crash. But he was helpless now to do other than go forward. Retreat would mean another shift of the plank bridge and a plunge to the ground.

Already he had caught the sill with his right hand. Now he pulled himself forward by the sheer strength of his arm and shoulder muscles. He balanced on the sill, wriggled quietly to bring his hands down on the attic floor. Something jarred beneath him, scraped for a second. There was silence and then the sound of some heavy object striking the ground below.

His feet and legs dangled over a void. The plank bridge had fallen. Would it bring Tony's wolves out to see what was happening? Spud drew himself inside, rose on hands and knees and looked down. For moments he rested thus, breathing heavily and listening for footsteps.

All was quiet. Once an automobile whizzed past. In the distance he could hear the coughing of switch engines in the yards.

Spud realized that his getaway was spoiled; he was trapped in the building. After all, that meant nothing. The odds were all against him anyway and, if he was forced to stay in hiding in the attic past daylight, the plank would have been a tip-off.

He reached up and slid the window back into place; felt about at his feet to make certain the floor was clear, then sat down, his back to the window to plan.

Sounds of music drifted up from below. At first he thought it came from a radio somewhere in the apartment beneath him. Tony or some of his guns had turned it on and left it in operation. That was why his entrance had gone unsuspected.

Rested, his senses again on the alert, he went to hands and knees, making his way through the darkness toward the coaming about the bathroom trap. It was out there in the darkness ten feet or so distant from him, probably about the middle of the attic.

Foot by foot he made his way forward, feeling carefully ahead of him with both hands for loose boards or discarded articles which might cause a rattle.

Apparently the attic was not in use. Only dust and grime met his questing fingers. The air was stifling; dust arose in clouds. Several times he buried his face in the crook of an arm to stifle the sneeze he could not control.

When his exploring fingers finally struck a projection in the floor he drew himself forward and felt about it with both hands. Instinctively he had gone straight to the trapdoor. He spent minutes, using his fingers for eyes, learning every inch of the vitally important covering.

It was of the hatch type, easily removable from above or below. Deftly Spud lifted it upward, pausing, listening after each slightest scraping sound.

Suddenly a blinding beam of light flamed into his eyes as one corner came free. It struck against his distended pupils like a blow.

He looked away into the blackness for a long moment before he lifted the cover farther back. It was only a crack, but through it he could see a part of the bathroom and a few square feet of the room adjoining.

Now he could hear voices, distinguish an occasional word. He bent forward, put his ear to the crack—snarled as he recognized the voice as Tony's. A terrific wave of hatred gripped him, nearly sent him catapulting down into the place below for the showdown he had come to seek. Reason told him this could not be.

He listened more calmly, catching a word here and there.

A knock sounded below. Instantly there was hurried movement.

"Get her into the bathroom and turn out the light!" The command was Tony's.

A second later feet scuffled out of the other room. It was Cokey Marron, Tony's chief lieutenant. In his arms he bore the form of the girl Spud had seen in that brief second when the curtain had moved. She was gagged with a towel and her feet were tied. Her hands, however, were free. Just now they dangled helplessly at her sides. Seemingly she had not regained consciousness.

The knocking was repeated. Cokey rushed back to the other room, clicking the bathroom light out but leaving the door partly open.

"Hello, Dugan! Sorry to keep you waiting."

Spud heard the silky voice of Tony more plainly now as he hitched the cover farther back.

" 'Sall right," the newcomer replied. "Bringin' you news, Tony. Spud's out. Crashed the county and shot his way out when we had him cornered in his home garage. Where the hell he is now we don't know. Figured he might come lookin' for you, eh, Tony?"

Spud frowned. That would be Detective Captain Terry Dugan. Probably had the place picketed. The cops knew damned well that Tony had provided the framed evidence for his own conviction; knew that he knew it too. There'd be a crew of them on watch all around the place.

Old Moll was right. It was his last night—and he'd make it a big one.

"Out, eh?" Tony was replying. "Yes, he'll come here, that big one, and he'll find his boy friend, Tony, waits to give him a party. Huh? Cokey, tell the boys a caller is coming—Spud McGrahan. I do not want to see him without bullet holes in his ugly face. Do you get me—plenty of bullet holes in his face."

The words were clipped, precise. Tony had had the benefits of an American public school education. This he combined with a pose of gentility. He thought it rather effective.

"Sure, Tony," Cokey replied. "Some of 'em will be mine. I got a bone to pick with 'at big Irish meself.'"

"Guess you can get away with it, Tony," Detective Dugan said thoughtfully. "If he comes here it's for just one thing, to get you. But I doubt if you see him. We've got the block surrounded and he'll never get this far. Use your head, guy, and don't smoke up any cops."

The outer door slammed. Tony came into the bathroom and stood looking down at the still form of the girl. Swiftly he stooped, lifted her into the bathtub—then arranged the shower curtain so that she would not be visible from the other room.

Spud's finger tightened on the trigger of his gun. It was pointed directly at the sleek, black head in the doorway. But his hate would not permit such a tame ending to his feud with the oily wop. They must be face to face, gun to gun when Tony went out.

Tony turned, lit a cigaret, thought a moment then walked across the room. Spud heard a door open, then close. He listened for long moments. There was no sound. Seemingly Cokey and Tony had been alone with the girl.

She was stirring now. Spud heard a gasping moan. The curtain fluttered and something fell to the floor. It was the gag from about the girl's lips. Damn it, probably she'd start screaming again!

Such was not the case. In a moment she stepped out of the tub, in her hand the curtain tie with which her feet had been secured.

She was a pretty thing, young, athletic. There were bruises on her arms and throat that stood out like welts on her fair skin. Seemingly she had fought, and was ready to fight some more. Somewhere within Spud there was a stir of pity. What a hell of a chance she had against those wolves downstairs! It was the night before hell for her, too.

Irishmen ever were romantic, eager to be of service to women no matter what their own plight. So it was with Spud. A force greater than reason dictated when he thrust the cover far back and whispered:

"Don't yell—but if you'll help me to get you up here I'll try my best to help you to get away from that scum."

Except for a sudden start and her quick glance upward, the girl retained her coolness. She let her eyes dart to right and left for some means of mounting to the ceiling.

"Throw up that towel and bit of rope to me first," Spud directed in a sharp whisper. "Then stand on the edge of the tub and reach up—I'll pull you through the hole." She obeyed and in another second was clasping her hands firmly about Spud's wrists.

There was strength in that grip, power in the young arms which caught at the coaming and drew her through after Spud had lifted her that far. He pushed her to one side, told her to sit down for a moment. Then he pulled the cover back, all except for a crack at one side.

"Who you?" he demanded in a whisper. "What are you doing with the likes of them, down there?"

"I'm Commissioner Millan's daughter," the girl replied. "The son of an old friend of his, Jeremiah McGrahan, was convicted today for a killing—"

"I know—I'm him," Spud interrupted. "And I broke out and come here to settle my own debts."

"Dad was going to do it for you," the girl replied. "He found out that this Tony Whatshisname had framed the evidence, and gave orders to the chief to smash Tony and his gang and run them out of town."

"He'd do that for me?" Spud whispered wonderingly.

"No—for the friendship he had for your dad," she said. "He thinks you're as bad as Tony."

"How'd you get here?" Spud demanded.

"Some gangsters trailed me as I was driving home, crowded my car into the curb, and brought me here. One of them took my car away somewhere to hide it. When I got here Tony told me he was going to keep me until Dad changed his mind about running him out of town. A while ago I got near a window and started yelling. Tony choked me senseless and tied me up. The next thing I knew I was in the bathtub."

"Ye-ah," Spud mused. "Tony would do a thing like that. I suppose some crooked cop tipped him off on what was coming to him."

"Why not?" the girl answered. Her voice was level, even. She had regained her poise. Breeding was asserting itself, even here. "But see, where do we go from here?"

Spud was silent. Here was an impasse. The plank bridge was gone. Probably the attic would offer nothing to replace it, either as a bridge or as a method of lowering her the more than forty feet to the ground. His decision was made quickly.

"You sound like a good sport," he said. "You'll have to gamble with me. I won't let even you get in the way of what I came here for. Hell's going to start popping when they find you're gone. Come on."

He took her hand, led her toward the rear. Another of his precious paper of matches went to show her the corner in which he wanted her to wait.

"Whatever happens—and it will be plenty," he said, "keep quiet—if it is for days. Lots of things have to be done before you can say 'Hello, Dad' again. Here's a gun—a cop's rod that came to me tonight. There are five shots in it. Use four and figure for yourself what to do with the other. Now I'm through with you. Be a good Mick, girl."

She reached out, caught his hand, pressed it.

"Thanks, Spud McGrahan," she said huskily. "I'm Irish, too."

He stole back silently to the cover of the chute; pulled the lid back. Someone came in and used the hand lavatory. Spud's gun was at the ready. From somewhere below a whistle sounded. The man with the damp hands dropped the towel he was using and ran out. Feet scraped, and the hall floor gave back the sounds of footsteps. Somewhere nearby a door slammed.

Silence followed. Spud opened the trap—pushed it shut again. The wop might come to the bathroom, discover the girl was missing and send his boys up to the attic. He sat in the darkness for a time that seemed hours. There was no movement, no stir. He stretched his cramped legs. One knee clicked, the protest of inaction.

A telephone burred its signal. Spud lifted the cover back. He heard a key snap into a lock, a door opening.

"Hello." The voice was Tony's.

"No, chief, I wish he would come," it said. There was a pause. "Do you mean it?" Spud noted the artificial note in the tone. "The commissioner's daughter! What a thing to happen now!" Spud could see the ironic smile on the wop's avid lips. "Maybe an elopement." The suggestion was worthy of the Sicilian brain which prompted it.

Spud stirred, grasped his automatic closer. His thumb moved to throw off the safety catch. His mind whipped back at his passionate anger. Slowly, sullenly, he let his muscles relax.

"I'll send the boys out," he heard Tony say. "Sure, chief. I understand. Commissioner's daughters cannot disappear like that."

Spud heard the telephone click back on its hook. Tony fumbled striking a match. The telephone clicked again.

"Beekman 0001," Tony said. Spud stiffened. That was the number of Tony's warehouse down on the waterfront. He leaned closer to the crack in the opening.

"You Slim?" Tony asked quietly. "Spud McGrahan's crashed out, may come there looking for me. If you see anyone prowling there—anyone— burn them down. I'm back of you. If it happens, tell the cops the man was trying to break in."

Spud grinned wolfishly. He had the wop covering. What a kick Tony had coming to him! The girl stirred back in her corner. Spud shot a sibilant hiss into the blackness. The noise ceased.

Spud turned back to the crack. Tony was standing in the bathroom door. Spud tensed his muscles for the leap which would carry him down through the trap and to grips with his enemy.

Someone rapped at the outer door. Tony whirled, hurried back to the other room. Spud gritted his teeth and poised to listen. He heard Tony.

"Listen copper, tell the captain I said not to bother me any more. I'm tired—turning in. Big game last night. He'll know if anything happens. Tell him to keep sniffing—visitors will mean gunpowder."

The door slammed. Spud eased his muscles again. Best get it over with now while Tony was alone. Footsteps again. Tony hurried into the bathroom, pulled back the shower sheet—stared and cursed. His hand snatched at his vest, brought up a whistle. Three shrill notes sounded.

Spud heard the sound of running feet. Men crowded through the doorway. Tony was mouthing Sicilian curses.

"Spread out," he snarled. "The damn girl's gone. Blonde—a kid. Get her, damn you, croak her if you have to. We're sunk if she gets away!"

He coughed, his anger and fear choking him. The gunmen melted away. Feet slogged across the floor of the next room. The outer door slammed.

Tony started from the bathroom, turned back. He looked at the tiny slit of a window and shrugged. His eyes slipped upward to the shaft in the ceiling, appraisingly. He set his feet on the bowl, reached upward. His hands did not come to the top of the flush tank.

Dropping back to the floor he stood pulling at his waxed mustache ends. Spud could almost read his thoughts. The stairways had been guarded for many minutes by his gunmen. No flesh and blood could stand the forty foot drop to the ground. The girl must have slipped her bonds and was hidden somewhere near at hand. Tony whisked back into the next room. Spud heard him pushing furniture about.

Spud gripped the corners of the cover and pulled it over. He sensed that Tony was back in the bathroom. Suddenly without any warning Tony pointed his rod upward and emptied the entire clip into the cover and the ceiling about the passageway.

One slug smashed through and burned the thumb of Spud's left hand. Another twitched at his trousers alongside his right knee. Several flew harmlessly by, each leaving behind it a pencil of light. The last smashed through the board on which Spud's weight rested, delivering a paralyzing thump on his spine.

Cordite fumes drifted upward through the bullet holes as men came tumbling back into the apartment.

All were shouting questions. Tony whirled on them, spitting curses.

"Get a ladder," he mouthed over and over again until he could make them listen. "Her only chance is the attic. You, Cokey, take a Tommy-gun and fan every foot of the place. She couldn't make it up there alone."

"The cops—" Cokey began.

"Damn the cops," Tony raved. "The rest of you hold 'em off if they try to get in. I tell you, we're sunk if that broad gets away. We've got to croak her now."

Spud drew up his knees slowly. The showdown was here. Using the hurlyburly of sound as a screen, he got to hands and knees at the left of the opening. He heard a step-ladder placed against the wall; heard it creak under Cokey's weight.

The cover moved, slid over to the right and clattered to the floor. Spud drew back into the shadows. Cokey would be blinded for a second or more. The gunman's head rose through the opening. Something clattered against the sides as he brought the Tommy-gun through and laid it on the floor.

Spud's hand stole out silently, lifted the weapon and drew it back. Cokey caught at the edges and pulled himself upward.

He grunted with the unaccustomed effort; wheezed in ghastly fashion as Spud's great hands clamped about his throat—lifted him clear. The thumbs dug in horribly. Spud, his feet braced wide, held the little gangster clear of the floor while he kicked and writhed in the death agony.

"What the hell—" Tony barked angrily. "Get busy up there."

For answer Spud dropped Cokey's inanimate body back through the hole in the floor onto the heads of the men crowded together below. He caught at the Tommy-gun, fell back into the corner. Despite his huge bulk he moved with the grace and quietness of a cat.

Cries and curses burst out after the first awed silence.

Tony was raving.

"UP!" he demanded. "Up—up there. Get her and whoever's with her. Up—quickly."

For answer Spud stepped three paces forward and, aiming by instinct, let a burst of fire pour through the flooring into the gangsters below. One screamed with the impact of a slug while the others fought to be first through the doorway.

Spud stole to the opening and looked down. A hand stole around the casement, holding an automatic. Its throbbing reports drew a new line of holes across the flooring at the point where Spud had stood a moment before.

He sent a single shot crashing down. The automatic went spinning while the gunman's hand disintegrated into a bleeding mass of smashed knuckles. A wail of pain followed the shot. He could hear Tony's bellows of rage over the excited shouts of the others.

Police whistles were shrilling outside now. Spud's face lighted with unholy glee. With the police below and with him above, Tony's race was about run. A new clamor sounded outside. The police sirens. Carrying the Tommy-gun, Spud slipped silently back to the corner where the girl stood. He put his lips close to her ear.

"The cops are coming," he said. "When I whistle, follow the walls around to the window—keep you from getting drilled. You'll have to—"

The words were silenced by a new burst of fire from below. Jets of light were popping up erratically wherever slugs tore through the flooring. Spud tiptoed along the wall to the farther corner, smashed out the window glass and then leaped quickly to the hatchway.

Heels scraped in the bathtub.

Score one against him. One of Tony's gunmen was planted there out of range from the scuttle, waiting, listening for a sound to betray the whereabouts of the intruder above.

Spud leaned forward, watching the doorway through the opening. A thin, lean hand, carrying a gun slipped into view. A snuff-colored sleeve, disclosing a silken cuff gave him identification. It was Tony. He brought up his automatic, held it steady while elbow, upper arm, came into view. For a split second half of Tony's face came into range but was jerked back before he could pull the trigger.

Patiently Spud stood immobile; watched the arm slide back again. His finger came back slowly on the trigger as the shoulder came into sight. Tony's arm was rising but he did not show his face.

So be it, Spud reflected; a bullet through the gun arm would ruin Tony's effectiveness. The heavy automatic roared; the gun below crashed on the tiled floor. The impact jerked Tony forward and for a flashing instant his head and part of his body were framed in the doorway.

Spud's gun belched twin slugs as his enemy fell backward. Spud leaped far to the left as the other gun in the corner of the bathroom sent a stream of lead through the floor where he had stood.

Avidly he listened for words from below.

"Where'd they get you?" someone demanded. Tony, a note of pain in his voice, replied: "Through the meat on my shoulder. No bones."

Spud slipped a new clip into his rod, stole across to the wall to retrieve the Tommy-gun. There were voices outside now, men were in the alleyway between that and the adjoining building. He slithered to the window and looked down. Someone pressed the button of a flashlight. Its beam showed the head and shoulders of a harness cop.

He turned, hissed a signal to the girl. Light as a feather she came up to his side.

"Give me your shoes," he demanded. There was a stub of pencil in his pocket. Casually he reached over and ripped away a bit of silk from her torn and damaged waist.

"Write your name and the word 'attic,' " he said. "You don't dare to call to 'em. I'll put it in your shoe, throw one down to attract their attention, then flip 'em the one with the message."

He leaned far out, waited until the group below was silent for a second and pitched the small suede shoe down. Someone grunted, a flashlight flickered on the ground.

"Girl's shoe," a voice said.

Spud felt behind him, took the other shoe, pitched it after the first. There was a moment of quiet, then words:

"Aileen Millan—commissioner's daughter—attic. Commish's around the corner."

A black figure detached itself from the group and sped away.

"Stay here," Spud commanded, turning to the girl. "I'll keep 'em off you. Use your gun if they get me."

He turned away. A tiny, determined hand caught at his arm.

"Goodbye, Spud McGrahan—you're a man," she whispered. "Don't let them take you back."

Spud's face was grim now. Seconds, maybe minutes remained for his reckoning. He closed his eyes, better to picture the bathroom below, the position of the tub. Police whistles were sounding everywhere outside. He tiptoed across to the point he sought, sprayed the floor with a burst from the automatic gun. The slugs rang against the bathtub like hammers on a boiler. He leaped back to the scuttle in time to see the gunman dash into the other room.

Far below there was a muffled, battering sound. The police were smashing through the heavy oak doors of the stairway. Shots were being exchanged somewhere. Tony's gunnies were serving warning from behind the thick barriers, he sensed.

The minutes were all too few. He felt in his pockets, slid two extra clips into the left vest pocket, thrust the warm muzzle of his automatic back inside his open holster and leaned over the opening before him.

Spud McGrahan was in the home stretch of his gallop with Fate.

Somewhere back in the past of his black and hairy Celtic ancestors there had been a streak of ruthlessness which manifested itself in an absolute contempt of death, and apparently fanatical belief in an imperviousness to thrusts and blows of deadly weapons.

Such was Spud's attitude now. Without thought of the number or capacity of his enemies, he went through the hatch and to the floor of the bathroom in a deadly, slithering rush almost unbelievable in a man of his bulk.

He was on the floor, snatching at his rod with one hand, throwing the light switch with the other before his opponents realized that here was a killer gone berserk—amok—willing to die; asking only the favor of taking as many as possible with him.

An orange stab of flame cut through the doorway. Spud roared his battle cry and shook his head angrily as the top half of his ear disintegrated. He crouched, gun tilted at the door jamb. The room echoed with the roar of shots as those outside combed the darkness with hot lead in the hope that a lucky ricochet might disable him.

From below came a prolonged crash, the quick tut-tut-tut-tut of an automatic rifle; a heavier explosion, another. The cops were using their riot guns. The firing died down. The persistent booming crash of sledgehammers started up again, nearer now.

Suddenly Spud stood framed in the doorway, his big shoulders filling it almost from edge to edge. A gunman lay on the floor in a corner, covering the door with a Tommy-gun.

Spud shot him in the same motion which brought him to view. The bullet made a gruesome "tunking" sound like a knuckle on a ripe watermelon as it penetrated the top of the gunnie's head.

Spud felt a solid, smashing blow low on his left side as he pulled the trigger a second time, the weapon pointed at a group of three standing in the middle of the floor. The pain was intense for a moment, then quieted as something warm spread about his side, ran down his thigh in a stream.

His second bullet took the center man of the group in the shoulder, spun him about—thrust him staggering against the wall. The man at his left ducked to the floor and started shooting under the table. The third, slower, staggered and fell, a slug in his throat.

Something rasped against Spud's right leg, tore it out from under him, threw him to the floor. But he was shooting as he fell. The rod on the other side of the table ceased blazing.

Another gat was in action now. A bullet burned across his back, thudded into the door behind him.

Spud fought down the sickness, the nausea caused by his splintered thigh bone, pushed himself backward with a thrust of his great arms so that he lay within the bathroom. There was movement out there in the other room. The big library table crashed over, its heavy mahogany top facing the bathroom door.

Spud caught a glimpse of Tony, coatless, a bandage around his shoulder, diving to cover behind it. With a flick of his hand he sent a slug over just in time to intercept the other in his downward plunge. A red smear showed across his forehead for a brief second before he plunged forward on his face.

There was more shooting in the hall. Spud, disregarding the stabbing pain of his wounds, began dragging himself toward the up-ended table. Four feet! Three feet now. He was almost there.

Tony, his face a grinning mask of crimson, came up suddenly from behind the sheltering table, leveled his gun full in Spud's face and pressed the trigger. The other twitched his head like a boxer rolling out of a punch. The bullet missed his face, entered the back muscles and caromed off his spine somewhere low around the kidneys.

Spud hardly felt the shock. Once, twice, his own finger twitched on the trigger.

Tony said "Don't!" and rolled away. He lay on his back between the table and wall, six feet distant.

"Got you—you stinkin' framer," Spud exulted. "Got you like I said I'd do. Now come on to hell with a better man!"

Tony's eyes opened. Bloody froth was forming on his lips.

"Get—well," he said weakly. "You—burn."

A great snarl came from Spud's lips. He tried to lift himself; slumped back. He was paralyzed from his chest down. One arm was useless. Oh yes, those smashed ribs.

Still gripping the automatic he snatched at the table leg with his right arm, managed to push it clear. Tony's eyes were watching his every movement.

"Bug—smashed bug," he whispered. "Lay there—see me—get well!"

Bullets were smashing through the outer door now, feet came rushing up the stairs from below. Spud summoned all of his failing strength, managed somehow to grip the carpet with his right hand. He tugged and his huge, useless body came forward a foot. He pushed the gun aside, half rolled his shoulders, pitched forward again.

Tony, helpless also, saw that deadly progress and screamed in fear.

"Yell, ye lousy—wop skunk!" Spud found breath for the taunt as he dragged himself forward another two inches. Something heavy smashed against the outer door, still holding by its heavy spring lock.

One more thrust. The lights went black for a moment but Spud had not lost consciousness. His right hand went out, felt for the soft throat of the enemy lying there before him.

Thumb on one side of the windpipe, fingers on the other—squeeze and keep on squeezing until the cops pulled you off.

There was a sickening, rattling sound beside him. Spud shook his head. The lights shone yellow again. Ha! That noise. Ye-ah! Tony and his death-rattle.

The door came in with a crash, two huge policemen tumbling across the room as the barrier gave.

Behind them came Commissioner of Police Millan, gray, disheveled and himself wounded about the head. His eyes flashed about the room, saw the light of understanding in Spud's eyes.

"The attic—my girl—where?" he demanded.

"Call," Spud whispered, his throat strangely paralyzed. "She'll come."

"Aileen!" the commissioner's voice trembled at the realization of her peril.

"Dad!" It was a glad shout. The official jumped to the bathroom door in time to catch his daughter to him as she swung from the attic coaming. For a brief moment she rested there in safety. Then she struggled free, ran to Spud;

raised his head against her firm young breast.

"Spud McGrahan, Daddy," she said. "He saved me from them, kept me up there until we could get word to the police. Then he dropped down among them and fought them single handed. He's a man, Dad Millan, a better man than any you've got under you."

The commissioner dropped on his knees at Spud's side.

"I knew your father," he said simply. "What can I do for his son?"

He heard the answer from the stiffening lips. "See that I'm buried first. I want t' beat that wop scut—out of purgatory—be in—hell—when he gets there!"

A police surgeon bustled in. "See to him," the commissioner ordered.

Spud's eyes opened again for a moment, gazed understandingly about the room.

"Turned cop at the last," he whispered. "Wish—I'd—never been—anything else."

Hellcat Buys a Stack
A Novelette of the Big Stem

He was a big hillbilly from Kentuck—all rod and not much else—and he was wanted by John Law and the Hellcat. Which one will get him?

REGINALD—"HELLCAT"—KILEY, SLENDER, DEBONAIR, with the innocent face of a cherub and an indefinable air of shyness, grinned happily to himself as he waited at Tenth Avenue and Twenty-eighth Street for the coming of Stanley Chambers.

It was to be a reunion, their first meeting since the year of the Armistice. Chambers, now a star of Broadway newspaper stars, had been his buddy in the Marine Corps; at Belleau Wood had saved him from death by carrying him out of the line when a German machine gun made of him a crimson sieve.

As he stood, watching southbound taxicabs for a sight of his friend, Hellcat reviewed those intervening years which had drawn him into the whirlpool of Chicago's gangland.

His nickname had been bestowed on him by his buddies in France, had been justified during his Chicago career. Everything he seemed to be, he was not. His mild appearance belied his salty temper; his slight form was a trap for the unwary who found in the apparent weakling, steel strength and an almost insane energy.

A cab pulled in at the curb ten feet distant. Stan, big, bluff, daredevil Stan, grinning happily, stepped forth, turned to pay the driver.

Hellcat started toward him. As he moved, a powerful arm caught him about the throat from behind, thrust a gat under his right arm.

Then it roared its death song—three times—blasted the life out of Stan with its stream of heavy slugs.

Hellcat saw the horror in his friend's eyes as the lead smashed its way into his chest. Instantly he went half insane with the seething, white-hot anger which had earned his nickname.

He was like one of the cat tribe, caught and held in a trap; forced to look on while its young meets destruction. He pitched, twisted, lashed out with his feet—almost succeeded in breaking out of the hold on his throat.

Stan's killer forced the side of his fist back against Hellcat's chin in an effort to throw him off balance. Hellcat shifted, slashed sidewise, wolf-like, managed to sink his teeth deep into the base of the other's thumb.

A gun crashed against his temple and he went deep down into the waters of oblivion—out for the vital seconds required for the other's escape.

Yet with him he took two clues. The man was tall—tall enough to top him by nearly a foot. And he used a cheap, highly scented soap. Hellcat had caught the heavy odor of verbena on the hand he had mangled.

Veteran of many violent scenes, it needed more than a single blow on the head to rob Hellcat of his senses for more than a few seconds. The cop on the beat and a group of bystanders were gathering about Stan's body when he lurched over to them.

"What the hell's this? Who did it?" the cop was demanding.

"He did—I guess," a bystander said, pointing to Hellcat.

"No, it was another guy; that one got socked too," another contradicted excitedly.

The cop turned to Hellcat, kneeling at Stan's side.

"How about it?" he demanded.

Hellcat looked up. The cop started back at the malevolent gleam in his eyes.

"I didn't see him. He grabbed me about the neck; shot under my arm. Then he cracked me over the head and beat it."

He said nothing about the perfume, the teeth marks on the killer's hand. These were his own clues.

"Wonder who this bird is?" the officer said. He stopped as though to go through Stan's pockets.

Hellcat pushed his hand away, wearily.

"Stanley Chambers," he said, still in the cold, emotionless tone of the man whose anger is almost past restraint. "Star reporter on *The Sphere*— and there'll be plenty hell over this. He was coming to meet me when they croaked him."

"Yeh?" The cop had a vision of promotion, a detective's shield. "Thasso? Now, who knew he was gonna be here at this time?"

Hellcat took up Stan's hat from the sidewalk, laid it gently over the dead face. Then he turned and glared bleakly into the eyes of the cop.

"That"—he spoke slowly, bitterly—"is something I'm going to find out."

He turned, started away. A bulky, middle aged onlooker stumbled against him.

"Judd Hanby—hangout upstairs," he whispered. He backed away, apologizing for the collision.

Hellcat was fifty feet down the block when the first police auto screamed its way to the scene. Then came an ambulance; other police cars. He looked over his shoulder. The harness cop was talking excitedly to the detectives, pointing in his direction.

A plainclothes officer stepped to the running board of a car, motioned for the driver to go ahead. Hellcat turned, began to retrace his steps. The detective dropped off beside him.

"Stick around," he snapped. "What the hell you lammin' for?"

"Going to see a man," Hellcat said crisply.

The detective stared hard at him for a moment, decided that this mild-seeming young man would not dare to kid him. Hellcat was eyeing him innocently.

"Well, he'll have to wait; we need you," the officer said curtly. "Copper says you knew this bird—did you?"

"My buddy," Hellcat said. "Saved my life once. He was coming to meet me when they got him."

"Reporter, huh?" the detective continued. "On *The Sphere*?"

"Yes."

"What sort of a looking fellow bumped him?"

Hellcat slouched along wearily, his mind in a ferment.

"I already told the cop I didn't see him. He had me around the neck; shot under my arm—then socked me on the bean with his rod. All I know."

"Ye-ah?" The detective seemed not to believe the story. "Is that it—or are you scared some gun'll knock you over if you talk?"

"Dope it for yourself—I've said my piece."

"Maybe if we take you down to headquarters and hand you a few, you'll remember better," the other snarled.

"Make it easy on yourself," Hellcat said dully. "When you're all through jabbering I've got some business to 'tend to."

"Hell you say! What business?"

"Find the man that croaked my bud."

"Well for cripes sake!" The dick beckoned to two of his brother officers. "Come over an' see what's gonna get the bird 'at got his buddy! He won't talk—but he's takin' the warpath."

The others came, grinning with the callousness of men used to the sight of violent death. Suddenly the elder of the two caught Hellcat's arm, spun him about.

"Name's Kiley?" he asked. "Chicago?"

"Yes."

"They call you 'Hellcat'?"

"Sometimes."

The old officer nodded.

"Probably he means it," he said. "He just beat a murder rap in Chi; cops say they can't use him there any more—too tough!"

"Well, Jimuel J. Gosh!" the first dick gasped. "And I thought he was some family's pet son!" He eyed Hellcat in surprise. "You suppose he knocked this guy off, himself?" he asked hopefully.

Hellcat turned, caught the officer's gaze. His eyes were glittering, baleful, unwinking, like those of a cobra.

"Stan Chambers was my friend—I said," he replied slowly, distinctly. "And I know damn well what to do about it—whenever you coppers get through running around in circles."

"Say—I gotta good mind—" the bull voiced dick began. A wave of the elder man's hand silenced him.

"The dead wagon's coming," he said. "You and Miller work independent of the others; see what you can dig up. Kiley and I will go to headquarters."

"Pinch?" Hellcat's voice was bleak.

"Not unless the inspector says so," the other replied. "It's a good idea to make it look like one, though; a couple of Judd Hanby's roddies are lampin' you pretty hard."

"Who's Judd Hanby?" Hellcat demanded. "Seems like I heard of him."

"In Chicago—maybe?" the other asked with a knowing leer.

"Maybe!"

"Or did Chambers say something to you about him?"

"No, he didn't. I hadn't seen him; just telephoned I was in town and he said he'd be right down. No names were mentioned at all."

The detective stared at him as though trying to read his mind.

"If that's all you know, how are you going to start out to find the man who killed him?"

Hellcat's anger flared forth, suddenly.

"Just like any dumb dick," he snarled. "Ask questions, keep my eyes open—trust to luck mostly—see what happens. Only difference between you and me is that I haven't any lousy stoolies to do my work for me."

The chief homicide inspector, himself, interrogated Hellcat. He was gravely careful to impress on the witness that the killing of a newspaperman meant a serious upset; that early and complete frankness was essential.

Hellcat, despite his preoccupation, for his mind was working furiously on his plans, was both clear and concise. At the end of the interview the inspector said:

"You've a hard record in Chicago, Kiley; much of it growing out of a violent temper. My advice to you is to be careful here. *The Sphere* has offered ten thousand reward for Chambers' killer. I think you can leave all idea of revenge in the hands of the police. Understand me?"

"I heard you," Hellcat replied sullenly.

"I can hold you in a cell as a material witness—" the inspector began.

"Use your own judgment," snapped Hellcat. "But if it's any news to you I'm going to get the louse that croaked Stan Chambers. I'll find him—and when I do, he won't be much trouble to you birds."

"What are you doing—putting in an order for an electric chair reservation?"

Hellcat wheeled on him savagely.

"No!" he said. "All I'm doing is asking not to be monkeyed with. Leave me alone—that's what I want."

When he had gone, the inspector called a stenographer and issued a confidential order to all inspectors and detectives in his division. It was an instruction to all detectives in the Chambers case to watch Hellcat on the supposition that he suspected the identity of Stan Chambers' killer.

Meanwhile Hellcat was whizzing in a taxicab to *The Sphere* offices. There, he felt sure, he could obtain the facts he needed.

He knew, intuitively, that only the owner or managing editor had authority to make definite promises in the name of the paper and it transpired that he made the proper choice when he asked to see Austen Strang, the owner-publisher.

Strang, a tall, distinguished appearing man with a youthful face and snow white hair, was cordial in his greeting.

"Mr. Kiley," he said, "something about the regrettable death of Mr. Chambers? Be seated and tell me what I can do for you."

Instinctively Hellcat knew that Strang was worthy of trust. He resolved to give him his confidence except such clews as pointed to the killer.

"I was in the same company in the Marines with Stan," he said, "and we got to be buddies. I am a gangster; he was a gentleman—but we were friends. I got in town tonight and telephoned him. He asked where I was, said for me to wait, and that he'd be right down.

"They killed him before my eyes, Mr. Strang; while they held me so I couldn't help him."

He stopped. Strang looked at him narrowly for a moment.

"I think I know what you're going to say," he said musingly. "Chambers was your friend and you're looking for his killer—ahead of the police. Am I right?"

"And if I am—would you try to stop me?"

"Under any other conditions I would," he said finally. "But like you, Stanley Chambers was my friend as well as my employee. I think it would be well for me not to know what you have in mind."

"But I do want some information. I want to see photographs of every big gangster in New York—I mean the leaders, the topside guys."

Strang nodded, took up an intercommunicating phone.

"Library?" he said. "Send at once to my office these photographs." He consulted a typewritten list which he took from a file, dictated the names to the librarian. Hellcat sat silent until they came.

Then, their chairs side by side, the newspaperman and gangster went over the pictures while Strang read their histories from his list.

"That's fine," Hellcat said at last and arose as though to go. At the door he stopped, turned back.

"I think he forgot one," he said hesitatingly. "Name's 'Hanby' or something like that."

Strang nodded.

"One of the worst," he said. "Ruthless—a double-crosser and thief; steals from his own kind. Half of the men found dead after 'rides' we believe met death at his orders."

He telephoned for Hanby's picture, handed it to Hellcat when it was sent in.

Hellcat picked up the others, ran through them again, juggling them about as he worked. Finally he put several in his pocket.

"Like to keep these," he said carelessly. "Thanks."

Four were of minor gang leaders, men who could not have been connected with the killing.

The fifth was a half profile photograph of Judd Hanby.

Hellcat's first act on leaving *The Sphere* building was to go to a quiet midtown hotel on one of the cross streets and engage a room.

The second task was one requiring more time. With a taxi driver for a guide he began a tour of the speakeasies known as hangouts for various gangs, searching for the face of someone he knew.

The eighth resort produced what he wanted. Blinky Dawson, a former Chicago gun—now A.W.O.L. because of a bail forfeiture in a major felony case—was drinking with two friends at the end of the bar.

Hellcat dismissed his driver and for some time stood alone, drinking an occasional beer. Finally he caught Blinky's eye but signaled him the holdback sign. Eventually he worked his way over to the other's side and whispered, "Next corner, right."

Dawson was treading almost on his heels when he reached the corner a few moments later.

"How long have you been here, Blink?" he asked.

"Six months. In now with a good gang and never going back," Dawson replied.

"Good gang? What one?"

"Cooney Wilson—alky racket."

"Yeah? I heard you was with Judd Hanby's mob."

"Not on your life, and if you're smart you'll lay offen 'em too. They's going to be hell over there some day—and I mean pretty damn quick too."

"Why?"

"Judd's got into the habit of knockin' off anybody he don't like, and the way he's been goin' lately it looks like he ain't got a friend in the world. He fans 'em down because he don't like the way they hold their face—or somepin'."

"Oh, yeah? Do his killings himself—or has he got a topside rodman?"

"Lookin' for a job, Hellcat?" Blinky's tone was jocular. Then he turned serious. "If so, that's a job that'll take some gettin'. Guy that's holdin' it down now is Big Fred Pitts, Kentucky gunny. He kills 'em just to see which way they'll fall."

"Hillbilly, huh?"

"Yeh. Dude hillbilly. Behind his back the gang calls him 'Stinky'—uses toilet water 'n things."

Hellcat's nostrils widened. Again, for a split second, he caught the odor of verbena.

"See—if you want to catch on with Cooney, I'll ask him," Blinky suggested. "He always wants another fast rod."

"Nix on the alky racket. Anyhow, I've got a dollar and time to spend it. So long, Blink. Find you in the same dump sometimes?"

As he strode away, inwardly jubilant, his tired body whispered of bed, but he felt, intuitively, that he must return to the scene of the killing. Maybe he would encounter the big fellow who'd given him the name of Judd Hanby.

Flagging a passing taxi he rode to Tenth Avenue and Thirtieth Street. Thence he strolled south in the shadows. There still was considerable auto traffic, but pedestrians were few and nearly all of the business places were dark. A block distant the flash of light on metal showed him a patrolman, also half hidden in the shadows.

At the Twenty-eighth Street intersection he heard voices, stopped, peered around the corner.

Three hard-faced youths, their backs to him, were arguing fiercely. Hellcat drew back, listened.

"I'm blowin'," he heard one declare. "Knockin' off grifters and John Laws is all right—but Judd messed things up when he bumped off this reporter."

"Aw, nuts!" another replied. "Yuh got goose pimples. They'll be a helluva splash a day or two—and then that's that. You know how Judd fixes things.

"If anybody's got somepin' to worry over, it's me—with the broad workin' the telephones at *The Sphere* office. She was the one that slipped the info to Judd when this guy made a date on this corner. Cripes! If that ever comes out, me and Myrtle's got a swell chanst to meet the big juice-guy at Sing Sing."

"You lettin' her stick on the job?" the third gangster asked.

"Why not? Ain't nothin' going to scare that twist off twenty bucks a day from Judd and four from the paper."

They began to move and Hellcat drew back into a doorway, grinning contentedly as he thought how beautifully the pieces of the puzzle were fitting themselves into place. He almost feared the thought of going to bed lest he break his lucky streak.

Then, a moment later, it seemed that he might retire at once—and forever.

A flash from the lights of a passing car fell on him as he huddled in the dark doorway—just as the gangsters rounded the corner.

In the fraction of a second he was covered by three rods; cornered. There was but one way out—and that was held by the men whose gats covered him. Yet he was quick to see his sole advantage. The moving light had passed on, leaving him, momentarily, only a shadow within a shadow.

His rods seemed to leap into his hands as he dropped silently to the floor, roared full in the faces of his attackers.

One fell limp with the first shot, bored through the throat. The second, staggering back, cursed, tried to bring his gat up for a shot. Then he twisted oddly, collapsed.

The third was pumping lead in a stream at the spot where the first shot had been fired. Hellcat, wise in the ways of Gunland had rolled to the opposite corner, his rods silent for the moment.

The store windows reflected back the flashes from the other's gun, outlining his form plainly. Coldly, as though driving off an offensive insect, Hellcat brought up his right hand; slammed three heavy slugs into the man's body just above the belt.

Then like a flash he leaped the prostrate bodies and sped to the other side of the street.

Footsteps were thundering down the stairs of the building he had just quitted. An upper window banged open, and he heard someone shout:

"There he goes! Across the street. Just one guy."

He was grateful for the deep shadows as he raced west on Twenty-eighth. A flashing glance told him the stairway was erupting gunmen. Their hoarse shouts came to him as they gathered about the three bodies.

When he was fifty feet down the block a stream of bullets whizzed past him. He did not even look back, contenting himself with zigzagging close to the fronts of the buildings.

Nearing the corner of Eleventh, he kept a wary eye out for cops attracted by the shots. He slowed, rounded the corner at a brisk walk; looked about him. Back at the other corner the glaring lights on an automobile stared after him. Dark forms were swinging to the running board. The chase was on!

Blocks down the street he could see the running lights of north bound taxicabs; too far distant to help him. A motor sang sweetly behind him. It was another taxi, swinging to the curb before a Coffee Pot lunchroom. The driver got out; looked at his tires, strolled inside.

Hellcat, moving like a ghost, slipped about the rear of the car and into the driver's seat. A glance behind showed that the pursuing car was almost at the corner. In the lunchroom the taxi driver sat chatting with a waiter, his back to the door.

Slipping the gears into second speed, Hellcat advanced the spark, pressed the starter. A second later he was roaring away up the almost deserted avenue. He was not a second too soon. Even as the gears meshed the pursuers' car swept around the corner, holding the moving taxi full in its lights.

Hellcat was unworried. They had not seen him enter the cab; their first thought would be that he had hidden himself in some stairway. A moment later he cursed, fed the engine more gas. The other car had slowed, but only to drop a squad of men to search the block. Now it was roaring along in his wake.

At Thirtieth, Hellcat rounded the corner on two wheels, heading east and jammed the foot throttle to the floor. He was almost through the block before the other car turned in. At Tenth Avenue he turned south; noting with relief that the block ahead of him was clear.

Cutting down his speed, he shifted into second, set the wheels parallel with the curbing; leaped into the darkness. Instantly he was lost in the shadow of a doorway showcase while the abandoned cab chugged merrily along, rubbing its tires against the right curb.

Hellcat was tense—ready—as the pursuers swept around the corner in a wide arc to avoid capsizing. He heard excited shouts, then the roar of the motor as the gangsters speeded after the slow moving taxi.

Without a glance behind, he sprang from his hiding place, across the avenue and toward Ninth. Behind him he heard a wild rattle of machine gun fire; then the crash of some heavy object.

That was the tip-off. In another moment they would be spreading out in all directions for a shot at him. Running lightly, he reached the corner before there was any sign of pursuit.

A taxi was dropping a passenger across the street. Hellcat slipped into the seat, called "Uptown" to the driver.

"How far?" the man demanded roughly, fearing a short haul.

"Broadway and Forty-second," Hellcat snapped, "with a finnif for you if you make fast time."

"Now you're talkin'," the driver said as he trod on the accelerator.

Hellcat turned to look back. The other car was rounding the corner of Twenty-ninth. It too turned north, raced along—hesitated—finally turned left into Thirtieth.

Judd's prowling gunmen had lost the trail. Hellcat settled back with a satisfied sigh.

He was miles ahead of the dicks and another day was coming.

"TEN THOUSAND REWARD FOR REPORTER'S SLAYER." The morning papers screamed the news in huge type. Hellcat read them in his room, slowly, painstakingly. His name was not mentioned; he was merely "an unidentified bystander" so far as the press was concerned.

It was nearing noon when he strolled into the street. Again he found himself without a definite plan other than the urge to be back to the scene of the killing to pick up what threads of information might be lying about.

His taxi dropped him a block from the hangout after rounding the square once to reconnoiter. He strolled about for some time, seemingly merely another of the quarter's loafers. Eyeing the various groups covertly, he soon picked out the gunmen and lookouts posted by Judd Hanby as guards outside the hangout. One or two, he thought, eyed him closely. He contrived a thoroughly vacant expression, lounged away.

Presently Hellcat started briskly down street. A door on the opposite side had opened and Hellcat had recognized the heavy-set man of the night before—the tipster he was seeking.

Hellcat kept even with him, crossed the street and followed when he entered a Chinese laundry. The man turned as he took his receipt from the Oriental.

"Hello, Jack," he said familiarly. "Got back, eh?" He let his right eyelid droop warningly.

"Yeh," Hellcat said. "Gimme my things if I come up now?"

"Sure," the other said placidly. "Took good care of 'em. Say—when you want good laundry work done, come here." He turned to the Chinaman. "This is my good friend, Ah Wong; mebbeso he ketchum shirt for you."

The Chink grinned hopefully. "Can do," he said. "You come back, huh?"

In the street again, the stranger spoke rapidly.

"Quiet—until we get to my room," he said. "You were smart in there—keep it up. Remember, you're my friend Jack Smith just back from Denver. Ever been there?"

Hellcat nodded.

"Did thirty there for bustin' a cop on the beak; guy was the chief's brother. Yeh, I've been to Denver."

"Damn if you haven't, brother," the other said with a chuckle. "You got your diploma."

As they reached the door, the other whispered:

"Third floor front; go up as though you'd been there before."

Inside the plain, poorly furnished room, the man said:

In another moment they would be spreading out in all directions for a shot at him.

"My name's Bates—yours is Kiley. I figured you'd be scouting for me and when I saw you, I came out."

"You know me, huh?" Hellcat said suspiciously. "What the hell, anyhow?"

"Listen!" the other drew him toward the window. "You and I have the same cat by the tail—so it's cards on the table with me. I'm a Department of Justice man, transferred from Chicago on a big dope roundup. I recognized you last night; that's why I tipped you."

"Fair enough," Hellcat said, extending his hand. "You saw the whole play?"

"From the moment you came out of the cigar store. I saw you spotted; saw the killer when he eased up behind—"

"Yeh," Hellcat interrupted. "Big, tall guy; dark, kinda skinny." It was Bates' turn to be surprised.

"How do you know? You didn't see him."

"Name's 'Pitts,' " Hellcat continued. "Kentucky hillbilly. Gangies call him 'Stinky' because he uses perfume. I smelled it on him last night. A guy told me all about him later."

"But you can't pin the killing on him because he smelled of scent," Bates objected. "Juries are tough these days."

"Sure!" Hellcat was impatient. "But he's wearing my teeth marks in his left hand. That don't mean a thing though—he'll never get as far as a jury."

Hellcat's tone was calm, conversational. He might have been saying, "Nice day, isn't it?"

"I thought as much," Bates rejoined. "I figured you'd be gumming the works for Uncle Sam if you get smoky too soon."

"Listen! Uncle flung me out on my neck when he got tired of using me for a target in France. He's owing me, not me owing him." Hellcat gave the other a bitter stare. "Get me right now! I'm knocking this big hillbilly off the first time things are right so I can tell him first what it's all about."

Bates produced a pair of high powered field glasses from a hiding place, scrutinized the building across the street. He turned and handed them to Hellcat.

"Focus them on the mirror back of the second window," he directed. "When your eyes get used to the distance, you'll see a man at a desk; another near him.

"The one at the desk is Judd Hanby. The other's Fred Ellis who acts as a go-between for the importers. There's a big shipment in now and we're waiting to cop Judd with the goods. See them?"

"Ye-ah. I'm carrying Judd's picture too. Think you've got him by the short hair?"

"Absolutely—a twenty-spot at least."

"Not enough," Hellcat snarled. "He ordered my bud on the spot." He was silent a moment, then flamed out:

"See here, Bates—what the hell did a guy like Stan Chambers ever do to that punk to get himself knocked off?"

Bates was silent a moment before he replied.

"All of this is under your hat. Chambers was on secret assignment to round up the dope gang; had been for months. He was the first to get the dope on Judd as one of the big money guys and a wholesaler as well. Somehow they found out—"

"Yes"—Hellcat interrupted—"and planted a gun moll on *The Sphere's* switchboard. She tipped off to Judd that Stan was to meet me last night."

Bates caught Hellcat by the shoulder excitedly.

"What?" he demanded. "Say that again—if you're sure."

Hellcat told him of the gun fight—the conversation he had overheard preceding it.

"What a break! What a break!" Bates exulted. "That makes Hanby an accessory to murder—and in this state he gets the same dose as the principal."

"Uhuh!" Hellcat said uninterestedly. "But he's another that'll never see a jury."

He stood, thinking, for a moment before he said savagely:

"See here, Bates, you've been square with me and maybe I'll lay off for a day or two—but Hanby and Pitts are mine, you hear me? If you lock 'em up in the middle of Hell, I'll still find a way to get 'em."

"You'll lay off until I say 'Go!'" Bates rejoined briskly. "Uncle Sam won't stand for any damn foolishness in this case."

Hellcat turned, stared out of the window.

"Oh no?" he said over his shoulder. "Listen guy—if you intended that crack for a belly-laugh, it's lousy."

A knock on the door interrupted them.

"Papers," a shrill young voice called out.

"Thanks, Sammy," Bates said a few seconds later as he handed the boy some small change. He tossed the *Telegram* and *Journal* over to Hellcat, turned to the window to read a tight rolled bit of paper he had palmed. He felt Hellcat eyeing him curiously.

"If you'll read your papers," he said, "you'll see that you only killed two of those yeggs last night. The third is dying in Bellevue—and my chief writes me the man thinks he's been double-crossed. His name's Shag Kennedy."

Hellcat was on his feet in a second.

"I'm going to see him," he snapped. "Where is Bellevue—and can I get to him?"

"Not unless I go with you," Bates replied. "My badge will take us anywhere."

And so it proved. The sleepy cop outside the gunman's door and the bored nurse both lost interest when they saw the bit of bronze.

Hellcat crossed to the gunman's side, looked down at him; saw the clammy perspiration on his forehead, the ghastly death-hue on his face.

"Poor damned kid!" he said sympathetically. "Going out—just because a crazy man thought he'd crossed him up?"

The sufferer's eyes opened.

"Jeez!" he exclaimed. "Another bull! A guy can't even die without some lousy dick smellin' up the place."

"I'm no cop," Hellcat said slowly. "I'm just another sap like you—selling my rod to nuts that'll blast me off most any day."

Shag's eyes were closed again. He was thinking of Hellcat's first words.

"What did you mean?" he asked, "—crazy man—double-crossed?"

"Just what I said, you poor punk! Judd Hanby planted his new heater-man in that doorway to knock you and your two pals over. He figured he had to get rid of you on account of the shooting of that reporter—and he wanted you out of the way on account of your broad."

Two pink spots showed in Shag's cheeks.

"Show me!" he demanded.

"You can see it for yourself," Hellcat said, leaning forward; speaking slowly, distinctly.

"As long as Judd kept his head, he did all right. But when the 'power' bug hit him he started building a gang with which to run the town. Then he began to learn what a lot of kings have learned—that you can't trust even the palace guard!

"He got so he didn't trust anyone—so far as you can throw a bull by the tail. On top of that he's a fool for the twists—on the quiet."

He waited a moment to let that sink in, then continued:

"What do you suppose he pays your moll twenty bucks a day for? Just to tin-ear on a switchboard? Because nobody else would do it cheaper?

"Hell no, Shag! You've been asleep. He's nuts over the jane and she fell for him. That's why you're going out—with three slugs in the guts."

It was an artful play on the dying gangster's emotions, done with the masterly talent of a veteran actor.

Shag's face now was a twisted mask of hate, his eyes flaming with the lust to kill.

"Myrtle!" he growled, "the lousy chippie 'at I fed an' dressed up! And—she had the guts to tell me Judd was trying to make her—and how she hated him!"

He caught his breath, shuddered with the pain, then lay quiet for a moment, resting.

"Gimme a shot of hooch," he asked at length. Bates got up and left the room in search of the nurse.

"I'm—gonna spill my guts—turn snitch, you hear me?" he moaned. "Snitch, I said. I'll belch every lousy, blamed thing I know that'll make it tough for Judd and that rat, double-crossing twist—"

He went into a spasm of cursing, quieting only when Bates returned with a graduate half filled with whiskey.

Hellcat took it, let some of the fiery liquor course down Shag's throat. The gunman lay back, gasping, his fingers picking at the sheet—certain sign of approaching death. Finally he spoke.

"Cris'!" he moaned. "Goin' on twenty-four and gettin' croaked over a rotten moll!"

"A moll you'd have ditched for a thin dime, too," Hellcat prompted. Shag began cursing again.

"Here!" Bates interrupted. "You're wasting the strength you need to fix Judd up for the hot seat." Shag quieted.

"Get some paper," he ordered. "I want to sign it. Hell with what the gang thinks about it when I'm dead."

Bates produced a memorandum book and fountain pen from his pocket.

"Go ahead," he said softly. "We'll start it off that you know you're dying and want to make the statement—"

"That'll go in court?" Shag asked. Hellcat nodded.

"And they can't cross examine you, either," he said.

An expression of satisfaction settled on Shag's face as he began:

"The reporter, Stanley Chambers, was killed at the order of Judd Hanby, who knew he was getting close on Hanby's trail in the narcotic game. The actual shots were fired by Big Fred Pitts, who received five hundred dollars for doing the job. That was his regular rate for killing men for Judd Hanby—some dozen or more of them."

Then Shag, pausing now and then to rest and collect his thoughts, went on giving approximate dates, names and, as far as he was able, Hanby's reasons for wanting them out of the way. The total was fifteen for a six months period!

Hellcat, during a rest period, moved over to Bates to ask:

"Hadn't I better get the girl angle to make sure of it?"

Bates frowned, shook his head.

"No. Make him talk about the dope. I'll question him if you don't care—but keep the girl until the last. It's hate for her that's keeping him alive now."

Hellcat gave Shag a little more liquor as he asked:

"Where does Hanby store his dope shipments?"

"Blueprint cases—round tin ones; keeps 'em in Helmertorg's architect office, Mammoth Building," Shag answered quickly. "They carry 'em in and out openly; nobody thinks of friskin' 'em. But if they did, they'd find cut ends of real blueprints in the ends of the cases."

"Damn neat!" Bates ejaculated as a wedge to get into the questioning. "Who's the Big Boy—the brain of the ring?"

Shag eyed him speculatively. "You're a bull, ain't you?" he demanded. Then he grinned evilly. "All the better," he went on.

"Judd sends telegrams to Robert Smith, Empire Building, Trenton, after each shipment gets in. Smith repeats 'em to a guy named Mortimer out in the lah-de-dah section of Brooklyn.

"I heard Judd and Fred Ellis laughing about it one time. They said the Smith telegrams go Western Union; then Mortimer repeats by Postal. In that way they figure it'd be hard to tie 'em together."

"One more question," Bates continued. "Did you ever handle any dope yourself?"

"Not for sale—just to pass it on to the mob when there was a big job on. Judd always sends his rods out coked to the hatpins. They get it just before they start."

Bates caught Hellcat's eye and nodded.

"Tell me how Judd learned that Chambers was on his trail," Hellcat said.

"Bartson, a stoolpigeon dick at headquarters; friend of Judd's. He learned it from a federal who talked too much. That's how Judd come to plant Myrtle on the switchboard at *The Sphere*."

He paused a moment, to think, when Hellcat said, "How?"

"Remember a girl, Mildred something-or-other, they found wandering around in the woods up in the mountains? She was the paper's 'phone supervisor, and Judd snatched her off, filled her up with coke and hyoscine. He had Ellis buy the job for Myrtle from a crooked supervisor Ellis knew."

"And it was Myrtle who told Judd that Chambers was coming to meet me?"

Shag blinked in wonderment. "Jeez!" he exclaimed. "You are the guy, aren't you? Yes, and when she told Judd where, he said: 'Now ain't that nice! Right on my own doorstep!'

"And she told him something else too. The reporter phoned some broad to call off a date right after he talked to you. He told her you was the angel faced guy he'd told her about; the one who looked like a willie and was so tough they'd flung him outta Chicago."

"And then?"

"They sent me out to scout you. I made you right away and Big Fred parked in behind you until the reporter guy showed up. It was Judd and Myrtle who—"

Bubbles of crimson foam appeared suddenly at the corners of his mouth.

He fell back inert. Hellcat caught him about the shoulders, raised him; wiped away the traces of blood.

"You've got to sign it," he said, over and over again. "You don't want Judd and Myrtle laughing at you, do you?"

A quiver passed over the dying man's body. Finally, out of the well of his hatred he summoned enough strength to beat back the death angel for another moment. He tensed for the last gesture of his revenge.

His trembling fingers closed on the pen; the point touched the paper— moved. Carefully as a schoolboy competing for a prize, Shag formed the words "Henry (Shag) Kennedy" below Bates' shorthand symbols.

Then he laid back quietly—dead.

It was Hellcat, the hardboiled gunman, who paused to close the dead eyes—to fold the flaccid hands over the still breast.

For the first time in his life he had no fault to find with a snitch!

Hellcat's hand on Bates' shoulder brought him to a halt outside the hospital.

"What's on your mind?" the federal asked. "There's nothing now to keep me from turning Judd and Pitts in to the cops as murderers."

Hellcat smiled wolfishly.

"Can it," he said. "Save the bull for the hopheads! You'll not spoil your case against Big Guy Mortimer just to keep me from burning down a couple of skunks."

"Pretty wise, eh?" Bates sneered. "Look! I'll make a deal with you. Lay off for twenty-four hours so I can finish my case and—"

"No!" Hellcat growled the word stubbornly.

An angry light appeared in Bates' eyes.

"I'm a federal officer," he said slowly, "and you've heard a statement concerning an unfinished case—"

"Yeh!" Hellcat took the words from his mouth. "—and so you're going to tell me you'll hold me for a material witness. Well—you won't."

He leaped back; snapped a rod from under his arm.

"You haven't said it yet, so I'm not resisting an officer," he snarled. "Now, keep your hands down and be on your way. Everything you've got, came to you through me, so it's your job to 'tend to your own business and leave me to mine. Beat it now, Bates—you're a good guy and I'd hate to plug you."

Bates stared back at him for several seconds, turned away.

"You win," he called back, "but—get in my way and its Leavenworth for yours."

Hellcat wasted no words in a reply. He stood waiting patiently until Bates took a taxi and turned west, then he entered one and drove directly to *The Sphere* building.

For a moment it seemed that a scholarly young secretary was inclined to bar Hellcat from Mr. Strang's presence—until he chanced to glance into the visitor's eyes. What he saw there—a malign gleam which boded him no good—stopped him cold. His jaw went slack with unspoken words as he backed into the inner office.

In a moment he was back, motioning for Hellcat to enter. Strang met him with outstretched hand.

"Something has happened?" he asked anxiously.

"Yes—something in your own office." Hellcat tossed the verbal bombshell nonchalantly. "A telephone operator—first name, Myrtle.

"She was the one who tipped off Judd Hanby that Stan was coming to meet me; who tin-eared in on another conversation and got my description. That's how they recognized me. I just found out that Hanby planted the girl here because Stan was getting close to him in the dope racket."

Strang started in surprise.

"I thought only Stanley and I knew of his work," he said. "And, this girl—"

"Send for her; get her up here—she's the new supervisor," Hellcat interrupted. "Hanby doped the other girl, turned her out to die in the mountains so he could get this one in here."

"But my dear man—" Strang began.

"Don't argue," Hellcat demanded. "As long as she's here, you haven't a private line on your board. I want that jane in here right now!"

Strang gave an order over an inter-communicating telephone. Five minutes later a slender, sharp featured girl was ushered in by the secretary.

"I'll talk," Hellcat said in an undertone to Strang.

"See a show last night, Myrtle?" he asked coldly.

The girl shook her head without replying.

"Too bad!" he continued. "The next big performance will have you in it—as the star."

"Is this a joke?" she mumbled. "A kidding match in the publisher's office?"

Hellcat regarded her curiously, much as a reptile regards its bird victim. She squirmed, turned white beneath her makeup.

"We've got it on you, Myrtle," he said at length. "Accessory to the murder of Stanley Chambers. You and Judd Hanby and Big Fred are going to fry up there in the Big House."

"Like hell!" the gang moll snarled, forgetting her character of telephone operator. "I'm not—"

"Forget it. You are. Whatever they get, you get some too. Shag died an hour ago—I was with him when he went out. We've got his deathbed confession—"

"And I get a frying on the word of a rat like that!" the girl screamed. "Listen, you! Try to frame me for the chair, will you? Why, Judd Hanby'd cut your heart out and show it to you—"

Hellcat raised his hand for quiet, turned to Strang:

"Satisfied?" he snapped.

Strang shuddered. "Yes," he said. "What next?"

"Hold her somewhere in the building with a trustworthy man and girl reporter watching her every minute. She mustn't get near a 'phone—"

As he talked, Hellcat had worked nearer to Myrtle. Suddenly he leaped, caught her hands, pulled them behind her.

"Take the gun out of her garter!" he commanded.

"I—really—" Strang began.

"Hell with that; she's dangerous as a man," Hellcat growled. He threw the girl to the left, caught her around the shoulders. A second later he tossed a stubby .25 automatic on Strang's desk.

He accompanied a veteran police reporter and an athletic appearing girl reporter when they took her to a storeroom; gave explicit orders for her care.

"She was in on Stan's killing?" the girl scribe asked.

"Yes!"

"Don't worry then; she won't get away. Stan was to have married my sister."

Back in Strang's office, Hellcat said:

"I want two promises from you; that no matter what happens to me, *The Sphere* will see that every louse connected with Stan's death is punished. The other is that you'll keep the secret that I'm going to tell you until it breaks. It's a scoop you're entitled to."

Then he told the whole story from the moment of the killing down to the present moment. When he had finished, Strang, whose excitement had been growing by leaps and bounds, came to his feet exclaiming:

"Great God! What a story! What can I do to repay you?"

Hellcat regarded him quizzically.

"Oh, I don't know," he said hesitatingly. "Maybe get me out of jail sometime."

He jammed on his hat, started to leave.

"Be seeing you," he said, "—maybe."

Soon after dark Hellcat reappeared in the Tenth Avenue sector. This time he came afoot, keeping a wary eye out for Bates and homicide squad men. He crossed at once to a Greek restaurant across the street from the Hanby hangout, taking with him the evening papers.

He chose a booth that commanded a view of the corner, ordered his meal and began reading. What he saw brought quick curses to his lips. Already Hanby and his crooked connections were attempting to blacken Stan's name.

"UNDERWORLD SAYS DEAD REPORTER WAS GRAFTER," a tabloid told the city in its biggest type.

"SLEUTHS PROBE CHAMBERS' DEALS WITH RACKETEERS," the *Journal* declared.

The stories were identical in form. Headquarters detectives, unnamed, were said to have given out the information. Their angle of the case was that Chambers had been connected as fixer with a dozen or more rackets; that he had broken with a gambling clique and had dared them to reopen without his protection.

Hellcat was still mouthing angry curses when his eyes fell on a tall, spare framed individual emerging from Hanby's stairway. Instinctively he knew the other for Big Fred. He grinned evilly as he saw the killer rubbing the base of his thumb with the other hand.

Big Fred crossed the street. In a moment he appeared in the doorway, chose a seat at a corner table with his back to the box partition. There he could watch the door, see the movements of everyone entering.

Hate, the urge to kill, surged through every fiber of Hellcat's body. This was not the time or place, but he wanted, more than anything else in the world to leap out, hold Big Fred under his rod, then blast him down with every slug in the clip.

Then a plan came to him. Big Fred, he was certain, was yellow, like a majority of other cold blooded killers. He slipped from the booth, tiptoed close behind the unsuspecting rodman. His right hand rested on the gat under his armpit. He jammed his left thumb roughly against the other's spine.

"Up with 'em—snappy now!" he gritted. "Eyes front too, you big punk!"

Slowly, carefully, Big Fred brought his hands into sight; put them on the table, fingers widespread. Hellcat reached across, pulled a heavy automatic from a shoulder holster; its mate from the hip. He touched the other's cuffs, feeling for sleeve guns, then slipped the clips from the confiscated rods.

"Here!" he said coldly, disdainfully. "Put 'em back where you carry 'em. I've got their teeth." He slipped into the chair opposite his prisoner.

Big Fred's eyes bulged as he recognized Hellcat.

"Chicago stuff, eh?" he snarled. "What's the game?"

Hellcat grasped his left hand, turned it over, pointed at the purple crescent bruise at the base of the thumb.

"I put that there," he said, "marked you so I'd know the right man when I put the heat to him."

Big Fred blanched.

"Heat?" he asked in simulated surprise. "Got something against me?"

Hellcat, leaning across the table, spoke coldly, with extreme slowness.

"Yeh," he said. "You've got something I want—it's your life, punk! And I'm going to take it when I'm ready. Tonight—tomorrow—next week—when I'm ready! I'm going to send you where you've sent fifteen better guys for Judd."

The nervous flicker of Big Fred's tongue across his white lips showed the strain he was undergoing. He let his gaze dart to the door, hoping for rescue.

Suddenly Hellcat reached across the table with his free hand, crashed it roughly across his mouth.

"Listen, fuzztail!" he snarled. "Be ready for me—I'm coming for you."

Big Fred's face was purple with anger. Of all the insults to a mountain-bred man, the slap across the face is most deadly. He was trying to flog his muscles into a leap at his tormentor. Hellcat read his thought.

"Do it!" he gritted. "You're yellow if you don't."

With the echo of the words his right hand described a half circle and his gat crashed against Big Fred's temple. The victim gasped, sunk forward on the table, his head on his hands.

Hellcat left the restaurant casually. His mood was one of elation. From now on, Big Fred would be watching, waiting for the coming of the avenging bullet. He would be leaping aside from shadows, trembling at strange footsteps in the dark.

But Hellcat failed to note the sudden start when a bystander caught sight of him; did not realize when the other glided out into the street and began to trail him.

The sidewalks were filled with pedestrians, loungers and the usual hodgepodge of children busy at play. Hellcat, seeking a quiet spot from which to continue his watch, turned into the side street.

He whirled at the sound of soft footsteps behind him; whirled too late. A dead-eyed, hard-featured youth confronted him; covered him with a rod.

"Get gay," the gunman said, "and I'll let you have it."

Hellcat's answer was to place his fingers across his vest. "What's the dope?" he asked coolly.

"Guy wants to see you; beat it ahead of me."

"You're wet," Hellcat demurred. "I've only been here two days."

"Yeh?" the roddie retorted. "But you was at this corner last night. That's where you made your slip-up."

"Oh! Like that, eh?" Hellcat was coming to realize the extent of his folly. Yet, when the other shoved him ahead, he did not resist.

"Cross the street—up the stairs next to the cigar store," his captor said.

"No funny moves; I don't want to burn you down, for the Big Guy wants to see you."

At the head of the stairs the gunman pressed a concealed button and two others came out. Hands caught him from both sides, removed the twin gats from under his armpits.

"Who's your han'some friend, Eddie?" one asked.

Eddie leaned forward, whispered something.

"Hell he is!" the other replied. "What a nice time he's going to have!"

"And how!" the first gunman replied. "I made him quick as a wink; knew him for the guy I saw run across the street after Red, Shag and Scar got the heat."

The door guard returned from an inner room.

"Judd says to bring him in," he said, motioning for Hellcat to move on. Eddie seized an arm, thrust him into the room with the mirror. He recognized Hanby at once, both from the photograph and the view he had had through Bates' field glass.

Judd sat leering at him, ready to play the role of the King Racketeer cat, toying with his mouse victim before the kill.

"Come in, gay-cat," he said silkily. "Glad to see you."

Hellcat elected to be sulky, wordless.

"Search him?" Judd demanded of Eddie.

"Yes, chief—two forty-five rods."

"Fan him good?"

"Hair to heels; nothing else."

"All right—beat it!" Judd ordered; turned back to Hellcat.

"Had a smoke party down in the street, didn't you?" he demanded.

Hellcat saw no use of attempting denial before this prejudiced court.

"Some," he said briefly. "They climbed me—and I knocked 'em back."

"But why?"

"I told you—they crawled my hump." Hellcat's tone was one of injured innocence.

Judd leaned back, hooked his thumbs in his vest.

"Spill it," he advised. "You knocked off three damn slick rodmen, which means you're good. I might use you myself."

Hellcat let his eyes flicker upward for a moment, surprised the sarcastic smile on Judd's lips.

"Nothing much to it," he said. "I was piping off a plan and heard somebody coming. I got back in a doorway and when they saw me when a car went by, they started smoking me up. I flopped and burned 'em. That's what happened."

"Sounds fishy to me," Judd replied. "Who are you?" Where did you come from?"

"Joe Jones," Hellcat replied instantly. "Jumped out of Baltimore on a rap. Just trying to stake myself to a dollar and keep going."

"Baltimore, eh," Judd said. "Know Billy Elliott?"

"Never heard of him; don't believe there is such a guy."

Hellcat was forced to make the decision with lightning speed. Intuition told him that Judd had made up a name to trap him in a lie.

"Right answer," Judd said. "I never heard of him either."

Hellcat kept silence. Judd puffed at his cigar, knocked the ashes off, studied the glowing tip.

"Like to connect with a live gang?" he asked finally. He paused, stared hard at Hellcat. "Always provided you check out O.K.?"

"Sure!" Hellcat looked Judd fairly in the eyes for a moment. What he saw there was disquieting: fear and suspicion. All he could do now was to stall.

"Talk to Stumpy Mitchell on long distance; he'll tell you all about me," he said, taking a chance that Judd had not read the papers. The late editions had carried a flash of the gangster's death in an automobile smashup.

"Stumpy, eh? I'll just do that little thing. Now you go and sit with the boys in the back room." His voice became deadly. "But don't tease 'em," he continued. "They'll make you feel like a lead mine if you make a wrong move."

"What the hell would I do anything like that for?" Hellcat demanded. "Ain't I takin' on with this gang?"

The gunman, Eddie, responded when Judd pressed a button.

"This may be an all right guy, Eddie," Judd said.

Hellcat, watching in the mirror, saw the wink which accompanied the words. Also he saw something else—the window of Bates' room, and for a split second the flash of some moving light on the lenses of his field glasses.

"Take him back with the boys," Judd was saying smoothly. "I'm calling somebody; then we'll decide where he goes from here."

As he ended the sentence, the telephone rang. Hellcat, on his way to the door, heard him shout excitedly:

"Big Fred! Sapped in the Greek's! Get him up here damn quick."

"New guy—chief's checkin' up on him," Eddie explained as he led Hellcat into the back room where Judd's gangsters were gathered. "Judd says he gets a good time unless he gets frisky. If he does, give it to him."

Hellcat dropped into a vacant chair. Across the room a gunman said:

"What do you mean, 'checking up'? He's a pal of Big Fred's. I saw 'em eatin' together in the Greek's when I passed ten minutes ago."

"What?" Eddie almost shouted the words. "Jeez! What a break for me.

And I copped him for the guy that burned down the boys this morning. Think of that!"

"Ye-ah. What about it?" the other demanded.

"Oh nothin'—much," Eddie replied. "Only that some guy bounced a billy or a rod off Big Fred's bean in the Greek's just now, and I gotta hunch this gink is it."

He whirled to the door. "Keep him covered," he called back. A moment later Hellcat heard the door of Judd's office open and close with a bang.

Now the fat was in the fire! Big Fred would beat him half to death with a gat, and then take him for a ride. He twisted angrily in his chair. Instantly he found himself covered by eight rods.

"Set quiet," someone snarled, "if you don't want the works."

"Aw scat, you blamed gutless punks," Hellcat snarled back at them. "You wouldn't put the heat on a blind cripple!" As well take it now as to wait for the session with Big Fred. It was a relief to be himself again, if only for a moment.

"Shoot 'em if they won't scare you," he taunted them. "Hell! If I had a rod I'd make all of you jump out a window."

The gangsters stared at him blankly, one by one returned their rods to their holsters. Hellcat kept his face blank, but listened intently for developments outside.

Presently he heard someone open the door a crack. He turned his head and encountered the leering eyes of Big Fred, a bandage about his head, his face still drawn and pale. They stared balefully at one another for a space of seconds, then Fred drew the door shut. Hellcat heard him say to someone:

"Yes, it's him; said he was going to get me for croaking the reporter."

A moment later Eddie and another of the guards came into the room. Without a word they fell upon him, twisted his arms behind his back, dragged him into the hallway. Another man stood holding a door open, revealing an unfurnished cubicle with close-set iron bars.

At the threshold the men shoved him forward suddenly, banged the door behind him. As he crashed against the opposite wall, he heard the click of a padlock.

Cat-footed, he made the rounds of his prison, listened at the three inner walls, chinned himself at the window. The bars were set in a steel framework. To escape that way would need stout tools and a rope. The whole fitting would have to be gouged out.

He realized that his position was hopeless, but suddenly content surged over him. True, his own race was run, but in telling Strang of his investigations, he had set in motion forces certain to take Judd and Big Fred to the chair!

Now, he reflected, he could go out—man-style. When they came for him he'd be quiet until he and Fred were face to face. Then, though he'd die in the end, he'd go trying to take Stan's killer with him.

He never knew when the tap-tap-tap-tapping on the window began, so lost was he in contemplation of his last minute plan.

A single, squirming thrust of his muscles brought him to his feet. Silently he slipped across the floor to the window. A dark shape was between him and the reflected street light, but he could not make it out.

Another tap on the glass, this time like a warning. Then for a split second the glow from a pencil flashlight fell on the face of the man outside. It was a stranger, perched on the rungs of a rope ladder.

Still another tap, then the bite of a glass cutter. The man outside waited until delayed motorists began blowing their horns in chorus. Then came a single muffled blow and Hellcat felt the cool light air on his face.

"Here's a rod and some extra clips Bates sent you," the man whispered. "He's on the roof now. We're going to raid through that room, but he's waiting for more men and says you've got to hold the fort until we can get in."

Hellcat felt the welcome touch of an automatic butt. Extra clips followed, and he was armed again. There was one more order:

"Bates says for you to keep behind the door so they don't sneak in on you," the man said.

Hellcat slipped obediently across the floor, listened. All seemed quiet outside except for the whine of screws being turned out of hard wood. Fifteen, twenty minutes passed thus. Then he heard footsteps in the hall, a knock on the door.

"Hey, you!" a gruff voice shouted.

"What?" Hellcat demanded softly, talking as though from across the room.

"Want some pink lem'nade and cake? You know—nothin's too good for the guy 'at sapped Big Fred."

"Got time to go to hell, you big floozy?" Hellcat snarled.

The other laughed, jeeringly.

"Set tight, guy," he sneered. "They're gonna give a party for you in a li'l while, and you're sure gonna learn yourself somepin'."

"All right, you big pansy, but you won't hear me do any squawking."

Hellcat grinned happily in the darkness as the epithet brought a roar of curses from his tormentor. Well he knew that "pansy" to a gangster is the killing word.

As the man retreated, Hellcat sped to the window. "Hear that?" he asked.

"Uh-huh," the other replied. "You'll get to use that rod yet. These damn screws come out mighty hard."

Hellcat returned to his post at the door, listened intently. His ears caught the sound of creaking stairs. The wolves were gathering for the kill. Judd's gangsters were slipping in, one by one. He could visualize their avid eyes, tongues flicking happily at slobbering lips as they pictured the spectacle to come.

He patted the rod in his pocket. Business was about to pick up.

The promised "party" materialized without warning.

Suddenly Hellcat heard the soft scuffing of feet, whispering outside the door as someone said softly:

"Slam the door open quick; light'll blind him. Be sure and tie his legs together like Fred said."

It was no part of Hellcat's program for the door to be opened. Better still, he must keep them away from the padlock.

Stepping back two paces, he sent four quick shots smashing through the door, midway of the height of the average man—directed to the left where he'd be certain to wing at least one.

His lips curled in a wolfish grin as a body slumped against the panels, slid downward with a grisly thud. At the same moment another howled in agony. There was a sound of running feet. Someone bawled:

"Cris'! He had a rod hid on him some'rs!"

Hellcat dropped to his knees, glued his eye to one of the jagged bullet holes. The man Eddie was leaning against the wall ten feet away, hands clasped over his stomach. Even as Hellcat watched, the man's knees buckled. He slid to the floor in a sitting position, back to the wall, moaning in agony.

Hellcat tried another peephole, looked along the hall to the door of Judd's office. A milling, shouting group stood there looking back toward the still forms by his door. Hellcat saw a chance for further terrorizing, and loosed three shots up the hallway.

As the roar of the explosions died, he heard more groans, cursing. He slipped to one side just in time to avoid the return hail of slugs from the gunmen outside.

He crawled back to the door, peeped out. A gunman was creeping on hands and knees down the hall. He carried a steel jimmy, one big enough to wreck the door with one giant twist.

Hellcat let him come on almost to the door, and drilled him through the jaw and throat. Another storm of slugs smashed through the door in answer. Silence followed.

Suddenly he heard Judd shouting:

"Got him now, fellows! Four shots first, three next—when he got Jimmy—another just now. That leaves him two to go."

A moment later he turned, called, "Fred! Come here!" The killer came out, leaned weakly against the wall.

"He's got just two slugs left," Judd said. "When those are gone I want you to go in and bring him out. You'll know what to do."

Hellcat's lips drew back from his teeth in a snarl. He raised the gat to one of the bullet holes, felt rather than sighted for aim, and sent one slug whizzing up the hall.

Big Fred raised his left hand, stared at it dully. The heavy bullet had struck the base of the forefinger; had torn its way across the hand, smashing the bones, leaving the fingers dangling, forever useless.

"Oh Gawd! Look—look—my hand—smashed!"

Big Fred screamed the words as a woman might.

Hellcat heard a crash behind him, turned. The grating was moving.

"Minute now," the man on the rope ladder whispered. "Hold 'em."

Hellcat went back to the door.

It was balm to his soul to see Big Fred, the killer, weeping like a schoolgirl over his smashed hand.

Bates, despite his white hair and great bulk, was the first of the federals through the window. He crossed the floor and wrung Hellcat's hand.

"Dammit," he said, "you've made my raid a little early, but it's all right. We got Mortimer at his home, with the goods. Ellis is in a cell and we're ready to clean up here."

In a few whispered words Hellcat put him in touch with developments up forward. A young operative set up a Thompson gun; five other heavily armed men came through the window and took stations as Bates directed.

"Crash!" The heavy table top collided with the door. The hinges groaned. Again—a third time it struck. Hellcat raised his rod and shot twice. Above the uproar Judd's voice rang out.

"Got him now," he roared. "Gun's empty. Get in that blamed room and snatch him out."

"Crash!" The table struck again and the weakened door sprung from its hinges. The men carrying it slithered into the room and died where they had stumbled.

The remaining gangsters, more than a dozen in number, had massed in the hall, secure in the belief that Hellcat's rod was empty. These, the federals' fire sent toppling, groaning, fighting to get out of range.

It was while the uproar was at its height that Hellcat dived headlong into the maelstrom of human bodies. Bates snatched at his coat—but missed. He cursed, drove his men to their feet and out into the hall.

"Watch out for Kiley," he bellowed. "He's making for the front office."

But Hellcat already was there.

Squirming, twisting, slugging and being slugged, he had won through to the place where Stan's killer hid out of range of the bullet streams.

Raging, snarling like some wild animal, he found Fred at last, crouched behind Judd's great desk. Like a panther Hellcat flew at his throat, flailing with iron hard fists at eyes, nose, chin.

Bates, gun in hand, ran in; tried to drag Hellcat from his prey. Hellcat hunched his shoulders, pitched, snatched the rod from the other's hand.

He emptied its clip full into the breast of the battered, cringing killer.

"Like it?" he snarled. "Here's some more."

He pressed the trigger again, but the rod was empty.

Actually, it didn't matter.

Stanley Chambers' enemy's soul was on the way to hell.

The Raspberry

They had gathered for the kill, this Wolf-Pack of the Underworld, with guns and choppers, besieging the man high above Broadway with none of the passersby any the wiser—a single life between them and the stake—two million!

CLANG!

A blow from a mighty hammer crashed against the steel latticework of the penthouse window at Shane Stevens' side.

He stirred almost wearily in his great leather chair to eye the barrier which still was quivering from the impact of a high-powered rifle slug.

That would be Krag Morrison, his onetime bodyguard, firing from a still higher building somewhere in the vicinity. From the window his gaze lifted to the left wall; to gouged scars which gave mute testimony to the accuracy of the gunman he himself had trained.

Shane's lips twisted into a sardonic grin as he put out his hand, snapped off the lights—switched them on again. That was at once his taunt and a warning; proof that the questing slug had not found him; warning that he still was master of the almost impregnable penthouse fortress.

This was the fourth day of the siege.

Outside for blocks around, as well as in the office building below him, furtive-eyed, hard-faced men watched—waited for him to break cover.

Among them were men who, a short week before, had obeyed him without question. One, Harve Roper, was the leader of this group. He knew that somewhere out there, Harve, his former lieutenant and confidant, was waiting in a darkened car; a chopper nestled in his lap.

There would be others in the tightly drawn cordon; others—once friends—now turned wolves at the prospect of bloodshed and enormous loot.

They had gathered for the kill—this wolf-pack of the Underworld—his Underworld, of which he had been the recognized overlord.

Two things they sought; two only. The life of Shane Stevens, racketeer czar, and the millions in cash and securities he had drawn, he thought secretly, for his getaway to Europe.

Roper had turned rat!

The thought brought Shane's strong teeth together with an angry click. Roper and Krag Morrison, hitherto beyond the power of threats or bribery, had gone over to the enemy. Worse, they had taken with them Shane's secrets—his two hidden ways out through the great building's sub-basement—and definite assurance to the enemy that in the penthouse Shane still had more than two millions in cash and securities.

A buzzer sounded at his elbow. It was a deep, musical note, far different from those other burring screaming sounds his alarm system gave off through an annunciator before him on the desk.

Shane hesitated, picked up the French instrument. He had good cause to know it had been "bugged"; that each word spoken to him was heard and treasured by the besiegers.

He shrugged; said "Hello!"

"Ben speaking, Shane." The voice was anxious.

"Wait!" Shane cautioned. "It's fine of you to call me, Ben—but they are on the line—listening to every word."

"Damn!" Ben Dwight fumed. "They've been threatening me—and Betty, Shane. For myself I don't care, but now it looks like we'd better call in the police."

Shane went cold at the words. Betty! The girl whose fine influence had brought about his decision to quit the Rackets. Betty, Ben's sister. Two friends whose loyalty never had wavered even in those hectic days when his path and theirs had strayed so far apart.

"The police!" Shane rapped out the words derisively. "A hot chance—with Captain of Detectives Cardloe and his strong-arm squad planted out around me this minute, to make certain that they get theirs! No, Ben—it's no good. The police can do nothing for me—will do nothing for you."

"But Shane! Betty—" Ben Dwight's voice was shocked, incredulous. "Surely you don't want her to—"

"God!" The word seemed torn from the very depths of Shane's being.

"Go home, Ben," he continued more calmly after a moment. "Stay there with her; don't let her out of your sight for a second. I know a way—she'll be protected within an hour at the most."

He paused to emphasize his next words; a stage wait.

"Think back to the kid days," he said finally. "Remember the name Betty had for me—the nickname? Think, Ben, but when it comes to you don't repeat it."

"I know—go ahead, Shane," Ben said almost instantly.

"That'll be the password for whoever comes from me," Shane continued. There was a world of relief in his voice. "Trust whoever speaks that word. He will do what is necessary to—"

The line roared. There was a scraping, crackling sound as of a new connection established.

"You there, Shane?" Ben asked anxiously.

"Shut up—you!" A heavy voice snarled the words before Shane could reply. "Listen Stevens, and you too, Dwight; we got your number, see? Either you kick in with the jack before dark or all the rods 'n' all the passwords in the world won't save your damned twist. She and the old woman are at home now—alone—I can grab her in three minutes. Speak your piece, Shane; jack, or girl?"

"Home, Ben—quick!" Shane snapped the words before the connection could be broken.

"The hell with Ben—and home!" the strange voice snarled. "Take your pick, saphead—jack or girl?"

"Come and get it; it's here," Shane said tauntingly. "And I'm here too, you filthy thug, waiting. I hope it's you that comes."

He heard a muttered curse. Then the line rasped again, went dead. Shane caught the reflection of his face in a pier glass; stared as at the countenance of a stranger, so white and drawn did it seem.

From the shuttered living room he turned impatiently toward the rear. At the window of the bathroom he paused; reconnoitered the surrounding buildings. He had been right. The thirty-six story Alcazar pile which was topped by his penthouse home, stood above all others on the north side. There could be no surveillance except east, west and south.

He smiled grimly, turned into the dressing room. From the back of a chest of drawers he produced a compact field-telephone set.

This of all his secrets was the sole one Harve and Krag had not known; his private telephone line to the desk of Mal Binford. In it now lay his one hope of safety for Betty. That came first, though until the moment of Ben's call, he had thought of it as his own "ace in the hole."

As he drew the telephone toward him he reflected anew on the utter general rascality of Mal, one of the Broadway type of private detectives, compared that with the man's unswerving devotion to him in many trying situations.

The telephone line had been Mal's idea.

"You'll need me quick some day, Shane," he had said. "Then the line'll prove worth its cost."

Shane pressed the button at the top of the portable case; held the receiver to his ear.

"Yep—what is it, Shane?"

The words snapped back in the twinkling of an eye.

"Listen, Mal," Shane queried, "know what's happening?"

"Not a know!"

"I'm cornered—sold out—ambushed. Krag, Harve, Spiro the Greek—Cardloe!" Shane talked rapidly, wasting not a syllable.

"Hell, you say! Be right over!"

"Wait, Mal!" Shane almost shouted the words to keep the other from hanging up. Mal grunted inquiringly.

"Never mind about me," he continued. "It's worse than that. For the moment I'm safe, but Harve and Krag have turned rat, and have teamed up with the Greek and now Cardloe and his strong-arm squad have cut in. They're out to croak me and roll me for every cent I have in the world."

"Just now I learned they're going to hit at me through Betty Dwight, the girl I'm going to marry. She's the sister of Ben Dwight of the Snowflake Bakeries chain. They've given me until dark to turn over the two million I had ready to beat it to Europe with, or they'll kidnap her.

"Mal, you're the only man I can trust. I want you to protect her. Take every man you've got or can get; picket the house; put a guard at every door and window—kill the first rat that looks that way."

"Where?" Mal also could be chary of words.

"Thirty-four eighty-six Kings Drive. Go there yourself, old man, and say to whoever answers the door that you're sent by 'Buvver'—Bu-uv-v-e-r, Mal. It's the password. Get it?"

"Sure! Three-four-eight-six Kings—Buvver," the sleuth answered. "Now what do you want me to do for you?"

"Keep somebody close to the bell there. I'll make out. And Mal—do your damndest, won't you, to keep Betty safe?"

"Damn tootin'," said Mal. "I gotta good plan already."

Shane stood, frowning thoughtfully for a moment after he had hidden the telephone set again. Lacking the opportunity to win free of his besiegers he had taken the only means of providing for Betty's safety. Mal, tested time and again, he knew to be reliable, devil-may-care to the point of reckless bravery. There was nothing now for him to do but to wait.

He made the rounds of the penthouse again, inspecting bars and locks; checking over the alarm system to make certain it had not been tampered with from without.

At the heavy bronze doors which cut off the stairway from the reception hall, he drew back a small swing-cover and put his eye to a peephole. Below him lay the broad flight of steps which led upward from the top floor of the building. The one elevator which served the upper levels stopped at the foot of those stairs. The doors giving onto the staircase could not be opened until someone within the penthouse pulled a switch which controlled the magnetized bar-lock.

Turning from the empty stairs, Shane checked for the twentieth time the rack of tear bombs on a table just within the door; the Tommy-gun and its extra ammunition and, lastly, the two Mills bombs he had provided for his last, desperate stand. All were in order. He retraced his steps to the living room.

As he crossed the threshold, the telephone buzzer sounded its deep note.

"Harve talking, Shane," a familiar voice said as he responded.

"You lousy dog!" Shane snarled. "Eat—"

"Take it easy, Big Boy," the other said calmly. "You know me, I'm looking out for Harve Roper first, last, and then some. That's why I'm calling you; I want a new deal. Cardloe's cut in and he's planning to cross me and Krag after we've got your jack, by knockin' off Spiro; then framin' us for the job. If you want, you can make a deal with me and Krag—"

"No deals with rats! Anyway I'm sitting pretty."

"The hell you are! Every exit's watched; they got Krag and some more crack shots with silenced rifles parked around in other buildings, rattlin' your windows. The building's lousy with roddies and Cardloe's dicks. You ain't gotta chanst."

"But before you get me, I've got to come out, you know."

"Yeah? Well, you'll come out all right, Big Boy. While we been talkin' they cut off your water line; you can't telephone nowhere for help—and in an hour or so we'll be bringin' your broad to the foot of the stairs for you to take a gawp at. They's startin' out after her now."

"Who's starting?" Shane asked with deceptive calmness.

"Some of the Greek's lads; they're gonna get her anyway if you don't kick in with the jack."

Shane caught his breath at the threat; fought down his anger, before he said:

"Oh, did you think to bid the boys goodbye before they left? You know, Harve, they won't be back."

Without waiting for a reply he hung up the receiver; looked anxiously at his watch.

Five-thirty! If Roper had told the truth, it would be a race between Mal and Spiro's thugs to the Dwight home. He paled as he thought of Betty in the hands of such as Spiro and his crew—Betty, beautiful, immaculate, the incarnation of everything sweet and wonderful in womankind.

His mind raced back to that night, three weeks ago, when Ben had come upon them in the library of his home, clasped close in each other's arms. Instead of muttering an apology and retiring, Ben had remained to say:

"Never again, Shane, while you're in your present game."

"I've just promised Betty to quit it," Shane had replied. "I'm through—cashing in."

Now, he reflected, the words had been prophetic. "Through—cashing in!" Cornered, unable to do more than fight to a ghastly finish; all of his dreams scrapped through the fear and cupidity of associates, rivals, and Cardloe, crooked dick.

An epic siege this, surely, high above Broadway, with none of the passersby, even the police, the wiser for what was happening. What a finish! And what a stake for such a battle; two millions—and but a single life between them and the wolf pack.

As he thought over the strange circumstances which had caught him in their net, a droning sound began beating against his eardrums. Startled, he came erect; listened. It was an airplane, close at hand, flying low.

Steadily the hum of the propeller, the crackling roar of the motor, increased in volume. Shane sat tense, trying to find some explanation of the federal and police rules governing flights over cities.

He leaped to a side window; looked out and up. It was dusk outside now, but directly over the building, descending in tight, steep-banked spirals came a cabin biplane. He watched it narrowly through a part of two circles; knew instinctively that the pilot was using the Alcazar building as the base about which to lay his circle.

Friend or foe? It could not be a friend; there was no place for the plane to land and take on a passenger. Then, too, only Ben and Mal knew of his predicament. Therefore, it must be an enemy.

In a flash the solution came to him—attack! With the thought, he leaped into action.

Which would it be, gas or explosive? He snatched at the handle of a master switch as he reached the doorway. Instantly wall and ceiling fans in every room began throwing air against all of the tight-closed skylights and windows. There was no wind to force its way inside. It followed that the fans would exclude any of the heavier poison gases.

An explosive bomb would be a different matter, though. For safety's sake, Shane sped along the hallway, flicked open the bronze doors and stepped into the stairway, closing the doors carefully after him.

Even in the stairway, the roar of the airplane motor sounded with increasing clearness. Shane estimated that it was within fifty feet of the roof now. From above came the sound of missiles—soft plops—and the sound of splintering glass or light metal.

Long minutes passed, and still Shane stood silent in the stairway. The drone of the airplane had softened; seemed to recede. Whatever his mission, the pilot now was seeking the higher and safer air lanes. Shane turned, unlatched the bronze doors, sniffed. There was no unusual odor though the fans were driving a heavy current of air through the open door.

In the same instant there came a crashing impact against the heavy door at the foot of the stairway. Shane saw it all clearly now—a gas attack from the air to make possible an assault from below. Like a cat he whirled inside the door, caught up the Tommy-gun; saw to it that it held a loaded drum.

Again some heavy weight crashed against the lower door. Shane's hand stole out, cut off the lights, then slid to the switch controlling the magnetic lock on the lower door. For a few seconds he stood thus in the darkness, poised, waiting.

A third crash brought his hand down like lightning. The bar swung up and the door, released, swung inward. To the attackers it would seem that the last blow had broken through.

With it came a toppling figure, sledge in hand. The big hammer clattered to the floor while four heavily armed men dashed in, one tripping over the hammerman as he tried to rise. Shane, his chopper muzzle protruding through the crack between the bronze doors, waited for a split second while the tangle reasserted itself. His eyes, narrowed now to flaming slits, took note of the grouping, chose for the first victims the men closest to the door.

His finger came back slowly, carefully.

The Tommy-gun stuttered its death croon, on and on—through the contents of the drum.

In turn the invaders threw up their arms, pitched forward until all lay silent, motionless at the foot of the stairs. And still the grinder coughed on. Bullets whipped into the quiet forms, tearing and smashing indiscriminately, beating at them until the last vestige of life was gone.

Shane lowered the muzzle of the smoking weapon; pulled over the magnetic switch. The lower doors swung shut and the bar clanged into place.

From the relocked inner doors, he went to the telephone.

"Whatcha want?" a gruff voice demanded in a moment.

"The coroner," he said softly. "There are five dead men at the foot of the stairs."

Shane had no illusions. The coming of the coroner and police would avail him nothing. He could not escape even in the midst of a police guard. One shot from a silenced rod in the tumult would finish him. Then Cardloe, Spiro, Krag and Roper would have easy pickings in the penthouse.

He decided to listen for the arrival of the police, throw off the lock on the lower door, then refuse to answer his doorbell. So far as he was concerned, he was back where he started, except for whatever advantage lies in striking the first, shrewd blow.

Presently he became conscious of a low, intermittent whining sound which blended with the beat of the fans in the still air. His thoughts suggested another airplane! Going to the window he looked out. The skies were empty, but around his windows there circled and eddied a cloud of greenish-yellow, greasy-looking vapor. Small need, therefore, for another gas attack. It would be possibly another hour before the last of the clinging gas had been carried away.

As he turned back, he sensed the sound again. It seemed to have the human quality of impatience—anxiety. He turned his head this way and that; caught its direction. The bedroom! Two strides brought him there. It was nearer now, louder. It came from the dressing room. He cursed himself for his denseness. It was the signal from Mal's telephone set.

Shane darted to the chest of drawers, snatched out the head phones.

"Cripes!" Mal's voice was anxious. "Thought sure they'd—are you all right, fella?"

"Betty!" Shane demanded. "Were you in time?"

"Yeh! Hadda knock over two-three Greek boys tryin' to jimmy the back door; they'd been watchin' the house all day. Girl's okey. Got her and the old lady in a safe place."

"Good, Mal!" Shane jubilated. "Where?"

Mal grunted—his nearest approach to a laugh.

"Here!" he said surprisingly. "Wanta talk to her?"

"God, yes!" Shane half whispered. "Hurry, man!"

In another second Betty's voice came to him over the wire.

"Shane!" she breathed. "Tell me, are you all right?"

"Yes, now!" he answered gratefully. "The last hour has been hell—waiting—afraid they'd—"

"They almost did; Mr. Binford came just in time. They were breaking in when he came and shot them."

"Good man," Shane growled. "Do what he tells you. Anyway, stay there until you hear from me. I've a bit more than half a plan of getting out of this jam."

"Tell me, Shane, dear; what can I do? You know, things wouldn't be worth while without you, my dear."

"Or without you!" Shane responded, his voice thick with emotion. "Just wait, dear—that's all there is to do now. I'll talk with you again later, but first put Mal back on the line."

Briefly he told Mal the events of the last hour, beginning with the gas attack and ending with the slaughter in the stairway.

"I gotta hunch I could bust through with eight-ten hard guys I know," Mal suggested hopefully.

"No good!" Shane negatived quickly. "If it was just a bunch of rods that might work. But Magnus Cardloe's in it up to his neck, which makes it police business. Nobody can afford to shoot it out with Cardloe's strong-arm squad, plus my own gang of rats who've turned on me because I wanted to quit the racket.

"If there was a fight, Magnus'd call it a police case, and if you weren't all killed, he'd send the rest of us to the chair as killers."

"Afraid you're right, Shane. Got any plan?"

"The makings of one. Right now, Mal, if you want to help me, see that Betty is safe, and somehow beg, borrow or steal an armored limousine; keep it somewhere near your office. If I ever make it away from here, I'll need the car as much as I'll need breath."

"That's easy! Harry the Finn owes me a good turn, and he's got a lulu. I'll have it here in thirty minutes, parked at the side. It's even got a Tommy in a turn-down case in the back seat upholstery. Give me the office when you make the break, Big Boy, and I'll have you covered nine ways from the jack."

"Right! And Mal, you know the place where I keep this field set. Just in case—you know—I'll be leaving a package there addressed to Betty. It's securities, negotiable; enough—if I don't make it through. You'll make it your job to get them for her in that case? What?"

"Yer, Big Fellow, but before that you'n me'll have a snort outta a bottle of Scotch I just got off a boat."

Shane breathed a sigh of relief at Mal's promise, couched as it was in words that would arouse no fear in Betty's mind.

"You're one right guy," he said. "I'll try to buzz you back later."

As he replaced the field set in its niche there came up to him from the canyon of Broadway the wailing of sirens. Police cars, bringing officialdom to the fringes of his private siege. He grinned caustically at the realization that the Law could do nothing to aid him.

He was as helpless as the dead men lying at the foot of the stairs.

Was he as hopeless?

Feverish activity marked Shane's movements during the next few moments.

Like a quick-change vaudeville actor, he already was tugging at the buttons of his clothing as he turned from the telephone. In the wardrobe closet he stepped out of his neat gray suit; drew from its hangers a natty golfing outfit.

Quickly, yet without lost motion, he donned the Scotch hose, plus fours, outing shirt and limp Panama; thrust his feet into rubber-soled greens shoes. From a corner he took his golf bag, removed several clubs and threw them on the bed. A suitcase yielded flat packages of greenbacks of high denomination; bundles of securities.

The money he fitted into the bag, thrusting in shaft after shaft; packing the bills about the handles solidly. The securities he put into a Boston bag, tagged it "For Betty Dwight"; hid it back of the chest of drawers.

The golf bag, with its precious load of cash, he concealed back of the shower curtain in the bath.

This done, he raced to the doors, peering through the peephole at the grisly mound of bodies below. All was quiet, but to Shane this meant nothing. On the other side of the closed door police would be scurrying here and there, seeking an answer to the report that there had been a gun battle somewhere in the building.

Pulling the switch which cut the stair lights, he touched another and watched the strip of light as the magnetized bar swung back and allowed the heavy doors to open.

Almost immediately he heard a shout, then scurrying footsteps. A uniformed cop stood outlined in the doorway, yelling to attract the attention of others.

Shane, watching at his peephole, gritted his teeth in impotent rage as the gross form of Detective Captain Cardloe appeared in the light.

For a moment hate nearly overbalanced reason. What would he not give for one shot at the police department's arch-crook! Another uniformed man, then several men in plain clothes appeared. Shane saw red again as he recognized the scrawny neck and hawk-like features of Harve Roper, peering over the shoulders of the others.

Suddenly the group divided, formed a lane, to make way for Captain McQuaid of the precinct station. In him Shane recognized a friend, the only friend he could claim in the building. Though they had known each other for years, Shane knew that the official would not swerve one iota from his sworn duty. Inversely, Shane realized that he would do nothing while McQuaid was there to bring injury to his friend.

With the coming of the district commander, the hurly-burly of shouts and questioning ceased.

"Know anything about it?" he demanded of Cardloe.

"Nothing!" the other grunted sourly. "Maybe Shane Stevens does, he lives up there." Cardloe pointed with a none too clean thumb up the stairway.

"Shane? H-m-m-m! Hardly a whole-sale killer," McQuaid said. "There's something fishy about this."

Cardloe turned; flashed him a suspicious glance.

"Meaning what?" he demanded.

"How did *you* get here so quickly?" McQuaid snapped.

"Official business in the building. Think I bumped these guys off?"

McQuaid's face was grim.

"As soon as I'd suspect Stevens," he said gruffly. "I'll go up," he added. A second later he turned, staring angrily into Cardloe's eyes as the latter turned to follow. Cardloe dropped back with an oath.

Shane watched the captain's progress up the stairway, his eyes glued to the masked peephole. He stood, unmoving, while McQuaid battered at the door; pushed innumerable times at the bell button.

"Nobody up here," McQuaid said over his shoulder.

"I'll get some of my boys and smash in," Cardloe suggested eagerly.

"Not in my precinct you won't, Cardloe," McQuaid said sternly. "Shane Stevens is just strong enough to get us both set down if I let you pull a stunt like that."

"Aw, hell, Cap—" Cardloe began angrily.

"Just what do you want in there anyway?"

Cardloe snarled and turned away at the question.

"You seem to be running it," he sneered. "You'll make the explanations too."

A moment later he added:

"Medical examiner and his assistants are here."

McQuaid turned; ran lightly down the stairway.

And now Shane's moment was at hand.

Below, for half an hour at least, all would be confusion. There would be more policemen, the medical examiner and his crew; reporters and photographers would be swarming everywhere.

Cardloe, Krag, Spiro and the others might watch for him as they willed, but in the confusion there was an outside chance that he might slip through.

Pulling down a heavy steel bar, he dropped it into beckets in each door-jamb; scattered the tear bombs about the floor where inrushing feet would be sure to smash them. The Tommy-gun he thrust to one side, but a hand closed on each of the Mills bombs.

These still represented his last-minute defense.

From a medicine cabinet he took a roll of absorbent cotton; packed liberal pads of it in each cheek. He settled his limp straw hat low over his eyes, swung the treasure bag to his shoulder and turned to the mirror. Good enough, he felt assured, to pass for a tenant of the building en route home after stopping at the office at the end of an afternoon of golf.

A drawer yielded a pair of heavy buckskin gloves. From a locker he took a coil of wire rope kept in reserve as added lashing for his big canopy in time of storms.

Thus equipped, Shane stole silently from the back door, kept close to the wall until he had reached a point under the bathroom window.

Darkness shielded his movements. He was invisible, he knew, except to prying eyes in higher buildings. That was something he must chance.

He knelt, knotted an end of the cable about a pillar; tossed the remainder of the coil over the low parapet, waited listening alertly, until the vibrations told him the line hung, unnoticed by late tenants.

He moved toward the edge of the building; paused as the thought struck him that he had not notified Mal and Betty that he was coming. Then he squared his shoulders resolutely. Far better to leave his Great Adventure in the hands of Fate. The next few moments would tell the story.

A moment later he stood calmly erect on the very edge of the parapet, gazing down into the brilliant, shimmering gorge called Broadway.

His figure was outlined eerily against the night sky.

A buzzing, droning something, like a giant bee, whizzed out of the darkness, snatched at the shoulder of his coat; nearly overbalanced him.

Krag Morrison, high in a nearby building, had caught sight of him against the background of Broadway's lights! The tiniest fraction of an inch had saved Shane's life!

He dropped to his hands and knees, crouching for a moment as he made ready for his ordeal.

Even as he moved, his eyes caught another lance of flame when it stabbed out from a high building a block distant. This time the bullet whizzed past harmlessly.

With a last vision of Betty's radiant face to strengthen him, Shane slipped over the edge and hung by his hands. With the right toe he managed to work a wrap of the cable about his calf and thigh. This done, he clamped the sole of his left shoe against the rope, worked it back until it rested against the instep of the right shoe. Now he had a brake of sorts.

Hitching the golf bag more securely over his shoulder, he drew a deep breath, caught with first one gloved hand, then the other, at the cable; started his downward slide.

He had planned a slow, measured descent. Instead he found the metal rope slipping through his hands with alarming speed; his feet and the clutch of his fingers seemingly powerless to stop him.

The braided metal strands burned his hands, the inside of his thigh and calf; scorched his ankle as he tried desperately to check his fall. He clutched ever harder on the slippery cable, bearing as best he could the almost intolerable pain of the burns.

Now he found himself swinging slowly about as well, with the cable as his axis; probably the uneven weight of the golf bag. In desperation he set the muscles of his forearms and legs, gripping down on the line with the last atom of his strength.

The added burning struck on his nerves—but he was slowing up—stopping. Perspiration was running down his face in streams, almost blinding him, when he managed at last to clamp his feet together and hold his position.

He looked down. Already his feet were below the tops of the windows of the second floor below the roof of the offset structure. Ten stories below was the top of the main building, itself more than twenty stories high. Darkness shrouded the intervening distance, saved him the sight of the long drop.

Slowly, gingerly, he turned his head; slid a few feet farther down. There was a light in one of the offices close at hand. He craned his neck for a better view; growled a curse—relaxed his hold and slid down another ten feet.

Another narrow escape! Spiro the Greek and two of his henchmen were there; the three standing with their backs to the window! A cold dew gathered on Shane's forehead. One whistling breath, the slightest sound, and their rods would be out—and he would be falling, filled with their slugs, to the roof below.

Once level with the windows of the next floor, he clamped hard on the line again with both hands and feet; realized instantly that he had gained too much speed again. He was sliding, sliding steadily downward; the terrible burning had returned.

For a second he managed to slacken the speed of his descent.

Then the sole of his left shoe clicked against the right; something slashed at his ankle, scorched a furrow along the leg—

Instantly the cause flashed through his mind.

He was at the end of the rope! Less than three feet of the line remained—and he was still slipping downward!

Desperately he shut his burning hands taut on the cable. He stopped, slid a few more inches—then came to a halt. He was hanging only by his hands now. The free end of the line was whipping about his hips.

He could not hang there interminably. He doubted if he had the strength in reserve to pull himself back enough so his feet could grip the cable again. No human could help him now. It was do or die—with his own resources standing between him and death on the roof below.

From somewhere he summoned new strength; shifted his weight so that he hung suspended by his right hand only. The left he forced slowly downward, past his chest, groping desperately for the free end of the cable.

At last his fingers touched it; brought the loop up even with the right hand.

Panting with the added exertion, he forced his fingers to carry the end twice about the rope, but below his hand hold. Now he had a swing—a bo'sun's chair—provided that he could hold on long enough to bring the bight of the cable through one of the loops.

His hands were horribly numb now; it seemed that his right shoulder was unjointed; that the tortured muscles and ligaments were tearing one by one. Searing pains fled downward through the muscles of his side and back as the arm thews quivered with the strain.

At last!

The knot slid home, tightened with a jerk. He caught a new grip with his left hand above the right, pulled his body upward until he could put a knee through the life-saving loop.

For a moment he knelt there, resting, catching his breath. He looked upward; shuddered as he saw the straight, silver line of the cable outlined in the glare from the office the Greek had preempted. They might see it at any moment.

Before him, distant two yards, were the windows of a dark office. Two yards! As well two miles!

He shifted his weight unconsciously and the rope began spinning again. Leaning out and back, he sought to counteract the motion. Instead he gave the line a pendulum effect. Now he was turning more slowly, but he was swinging back and forth, parallel with the face of the building.

To offset this, he caught a higher hand-hold, tilting his shoulders back and thrusting forward with the lower part of his body.

The effect was instant, though not what he wanted. He had increased the length of the swing, but still he was only quartering toward the face of the building.

Suddenly there flashed into his mind the picture of a gymnast he had seen recently; an aerialist whose varying swings enabled him to change his direction at will.

His was the same task now, complicated by his inexpertness and the length of the cable above him.

Shane closed his eyes, waited for a moment for the swinging motion to slow down. Then he arched his back, took up his weight on his hands; thrust mightily with his legs toward the nearest window. He must work up a sufficient impetus so that, at the last moment, he could release his hold and pitch himself through and into the darkened office.

The first swing took him directly toward the sill. The second brought his knee against it with a sharp thump.

Now he lifted on the outward cast—poised for the supreme effort.

Up—out—he swung over the darkened void below. Dimly he sensed that a telephone was ringing furiously somewhere above him.

At the end of the outward arc he hung poised for what seemed an eternity.

Then he felt the night air rushing past his face as he swung down—in, with ever increasing speed.

In the last fraction of a second, when it seemed that the face of the building was leaning outward to meet him, he disengaged his knee from the loop; thrust his feet up and forward—made ready for the leap.

He felt his feet strike heavily. Then came the crash of breaking glass; on top of that a numbing crash against some hard object; the feeling of a thousand lancets stabbing at his back.

He struck heavily, rolled over and over; brought up against the corner of some heavy piece of furniture.

He was safe! Nothing else mattered. He never knew when he had released his hold on the cable; what instinct told him when the proper time had come.

He staggered to his feet, clung to the sash of the splintered window; gulped in great breaths of fresh night air.

A voice—shouting excitedly in the office above him where he had seen Spiro and his men, brought him back to reality.

"Chris'! Deesa Steve' hees got away!" he heard Spiro bellowing. "Scatter out! Keel heem! Krag's seen him go down a rope!"

Shane shook himself together with a muttered oath.

His troubles were just beginning!

• • •

The hallway was deserted, lighted only by an occasional lamp globe, as Shane emerged from the office he had entered so strangely.

His rubber-soled shoes made no sound as he ran lightly along toward the red light which indicated the built-in fire escape. There, for a moment at least, he might be safe. It even was possible he might work his way down far enough to evade Spiro's thugs.

He hitched the golf bag well around on his left shoulder; slipped the muzzle of one of his shoulder guns under his trousers band where his fingers could clutch it in a flash. He paused for a second longer; listened, adjusted again the pads in his cheeks which changed the entire contour of his face.

Then he caught a deep breath, began running nimbly down the concrete steps. He rounded turn after turn, keeping accurate count of the floors as he passed them. At the eleventh, he slowed his pace to a walk; stopped at the next hall to listen carefully.

Instantly he stiffened. There were voices outside; gruff, raised in acrid discussion. He could not distinguish the words, but his reason told him he must continue farther before testing his semi-disguise in the hallways.

Another flight; a second. Now there was nothing left him but to emerge, for the fire escape well ended here. That serving the main building would be further down the corridor. Again he listened and heard movement and voices.

But haste was imperative. Nick and his crew might be ahead of him even now. Far better to risk all on one desperate chance than to wait until Nick and Cardloe had joined forces. Their first act would be to start a search of the building from the ground upward.

He lifted the latch, let the door swing open a few inches. Down the hall to the right, scrubwomen were cleaning the floors. To the left a group of workmen toiled at a repair job in the tessellated floor. No lights flowed from within the offices in either direction.

Shane spent a few precious seconds obliterating as best he could the marks of his exertions. Then, assuming a swagger foreign to his usual carriage he slipped out into the hallway.

Some men have the impulse to move to the right; others to the left. Shane let instinct guide him; strode, whistling, toward the scrubwomen. They were four, making a line across the hall. One drew her bucket aside; looked up at him with a toothless grin.

"What's all the noise up above, mother?" Shane asked pleasantly.

The dame's scrawny shoulders lifted in a shrug.

"They do be strange doin's the night," she quavered. "Policemen an' other bums runnin' here and yonder; trackin' up the floors. Wan av 'em's ridin' wit' each elevator lad also; seems like they do be lookin' fer somewan."

Shane tossed a bill on the soapy floor beside her.

The news was well worth it. But for that he would have run into a trap. No time now for further recourse to stairs. He must take a chance on the elevators.

They were just about the turn in the hall. The cables of three showed they were down. The fourth was higher in the building. He was wise; waiting for that one to pass before ringing the "down" bell. As it passed he thrust out his head curiously. He had been right. It was filled to overflowing with harness cops and men in civilian attire. Officialdom, without a doubt.

He pressed the down signal; noted immediate response as the cables started singing upward. He pressed close to the door, caught sight of the glare of rising lights.

Through the open grid in the top of the cage he could see the operator; another form was squeezed back into the left corner!

In another second the lift slid to an easy stop; the door tripped back. Shane, his golf bag pressed awkwardly against his stomach, was singing the golfers' anthem, "A Hole in One," boisterously. He leaned unsteadily against the grillwork as though a bit the worse for a prolonged stay at the Nineteenth Hole.

Actually he was tense, alert! The man in the corner was Eliason, one of Cardloe's dicks, a ruthless gunman and slugger despite his police star.

Still bellowing his rowdy song, Shane lurched forward unsteadily. His hand flashed to his trousers band; came up with leveled rod.

"Up, Eliason!" he snapped. "Turn around."

The detective's hard mouth opened in surprise. His eyes lighted with an angry fire as he recognized Shane; knew he was helpless.

"Turn, dammit!" Shane gritted, taking a step forward.

Eliason complied, but kept his head turned watchfully over his right shoulder. Shane leaped in, thrust heavily at the dick's shoulder, forcing him, grunting curses, into the corner.

His arm rose—fell. The barrel of the automatic caught Eliason over the temple. He crumpled with a groan; lay still.

Shane flashed about at the operator; covered him.

"Down—basement!" he demanded. "No stops."

"Yuh—yes!" the man quavered. "Please dud-don't hurt me."

"Then hurry!" Shane crowded close to the pilot, in the corner; his left hand poised over the other's right should he attempt to shift the control to stop.

They flashed downward through what seemed an eternity to Shane; past floor after floor, past cars rushing upward. Watching closely he saw the numeral four; counted two other flashes of light, then saw the glare of the main floor as they slid past it.

The safety chains caught and stopped the car. Above them Shane could hear someone bellowing profanely, shaking the doors, commanding the operator to return.

Shane caught the man by the shoulder, dragged him out into the dimly lit corridor.

"The back way—show me!" he snapped. He knew his secret getaway was guarded. The man hesitated. Shane dug his rod into the fellow's spine. "Quick—or take a slug," he said.

As though galvanized, the man rushed down the hallway, around a turn, down another passage which ended in a flight of concrete stairs. "There," he said, pointing.

"Go ahead," Shane ordered. "And no tricks."

At the head of the stairs, the man fumbled with the door fastenings; finally threw it open. Shane looked out. Before him lay a brilliantly lighted tunnel; a passage to the street.

Dangerous, that, he reflected. It might be a trap.

"Where's the light switch?" he demanded of the operator.

"Main board—engine room," the other quavered.

"Wait!" Shane said.

He snatched a putter from the bag, sent the globe flying into fragments with a blow. Twice more he struck, battering loose the brass-edged collar of the fixture, opening the way to the contact point.

He glanced about, fixing the route in his mind. Raising the metal head of the club he forced it into the light fixture. There was a hiss, a flash of blue flame. Instantly every light in the passage went black.

Shane loosed his hold on the operator's shoulder, pressed a bill into his hand.

"Stay here five minutes," he commanded. "Tell them I stuck you up; that you didn't hear me leave."

Ten seconds later he stood just within the dark maw of the passage, looking out into the street. The sidewalks were crowded with early evening pleasure seekers. A majority moved toward Fifth Avenue. Mal's office, with Betty awaiting him, was in the opposite direction, just off Madison. He did not dare to force his way against the trend of the crowd. To do so would make him a marked man.

Perforce he stepped out and fell in with the crowd, working his way quickly to the outside. Fifty feet from the corner he stopped, cursing angrily under his breath.

Harve Roper was posed watchfully at the corner, his tall ungainly form ready for instant action.

In golf clothes, and with the contour of his face changed, he might fool many—but Roper, his lieutenant for two years, would be difficult to deceive. An empty taxi stood a few feet ahead at the curb. Shane slipped inside.

"Eighth Avenue, north to Fifty-ninth; then Madison," he directed.

The man half turned to listen and Shane's hand snapped to his rod. The driver was "Speck" Ashton, one of the Greek's gunmen—apparently another watcher.

"I ain't takin' no short hauls," he growled. "Anyhow I'm waitin' fer a guy."

For answer Shane slid forward, bored with his gat in the back of the man's neck.

"Move!" he gritted. "That—or croak!"

The driver's eyes lifted to the rear vision mirror, caught those of Shane; widened in recognition. Shane, sensing treachery, saw the man's plan in a flash—the stalled engine—a sudden dive from his seat.

There was but one answer. Heedless of the passing crowd, Shane snapped his gun back, snapped home a crushing blow on Ashton's head. In a single darting movement, Shane slipped out, crowded into the driver's seat and pitched Speck's inert form down under the dash.

He kicked the engine into lift, started in second gear with a shrill screaming of cogs; nosed in ahead of a private car.

Then the traffic lights went red!

Here was disaster. He could not expect to stand there for thirty seconds without detection. Someone would see the quiet form huddled at his feet, or some flat-footed cop would note that a civilian was driving a taxicab.

Something must be done to distract attention. He half set the emergency brake, put the lever into low gear. Then, moving with the speed of light, he slipped to the street and past the nose of the car next on his left. At the same instant the taxi moved forward and bumped heavily against the car ahead of it.

Instantly there were excited yells. The crowd rushed to the scene of the new excitement. Someone shouted, "Dead man!"

Shane whipped about the corner, signaled a cruising taxi as it was passing him.

It was the theatre hour and north and south regulations applied. They must go north until a right turn street was reached. He motioned up the avenue and the driver let in his clutch.

Then there occurred one of those unexpected happenings common to New York traffic.

The cop at the intersection, trying to straighten out the snarl caused by Speck's cab, chose to flag down all avenue traffic as Shane's cab was just across the line. He motioned for the driver to pull to the curb to clear the way for exit from the cross street.

The cab slowed; came to a stop beside the one man in New York Shane wished to avoid. He looked up, found himself staring into the beady, murderous eyes of Harve Roper!

●　●　●

Harve's right hand snapped to his armpit; the other caught at the door handle.

Shane shot him through the heart, his hand moving like a lightning flash.

Harve's body stiffened, but the murderous mind would not be denied. His rod flamed, roared its death song within the cab.

Shane knew he was hit; felt the slug tear through the upper part of his right lung. Yet the second report from his rod seemed to blend with Harve's shot.

That slug also went true. It struck Roper full in the mouth, slanted upward through the brain. When it emerged it carried Harve's hat with it.

Women's screams, men's curses, the clatter of shots and Roper's falling body, brought pandemonium. Shane switched the muzzle of his still smoking rod to the chauffeur.

"You're next," he snapped, "unless you get me out of here."

A roar from the motor, screaming of gears, was his answer. The taxi leaped from the curb, tore the front fender from the car next on the left, skittered through between two other cars and roared upstreet.

Shane leaned back; tried to collect his whirling senses. The chest wound was serious; that was all too plain. Already blood was soaking through his shirt and coat; running through and coursing down his body.

"Next right," he croaked at the driver. "Madison—down two blocks—northeast corner."

Miraculously the way seemed to open for them. The lights were green at Madison for a right turn; right again at the next corner. Brakes screamed shrilly as the driver pulled up before the entrance to Mal's office building. A block distant a small police car, siren screaming, was swinging into the avenue. Another car, dark, low-slung, sinister, clung in its wake.

"Fifty for you—beat it!" Shane gasped, as he dragged himself feebly to the pavement. Before he had taken two steps the getaway car was around the corner, lost in traffic.

"Eighth," Shane said to the night elevator man. The other was staring at him, agape at the spreading crimson stain on his shirt-front.

"Nobody up there but Binford," the man said.

"He's the one," Shane replied wearily. He caught at the grillwork to steady himself as the car shot upward.

"I'm one of Mal's men," the operator said. "Anything I can do?"

"Yes—forget you saw me," Shane gasped. "If you're on the square."

"Mal'll tell you," the other said. He grasped Shane's arm, steadied him to Mal's doorway; threw the door open without knocking.

"Oh, chief!" he called. "Man here—hurt."

"I got Harve—he plugged me in the lung," Shane gasped as Mal came running from an inner room. "Some of 'em are just behind me. Hold 'em."

Mal whipped a supporting arm about him, turned to the elevator man and snapped:

"Nobody's come to this floor. Keep 'em back as long as you can."

"I'll stick the car between first and second," the other said and ran back to his cage.

"Betty—?" Shane gasped the name.

"Back in the rear office with her mother. Eight of my boys are on the job," Mal replied. "I've got a young doctor friend on the floor below; that'll be a good place for you for an hour. Think it's pretty bad?"

"Bad enough—but not the Big One." Shane's voice was stronger now. "I think I'm beginning to get the breaks."

His eyes fell on the golf bag which he had dropped.

"Hide that," he ordered. "And don't tell Betty I'm hurt. Just say I got away and I'll be seeing her soon."

Mal called one of his men. Between them they got Mal to the floor below. Fifteen minutes later as the bandaging was complete, Shane heard the physician whisper to Mal:

"Clear through the right lung. I got the slug out from beside the shoulder blade. Rest and quiet—he'll be all right in a week."

A week! Shane shrugged. Why not a century?

Mal signaled he was returning to his office.

"Can't he rest here awhile, doc?" he asked. "And privately? Get what I mean? It's worth five yards to you."

"It's a doctor's duty to see that his patients are not disturbed," the physician replied with a knowing wink. "Expecting someone?"

"Just a few tough gunmen and some thug cops; I'll send a couple of my men down to do the arguing."

The doctor switched off the lights in the surgery; went with Mal to the door. Shane closed his eyes wearily; tried to think. Had he escaped from one trap, only to fall into another, even less beatable?

As though in answer he heard the thud of heavy feet running up the stairway; curses—another rush to the floor above, then argument.

In a few moments there came a soft tapping on the outer door. The physician tiptoed in. "What do you think?" he asked.

"May be Mal," Shane whispered. "Better take a chance—but give me my gat first." He fumbled, slipped in a new clip; drew himself erect.

"Now!" he said.

The doctor braced himself, pulled the door open an inch, then swung it wide.

"Mal's men," he said over his shoulder. Two hard-faced men thrust their way in.

"Cardloe's up there"—one said out of the corner of his mouth—"raising hell. They was blood spots leading into the office. He found 'em. Girl's gone down the back way.

"Mal says to get you to hell away from here. Harry the Finn's car's waiting. Let's go."

Shane, with the aid of one of the men, struggled into his blood-smeared coat. The second man reconnoitered in the hallway. As they left, the doctor handed Shane three tablets.

"Take one now," he said; "another if you feel yourself slipping. Use the third on top of that if you've got to have your senses for a few minutes longer. Good luck, Big Fellow."

The three stole into the hall silently, down to the freight elevator. Upstairs Shane could hear men cursing; milling about, threatening. Suddenly he heard Mal's bull voice bellow above the uproar:

"You'll come in when and if I say to. Damn you, Cardloe! The only little thing you'll need is a search warrant and a lot of good luck—you stinkin' blot on the good name of decent yeggs."

The detective mouthed some obscene reply, then shouted angrily:

"He's stalling! Scatter out, you guys. Two to a floor. Burn that bird down the minute you lay eyes on him."

Mal's companions tugged at his sleeves. One pulled the elevator door back soundlessly. Feet, clattering on the stairs, drowned out the slight sound of the gears as the elevator started down.

The cage finally slid past the blank doors of the first floor; came to rest at the basement level.

Instantly there was a rush of feet and Shane found himself held tight in the arms of Betty. Beneath her superb eyes were dark circles of worry. She was pale and shaken, yet, despite his wounds and the present danger, Shane glowed with the thought that this beautiful thoroughbred was forsaking her world, to go down to hell with him—if need be.

"Oh, Shane dear!" she murmured. "I knew you were hurt; that you'd need—"

"Aw, can the mush!" One of Mal's men hissed the words. "This is a hell of a good place to be away from." He twitched uneasily at Shane's sleeve.

A short flight of stairs taxed Shane's strength to the utmost. They stopped behind a corrugated iron door opening onto the cross street. There was movement outside, but seemingly it was the steady tap-tap of folk going about their private affairs.

"Get ready to lam," the detective grunted. He grasped the bottom of the door, slid it up with a rush. He leaped out, followed by Betty, who ran straight to the big blue limousine at the curb. Shane came next, with the second of Mal's men bringing up the rear.

What followed seemed to Shane like a hophead's dream; a kaleidoscope gone wild.

Shots roared, seemingly from all sides. A slug snatched his hat from his head, sent it sailing into the street. The dick in front of him loosed half a dozen shots to the right; grunted with pain; slumped to the pavement.

Shane's rod leaped into his hand as he glimpsed Spiro the Greek crouched over a hydrant, ten feet distant; his rod spitting flame and slugs. One slashed Shane's cheek, even as he sent his own bullets streaming at the crouching figure.

One, at least, went true. Spiro's gross face turned blank with surprise. His hand flexed; let the rod fall. Then he straightened, took two more of Mal's missiles in the face, and toppled over backward.

Mal's second man still was in the fight; his rod barking evenly a foot or so to the rear. There was a hurried scattering of pedestrians. Police whistles were shrilling everywhere. Over the tumult, Shane heard Betty's voice, calling his name. He whirled, anxious for her safety.

She stood at the front door of the car, holding it open; beckoning. He heard the detective behind him shout: "You would—would you?" There was a double roar of gats; the man pitched forward, lay dead beside him. Another, behind him, was coughing out horrible curses. Shane caught a glimpse of a gunman's face; bullet-torn and gory. His lower jaw was shot away.

Shane was alone, except for Betty. Another few seconds and they would have him. Yet, once inside the bullet-proof motor, he and Betty would be safe from everything short of explosive missiles. As he leaped forward he saw Betty slip into the car and under the wheel.

A slug smashed against the edge of the door as he closed it. The bullet hummed off into the shadows, its sound mingling with the staccato beat of the motor as Betty shot the gas to the cylinders.

The big car leaped forward, narrowly missing another which was making a dash to safety. A figure leaped out from the sidewalk; brandishing a rod.

Betty's firm hands twitched at the wheel. The mudguard slithered over, caught the man at the hips, threw him hard against a parked car.

Then they were free, for the moment; rushing across the side street to Fifth Avenue. Shane twisted in his seat, gasped at a sickening twinge from his wound, succeeded in focusing his eyes on the street behind them.

There was a jumble of cars, with men and women running wildly here and there among them. Despite this he saw a small car wriggle through the press and straighten out after them.

More pursuers! Would the chase never end?

He was faint from exertion, excitement, loss of blood, but one glance at the gallant girl beside him brought him new strength. Betty's bobbed, golden hair was blowing about cheeks pink with the excitement of the chase. Her slender, beautifully formed hands held the wheel firmly, moving it gently, surely back and forth as she slipped through holes in traffic like a veteran race driver.

She felt his gaze, looked over her shoulder at him briefly; said:

"Where, Shane?— And are they gaining?"

"Zigzag a few blocks," he answered. "Then slip into a hole around a corner and park—dark. It may give us a chance to double back."

She nodded; trod firmly on the foot throttle. The big car literally leaped about the next corner on two wheels, to spin back toward Madison Avenue.

The red light turned against them. Betty threw the wheel left, cut in ahead of another car, ran along the line and was but three cars distant when the lights changed at the corner. Also she was in proper position for a left turn, a maneuver she executed suddenly in the middle of the avenue. But the pursuers were not caught napping. It was a matter of seconds before they too turned sharply. Another car turned out from the curb. In a second there was a grinding crash and Shane saw the light car wabble to the left, stop momentarily and then swing crazily along. Its mudguard and running board were torn off in the smash.

"Now!" Shane said. "Right—and park if you can." Twenty feet inside the turn was an open parking place. Betty snapped off the lights, drifted in, trod on the brakes, all in the course of split seconds.

"Down!" Shane emphasized the words by pulling Betty below the window level. As they crouched there, they heard the other car limping by, the smashed equipment rattling and clanking. When they had passed, Shane peeped out; saw three of Cardloe's squadmen peering ahead as the car rushed down the block.

"Let's follow!" Shane suggested. "As long as we're behind them they can't chase us."

As they neared the corner, Betty slowed down, pointed ahead. The police car was stopped in the middle of the street. The pursuers were asking questions of the traffic cop. Finally he pointed onward toward Lexington. The smaller car rushed ahead.

"Fine!" Shane jubilated. "Down Park now, over the ramp; we can lose ourselves in lower Sixth before they can pick us up again."

She obeyed instantly while Shane leaned back, closing his eyes wearily. Dazedly he realized that she was watching the lights, making right and left turns scant seconds before they changed, always working southward, never halting to give the others a chance to catch up with them.

Betty put out her hand, touched his arm, nodded toward the street behind them.

"A big, black car," she said, "running with cowl lights only. They followed the other car, and they've made every turn we made."

It was true. Shane's mind turned back to the few seconds before he entered Mal's building. There had been a black car following the smaller police car.

For a moment his spirits reached their lowest ebb. Unquestionably more of his pursuers kept to the trail, waiting for darkness—a quiet street—before bringing the fight to him.

Suddenly Shane remembered the Tommy-gun in the back of the rear seat. Despite the pain of his wounds, he managed to clamber over the front seat; fell on his knees across the foot-rail. He waited for a moment to collect his strength, then sent his fingers questing for the hidden catch of the gun compartment.

He found it beneath an arm rest; a short, blocky lever working on a ratchet. There was a click and the upper part of the upholstery folded down, revealing a new model grinder and extra drums of slugs.

Shane slipped one of these home, drew himself half erect and called to Betty.

"Over to Second Avenue as quickly as you can; stop just short of Thirtieth. There's a dark block there."

He was resolved to make his fight while he still had the strength. Strength! The word reminded him of the doctor's parting words. He drew one of the tablets from his pocket; swallowed it. Soon his heart ceased hammering, a delicious feeling of strength came to him. His hands clamped down hard on the stock of the grinder.

They were near the place now. He looked back, found the long, black car was pulling closer. But a half block separated them. Ahead was a high brick warehouse, shadows lying long before it.

"There—the dark," he called to Betty. She flicked off the lights, jammed on the brakes at just the right moment. Shane touched her shoulder, motioning her down. She obeyed, crouching below the window level. Shane dropped from the car on hands and knees, pushing the Tommy-gun before him.

The driver of the pursuing car was swinging the lights from right to left to guard against surprise. Someone shouted excitedly and Shane snarled with anger.

The huge bulk next to the driver could be none other than Magnus Cardloe—Cardloe, patiently playing the lone hand; seeking the showdown away from the others; the swag all his if he was victorious.

Hatred, the implacable urge to kill despite the consequences, surged through Shane. No longer was he cool, calculating. Within him there seethed only a seething demand for the life of this, his enemy. In his rage, his finger tightened on the trigger.

A burst of slugs struck the pavement; screamed off into the night.

Frantically Shane jerked the muzzle of the weapon up into line with the front seat of the enemy car just as three jets of flame bloomed from the rear seat. Shane felt a numbing blow in the thigh—the left—gave it no heed. Instead he snapped the grinder into position, began hosing it from windshield to rear with continuous burst of fire as the other car rolled past.

Now another Tommy was clattering its dirge. Slugs were rattling against the glass and body of the blue limousine. Some ricocheted off the pavement and screamed against the front of the warehouse as the enemy gunner tried for Shane's legs beneath the car.

He heard the front door of the car open; heard Betty call to him. But even his love for her could not swerve him from his purpose—to even things with Cardloe, to mangle him—let his stinking soul out through a hundred bullet holes.

He snapped another drum into place; stepped boldly out into the street. As he moved, the nose of the chopper flamed anew. In answer, a heavy weapon—the Tommy from the car—fell with a crash to the pavement. A second later the rear door of the attackers' car fell open; an inert body toppled out.

Then the other engine roared into life; the black car started speeding off. Shane elevated the muzzle of the grinder for a last try at the men in the front seat. It grew heavier with the passage of each second. Try as he might, he could not keep the proper elevation.

Red and blue flashes of light stormed before his eyes; the pavement rose to meet him. He fell across the hot muzzle of the grinder, out momentarily.

Dimly he sensed the tug of strong, young arms about him. He drew a deep breath, forced his muscles to obey the impulses from his mind. Betty was beside him, his right arm drawn over her shoulders, fighting to draw him back to the safety of the armored car.

Legs—strange, numb legs—enabled him to stagger the intervening feet. He fell prone in the rear; groaned as Betty thrust at his wounded leg as she tried to close the door. He lay where he had fallen, twisted, suffering intensely from the lung wound and the newer hole in his thigh.

He felt the big car leap forward. Shane groaned as it made a flying turn toward First Avenue; half rolled onto his face at the next turn and the increased speed as Betty flashed into the straightaway.

He neither knew nor cared what her plan was. Dimly he got a sense of long distances as light after light flashed by. The engine was singing a high note of speed; any corner might bring disaster. Yet he lay there, weakly, huddled against the foot-rail.

He was breathing easier now; somehow found the strength to drag his body to a sitting posture. A brilliant white light flamed through the rear window and he felt the car beneath him leap into an even greater speed.

Over the roar of the engine he heard pulsing reports. The pursuers had picked up their trail, were trying anew to burn them down.

He raised his hand to run across his tired, light-dazzled eyes. Betty's clear voice came back to him over her shoulder.

"Shane, dear—Shane!" she was calling.

He mumbled a response.

"Hold tight!" she said. "Our last chance!"

He felt the brakes bite down hard; heard their shriek as metal crushed heavily against fabric. The sudden slowing threw him forward—then back with a spine-snapping smash.

Slugs were slapping against the sides of the car. Then he sensed the other car slipping by them, its brakes screaming also. The limousine swung sharp to the left, gathered speed.

There was a sickening crash. He lurched heavily against the front seat to the tune of howled curses, rending metal. It seemed that the world was one great red and yellow blaze.

Doggedly he resisted the impulse to forget it all in the Elysium of unconsciousness. He felt the front of the limousine lift dangerously, slide, grating and tearing, off to the right; then it bumped forward again, gathering speed. There were more shots and the trilling of a police whistle.

Also there was a new danger. No longer was the blue car's progress smooth. It pounded and bumped alarmingly and Shane realized that both front tires had blown out when Betty had smashed into the other car. The wheels wabbled erratically, yet the girl fed the cylinders more and more gas.

"I turned them over," Betty called back to him. "Quiet now for just a few moments—I've a plan."

Shane dropped back thankfully. He realized that his chest wound was bleeding again; that his left leg was soaked with blood from thigh to ankle.

In another few seconds he felt the jolting, swaying car swing sharply to the right; wondered dimly where they might be.

Again the car lurched. He groaned as the flat tires ground and clattered over cobblestones for fifty feet. The lights clicked off. He heard Betty fumbling at the front door, then the one at his head.

"Try, Shane—" she commanded. "Just one more—and then you'll be all right." She caught at his extended right hand; tugged excitedly.

Summoning the last reserves of his strength, Shane managed to struggle to his knees, then toppled into the alleyway as his legs gave way beneath him. The shock helped to clear his head. From near at hand a pleasant odor came to his nostrils. "Raspberries," his subconscious mind said to him, and "Pies," another brain cell added.

It all began to make sense. "Bakery!" Betty had managed to get him to one of Ben's chain of bakeshops, somewhere down near the easterly tip of Manhattan Island!

She was speaking again. Words! Words! They came clear at last.

"Help me, Shane dear," she was repeating over and over. "Just a few steps—just a few—"

He managed to struggle to his feet. His arm about her shoulders he mastered the job of walking. Lights blurred through high windows; a ghostly white shape loomed before him. He heard a click and something collided with his shoulder.

"One of Ben's delivery wagons," Betty whispered. "Get in; they won't look for you there."

A shaft of light cut through the shadows of the alley as the rear door of the bakery opened and a white-clad worker came out with a tray of pies. He stopped, stared at them.

"I am Miss Dwight," Shane heard Betty say. "I need help. We have been in an accident—something serious—and we must get away."

"Jeez! De boss's sister!" the man gurgled. "Soitenly, lady. Duckin' de bulls, hey?"

"Yes!" Betty answered quickly. "Now help me get my friend into the back here. Then I want you to drive us to Number Five so I can 'phone my brother. And you won't let anyone stop us—will you?"

"Damn—I mean—sure, lady," the man replied. "Dey won't be botherin' wit' a delivery wagon. Will ya say a good woid to de boss fer me?"

Shane pressed a bill into Betty's hand.

"I certainly will—and there's fifty dollars for your trouble," she said. The other took the bill, whistled, leaned over and caught Shane about the thighs, lifting him bodily.

"Fifty iron ones," he grunted. "Fer fifteen blocks. Jeez!"

Shane leaned against the racks of still steaming pies, felt Betty clamber in beside him. Then the door clicked to and the engine roared.

Something hard was pressing against Shane's side. He felt inquiringly in his pocket. It was the Mills bomb he had taken from the hallway of the penthouse.

He let it drop back into his pocket.

The night wasn't over—yet!

The bouncing half-ton enclosed delivery truck might have been a huge success in pie-handling, but to Shane it proved only an instrument of torture as it jounced out of the alley, along the cross street and thence north on First Avenue.

Shane lay at full length, his head in Betty's lap, but despite this happiness he had to fight to suppress an occasional groan as the wheels hit holes in the pavement.

They had progressed thus for fully five minutes when they heard the driver's knuckles rapping thrice on the end of the truck body, their prearranged signal to indicate trouble ahead.

Then the truck slowed and they heard the driver say:

"Hello, Cap! Lost in de big city—or wanta pie?"

"Don't get young with me," a gruff voice replied. "Seen anything of a man and girl beating it outta this district? Man's hurt—the twist's a good lookin' blonde."

"Only womenfolks I ever see's me own wife—'n her mother, and say, Cap, you oughta see her! What a guy she is—that ol'—baby."

"Yeh? Well, you didn't see 'em then, huh? Then what the hell you standin' here for?"

Betty peeped through the rear window as they drew away.

"Two big men—not in uniform," she said.

Shane frowned to himself. Cardloe had lost no time in putting out a general alarm for them. That meant that depots, air fields, tunnels, subways, bus stations and all avenues leading out of town were picketed with men having a description not only of himself—but of Betty.

He still was puzzling over this new danger when the truck slowed. Betty touched his arm and said, "Here we are, Shane. Now I'll get Ben."

Number Five proved to be the largest of the Snowflake chain. There was an enclosed loading platform with sliding doors to shut out inclement weather.

Once within, Betty left Shane and hurried to the telephone. She was back in a few moments, starry-eyed and breathless.

"Ben left word at all the branches that he was at Mr. Steven's office," she said. "They're on the way here now, with a doctor."

Shane flogged his senses back to the world of reality. He put an arm about her shoulders as she stood leaning against the truck; drew her close.

"What a thoroughbred you are," he whispered. "No other girl—"

"Hush!" she answered quickly. "You see, silly, you happen to be my—my man!"

Thereafter it seemed but seconds before Ben and Mal came hurrying into the loading room. With them came the same doctor who had attended Shane earlier in the night.

It was the physician who interrupted a barrage of questions by demanding instant opportunity to see to his patient.

"You've been collecting more bullets," he said "What d'ye think this is—another World War?"

Shane smiled wearily, but lost all interest in humor as Mal and Ben half carried him to the private office. The thigh wound proved to be superficial. When it was dressed and the chest bandages had been renewed, the others entered for a council of war.

"I brought the golf bag," Mal said, cocking a jocose eye at his friend. "Thought you might need it where you're going?"

"What's that?" Shane asked.

"Europe—where you started for," Mal said, clicking his big teeth together determinedly. "Ben and I've been talking it over and between us we got last minute reservations on every ship leaving here the rest of the week. Name's Harry Jones, too."

"There's a 'general' out for Betty and me," Shane interposed.

"And how!" Mal replied. "It'd take a high wind to get even a Jersey mosquito back home this night, the way they're watching."

"Well, then—" Shane began inquiringly.

"Keep your weight on the seat of your pants, fella," Mal replied. "I'm doin' this. The *Carthuria* sails at 1:50 and in her bridal suite'll be Mr. and Mrs. Harry Jones. We been doin' some fixing, guy. Captain's going to perform the ceremony soon's you're three miles outside Sandy Hook—me and Ben'll be bridesmaids—or what have you in the icebox. Didn't tell you we was goin' too, did I? Well, we are."

"Great!" Shane's voice was tremulous with joy at the prospect. Then all of his doubts returned. "But how're you going to put it over?" he demanded.

"I told you your alias was 'Harry Jones,' didn't I?"

"Yes—but what's that—"

"There's another one, also. It's 'Raspberry Pie.' "

"That's how you're going to get aboard— We're gonna give the ship the raspberry—and you can give it back to Cardloe when you pass Sandy Hook."

Few among the thronging crowds on the deck of the giant liner *Carthuria*, or the other milling group on the pier, gave more than momentary attention to a luxurious ambulance which rolled gently up the dock and to the main gangway.

Police automatically took charge, cleared the way and held the onlookers back while a stretcher, bearing a woman's form, was carried aboard by two attendants. A physician and a nurse, followed to a stateroom on A deck.

Once there, with the door safely closed, Betty Dwight threw off the concealing coverings and said to Mal's operative who had taken the role of the doctor:

"Please don't wait any longer. Go back—and help Mr. Stevens to get aboard."

With a meaning glance, the detective handed the girl operative a stubby automatic, and said:

"There's nothing to worry about. Mal doesn't flivver on jobs like this."

The nurse slipped the rod into the starched folds of her uniform; locked the door after him.

At exactly the same moment, a huge Snowflake truck rolled along the pier, backed and came to rest almost against a loading port.

"Thousand raspberry pies," the driver shouted. "Come an' get 'em."

At the shout, three white-coated men shoved out a portable runway on rollers. One, who bore a suspicious resemblance to Mal Binford despite the steward's uniform, unlocked the truck doors.

"Up with 'em; I'll see what's in that truck myself."

The words, barked from the nearby shadows, brought the group to a standstill.

Grinning his derision, Magnus Cardloe—at the last playing a lone hand—stepped from behind a pile of boxes. Two heavy rods covered Mal and his two assistants.

"Smuggling the Stevens bird off to Europe disguised as a raspberry pie, eh?" he snarled. "Well, I've got a better idea."

"But mine's still better," a voice interrupted from the darkness. Shane, who had slipped around the truck from his hiding place in the driver's coop, swung a gat heavily against the side of Cardloe's head.

The big detective wavered unsteadily, half-turned; fell to his knees. Mal leaped forward and snatched the rods from his half paralyzed hands. Then with the speed of the wind he manacled Cardloe with his own cuffs, caught up a coil of light line from the dock and secured his ankles and knees.

"Next?" he said, turning to Shane.

"Only this," Shane replied, reaching into the truck. His hand came forth, bearing a raspberry pie. He slipped it from its paper plate, balanced it on his right hand—smashed it full into the face of his arch enemy.

"The raspberry for you—you lousy thug," he gritted. "Now"—he turned to the driver—"take him out into the high weeds somewhere and lose him."

His hand stole to his pocket, produced a round object which he placed in Cardloe's coat, jamming one of his personal cards tight around a metal pin which projected from it.

The parting gift was a Mills bomb! That, on top of "the raspberry"!

While
Choppers
Roared

SHORTY BREEN, GET-AWAY DRIVER FOR THE BULL COLEMAN GANG, was keenly alive to the trouble hunch which had been riding him all afternoon. So it needed but the touch of heavy fingers on his shoulder to send him jerking, leaping, twisting through the crowd on Fourteenth Street.

His first spring carried him through a group of chattering women. In a few seconds more he was clattering down the steps of the subway. Behind him was the usual chorus of "Stop, thief!" but over all resounded the bull-like roar of Police Captain McGrehan.

It's a hell of a thing to be waiting for the rubber hose in your B.V.D.'s and suddenly see yourself looking into your cell at you, with blood all over your face!

An express train was standing in the station. Shorty dropped a nickel in the turnstile, dashed aboard as the doors closed. Damn McGrehan anyway. Two nights before he'd caught Shorty in a dark corner and given him purple hell for playing with Bull's gang.

"Damn ol' goat," Shorty growled. "Where's he get 'at stuff? You'd think he was me ol' man, instead of him being just a guy 'at wanted to marry Mom w'en she was a goil!"

At Thirty-fourth Street he slipped from the train and cast a furtive eye over the crowd. Hell's fire! There he was, getting out of the last car! There was no mistaking the blue uniform with its captain's bars and stripes in gold, nor the heavy, squared jaw above it. Shorty dashed up the stairs two at a time, made the first half block at a rapid walk. Then he slowed, but no police uniform showed behind him.

At Eighth Avenue he turned south, stopping for a final survey of his back trail. He was safe. McGrehan had lost him. Heaving a sigh of relief, Shorty started to stroll along toward Finnegan's café and Bull's headquarters above it.

For the moment his underworld guardian angel was not on the job. He stopped at the curb to light a cigarette in the lee of a parked Checker cab. He gave the cab and driver no attention until he sensed a flurry of movement. He started to turn but it was too late.

A blue clad arm shot forth, clamped iron fingers on his shoulder, dragged him, struggling, into the cab. A split second later he heard the order.

"Down to Center Street, lad; drive right intuh the garage."

Shorty didn't need to see his captor's—McGrehan's—face. He couldn't, had he wanted to. His face was jammed into a corner of the seat, his knees were on the floor. The pressure relaxed; Shorty heaved himself erect, only to suffer the shame of being shoved back, slowly, relentlessly into his former position.

"You're a tough guy, Clyde!"—Jeez! how he hated that pansy name Mom had given him—"But I'm tougher than all of you gaycats. Now sit you down and listen to me."

The big hands heaved again, slammed him back onto the seat.

Captain McGrehan's eyes were blazing; steely fingers were digging into Shorty's shoulder muscles. Shorty tried to out stare the cop; his eyes fell first.

"What th' hell?" he growled. "This a pinch?"

"What does it feel like—a swimmin' lesson?"

"Aw, what have I done? You got nothin' on me." The old formula between cop and crook the world over.

"I have me hand on you, which'll do for the present," McGrehan responded with heavy wit. "It looks like a tough night for you, Clydie."

Shorty winced again at the hated name. "Clyde!" for the speedball who drove the chopper car last week when Bull Coleman's rodmen shot it out with The Yid's organ grinders, hijacked two trucks of alky. Uh-huh. Two cops had been killed, but that was their hard luck.

"You don't take kindly to th' name a good mother gave you, Clyde." There was contempt in the Captain's sarcastic drawl. "Well, it's a hell of a name for a gangster—and it's a hell of a gangster you'll be after this night."

Shorty stirred uneasily. Jeez! Suppose some of Bully's scouts saw him riding with McGrehan. They'd be calling him "Canary" and tomorrow taking him for a ride. Yet he hated a "chirper" worse than anyone, almost.

"Lissen, Cap," he pleaded. "Lemme go. Jess because you'n Mom went to school together's no reason fer youse to get me put on the spot."

"The spot, is it now?" The reply was a bellow of derision. "You'll be wishin' for the spot before tonight's over. It's the Third we're fixin' up for you."

Shorty's blood turned cold within him. The dreaded "third." And at the hands of this ramping, raging old Mick on whom he'd always looked, though from a distance, as a family friend!

"Yuh can't give me no hosin'," he said. "Whaddyuh think you got on me?"

McGrehan's lips didn't move; his hand did. It slid down to a point on Shorty's arm between elbow and shoulder. The fingers tightened, dug into the nerve center under the biceps. Shorty tried to jerk loose. The movement brought a howl of pain from his lips. McGrehan was pitiless. Slowly the grasp tightened. Horrible searing pains flashed down the arm to the finger tips, up over the shoulder.

"Enough?" The Captain growled the word. Shorty nodded in mute agony.

"Listen to me, then. Don't you start tellin' me what I can or cannot do this night. In five days more I retire on pension. Nobody can change that. Them five days is to be given to runnin' down some rats that killed two brave men recent—and to makin' a man out of Mary Ann Breen's lousy brat—or killin' him."

Shorty sunk down in his corner. Suddenly he felt terribly alone. McGrehan he knew was tough, iron hard. It was said he preferred a billy to a rubber hose—and followed his liking.

"Yes, Clyde," the Captain's tones were silky now. "It'll be a tough night, and here we are ready for it to start."

The cab swung across the curb, into a big room filled with riot cars, prowl cars, the fast buses of the strong arm squad; the big racers in which the Commissioners and Brass Collars buzzed to danger points. McGrehan handed the driver a bill, pointed over his shoulder with a big thumb.

"Out," he growled.

As the automatic doors closed, he spun Shorty about, crossed his pile-driver right to the button with a snap.

Shorty went limp. McGrehan caught him, did not let him fall.

"Poor, dumb lad," he half whispered. "Spoiled as he is, I wish he was mine."

Two plainclothes men came from the shadows, took the drooping form, carried it to the silent cells where there is only silence.

While Shorty still was unconscious, the detectives stripped him of coat, hat, shoes, collar, trousers, hat and tie.

"Cap said to leave him his cigarettes and matches," one of the searchers said.

"Yeh?" his mate replied. "The ol' boy's gettin' soft. Wouldn't be surprised to come down here in a day or two an' find he's been getting drinkin' water."

II
DOUBLING FOR SHORTY

"McGREHAN SPEAKING, SIR. I have the lad. May I come up?"

"In five minutes, Captain. I'll ring." The Commissioner's voice was curt but friendly. "Any trouble?"

"For him, not for me, sir."

McGrehan sensed the beginning of a chuckle as his superior hung up the receiver.

Commissioner Van Voort turned back to the stockily built, severe faced man opposite him, Captain Michaelson, Chief of New York's Secret Police.

"That was McGrehan," Van Voort said. "Reporting he's turned in the Breen boy. Dammit, Michaelson, I don't like the thought of Springer and Haddon taking such chances."

"Nor do I." Michaelson's face was granite hard. "McGrehan's plan to save this little Breen rat is apt to spoil it all. But we're ready—checked and rechecked on the plan."

"Yes, we're too deep in now to change," Van Voort replied. He drew a map toward him. "We'll go over it once again; then you can get your crew together. Here's the district, with the route marked in red arrows.

"The point marked 'J' is where the truck will be, with tools, tear bombs, extra ammunition; whatever's required. When Bull's third car passes, the boy who's been trying to start the engine will slip around the corner and signal Lieutenant Henry. The signal to close in will be a burst of blank cartridge machine gun fire. Right? All clear?"

"Perfectly, Mr. Commissioner. And in the meantime the other group will surround Bull's headquarters over Finnegan's. When the word is passed that the warehouse raiders have been mopped up, we'll hit Bull from all sides and the roof."

"Good, Captain. Goodnight and good luck."

A touch on the button brought McGrehan from downstairs.

"Good work," the Commissioner said. "Anyone see you get him?"

"Not a chance, sir. I snatched him offen the sidewalk before he could squawk. He was goin' to Bull's; thought he'd ditched me in Thirty-fourth Street. I hopped a cab, beat it the other way and copped him on Eighth Avenue."

The Commissioner stared for a moment at the stubborn old face before him.

"See here," he said. "It's a devil of a thing you've made me ask of Springer—to gamble his life for a crook like that."

"Wait 'til you've seen Springer in his clothes. They're enough alike to be twins, except their eyes is different. Springer has painted a couple of fine blue bruises on his lamps to take care of that. You'd swear he'd been in a pip of a fight."

"It's a terrible chance—" The Commissioner paused.

"No worser'n any other man of the Secret Squad's takin' every day, sir. No more than the other boy we shoved in on Bull's gang. It's all risky; that's how we're cleanin' up on the tips they get."

"I hope you're right, McGrehan. Anyway, after tonight there'll be no more cop killings by the Coleman gang."

"Which'll be a blessin' in a wicked world, Mr. Commissioner."

McGrehan saluted, about faced and departed.

Thirty minutes later the lookout at Bull Coleman's headquarters opened the peep panel, recognized Shorty Breen and admitted him.

"Where th' hell youse been, punk?" the lookout demanded. "Bull's been askin' for youse."

"Aw hell! I had a fight wit' a guy over a pool game," Shorty replied out of the corner of his mouth. "I got a pair uh shiners."

"Damn if you ain't—an' maybe Bull won't slap youse down fer that."

Shorty did not reply. Instead he shambled across the room and, dropping into a chair commanding a view of both the office and entrance doors, he seemed to doze.

III

THE STAGE IS SET

SHARP AT TEN O'CLOCK BULL COLEMAN opened the door of his private office to crook his fingers at four of the loungers. Shorty followed Ginger Olsen, Chopper Allen and Sid Haddon into the room.

"Shut the door, kid," Bull growled. "All of youse set down and hang out an ear. Everything's set. Sid'll drive the lead car wit' two roddies an' Chopper wit' his grinder. Shorty's to drive the guard car. He'll take two more rods, an' Ginger wit' his Tommy.

"On th' way youse'll pick up the third car, which'll run between lead an' guard. That one'll back into th' shippin' alley beside the warehouse. Shorty pulls down th' street half way of th' block, headin' east. Sid heads back west and pulls near to the corner. That way, if they's a ruckus, they won't burn each other down.

"Now lissen. That gives a guard car headed whichever the dope buggy heads when it comes outta the alley. The other one'll swing an' follow. Get me?"

All nodded, but Bull, himself a strategist, duplicated the scene of a few moments before in the Commissioner's office, when he produced a rough map of the route to show the course to be taken.

To one man in the room the scene had its element of humor. It was his second view of the maps—one down in Center Street, the other in Bull's office. For Sid Haddon was the "other fellow" mentioned by McGrehan—a member of the Secret Police, planted on Bull's gang through clever plotting.

Something warned Haddon. He looked up, caught the burning eyes of Chopper Allen studying him intently. Instantly he let his face go blank, gazing back almost stupidly at the other. This simply wouldn't do. Allen never had been friendly. Just now it is possible the man had caught the half grin on his face.

Bull's bellowing voice brought the duel of glances to an end.

"Everybody out now," he said. "But stick around. Youse know th' rules. I'll tell youse when it's time."

That was Bull's method. At the last moment he outlined his plans in detail. After that no one was allowed to leave the hangout or to telephone. Even then the exact hour was kept secret until the moment of departure.

At the door, Chopper turned back.

"See you a moment, Bull?"

"Yeh. What youse got on your chest?"

Chopper saw to it that the door was closed. He returned to the desk and leaned forward.

"It's that guy, Haddon," he half whispered. "Lemme knock him off, chief; he's poison. Don't ask me how I know. I just feel it. I've seen him in my dreams putting the cuffs on me. Every time he comes near me I smell the cops."

"Aw cripes, Chopper, you're nuts," Bull answered. "He was sent to me by Mickey the Harp from Chicago after he got into a jam there. I had him watched plenty, and I know he's all right. Just because you're a damned old woman's no reason for me to lose a guy with th' kinda guts he's got. He'll go down intuh hell if I send him—'n come back wit' a bottle of pre-war in each hand."

Chopper shrugged, started for the door; turned back.

"Lissen, chief—" He was bitterly, insanely angry now. "When this guy sends you to the Big Squirm up in Sing Sing just remember that I told you to get rid of him."

Bull's heavy face crimsoned, turned purple.

"Get th' hell outta here, you damned croaking louse," he shouted. "When anybody sends me to the Hot Seat it'll be some rat like youse, afraid of his own shadow. Mebbe you're th' one 'at needs his horns knocked off—"

Chopper shivered involuntarily.

"Forget it, chief," he said placatingly. "It's you I'm worryin' about; not me. When do we start?"

"When I send you, rat," Bull snarled. "That good enough for youse?"

Chopper slouched to the door, white-faced, humiliated.

The stage was set for the third act of the drama of Secret Police versus the Coleman dusters.

IV

THE ATTACK

ZERO HOUR WAS 1:30.

Bull strode into the main room, followed by Ginger and Chopper, each carrying his favorite sub-machine gun.

"Smitty and Shuffle!" he barked. "Get your rods and go wit' Ginger. Dutch and Ike, you go wit' Chopper. He'll tell youse what to do."

"Come on, punk; get your driving eye alive," he snapped, halting before Shorty's slouched form. He stopped and peered under the boy's hat brim.

"Jeez, you would pick a night like this to get slapped up," he snarled. "One slip-up from you, gaycat, and I'll knock youse off myself. Kin you see well enough to drive?"

Shorty spat nonchalantly. "Sure!" he responded. "What's a shiner got to do wit' steppin' on th' gas?"

"Hell! Get goin'," Bull demanded. "Ginger's grinder in your car. If he tells you to drive offen a dock—do it."

Quietly the four slipped through the outer room, down the rear stairs to the alley garage where waited a stolen Packard touring car. Shorty wriggled under the wheel, touched the starter, listened for a moment to the motor's purr. He cut the switch, looked about him tranquilly.

The outer door opened. Sid Haddon entered, followed by Chopper and the two rodmen. Beside the opposite wall stood a Buick. Half way there, Haddon whirled and said to Shorty:

"Slip us a pill, kid, I'm all out."

Shorty obligingly extended a package of cigarettes to Haddon.

Before returning it, the other snapped his pocket lighter and set the fag going. Stepping close to the side of the Packard he handed the package back to Shorty with his right hand. At the same time, with a deft twist of his left, he tucked a squat automatic between the padding of the front seat and Shorty's leg.

"Thanks, kid—see you in church," he said nonchalantly, turning back to the other car.

Shorty's eyes flashed to the rear vision mirror. Had Ginger or the other two seen Haddon slip him the rod? It was Coleman's rule that drivers of get-away cars must not be armed. Thus, if they started any treachery, they'd be at the mercy of the other gunmen.

Seemingly Haddon's sleight-of-hand had gone unnoticed. Dutch Schmaltz, who had been standing at the right of the car, slipped in beside Shorty. He inspected his automatic, lighted a cigarette and wriggled to a comfortable position.

"All right—let's go," Ginger said in a moment. "Follow Chopper half a block behind, When we pick up the other car on Eleventh Avenue slide back a little further; don't want it to look like a parade."

The garage doors swung open on oiled hinges. In another moment they closed behind the two dark cars. The side curtains were up on both, but a touch on the bottom buttons would open them for the death-spewing choppers. Otherwise there was nothing to distinguish them from the other motor-cars of the night.

Shorty kept a watchful eye on the red tail light of the Buick. He speeded up when the other driver found a hole in traffic; slowed when the lights caused a temporary jam.

On Eleventh Avenue, where traffic was light in the early morning hours, a dark shape curved out of an intersecting street, buzzed up alongside the Buick, then dropped into line. It was the raiders' car. Shorty slowed down to give it room behind the lead car.

"All set now," Ginger barked. "Remember, when we get to the warehouse, you pull east and stop about fifty feet past where Sid turns and heads west. Let the engine run and be ready for a quick lam."

"Gotcha!" Shorty grunted. "Second corner, ain't it?"

"Yeh. What th' hell's that ahead of us?"

At the curb ahead the lights had picked up an unlighted black shape. As Ginger spoke he saw the twinkle of a flashlight and lifted the grinder from the floor. Shorty gave the engine more gas, swung so that his lights also lit up the scene.

By the curb stood an ancient Model T Ford, seemingly broken down. The hood was up and an elderly man, overall clad, was looking on as a youth tinkered with the engine.

"Breakdown," Shorty called over his shoulder. " 'Sall right."

"It is—like hell," Ginger growled "It's punks and old apple knockers like that who'll remember seein' three cars come along and turn the corner."

Grumbling, he glared back through the rear window. Shorty swung his car on the trail of the other two. He cut his lights as he saw the first car turn west. The second was backing into the loading area.

Fifty feet farther on he drifted to a silent stop, jazzed his engine to blow out the last vestige of carbon, then let it purr sweetly while they waited.

In the rear vision mirror he could see the outlines of the Buick at the opposite curb behind them. He grunted as he reached for a cigarette and remembered the orders were: "No smoking."

As he sat there in the darkness, he felt his nerve tauten as he visioned dark forms creeping through the warehouse, stalking the watchmen, ready to hijack the trunkful of cocaine and hyoscine Snuffles Thornton had stored there three days previously.

Wriggling about as though he tried to see farther up the street behind him, Shorty succeeded in getting the automatic under his coat and thence to the holster under his armpit.

Ten minutes passed, fifteen, twenty. Still there was no sound from the warehouse, no movement in the street.

"Looks like a pipe," Ginger whispered. "They've got the watchman by now, an' if there's any dingdongs, they've beat 'em. Pink Tiernan's the best man in the world on alarm systems."

Another five minutes dragged by. Suddenly three bird notes sounded shrilly. It was the "Get Ready" signal—a special whistle carried only by lieutenants in charge of a job.

It meant that the raid had succeeded, that the others were coming out. In a minute or so the trunk would be tossed into the rear of the raiding car. In thirty minutes it would all be over.

"Hold 'er, Shorty," Ginger warned raspingly. "See which way they turn. Only one man knows. That's Bull's system."

With the last word every man in the car stiffened to attention. From somewhere in the distance came the muffled tac-tac-tac of a machine gun—a sustained burst which ended as suddenly as it had begun.

"W'at th' hell?" Ginger growled. Shorty unlatched the door and looked back up the street. When he resumed his seat he saw to it that the latch did not catch.

"Sounded like a grinder to me," he said. "Long ways off, though."

He let his eyes probe the darkness ahead. There were shadows, he thought, shadows in the heart of shadows out there; flitting forms, or did his eyes play him tricks?

He turned his head, spoke over his shoulder to the others.

"Prob'ly somebody else turnin' a trick," he said. "This'll be a damn good part of town to get away from quick."

Ginger grunted assent, moved uneasily.

A shot crashed somewhere near at hand. Then it seemed that the whole world went mad. Orange and blue streamers of flame sprang out of the night everywhere. Ginger howled curses, thrust his weapon out through the curtains.

"Now or never," Shorty whispered to himself. He gathered his body into a compact ball, slid the door open another inch; fell against it and to the ground.

• • •

As he struck, instead of leaping to his feet, he rolled under the body of the car, lay there quiet. Fifty-feet distant Sid Haddon was executing a similar maneuver, warned by the crash of the first shots. Now the two cars were driverless, helpless until one or another of the rodmen took the wheel.

Heavy feet scraped the pavement in the darkness nearer and nearer at hand. From doorways service guns were belching streams of death. Ginger, still howling curses, shifted his grinder to the left door, sprayed the shadows with red-hot bursts of fire.

Somewhere in the darkness a moan told of a stricken man's agony. A pistol fell to the pavement, followed by the thud of a falling body.

Over the staccato barking of the rods and the deeper growl of the Tommy guns, grew a new sound. Motors were dashing up from every hand. It was but the second minute of the attack but already scores of blue-clad cops were out of hiding, converging to add their share to the death din.

Bullets were thudding now into the body of the car above Shorty. Something wet flowed along and soaked his coatsleeve as he lay hugging the pavement. A strong odor assailed his senses. Gasoline! A cop's bullet had punctured the gas tank. Shorty dragged himself a bit to one side. It wouldn't do to soak up a lot of that stuff and then get in the way of a pistol flash.

The body of the car above him swayed and groaned. Someone put his weight on the running board, dragged something from the tonneau, pattered across the sidewalk. A moment later Ginger's chopper began chattering from a recessed doorway where he had taken up his position.

The value of his strategy was proved instantly. Entrenched as he was, he could hose death at the compact group of police across the street. Wounded men shouted, fell. The group melted, tried to re-form; melted again. Viciously Ginger swept the muzzle of the chopper right and left.

Bullets from service guns slithered off the brick walls of the entryway, ricocheted. Ginger stopped only to change clips, then resumed his firing.

"Dammit—get that guy!" The command was bellowed from somewhere near at hand.

Shorty swung crosswise under the car, lifted the muzzle of his rod; tried to peer back of the spitting flashes to get a bead on Ginger. It was no use. Another agonized shriek came from the ranks of the attackers. Shorty loosed two shots from his rod at a point beside the spitting muzzle of the chopper. His answer was a burst of slugs which spun from the pavement near his head. Ginger was not to be caught that way.

Shorty raised his hand to rub his dust-filled eyes. The odor of gas was strong again.

That was the way! He lay for a moment, trying to think clearly. Yes, he could do it—provided the cops did not kill him the first second or two after he had acted.

• • •

Rolling out from under the car he came to hands and knees. Overhead was the sound of the passage of swarms of giant bees. The smashing impact of slugs against the car's riddled sides was nearly deafening. The roll of pistol fire was thunderous.

Shorty snapped his gat back into its holster. His right hand felt for and brought out his pocket lighter. Holding it within his cap, he spun the wheel. The first spark failed—and the second. Then the wick caught.

Deftly he skidded the metal box across the pavement, then dropped flat, rolling rapidly toward the opposite curb.

Almost there he collided with someone's legs. A great weight descended on him; throttling hands caught at his throat.

"Springer—headquarters!" he gasped.

The hands still held for a split second. The flame from the lighter snatched at a drop of gasoline. Instantly the opposite curb for a distance of twenty feet burst into flames which eddied and danced, making the scene light as day. Whoever was holding Shorty loosed his grasp. A tongue of fire ran along the pool, under the tank, leaped up and enveloped the container. The force of the outpouring liquid was too great as yet to permit the fire to enter.

With the lift of the blaze an exultant shout rang out.

"There he is—that doorway! Get him, men!"

Shorty stared across the way. Ginger and his chopper were outlined as on a motion picture screen. For a second he squatted there, staring dully at the blaze. Police guns barked. Ginger instantly fell prone, sending his stream of death back full in the faces of the attackers.

It was a moment of intense drama. Outnumbered, knowing that he could not escape—that the infuriated police would stop shooting only when he was dead, Ginger lay there coolly, firing methodically into the shadowy groups across the street.

The car's body was burning now. Flames burst from underneath the hood and chassis, climbed up the sides, caught at curtains and top. One of the rodmen, badly wounded, pitched out through the flaming curtains, his clothes smoking. Police guns rattled. Dust spots billowed from his clothing in a score of places.

He twitched, died. As the curtains burned away, another huddled form could be seen in the tonneau. Death had been merciful to one gunman.

Ginger was still in action, but he was firing jerkily now. A passing gust of breeze made the light lift, grow stronger. It showed a hate-twisted, bloody mask, little resembling a human face.

A dozen police pistols crashed simultaneously. No one possibly could live through that storm of lead. Expectantly the cops held their fire.

There was a moment's pause, then an unbelievable burst of shots from the doorway. "Tac-tac-tac-tac-tac!" Twenty-five, thirty times the grim chopper sang its song of menace. Silence at last.

The police guns roared again. One man, braver than the rest, charged into the doorway, firing as he ran. In a moment he was out, waving his hands excitedly. Others rushed to him.

"He's dead!" they shouted after a moment. "Croaked with his finger on the trigger."

They dragged the body into the light, marveled that one so torn and mutilated could have the spirit to continue fighting.

"All right, men." It was a captain calling. "That mops up this bunch. The others are inside yet. We've got 'em from above and from all sides. Get in there. Don't let one get away."

Shorty turned dazedly, walked a few steps toward the Buick. He realized now that the firing there had stopped long before. In the darkness he collided with someone in civilian clothes.

"You, kid?" the other asked.

"Haddon!" There was joy in the tone. "You got through all right, too!"

"Yeh—just a few scratches. Better duck now. You know the orders— under cover with cops as well as civilians. They'll mop up this mess, and anyway I want to be in on the raid on Bull."

Together the two Secret Police melted into the darkness, caught a nighthawk cab and speeded back to the vicinity of Finnegan's.

"I had to tell a flattie I was from headquarters after I'd touched off the gas," Shorty said after awhile, "but he didn't get a good look at me. Everything's jake."

"Nice party," Haddon said reflectively. "Wonder what the real Shorty'd have done in your place!"

"That fuzz-tail!" Springer's voice was hard. "He'd be dead back there with the rest of 'em. Wonder why McGrehan wanted to save him?"

"Damfino! Hell with that. If you want something to fret about, figure what the newspapers are goin' to say about half the department layin' for a bunch of thugs and knockin' 'em off. Them and the reformers. Hooey!"

"I can see 'em now," Springer answered. "And I'm damn glad I'm on the Secret Police instead of the regulars."

The taxi rounded the last corner, skidded to a stop. Uniformed police blocked the way. "Broadway or Tenth," they chanted monotonously. "Don't turn up Seventh or Ninth."

The trap was being sprung at Finnegan's then, according to plan. Haddon and Springer, ex-Shorty, dropped out and paid the driver. For two blocks the avenue was free of moving traffic. At the corner nearest the hangout stood several armored motorcycles, police prowl cars, and two of the big armored trucks used by the riot squad.

One of the flatties came over to them.

"What're youse guys hangin' 'round here for?" he demanded truculently.

"Sixty-six," Haddon replied, giving the code word which in the department on that particular night meant "on special duty."

The word changed nightly. Only men within the department could know it. It was whispered to each relief on leaving the station.

"Oh, yeh?" the policeman said. "Well, youse guys better crawl intuh th' ol' tin vests if youse're gonna stick aroun' here. Know what's doin'?" He leered at them craftily, with the curiosity of the harness bull as to what the plainclothes men were doing.

"No, handsome; what is it?" Haddon's reply was like a slap in the face.

"Ahrrr, nuts!" the cop replied. "Kiddin' somebody, aintcha?"

Turning, the two scurried along the darkened store fronts. A rhythmic pounding, somewhere ahead, came to their ears.

"Smashing down Bull's steel door in the middle of the stairway," Haddon said.

"That's a tough spot," Springer replied. "Be plenty hell when they finally get through."

His words were prophetic. Guns were in action now, their spatting sound curiously muffled by the building's walls. From higher up came a crashing, rending sound. The roof detail was smashing a way through to the upper floor. Across the street someone opened a window on a fire escape. Two cops with a machine gun stepped out onto the landing, trained the weapon on the windows opposite.

The armored motorcycles made a crescent before the open doorway. Each carried a passenger in its protected tub; each passenger carried a Tommy gun. The men in the saddles crouched forward behind their shields, automatics ready for business.

The shooting, which had died down after the first few shots, crashed forth again. A policeman, his right arm dangling loosely, blood dripping in a stream from his fingers, staggered from the doorway.

"They're givin' us hell in there," he said through set lips. "Door's down but they're hosin' the stairs with a rapid fire from back of a steel shield set on the second flight. Never get 'em this way."

Springer turned on Haddon, jerked his head. Haddon nodded.

"Try it, anyway," he said.

They raced toward the front of the place but were stopped by a captain.

"Sixty-six," Springer whispered. "My friend thinks he knows a way in through Finnegan's. There's a half balcony there and a doorway that's been boarded up. We'll signal through the window."

"Good! The other way's suicide. See what you can do, boys."

In the rear of the hallway, under the old-fashioned stairway, was a descending stairway leading to the Finnegan half of the basement. Haddon clicked on a pencil flashlight; inspected the lock. Springer flicked out a bunch of skeleton keys, turned the lock with the second.

In a moment they stood in the cellarway. A heavy partition divided the two halves of the basement from left to right. Along this stood a table where peelers prepared the vegetables. At the left, at the wall, was a narrow stair—hardly more than a ladder.

Springer led, tried the door at the top. It was held by a bolt on the other side.

"Hold my feet so I don't slip," he said. Swinging as far back as he dared, he launched his wiry shoulder against the barrier. It creaked but did not give. A second thrust splintered a panel.

Three or four driving blows with his palm made a hole big enough to admit his arm. The bolt clicked back. They were in the café now. Outside the Captain stood shading his eyes, peering into the window. Springer seized a bill of fare, wrote on it; ran lightly to the front.

"HALLWAY. THROUGH CELLAR AND BACK UP HERE," the Captain read by beam of his hand torch. He nodded, ran to the doorway, beckoning others to follow.

Springer looked about. Haddon was at his side. "Boost," he demanded.

"Right, kid," the big fellow said, catching the smaller man by the cloth at his hips; boosting him straight up as one might raise a chair.

Springer's hands caught the cross-piece; pulled him up.

"Go up the stairs," he whispered. "Feel along the wall from the stair head toward me. I'll work back. There's a boarded up door somewhere."

They met, but without result. "It's farther back," Haddon said. "I remember now."

It was almost at the back corner. They ripped away the light deal casing.

"This won't get us anywhere," Haddon whispered. "They're still on the floor above us."

"Old building," Springer grunted. "I'm gambling the stairs are built all the way up on a scaffolding. You know the old system. Four-by-fours, with two-by-four supports; like a grandstand. Get under there—shoot hell out of the choppers from underneath."

"Sure's hell something there, or there'd be no door," Haddon replied.

"Cripes, listen to those flatties stumble up the stairs!" Springer said. "Good thing everybody's shooting."

He flashed his torch to outline the way to the stairs. Three men accompanied the captain. One carried a chopper. The other had a sawed-off shotgun and a net of tear bombs.

The third attacked the door slit with a jimmy. The old wood gave readily. Back of it, as Springer had surmised, was a dark passage which led toward the rear of the building under the stair supports.

One of the flatties produced a long-beam flashlight, disclosing twenty feet back, the outlines of the second floor landing.

"I'm going up," Springer said quietly. "When I find which step they're on we can shoot 'em loose in two seconds."

He dropped his coat, set the pencil flash upright in his vest pocket; shinned up to the first cross support. From there he swung like a monkey, up and back to a point a score of feet above the others' heads.

Their flashes revealed him as he balanced on a two-by-four, clinging with knees and one hand. With the other he felt of the risers and treads until vibration told him where the gunmen rested for their shooting down the stairway.

Still clinging precariously, he took out his flash and counted the stairs. It was the seventh. A moment later he dropped to the floor, dripping with sweat, his palms bleeding from a score of sliver wounds.

"The seventh stair," he said, "but there's no use shooting them out of there until the cops are set for a rush. Get word out to be ready."

"That's the dope," the Captain replied. "I'll send word for the boys to be ready. Here, Wilkins, get out and tell 'em what we're doing. When they're ready to rush, wig wag me with a light and when you hear my whistle, you other boys blow them rats to hell outta there."

The police machine gunner took up his place back in the darkness, found a rest; set his weapon with the rays of a flash so he could spray his death hail through the rotting wood of the stairway.

It was stifling in the narrow passage. The minutes dragged terribly. At intervals firing was resumed in the stairway. Also there was firing at some distant point; probably the roof crew fighting their way downward. Below, in the rear, were other smashing sounds as the basement was occupied.

Haddon, his nerves ragged from waiting, started toward the balcony. Before he had taken three steps, a shrill note cut through the medley of other noises.

Springer and the harness cop threw their flashes upward. The gunner's finger compressed on the trip and the Tommy-gun began its death chatter.

Its barking roar smashed on their ears like the turmoil of a boiler shop. Orange flames spurted in a continuous stream from its blunt muzzle. The tread of the seventh stair seemed to lift under its smashing blows. Men bellowed in agony and a heavy object clattered downward. The stairway creaked. The tread flew apart; became a mass of splinters.

Springer touched the flattie's shoulder; mentioned for him to sweep the remaining six steps to blot out any lurking thugs.

He obeyed. Other yells of pain or anger burst out in answer. He hosed every nook and corner where a gunman might be hiding.

"Hold it!" Springer barked the word. Heavy footed men were pounding up the stairway from the ground floor. It wouldn't do to shoot down any of the attackers. The cops had gained the hallway now, but were being fired on from within the gang's assembly room. From farther back came the chatter of guns as well.

"Bull's holed up in the office," Haddon muttered. "He's cornered, but it'll take a hell of a lot of lead to get him out. He's shooting from behind the big safe; that's a bet."

Springer shrugged. "Let's get going," he said. They slipped back through the café and cellar, into the hallway.

The heavy fumes of cordite made it almost impossible to breathe. The stairs were heavy, slippery with broken plaster, pools of blood. At the top the cops stood massed out of range of the death hail from inside.

As they watched, Springer and Haddon saw three men raise the steel shield from behind which the defenders had held the stairway. Others fell in behind it, pushed it through the open doorway of the clubroom. The others thrust forward. Springer nudged Haddon, pointing.

Three dead men lay at the foot of the second flight of stairs. Another sprawled grotesquely over the splintered tread.

"Must have got them with the first burst," he said. "Wonder if we can drive Bull out the same way?"

"Nope. Safe's on a steel plate about seven by four feet. It stands across the corner. Anyone behind it, with the doors open might as well be shooting from a battleship."

"I've got it through the wall." Springer rushed back along the stairway, returned in a moment, cursing. "Hall only goes part way back; they've built a partition there," he said.

"Above then," it was Haddon's turn now. "There's some way for us to get at that rat."

They ran up the stairs, shoving the body of the dead gangster aside as they went. Springer leaped to the door at the head of the stairs, opened it, slammed it again—dragged Haddon down flat on the floor.

Lead smashed in a stream through the panels at the height of a man's chest. More of the defenders were in there, holding back the crew attacking from the roof.

A battered broom stood in one corner. Springer tiptoed over to it, tore loose the cord of a droplight and wound it about the handle, leaving one end free.

"We'll pen 'em in there," he said. "Door opens inward. When it comes time for them to smash us from the rear, they can't get out."

Silently he slipped to the door-casing, laid the broom across horizontally, motioned for Haddon to hold it level. He wound the wire several times about the doorknob, then about the broom, tied a granny-knot. Purposely he jiggled the handle. More slugs crashed through, then someone tried to pull the door open from the inside. It held.

"That'll keep 'em off our backs. Come on," Springer barked. They ran to the rear of the hallway. The attic scuttle stood open. Back in the shadows he could make out the outlines of a face.

"Up with them—I've got you covered," a voice commanded.

"Sixty-six," Springer replied. "Drop a couple of men down here into the hallway to help smash into them from the rear. I've got the door barred from this side."

"How'll that help," the other demanded suspiciously.

"Easy. They figure they can hold us off, while Bull stands your fellows off from back of the safe in his office. We've got to smash this bunch and then get Bull through the floor from above."

Long, blue clad legs appeared in the opening. The cop swung for a moment by his hands, fell to his knees. Another followed with drawn gun.

"All right, Bob," the first said. "Headquarters, special service men with the password."

"Get a grinder," Springer interrupted. "We'll never get anywhere with hand guns."

The second cop was still suspicious.

"Say," he demanded. "Who in hell are you anyhow, young fellow? You look a helluva lot to me like a punk that hangs 'round with this gang."

"Yeh!" Springer snapped. "And if it means anything to you, I look a lot like my father too. Come on! Get busy. Introductions can wait."

Still surly, the copper went back and called to someone above through the scuttle. In a moment a third policeman swung down, holding by one hand while he passed over a Tommy gun.

"How many in there?" Haddon asked. The policeman rubbed his nose reflectively.

"Half a dozen anyway. We got into the attic all right, but they pumped so many holes around our feet that we couldn't break through. Four of our boys are up there, shot up. They burned the hell out of us every time we started."

"What's the layout?"

"Two big rooms with a door in the center of the partition. Two rooms on this floor, three in the same space on Bull's floor."

Springer pointed to the door with its broom-and-wire lashing.

"By now they've found its barricaded," he said. "That gives us a chance to surprise 'em. Put the guy with the grinder on the stairs, with just the tip of the gun showing over the landing. You others plant back in the dark and knock over the ones he don't get. I'll loosen the bar and kick the door open."

The firing within was intermittent. It seemed that the gangsters were satisfied with a stalemate; glad to hold the raiders from the roof on the attic floor. Springer's hands were working now at the wire lashing. Silently he released the broom but retained his hold on the doorknob. Flattening himself against the wall he waited for another burst of firing.

When it came he nodded to the others, turned the knob and sent the door sweeping back against the inner wall. Someone inside loosed a scattering spray of shots from an automatic through the opening. The copper on the stairs withheld his fire for a second, while the others, waiting for his first burst, stood silent.

Springer looked over his shoulder and unconsciously flinched aside from the doorway as the Tommy-gun went into action. He could feel the death-draught of the flying lead.

A medley of cries came from within. A bullet or two buzzed through the opening, smashed harmlessly into the plastering.

Haddon and his two supporting cops leaped forward, but Springer was first into the room. Four men were prone on the floor. A fifth, his legs shot from under him, was trying to crawl into the second room.

Springer's gun belched twice. The crawling gunny squirmed; lay still. Feet were thudding on the floor inside as the cops dropped from the low attic opening.

Springer turned and ordered the man with the Tommy-gun to keep on firing erratic bursts so Bull and his group could not know that the cops finally had occupied the floor above him.

"Give me a jimmy," he gritted. "I want to tear up the floor in this corner." He cast his eyes about the two rooms. Roughly they approximated the three of the gang headquarters below. Therefore the southeast corner would be directly above the spot where Bull was holding out against his attackers.

One of the cops disappeared; returned almost immediately with a jimmy big enough to wreck the City Hall. Springer snatched at it hungrily; turned to the corner baseboard. His agile shoulders twisted. The baseboard came loose. Another wrench. The inside flooring board flipped back in splinters. Another. Another. Haddon slipped to his knees beside Springer.

"Easy does it," he warned. "You're tipping your mitt. Can't you hear? They've stopped shooting downstairs."

Springer stared at him, wiped the sweat from his forehead.

"Who the hell cares?" he snarled. "I'm going to get Bull."

"Be smart," Haddon said and caught at his wrist. "Don't be a sap. We've got all night—but we've got to put this thing over or the Commish is sunk."

Springer nodded in understanding. He slipped the jimmy under the next board and levered it up carefully. It ripped loose at one end. Haddon slipped his fingers beneath the edge and wrenched quietly. Another board gave. Springer arose, wiped the sweat from his eyes.

"Enough?" he said, indicating the opening. Haddon shook his head. "More," he said. "At least three feet. Safe stands across the corner, you know."

Springer loosened two more boards, then a third. Haddon levered them out, keeping the nails from creaking. Then the firing started up again on the floor below, Springer motioned to the copper with the Tommy.

"Lie down," he directed. "Listen carefully and see if you can tell from the sound just about where he's standing."

The cop complied, laid there a matter of moments, then arose, grinning.

"Bet I knock a hole in his skull first thing," he boasted.

"Then get at it," Springer snapped, passing the gun to the man's waiting hands. "There's a big safe across the corner that he's using for a shield. Sponge out every inch behind it."

The cop up-ended the weapon, stopped to kick loose a sliver of board from a cross beam. He grinned over his shoulders at the others.

"Watch this," he said.

He brought the trigger back; drew a jagged line of holes straight from the corner back almost to his feet. The slugs tore through the plastering as a knife cuts whey. He moved the muzzle patiently from left to right and back again, probing into every possible corner. Suddenly there was a dull crash followed by a white dust cloud. A square yard of the ceiling had fallen.

Several slugs from automatics buzzed through the opening and crashed into the attic flooring but Haddon, unmindful, leaned forward to peer down. Springer shouldered him aside roughly.

The top of the safe was heaped with fallen plaster, as was the floor beside it. Two huddled forms were slumped against the wall. Springer detected sudden movement and dragged Haddon back as one of the two fallen men jerked half erect and emptied a clip from his rod at the faces above him.

Feet dashed across the floor below. Rods spoke their death word and the gangster, riddled anew, pitched forward; lay there quietly.

"Come on—it's the finish." Springer snatched at Haddon's arm and raced to the stairhead. In the club-rooms below they came upon a scene none of the living participants forgot for days.

Five wounded or dead police lay in a corner where they had been dragged by their comrades out of the line of Bull's murderous fire. The door and partition between the two rooms were splintered wrecks. The steel shield, used first by the defenders and then by the attackers, lay overturned near the doorway. Hardly an inch of its surface had escaped a scoring by flying lead and steel. Back of it lay one of the police, one side of his face shot away by a long burst of fire.

Within the inner room the walls and furnishings had been torn to fragments by the hail of bullets. Bull had left open the big doors of the safe as an added protection against police guns. The drawers and pigeonholes were wrecked, their contents smashed and torn until they were mere heaps of waste paper and rubbish.

Three dead gangsters lay in a corner back of a heavy oak table which they had up-ended to use as a shield. Another lay beside the safe, at the left.

A policeman caught at a pair of feet protruding from behind the safe and dragged out a wounded man. His head was smashed, but he still breathed—horribly, bubblingly.

Springer wriggled through the press and caught Bull's inert form by the collar. The gang leader was badly slashed about the head, either by grazing bullets or falling plaster. Blood gushed, fountain-like, from a wound in his left shoulder. One wrist was smashed. The hand hung, grotesquely, like a wet glove.

The movement roused the gangster to consciousness. He gazed, dazedly at first, at Springer. For a moment hope leaped into his eyes. Then he saw the police uniforms and realization came to him. Hate distorted his blood smeared features; his hand clawed at his trousers band for the spare rod he carried there.

"You damned, stinking, lousy rat!" he whispered. "Turned stoolie—gave me up to the bulls, damn you! I'm goin' out—but I'm takin' you with me."

Bull's great body surged forward, his right hand clutching at Springer's throat. Then, forgetful of his wounds, he tried to put his weight on the smashed wrist. The bones grated against the floor; sent him crashing back onto his face. The others were gathering up the injured policemen, only Haddon standing by.

Springer jerked Bull erect into a sitting posture again. The gangster's eyes shifted to Haddon's face.

"Another—rat!" he whispered. "Stool! Snitch! And I—I was warned. You—Shorty—lice, both of you!"

Springer leaned forward until his face was within inches of that of Bull. Hatred blazed in his eyes.

"No, not Shorty, Bull," he snarled. "His double. Eddie Springer, son of one of the cops you and your rods knocked off two weeks ago. Take that down to hell with you—and see how it tastes for a kid to make things square for his old man."

Bull's eyes widened in utter unbelief. "Liar!" he mumbled. "You're Shorty—and a stool." He sagged back hopelessly. Springer shook him viciously.

"Your mob's gone," he gritted. "Every one at the warehouse, everybody here. They're all finished—like you'll be in a minute."

Bull sighed. Suddenly his body went limp.

The Bull Coleman gang was wiped from the roll of "men wanted for major crime."

V

SHORTY'S AWAKENING

DAYLIGHT! SHORTY BREEN AWOKE, shivering in his underclothing in the silent cell. Slowly his mind grasped his predicament. He was A.W.O.L. with Bull. That meant he'd have to duck the town or take a one-way ride with some of his former pals.

Damn old McGrehan! Just like a thick-headed cop to get a fellow into a jam like this.

Feet resounded eerily down the corridor. Shorty strained his ears to hear. Then he leaped upright, gibbering with fear.

His senses told him that he was sitting erect on the hard board in the cell, *yet there he stood outside the locked door, dressed in his everyday suit, peering in through the bars at himself!*

For the first time in years, Shorty made the sign of the cross. The figure outside stood leering at him, wordlessly. Shorty tried to mouth a question— ended with a shrill scream. The words would not form in his mouth. His throat was a frozen waste. With the sound the other Shorty moved soundlessly aside, disappeared.

Long minutes passed. Never ending minutes. Once Shorty thought he heard whispering in the distance.

The boy fought to still the trembling which shook his every nerve and muscle. He lay back, eyeing the steel grating above him. It was a trick, a dream; something they were doing to crack his nerve. Well, damn them, he'd fool them.

Then, while he promised himself they wouldn't frighten him again, there was a loud click. He snapped erect, gazing in wide-eyed horror; burst into a shrill torrent of screams.

The other Shorty—his counterpart—was back, unlocking the door— coming in after him. He covered his eyes with his arms, cowered back against the cold steel wall of the cell. The other was inside now; probably come to take him down into hell.

A heavy hand clutched his shoulder, dragged him up, and out, and into the corridor.

It was more than even gangster flesh and blood could stand. Convulsively, squirming like an eel, Shorty broke the hold, ran down the corridor at a shambling pace, rounded the cell block—smashed full into the burly form of Captain McGrehan.

Clyde Breen, ex-speedball and gangster, burst into tears.

He forced himself to look into the eyes of the double who now stood at his side. His face was bloody, his hands gory and torn.

"Get goin'; the Commissioner's waitin'." Captain McGrehan was speaking for the first time.

"Here he is, Mr. Commissioner," said McGrehan, thrusting the half clad Shorty opposite the official.

For a long moment the Commissioner stared appraisingly into Shorty's eyes. Finally he spoke.

"Of all the Coleman gang, Breen, you only are alive today."

Shorty stared at him, unbelievingly. The toneless voice continued:

"We trapped them in the warehouse raid, surrounded Bull and the others over Finnegan's in the hangout; killed every one of them. Captain McGrehan saved you—for your mother's sake."

"Why? How?" The words were whispered. Shorty's world had come tumbling about his ears.

"Why did we clean them out?" The Commissioner's tone was savage. "Well, you know why. You drove the chopper car on the raid on The Yid's trucks. That night two policemen were killed. One of them was the father of Springer here—this boy who wore your clothes, pretended to be you tonight—and drove one of the cars to the warehouse."

Shorty turned and stared wonderingly at Springer. Within his mind he said one word. It was "Guts!" The Commissioner's dead voice continued tonelessly.

"Better men than you'll ever be, died tonight, Breen. They'll lie and mold in their graves while you go on living, breathing, maybe loving.

"Captain McGrehan convinced me we should save you for two reasons. The first is to keep your mother's heart from breaking. The other is that you're going to sit down now and tell a stenographer about everything you know that the Coleman gang did in a criminal way, including the death of the two policemen. You hear me?"

"I hope he says 'no,' Mr. Commissioner. I want a chance to slap him down until he's only two feet high."

Captain McGrehan, fists clenched, was advancing from the doorway.

"Get square, kid; start all over again—we'll all help." It was Springer who drove the clinching nail.

"I'll do it," he said.

Shorty saw the Commissioner but once more.

That was the day when Mom and Captain McGrehan went before the good Father O'Grady and rectified the mistakes of their younger years.

The Commissioner was best man. Shorty gave the bride away.

At the end of the ceremony, the Commissioner said good-bye to Shorty last of all.

"Keep your head up, boy," he said earnestly. "You'll make it all right."

"An' damn well you know it," his new father growled. "He's ji'nin' th' Navy tomorruh."

"Uh—uh—why, sure!" Shorty replied.

The Angel
From Hell

"Snell: You did something for me—I'll do something for you. Take this to the dicks and they'll be your friends for life!" And "for life" was underlined.

SOMEWHERE OUT THERE IN THE OPPRESSIVE STILLNESS of the night "Angel" Refkuski sensed movement, stealthily menacing, like the nocturnal padding of a cougar.

It had been there, at intervals, for more than an hour now, a deadly sentry-go that told of the Black Camel of Death waiting, ready to carry his killer soul off to that far land where such as he go after death.

Men were stalking him out there in the blackness, but Angel Refkuski had been first. He was stalking them with all the tireless patience, the unblinking watchfulness of one of the cat tribe. In his hand was a weapon—an acid gun—the butt of which was a bulb; the contents brittle containers of nitric acid which, finding their mark, would sear and burn deep into tissues and eyes.

Angel had left the shelter of his four walls with the coming of darkness. Wraith-like he had taken up a position under an overhanging shrub.

Unmoving, serene of face, he still lay there hours later, waiting for the almost soundless footsteps to draw nearer.

Serene of face! The most hardened of gangsters shuddered at the hideously perfect, unchanging beauty of the Polish killer's countenance. Two years before, a pineapple had exploded near him, tearing and blasting his face into a pulpy mass.

Plastic surgeons—some of the best—sent him back to Gangland months later with the angelic countenance of an altar-boy; spiritual and saintly in expression.

Yet it was unchanging, an unmoving mask incapable of showing emotion. They could and had rebuilt the tissues, but there science ended. It was impossible to remake the muscles and their governing nerves which, under stress, would have unmasked him for a vicious, relentless killer.

For Angel killed for the sheer joy of the hunt; the death-thrill—killed until even Snell Mahaley, racketeer chief and Angel's patron, had come to shudder at the sight of the bland, cherubic face which hid the seething hell of Angel's twisted, hate-driven mind.

Also—and far worse, there was a guilty secret between them, a secret shared by still another gunman—Dominic Repossito. The three were there when a finger compressed on trigger and sent a slug crashing into the heart of Emmett Rothgreen, King of Broadway.

As a result of that shot a police chief had been dethroned, the administration had suffered an upheaval, scandal hovered over America's greatest city. And thus far there were no clues.

Today a whisper had come to Angel. Snell Mahaley had "passed the word" on Dominic. A spark took fire in Angel's mind. Snell was too wise to be caught in a police trap baited with one or more confessions. For an hour that afternoon Angel and Snell talked in the hangout, Angel watching, studying Snell's face. There was death there, he saw. Snell was too elaborately casual in manner, too placating. He talked mysteriously of a big job he had in sight for Angel—a big money job, with a scram at the end of it; then months of well paid idleness in some distant city.

Angel nodded, said "Check!"; strolled through the door and into the street. For a second he had seen Snell's face in a mirror—the eyes leering, hate-filled. Nothing more was needed to verify his suspicion. He, like Dominic, was "on the spot."

Now the surge of his murder-lust came back to Angel as he caught the faint whisper of a shrub against fabric. Slowly but surely the enemies were ringing him in, setting themselves for the dash that would make the house theirs.

Off in the distance lights shone against the sky, giving him an opaque background for his eyes as he lay huddled close against the ground.

Presently a darker shadow came out of the blackness. A squat pair of shoulders, a human head covered with a cap stood out against the lighter patch of sky.

A second later Angel caught the sound of heavy breathing behind him. That meant a second enemy. Snell wasn't taking any chances. He'd sent enough men out, *and in pairs*, to make certain that dangerous lips would be closed forever.

Angel brought his knees up under him, lifted his torso until the lower branches of the shrub touched his neck.

Then the man at his right moved slightly; a whisper cut through the blackness.

"Come on," it said. "They've had lotsa time to get in through the back. Give Murph and Blackie a chirp."

"Murph and Blackie!" Two more there at the front! Angel set his teeth, then let his lips relax in a smile. Four in front, at least an equal number at the back. Eight—all of Snell's tried-and-true rodmen except himself and Dominic. What a tribute to his own deadliness!

He inched forward, cleared the shrub; came erect. Silently he brought his hand up, pointed the force-gun at the head of the man at his side. Slowly, deliberately, his fingers pressed the bulb.

There was a sound like a hissing sigh, a pause; then a strangled scream of agony that changed instantly into howls of anguish.

Angel twisted in the same split second, let two more of the brittle missiles go in the direction of the second man. He scored again, he knew, for he heard the double plop of the containers.

"Whatthe—!" the second man started to ask; then lost the words in a bubbling scream of anguish as the acid ate through his clothing and attacked the sensitive tissues.

Now the first man was on the ground, thrashing about, shouting that his eyes were afire, burning into his brain. The second man was rushing back and forth, slapping at his chest; yelling his agony.

Angel backed slowly about the shrub, his senses attuned to catch the first alien sound. Almost instantly it came, a low growl from near at hand.

"Cripes, can de racket!" a voice hissed. "Wanna tip us off?"

Angel crouched, watching the horizon. A second later two forms materialized before him. Instantly he squeezed the bulb twice—then twice more.

The acid slug struck the nearest man in the face, sent it cascading against his lips. His first shout was a mad, bubbling yell of anguish. "Mouth" was the only word distinguishable.

The fourth man fled, but without a word. Angel knew his acid slugs had missed.

In a second he was in motion, diving through the blackness in the direction the other had taken. Before him he heard a spatter of curses, the sound of a body crashing through the hedge.

Guided only by his cat instinct, Angel dashed silently across the lawn to the corner, swung lightly over the hedge and lit, running, on the parking strip between hedge and walk.

Twenty feet distant he could make out the form of the fugitive. It was a small man, incredibly swift. The sound of his pounding feet was like the rapid beat of a clog-dancer's feet simulating a drum roll.

Angel, head up and shoulders forward, dashed in pursuit. He too was swift of foot. In the first half block he gained enough to identify the runner as the little rat gunman, Murphy.

At the corner Murphy slowed, turned into the cross street. Angel cut across the corner of an unfenced lawn, leaped up and out; came down with Murphy under him, the little gunman's scrawny neck in the crook of his arm.

The prisoner kicked, threw himself about, gurgled as he fought for breath inside the tightening, throttling arm.

Angel came to his knees for leverage, loosened his hold; let his cupped hand slip back to the other's chin.

Then he brought the right up, laid it firmly against the back of his victim's head—and wrenched suddenly.

Then Murphy lay quiet. His neck was broken.

Angel arose, dusted the knees of his trousers, walked back to the drain-hole at the corner. He took the acid gun from his pocket, a metal case containing other projectiles; dropped all down into the sewer.

Behind him he heard sounds of turmoil. Someone nearby thrust up a window. A woman's voice began shrieking for the police.

Angel shrugged; began putting distance between himself and the living and dead victims. A crosstown car carried him to the East Side. There he took a taxi, rode awhile; dismissed it and took another.

In the middle of a long block on Christopher Street he signaled for the driver to stop, paid him and entered the lobby of a rebuilt studio building. He passed out at the back, slipped over a low fence and made his way back toward the East River.

He stopped at a corner cigar stand, eyeing the loungers appraisingly before proceeding to a telephone booth.

A feminine voice responded to his call with a musical, "Yes?"

"Alone, Gail?" he asked in a low tone.

"Yes, who is it?"

"Refkuski—Angel!" He smiled inwardly at her stifled gasp of terror. "I can help you," he said tentatively. "We've got business—together."

"No!" she said. The line went dead with the word.

Patiently he deposited another coin; called the number back.

"Don't hang up," Angel said gently a moment later. "They're fixing to hang the Rothgreen thing on you; the cops've found you were with him when he was croaked."

The line was silent for several seconds.

"Why—?" The woman began a question; stopped.

"Why should I bother?" Angel said, completing the query. "Something's happened that makes it my business. I've got to talk to you."

"Tomorrow!"

"No, now! It's 11:15—I've got to see a man. Meet me behind your apartment house at 1 sharp. If you're afraid, call a cab and ride round and round the block until you see me."

Angel hung up without waiting for an answer.

Ten minutes later he climbed, catlike, up the rusted fire escape of a cheap tenement facing on one of the side streets just off Second Avenue.

The rear fire escape window on the fourth floor was open. Angel listened for a long minute before he slipped noiselessly through. He felt his way around the walls to the door, drew his rod; clicked the electric switch.

A figure, bulky and bloodstained, lay across the bed, unmoving.

Angel let his eyes flicker about the room. It was empty, except for the body. Without turning, he felt for the door handle. It was unlocked. A moment later his fingers found the retaining latch and let the tongue of the lock shoot home.

Three steps brought him to the bed. He turned the quiet form over; saw where four slugs had torn through the chest and stomach.

The movement brought back the victim's life flame for a moment. His eyes opened to stare, horrified, at Angel.

"Lousy—yegg!" he gasped. "You—did—it!"

"No!" Angel barked the word. "Some of Snell's mob. They got you and tried for me because we know about Rothgreen!"

Dominic Repossito's glazing eyes opened; burned angrily for a moment.

"Write—I'll sign!" he gritted. "Snell Mahaley killed Rothgreen!" He fell back, let his jaw slack.

Angel whipped a notebook from his pocket; bunched the nerveless fingers around a pencil.

"Write—sign—sign!" he gritted. "Damn you, Dominic, you don't dare to croak without signing!"

The words reached what little of consciousness remained. Angel felt a tremor in the flaccid fingers.

"Get him—get Snell!" he hissed.

Dominic caught at his breath sharply. The fingers moved, formed the letter "D," paused. In a second they moved again, slowly, desperately fighting with the formation of each letter. When it was done, Dominic gasped, and was gone.

Angel looked at the blank page with the signature at the bottom; stood in thought for a long moment. Presently he moved to a table, sat down and wrote rapidly. When he had finished, he tore a corner from the sheet, put it carefully away in his purse, and wrote another brief line.

When precinct detectives came in answer to a mysterious telephone call an hour later, they found the dead body of Dominic Repossito. Pinned to the shoulder was a page from a note book on which was written:

> "I was there when
> killed Emmett Rothgreen.
> The other fellow with me was
> We both saw the killing. Get him. This
> is my dying statement.
> DOMINIC REPOSSITO."

Below the first sheet was a second. On this was written:

"I found Dominic dying, and tore two names from his note. Maybe some day I will give it to you cops. Maybe not. It was a man who killed him—and I saw it."

There was no signature.

Before dawn Centre Street sent out an order to all precincts to search all incoming prisoners carefully for a scrap of paper bearing two names. Dominic's original note was put between two heavy plates of glass to preserve the torn edge so it could be matched when the missing scrap appeared.

Gail Jacoby's slight form was almost hidden in the right corner of a Packard taxicab when it swerved to the curbing in a dark spot. The door opened. In the reflected light she saw the pale features of Angel.

The girl's hand settled firmly about the butt of a small automatic she held in her lap under an envelope purse. Swiftly she shifted her position to give her arm free play.

Angel lunged across to the opposite corner, barked the single word "Park!" into the mouthpiece of the speaking tube. He lit a cigarette, turned and surveyed Gail approvingly. There was good reason. She was petite; a brunette with a wealth of blue-black hair and eyes soft and languorous in expression; but eyes, as Angel knew, capable of flashing fire when need arose.

"Well, how's the Mystery Moll?" Angel tried to put friendliness in his tone; failed.

"What do you want?" The girl's tone was hard, suspicious.

"Congreve's framing you for the Rothgreen croaking; the Commish is on his neck. It's a case of produce a likely suspect or take the axe from the captaincy. You were there when it came off—"

Angel's words brought the quick light of fear to the girl's eyes.

"There?" she repeated. "How do you know?"

Angel stared into her eyes steadily; let a hand creep out to touch hers.

"The man who shot Emmett stood on my shoulders to reach that little French window. He shot, dropped the gun inside and pulled the window shut with a T-hook. There's a patent catch on the sash. That's why they called it an inside job."

The girl kept silence. Angel waited patiently.

"The man was—" Gail began, stopped with a shrug.

"Let that go," Angel interrupted. "Rothgreen's been in the ground three months now. What sort of an alibi have you got? You're a bigger sap than you get credit for being if you're not fixed pretty by now."

Gail touched the dome-light; searched Angel's immobile face with eager eyes.

"Why the friendship?" she parried, snapping the light off again. "What do I mean to you?"

She felt Angel's eyes searching her face in the glow from the street lamps. His silence annoyed her; for a moment brought a chill of fear.

"If you're smart—if you team up with me—we can take this town like Paddy took his liquor. I can spring you out of the Rothgreen mess and I can knock off some heads that are in my way. I'll be king! Do you hear me? King!"

"Who's in the way?" Gail asked.

"Who's on top of the heap right now? Snell Mahaley and a few cheap racketeers who'll follow me as quickly as him. With Snell and a couple of guys in the Bronx and Brooklyn put on the spot, I can slide in at the top overnight."

"Yes, with Rothgreen gone, too."

Angel twitched about in his seat, let his eyes devour the girl's face. Suddenly his hand came up, snatched purse and rod from her lap.

"Damn you!" he gritted. "Just what do you mean by that?"

Gail's gaze locked with his.

"It's a fact, isn't it, Angel? Until Emmett Rothgreen was out of the way you couldn't get at Snell Mahaley or the little fellows, and have it count for anything."

"Go on!" He snarled the words viciously.

"Now Emmett's gone, there's only Snell between you and the throne. Emmett, one; Snell, two—then a couple of little fellows and you're 'it.' Three strikes and out."

Angel puffed slowly at his cigarette. His eyes never left Gail's face for an instant. Presently he dropped the cigarette into the ash receiver, picked up the speaking tube.

"Back to where you picked me up," he ordered and turned back to Gail.

"You're the 'Mystery Moll' to everybody but me," he said slowly. "I've got your number, and I'm through asking for things. Take your choice tomorrow; tell me when I call you. Team up with me or I'll let you go through on the Rothgreen rap. If you do take the pinch, you're due for the Hot Squat. Play along with me, and while I'm living and packing a rod, you'll be bigger than the Vanderbilts and Harrimans."

He tossed the purse and rod back into her lap contemptuously.

"You wonder what I want," he went on. "It isn't what you think. I don't care a damn for women; there's nothing soft about me. But"—he raised his voice, let the words out slowly—"you're the best Finger on Broadway today. The only thing it needs is a good Finger, one I can handle, like I can handle you."

Noon of the following day found Angel reading in bed in a room in a Newark hangout he occasionally patronized when Gotham proper seemed unhealthful for him.

The morning editions of the New York papers lay scattered about the bed while Angel concentrated on the final edition of the *American*.

"ACID THROWER BLINDS TWO VICTIMS; SERIOUSLY INJURES THIRD; SLAYS FOURTH GANGSTER WITH BARE HANDS," a three-deck streamer head across the eight columns screamed to a sensation-loving public.

There was little meat in the story which followed. It told of a police call from residents in the vicinity, and of finding three acid-burned victims in the yard of a residence rented by unknown persons several weeks before.

The police denied knowledge of the tenant's identity and, according to the paper, were not prepared to admit that Murphy, found dead a few hundred feet from the scene, had died by the same hand.

The reporter, however, pointed to the fact that all four were known members of the Snell Mahaley mob; gave color to the theory by appending the story of Dominic Repossito's death as proof of some eerie fate which was dogging the steps of the Mahaley rodmen.

For a while Angel lay back comfortably, jubilating as he considered what Snell's fury must be after the setbacks of the night. Presently he uttered an exclamation of joy, dressed and hurried to the street.

Five minutes later he was in the back room of a photograph gallery, negotiating with the aged, half-starved owner to copy two bits of handwriting. The man agreed readily. Angel waited until the prints had been made, handed the man a yellow-backed bill and unceremoniously swept prints and plate onto a sheet of wrapping paper and walked out.

Late that afternoon, Snell Mahaley, rocking under the load of liquor his black mood had induced him to drink, received a special delivery parcel bearing the cancellation stamp of the New York main post office.

He studied it owlishly for a moment, ripped it open. Unfolding a tissue paper wrapper he stared at the contents for a moment, then launched into a burst of mumbled profanity.

He held before his blurred eyes the photographic print of the corner of a sheet from a pocket memo-book. At the top was his own name; below it the words in the same handwriting, "Angel, the Polack."

A plain card was enclosed with the print. On it was scrawled:

> Snell: You tried to do something for me last night. Now I'm doing something for you. Take this to the dicks at Centre Street and show it to them. They'll be your pals <u>for life</u>.

The signature was "Angel."

The words "for life" were underlined.

Snell knitted his brows; went to the telephone.

"Mac?" he demanded a moment later. "Snell talkin'. Lissen! Was they somepin' las' night about a paper wit' part of it tore off? My boys was tellin'."

"Damn tootin'," McMann, one of the Central Office men replied. "Keep it under your hat. Letter pinned to Repossito's shoulder when we found him." He whispered the words, added: "Know something?"

"Hell, no!" Snell barked. "Not up that alley. Fergit it 'n they's two-three yards waitin' for you at th' hangout tomorrun."

He mopped his streaming forehead; pressed a buzzer.

"Send for Shiv Johnny," he ordered weakly.

"You know Mame Baker's plant up there on West Forty-Fifth Street?" Snell demanded of the visitor when Shiv Johnny finally appeared.

Shiv nodded. He was tall, gangling, rat-faced; one of the few gangsters in New York who boasted that he never had carried a rod. Yet he was one of the Underworld's deadliest killers—as his nickname would indicate—a knife slayer.

"Mame Baker's?" Shiv repeated. "Hell, yes. I holed up there for three weeks oncet. That was after I'd carved up a harness bull 'at stopped me comin' off en th' Queensboro bridge. An' 'at blowser flang me out when me jack was gone. Sure I know Mame 'n her hideout."

At a gesture from Snell, Shiv dropped into a chair; flicked his throwing knife from his sleeve; began idly tossing it into the air and catching it by the point as it fell.

It was a needle pointed blade, with a weighted ball in place of a handle. Snell shivered as he watched the gleaming blade twisting in the air, as he recalled the tales men whispered of the unerring accuracy of Shiv Johnny's killings.

With an effort Snell collected his thoughts, pulled a handful of crumpled bills from his pocket.

"Here," he said, pushing them across to Shiv Johnny. "Take this and go back there. Tell Mame you've got into another jam 'n that Snell Mahaley sent youse."

"And then?" Shiv demanded suspiciously.

Snell's bloodshot eyes bulged as he sought to fight back his anger, fought to disguise the importance of the mission from the visitor. Finally he cursed explosively.

"I want youse to whittle a guy's neck fer me," he gritted. "Croak him 'n you get a grand; bring me his head and I'll make it two, the—" Again he lapsed into a torrent of cursing.

"Gimme three dollars more 'n I'll bring you George Wash'nton in pink peejimmies," Shiv snorted boisterously. "You talk like this geek had a tin hat 'n a solid steel shirt. Who is it, anyhow?"

"Angel, th' blankety-blank rat," Snell roared.

"Oh, ye-ah?"

Shiv Johnny snapped the throwing knife from his sleeve, caught it by the point; sent it whizzing across the room to bury it point squarely in the corner of the wall.

"Look him over careful," he said as he rose to reclaim the knife. "He'll have a hole in him—and it won't be in the front. I've saw that guy throw lead, but I know damn well he can't shoot through his collar button."

Snell's liquor was making him captious.

"Brave, hey?" he demanded. "Job too tough for youse?"

Johnny's wrist flipped over. The knife pinned Snell's coat to the arm of his chair.

"Uh-huh!" Shiv answered. "I'm scared to death—of you; maybe you won't pay when the job's done."

His left hand flashed to Snell's inside coat pocket, drew forth a thick pad of fifties. He thumbed them, took twenty; threw the rest on the table.

"You get your job done—now," he said, jerking the point of the knife loose and backing from the room.

When he was gone, when the door at the head of the stairs had clanged behind him, Snell pulled himself together; called a number on the telephone.

"Slip the word around," he said softly, "that I'm holed up at Mame Baker's; spread it good."

• • •

Shiv Johnny, shoes off and with the collar of a dark coat turned up about his throat, crouched in the darkness at the head of the stairs just outside the black outline of his open door.

He welcomed the order to rub Angel Refkuski out. It was a pleasure he had promised himself for months; now he was being paid for it. Within the house all was quiet save for the steps of someone on the floor above pacing about in his room. Johnny moved to rest protesting muscles, listened as a clock struck the hour of midnight.

Deft questioning had brought the information from blowsy, gin-sodden Mame Baker that Angel, unlike the rest of her well-paying guests, maintained a room there all of the time. The others, when police became too inquisitive, holed up there for varying lengths of time, paying twenty-five dollars a day for the protection she gave. Somehow, probably through having something on a precinct police official, she managed to evade searches of her joint.

Another hour passed; then, a distant bell tinkled softly.

Shiv Johnny wriggled to his knees as Mame opened the door.

"Oh, h'lo, Angel," she muttered. "Wasn't lookin' for you. Whatcha want, hey?"

Angel thrust inside, flashed a rod under his coat. There was a sound like a muffled hand-spat—and Mame's body, dead now, sunk to the floor. For a moment one hand clutched at Angel's trouser-leg.

He kicked free, snarled: "That's what I want here, blowser. This is my dump tonight; I've come rat-killing."

Angel, rod in hand, kicked open the door of Mame's rooms, felt inside the door casing; snapped off the lights. For a moment he stood listening; staring curiously, warily, into the darkness above. Then he began mounting the stairs, walking at the inner edge of the treads to prevent squeaks.

Shiv Johnny, prone on the floor, drew his heavy knife; pulled his coat over the side of his face to make it invisible. He dared not raise his head; contented himself with counting Angel's soft footsteps.

At nine he shifted the coat. Angel's cap was just below the level of the floor. Silently Shiv brought his right knee up under him, braced his weight against the left palm and elbow, ready for a quick thrust upward.

Before he could move further, Angel flashed into action, taking the remaining four stairs with a rush. In a split second he had melted into the darkness along the farther wall.

Shiv Johnny slipped back to the floor; held his breath. He dared not move, though he knew, instinctively, that Angel would pick him out of the blackness as soon as the other's eyes became accustomed to the darkness.

Cautiously he set his muscles; tried to roll back toward the open door of his room. A board squeaked. He heard Angel's feet move on the worn carpet. Shiv came to his feet, threw himself into a twisting leap which should have carried him into his room.

Instead, he caromed off the doorframe; stumbled noisily.

Angel's rod coughed once, twice—that Shiv Johnny heard.

The third slug, struck the point of his jawbone; tore through his ear; dropped him to the floor, senseless.

When he regained consciousness he lay on his own bed. His feet were tied together securely.

Angel, stony-faced, leaned across the foot of the bed. He was tossing Johnny's throwing knife into the air; catching it deftly as it fell.

Johnny shivered at the frozen beauty of Angel's face as their eyes met. Somewhere deep in those of the Polish killer, fresh from croaking Mame Baker, was the lust of the killer, and with it the red gleam of Angel's hatred for his prisoner.

Angel tossed the knife upward again, caught it nonchalantly; let it slip point downward and fall a hair's breadth from Shiv Johnny's stockinged feet.

"I'm pretty good at it, too," he said softly. "Back in Poland we use knives—because we can't afford gats and cartridges."

Shiv had no answer for him. Angel raised his head; stared at him frostily.

"Where's Snell Mahaley?" he demanded.

"Snell? Dunno. Ain't seen—"

Angel let the smooth edge of the knife slide along the bottom of Johnny's right foot. The severed sock fell away; a thin red line showed on the thick skin. Shiv Johnny uttered a howl of protest; stopped in mid-cry.

"Where?" Angel gritted. He poised the knife inches above the bare foot.

"Cripes—I dunno! Is he—?"

"Where?" Angel reiterated coldly. He pushed back the split sock; jabbed shallowly with the knife blade a half-dozen times into the tender skin over the arch of Shiv's foot.

"I tell you I—" Shiv protested; changed to a howl of utter agony as Angel reversed the knife; brought the metal knob smartly down on the metatarsal bones. Angel waited several seconds, rapped the foot again—in the same place.

"Talk!" he snarled. "Where's Snell?"

Shiv's agony sent him twisting about, jerking in an effort to win free of the unendurable pain of Angel's hands.

Angel caught Shiv's feet, lifted them; surged backward. Shiv slid down the bed, struggling. It was hopeless. Angel stopped when his victim's knees were at the foot of the bed; bent the legs downward and leaned against them.

"Now you'll talk," he sneered. He sunk a hard thumb into the nerve center beside the right knee; began drumming brutally on the kneecap with the knob-handle of the knife.

Shiv bit his lips until the blood came before he sagged; screamed his agony in a howl that rang through the house.

"Where's Snell?" Angel leaned forward, prodding at Shiv's knees with the needle-pointed knife.

"Gawd!" The word burst from Shiv's lips like a prayer. "I don't know—Angel—I don't know!" he mumbled. "Please—please Angel, I don't know."

Angel stared at him, half believing.

"He's holed up here!" he muttered. "I got it straight."

"No, not here!" Shiv jerked his legs to quiet the pain, raised himself on an elbow. He was cooler now. Snell Mahaley's money was in his pocket. What difference, then, what he told Angel? The deal was off anyway.

"Tell you why," he continued, the words falling over one another. "He sent me here to get you, Angel—so he's making his alibi somewhere else. Ain't that right?"

"How much?" Angel barked. "What's the price for my neck?"

"A grand—here." His fingers touched his inside pocket.

Angel leaned forward, removed the sheaf of fifties; dropped them into his own pocket.

He caught at Shiv's collar-band, twisted it brutally; thrust him back onto the bed. Holding his victim thus, he pawed behind him for the knife.

"Get ready," Angel hissed. "Snell's paying for your neck—rat!"

Shiv Johnny's yellow heart cracked under the threat.

"Gimme—a—break!" he begged, fighting for air; gulping the words hoarsely. "I'll stick—Angel—gimme—chanst!"

Slowly Angel's hand relaxed. The congested blood receded from Shiv Johnny's face. He lay there panting.

"Lemme help—you," he begged after a moment. "Snell ain't nothin' to me. I'll help you frame him."

Angel loosened the knot; slipped the rope off Johnny's ankles.

"Get on your shoes," he commanded. "We'll just do that thing."

Johnny groaned as he pulled the shoe over his aching foot; gritted his teeth as he touched his damaged ear; felt the clotted blood on his face. "I'm hurt!" he babbled.

"It'll make your story good," Angel answered. "You're going back to Snell and tell him you cooled me. Show him where I shot you while you was doing it."

Shiv Johnny nodded dully. "Aw right," he said. "That all?"

Angel waited long seconds before replying.

"I'm going with you," he said at last. "I'll be outside Snell's door. When you come out—I'll go in. Get me? I'm going in and croak me a rotten, lousy drain-rat."

Snell Mahaley's private room, office and personal hideout from unwelcome visitors was in the rear of the speakeasy he operated as a headquarters for his mob and their allies.

The place, in the pre-Volstead days, had been a restaurant. It was a long, narrow room in a corner building. At the back was what once had been the mezzanine office of the proprietor. Snell had caused this to be extended and walled in. This gave him a safe hangout half a floor above the street—and with the surety of a goodly number of gat-toting guards at all hours of the day or night.

A steep flight of narrow stairs led to the barred door, which could be opened only from the inside, or with a secret key which thrust in through what seemed a nail-hole high above the door handle.

En route to the place Angel gave Shiv Johnny explicit instructions; stopped at a drugstore and, crowding into the booth with Johnny, made him telephone to Snell that the job was done.

"Shiv Johnny, Snell," he said. "I sent yer laundry out, like you tole me!"

"Keerist!" Snell whooped. "C'mon down 'n tell me about it."

Angel and Johnny reentered the cab; left it a block distant from the hangout.

Just outside the door, Angel caught at Johnny's shoulder, twisted him about viciously.

"I'll be right behind you," he snarled. "Don't figure to cross me or I'll blow you down while I'm taking mine. Louse on me, guy—and you croak—even if Snell goes free."

"I'll stick," Shiv Johnny said uneasily. "I'm wit' youse, Angel; hell to breakfast."

Angel entered behind Shiv Johnny, secure in the knowledge that Snell would keep his plans to himself until there was definite news that Angel Refkuski had gone to join the rest of the bad-man crop.

Here and there a hanger-on looked up and nodded. None of the rank and file of Snell's gang cared for the slightest contact with the viciously deadly Angel. Sullen stares and averted eyes, as always, proved to be his welcome.

Shiv Johnny proceeded up the stairs with Angel at his heels. The latter, wise to the methods of Snell, kept his fingers under the banister on the right side, found and pressed the button which announced the approach of someone in the know.

At the head of the stairs, out of sight now of the loungers below, Angel slid against the blank wall beside the door; motioned for Shiv Johnny to knock.

In a second the door was snatched open. Angel heard Snell husk:

"C'mon in, Johnny—you got the damn rat, eh?"

"Yeh! Like I said—'n he pretty near got me—look at me ear where his slug hit me."

The door swung to. In an instant Angel had his ear pressed to one of the panels. The voices from within came to him plainly.

"Never mind the flapper," he heard Snell say. "Another grand'll mend that fine, hey? Go on 'n tell me about it. Wish't I could have been there to see it."

"Well, it was like this," Shiv replied. "He come sneakin' in. Me, I was layin' at the top of the stairs wit' me shoes off. I gets all bunched to hop him, but he musta heard me move, for he swung around wit' his rod coughin' when I sunk the sticker in his neck.

"He goes down. Blood was runnin' from his mouth, but he slings another slug at me. He'd 'a got me, too, on'y I was duckin'. It hit me on th' jawbone 'n damn near tears me ear off. I was kinda goofy fer awhile, but when I come to, Angel was all through. Gimme me other grand now, Snell—I wanta blow before they find him."

"Cheap at twice the price," Snell replied. "Here y'are—but you ain't got no reason to scram; nobody knows I was out for Angel's neck but four of my own men. I ain't tellin' my inside dope to them rummies down to the bar. They're just muscle; me, I use brains."

"Well, thanks, Snell; I'll—I'll be runnin' along—"

Feet scraped along the floor, fingers touched the latch within. Angel pulled back out of sight, waited, poised on the balls of his feet for the door to open.

"I got a place for youse any time, Shiv," he heard Snell say and then the hinges creaked.

Angel tensed his muscles for the move; flashed a glance downward. Nobody was even looking his way.

The door swung wide. Angel leaped, put a hand in Shiv Johnny's back; thrust him heavily against Snell.

Another split second and he was inside, backed against the closed door, his rod swinging back and forth between Snell and Shiv.

"Here's your laundry, Mr. Mahaley," he said tauntingly, "the laundry Shiv Johnny sent out." He stared into Snell's fear-clouded eyes, tried to twist his seemingly frozen lips into a derisive grin.

"Ain't I a nice looking corpse?" he snarled; "the two grand stiff you bought and paid for, you sap." He flashed around at Shiv. "Now tell him what really happened," he demanded, "so he'll get his money's worth."

With the words he put out his hand, shoved Snell roughly back into the swivel chair before a high, roll-top desk.

The chair creaked with the impact, went on over. Snell fell clear; struggled to his hands and knees.

And then he was gone!

With a single, convulsive thrust of his muscles he threw himself past the corner of the desk; behind it.

With an oath, Angel darted to the opposite end, rod in hand.

He was too late. Even as he moved, he saw the top of a narrow door open in the wall back of the desk; heard a bar clang into place as the aperture closed again.

Rushing to the window, Angel beat the glass from the frame with the muzzle of his gat. A counterweighted iron fire-escape ladder was just swinging back into place.

From the street below, out of shadows his eyes could not pierce, there came a mocking laugh!

Angel turned back toward the door, cursing. He was alone. Shiv Johnny, with a grand of Snell's money in his pocket, had chosen to make his exit while Angel was tracing Snell's getaway.

Reason told Angel that he had seconds only in which to make his getaway from Snell's stronghold. As he moved toward the door he snatched up an evening paper from a table, thrust his rod into the center of the "V" he contrived by folding the sheet twice.

Then, holding it in such a manner that the butt of the rod was within inches of his right hand, he calmly walked out and descended the stairs.

Curious eyes lifted; searched his face. Out of the corner of his eyes he saw one of the bartenders turn his back ostentatiously and make some remark over his shoulder.

Angel, alive to his fingertips with suspicion, eyed each group he approached for the slightest sign of hostility; listened to the sounds behind him. No one moved.

Just short of the outer door Angel paused for a moment. A drunken gangster slumbered in a chair back of the six foot screen which cut off a view of the bar from the doorway.

Angel caught the man by his collar; shook him brutally. The man muttered something, found his footing and stood swaying.

"Come on—I'm buying!" Angel growled. He took the man's arm, propelled him toward the door instead.

He worked the latch, thrust his head out and for a moment stood looking searchingly about. Then with an indescribably swift movement he turned, jammed his gray cap onto the drunk's head and thrust him out into the street.

Instinctively the other took two swift steps forward; brought up in an effort to catch his balance.

Three coughing explosions sounded from the corner of the building; three spurts of dust arose from his coat between the shoulders.

While he was falling a fourth spatting sound mingled with the thud of lead against bone. The victim's head jerked; the cap lifted and arched out into the gutter.

Angel waited. There was the sound of running feet.

Quietly he opened and closed the outer door. He peered about the corner of the building. The street was empty in both directions.

A leap took him over the body and into the street. When he stopped running he was in the middle of the block. For a moment he stood watching, then strolled unconcernedly away as the door of Snell's place opened and men gathered about the fallen body.

At the next corner he turned, made his way across to Fourth Avenue. In a speakeasy where he was known he called back to Snell's joint.

"Lemme speak to Snell!" he said in hoarse tones.

"Who wants him?"

Angel bellowed the next words.

"The guy he didn't kill twice tonight," he roared. "Tell him I'm coming back—to get me some Irish turkey!"

Gail Jacoby blinked in the soft rays of the night light; reached for the telephone.

"Yes?" She spoke softly. There were shreds of sleep in her voice.

"Angel— Coming up!"

"No!" Gail, wide awake now, spoke sharply. "Tomorrow—"

"It's tomorrow now; here I come!" The line went dead. Gail threw on a heavy robe, donned stockings and warm juliets. A light tapping at the door announced Angel.

Gail thrust her small automatic between her arm and side under her robe, turned the door handle.

"Where did you call from? How did you get here without anyone seeing you?" she asked angrily.

"Three guesses!" Angel taunted. "Nobody saw me, though. It's a way I have."

He crossed to a chair, ran his hands through his rumpled hair.

"Lost my cap," he said amiably. "It was a trade—I saved my neck."

Gail kept silent; watched him narrowly.

Angel stared back at her; read the unspoken question in her eyes.

"I came for your answer," he said at last. "I've got to know before daylight. If you're sticking with me, I'll do one thing. If not, it will be two others—and you'll be one of them."

Gail fought back the questions which came flooding to her lips. She even managed a detached smile.

Angel came to his feet, his hands working spasmodically.

"Talk, you damn image," he gritted. "Tell me what you're—"

"Image?" Gail spoke the word softly, sarcastically. "Did you say 'image,' Angel? At least I'm not a frozen-face—"

With the words she flashed the automatic from under her robe; covered him. The weapon pointed at his throat, held there a moment, traveled downward until the muzzle was on a line with the solar plexus.

Angel flinched. A second before he might have dared the tiny .22 caliber slug in a dash to overpower the girl. Now he knew that the impact of the bullet in the great nerve center between the ribs at the breastbone would paralyze him; leave him at her mercy.

"Out!" Gail snapped the word viciously. "Out, you rotten Polack murderer." Angel, watching narrowly, saw her finger whiten as it constricted on the trigger. He took two steps backward, raised his hands, palms outward, above the line of his shoulders.

"You're nutty," he said. "I can help you. Listen to me—"

Gail nodded. "Throw both your guns on the divan," she ordered; "right one first. Don't touch the handles, or I'll bore you."

Angel obeyed meekly, lifting the gats between thumb and forefinger, giving them a quick toss to be rid of them.

"Sit down there," Gail said, indicating a low, heavily tufted rocker. When Angel was seated she moved a straight chair with one hand, threw it over so that the heavy back rested in his lap.

"If that chair moves, I'll shoot," she said. "Use your own judgment. Now talk!"

She took a seat a few feet distant behind a flat-topped secretary-table; held the gun loosely on its polished top.

"You're plenty smart," Angel said placatingly. "What started you for your rod?"

"Threats—yours!"

"Wrong, Gail, what I meant was that if you didn't play with me I'd have to take the Rothgreen rap; cut you loose."

Gail grinned at him maddeningly.

"It don't add up," she said. "Somebody's been peddling you a big-city line. How can they tie me up with the Rothgreen croaking?"

"*Because you were there!*" Angel barked the words roughly. "He was at one side of the table; you at the other with your back to the door. The waiter came in and served the dessert. Rothgreen went to his coat for a cigar. Then he got the works."

For a second Gail's face went pale. The hand on the butt of the automatic trembled. With an effort she fought back self control.

"The answer is 'no,' " she said softly. "Somebody's been stringing you, Angel."

Something of the devil-fury within him burst its bounds. The color drained from his face. Trapped there by this woman and her tiny automatic, barred from a surprise attack by the chair up-ended into his lap, he could only sit there and beat impotently with his fists on the arms of his chair.

"Damn you, twist!" he raged. "I was there—I saw you. Dominic was with me; Dominic and the guy that did the croaking. I climbed up first to the lower roof to see that Emmett was there."

"And?" Gail prompted.

"Before Dominic died the other night he—spilled the—dope. Another guy, a friend of mine, tore two names off the top of the confession he wrote, then left the rest of it there to tease the bulls."

"I think you're lying, Angel." Gail leaned forward across the table. "I'd have to have proof of that; have to see the names before I'd believe you."

Angel moistened his dry lips with his tongue.

"I can get 'em; show 'em to you," he countered. "If I do will you team up with me?"

"Probably," she said. "Anyway, you can tell me what you're planning. You said the other night I was the best Finger on Broadway. If that's so I'm no stoolie."

Angel's searching eyes probed at Gail's mind, chilled her with the intensity of it. Presently he nodded, started speaking in a tone which carried but few feet.

"You know plenty about me," he said, "but not all. My dad was a pretty big guy in Poland; mother was—well, they weren't married. After the war I went back to the home town. She was dead and he was a general, and the Big Noise of the district.

"He knocked me cold when I went to him for help; threw me into jail and finally had me run out of the country. When I got here the word had come ahead of me. There wasn't a Pole in New York who'd spit on me if I was afire.

"Three months after I lit here they needed a fall guy in a stickup. Inspector Kolasinski got the tip I was anybody's dub and they hung the rap on me for three years. When I got out of Sing Sing they sloughed me into the can every time I stuck my nose into the street. I got more third degrees than all the other crooks in New York put together.

"One time Kolasinski gave me 'the fish.' When I came out of the cells two days later, they took me to Bellevue with a cracked skull. I guess he cracked something inside my head, for while I was getting well I did it just to get on the streets again and get Kolasinski."

"And you did—" Gail interrupted with an almost admiring note in her voice. "Somebody smashed in his head with a blackjack."

"Yeh!" Angel's tone was jubilant. "Just like he did mine—only better."

He waited, thinking for a moment.

"After that," he went on, "I traded with 'em. When somebody did me dirt, I did the same kind back at 'em. I was Barney Quinn's bodyguard until he got drunk one night and sloughed me with his gat—I put him to bed and he stayed there, until they came and planted him."

Two faint spots of color glowed in Angel's cheeks now. He was breathing rapidly, drunk with his self-inspired thrills.

"You like to kill, don't you, Angel?" Gail put the question with just the right amount of admiration in her tone to feed the flame of his vanity.

"Hell, I'm not caring," he gritted. "I'm not letting anybody, anything, get in my way. I'm headed for the top. I'm going to make New York a one-boss town, and I'm it. They're afraid of me, those damn heisters, and hijackers and racket-boys; they know I'd sooner bump 'em than look at 'em twice.

"Month by month I'd knocked 'em out of my way; put 'em where they can't shoot back."

His hands began twitching; here and there a dormant muscle in his frigidly expressionless face came to life for a split second, then quieted.

"There's only one left," he went on, the words tripping over each other in his haste to finish. "Snell Mahaley. He's tried to get me twice tonight; once while I was in his hangout trying for his neck. The lousy yegg—*he's the bird that knocked Emmet Rothgreen off, Gail; he stood on my shoulders while he did it.*"

"Snell Mahaley!"

Gail breathed the words through tense lips, but Angel seemed to sense her agitation

"Yeh!" he taunted, "Snell Mahaley, who was supposed to be running things for Emmett downtown."

"But why, Angel—why?"

"For the same reason that I'd have knocked him off—after getting Snell," Angel said acidly. "To get the top guy out of the way so I could be top guy. Snell just beat me to it, that's all."

Then, while Gail stared at him with affrighted eyes, he switched back to the subject of his plans again.

"What do you care?" he demanded. "When they're planted, they're through. A day—two days—and there'll be only Angel Refkuski, the king with the frozen face, for you to worry about.

"And I can handle 'em; *how* I can handle 'em, every last, rotten rat of 'em. I don't need a bunch of rodmen; a mob to take care of me. I'll croak enough of the rats to keep 'em away from me.

"In a year I'll have New York where I can shake grands out of it like a kid shaking dimes out of a toy bank. There'll be enough chiselers and muscle-guys knocked off so's the Undertakers' Association'll vote me a pension. That's how I'll handle 'em; knock 'em around; keep 'em afraid to draw a breath unless I say they can."

Gail shuddered inwardly. Suddenly she realized the stark insanity which seethed there in Angel's gnarled brain. She managed again to control herself; to ask, quietly:

"Why tell me all this, Angel? I can't help or hinder."

He thrust the chair from his lap, came to his feet. Gail did not protest. She even forced herself to keep from moving her gun hand.

Angel stopped at a distance of several paces, stood with his feet widespread; thumbs caught in his vest pockets.

"Because you're—the rest of it," he said slowly.

Gail elevated her eyebrows, smiled inquiringly.

"Yes!" Angel said quickly. "The Finger. You'll be King Refkuski's wire, listening, snooping, framing day and night, for me.

"Far's I'm concerned you're just another twist—from your neck down. From there up you're what I need to put me over. With you on the outside, I'll know what the framers are planning before they even begin to think hard. I'll throw grands at you like confetti; you'll be richer than Hetty Green and her whole damn family. And then, when we've got New York good and tame, we'll—"

"Wait, Angel!" Gail interrupted. "Before you take in too much territory, show me the names you spoke about—the proof that Snell Mahaley killed Rothgreen."

Angel's hand went to his pocket, came out with a seal-leather purse. From it he extracted the scrap he had torn from the statement in Dominic's death-room. Gail took it, studied it intently for a moment; passed it back.

"What do I do first?" she asked.

"Your first job's to rope Snell," Angel answered jubilantly. "Here's what I want you to do."

Snell Mahaley, hidden in the darkness of his curtained, steel-armored limousine, by a strange trick of fate was driving around and around the same block in the vicinity of Gail's apartment which she had traversed three nights before while waiting for Angel.

Snell, wary as an alley rat, was torn between the necessity for seeing the Mystery Moll as she had demanded, and fear of a frameup with his life as the stake. Angel, he knew, was in action.

"See me at ten tonight—about a missing scrap of paper, Snell," was the message she had given him over the telephone. Then, with characteristic abruptness, she had broken the connection.

Now he was out of hiding, checking up his outer defenses before entering the building. One by one his mobsmen had slipped out of the hangout; had taken up points of vantage about Gail's place. When he left the armored motor car three of his best rods would be in the foyer of the apartment house; two would ride with him to the ninth floor and do sentry-go outside Gail's door if she refused to admit them.

Two others were on the roof of a private garage across the street with a tommy-gun to protect him on the getaway if there was a plant to get him after his talk with the girl.

Finally, satisfied that everything was as he had planned it, he tapped on the glass; motioned for the chauffeur to pull up at the door. Someone, a man in evening clothes, was leaving the building. Snell sat back, watching past the edge of the curtain, until he was gone. A quick glance up and down the street reassured him. The driver slipped to the ground, opened the door.

"Okay, chief," he said out of the corner of his mouth. "All jake."

Snell was out and across the walk in two bounds. The outer door swung open. A blue-uniformed negro attendant stood there grinning. Behind him, hands in outside right pockets, stood Cropsey and Blackie. These fell in behind Snell as he went to the elevator, stood before him as the lift shot up to the ninth floor.

Snell mopped his face nervously as he pressed the button at Gail's door. Thus far he was safe but beads of nervousness leaped back instantly to his forehead. At a touch on the door handle, he settled back, motioned for the guards to close up before him.

Gail stood revealed—alone—as the door opened. She looked inquiringly at the two rodmen, centered her gaze on Snell.

"I said 'alone,' " she said significantly. One of the roddies shouldered past her; reappeared a moment later.

"Oke, chief—she's alone," he said. Snell motioned both down the corridor with a flick of his thumb.

"Things is tough, believe me," he said apologetically. "I ain't takin' no chances. One or two guys out after my neck; pretty near got me las' night."

"Angel Refkuski, for one," Gail said as she closed the door, indicating a chair.

Snell jerked as though she had struck him.

"Yeh? How'd you get so wise?" he demanded.

Gail smiled disarmingly.

"Oh, one hears things—sometimes," she said. "Even I. You see, Snell, you're a Big Shot now that Emmett Rothgreen's out of the picture. That was a lucky break for you, wasn't it?"

Snell's evil eyes studied her intently while he stifled the curses that welled to his lips. His mind raced back over the few facts he, in common with Racketdom, knew of her. "The Mystery Moll," a free spender, going and coming as an accepted factor of the Underworld, vouched for as one to be trusted.

But who was it who had vouched for her? Search his memory as he would, he could not pin it on anyone. The fact remained that for two years she had been a part of the rackets, of them, yet seemingly never inside.

She sat now a yard distant from him, composed, perfectly poised. Her face wore an expression of polite interest. There was nothing to identify her as an enemy.

"That's how Emmett got to the top," he said heavily after a long pause. "Somebody else got his and"—he expanded visibly—"it takes a strong man at the head, you know, girlie."

Gail showed no annoyance at the familiarity, even smiled as though flattered that the Big Shot had unbent.

Snell hitched his chair a foot closer to hers.

"Lookit!" he said thickly. "I been sluggin', shootin', knifin', my way to the top two-three years now. It's all been killin' 'n keepin' from gettin' killed. Now I'm there I want some fun outta life. How about you'n me teamin' up, baby?"

Gail studied the question for a moment, her gaze averted. Snell let his lewd eyes feast on her loveliness, the swell of her mature breasts, the lissome figure; the silk-clad legs half revealed by the filmy dress she wore. For the moment his lust swayed him, divorced him from his suspicions, his habitual craftiness.

"I don't know—Snell," Gail answered. "I'm not a cheap racket-moll. Nobody ever will say that Gail Jacoby went from one man to the other, and ended up finally in a dope-joint. If I say 'yes' to you, it will be because you're the strongest man in the game; because I'm willing to gamble my future with you."

Snell started to speak; stopped at sight of her uplifted hand.

"Wait!" she said crisply. "I've thought about you—in that way, but somehow I can't trust you. You've double-crossed too many friends, Snell. I think you're yellow at heart. I don't think you've got the guts to go to hell for your girl."

"I had the guts to get to the top," Snell muttered thickly, divided between anger at her plain speech and the desire that burned in his brain. "Tell me somebody else that's done better."

"Angel Refkuski's got everything," Gail went on musingly, "but he scares me with that frozen face of his." She stopped, laid her handkerchief on her lap, smoothed it; folded it primly.

"It's you—or Angel, Snell," she said finally, "just you two, for me to choose between."

Snell came out of his chair, lumbered toward her. Gail fixed him with a cold glare, stopped him at the second step.

"Don't paw me!" she grated. "I'm trying to talk sense to you. Anyway—I haven't told you what I telephoned you about."

Snell dropped back into his chair. Suspicion was in his eyes again.

"You said, 'A missing scrap of paper,' " he said tensely.

"Yes—one with two names on it; the cops have the other part," Gail answered. "There's two names, Snell—yours and Angel's. It says one of you handled the rod; the other was there when Rothgreen was knocked off. One of you had guts; the other just stood there."

She moved closer to Snell; studied his suddenly pallid face intently.

"Which was it?" she asked, "which one threw that slug?"

Snell let his wary eyes flicker about the room, probe into the lighted spaces adjacent. Caution was tugging at his sleeve, warning him that he was Samson—here might be his Delilah.

"What's that got to do with you 'n me?" he demanded heavily. His forehead was wrinkled, his shifting gaze betokened perplexity.

"Everything!" Gail was content with the one word. She put out one shapely hand as though to touch Snell's arm; withdrew it.

"I'm not talkin'—even to you," Snell answered. "If that's the price, I'm out of it."

Gail crossed the room, stood near the door.

"There's nothing more for us to talk about," she said. "You've shown me that you're yellow; even more yellow than I thought. You see, Snell, you've got to trust somebody—all the way—if you want to be trusted. All I wanted was for you to say you threw that slug; *I've seen the proof of it already!*"

Snell ripped out a curse. Gail shook her head.

"That doesn't mean anything," she went on coolly. "Angel has the piece of paper that fits the note the cops found pinned to Dominic's shoulder.

"The whole sentence reads, 'I was there when Snell Mahaley killed Emmett Rothgreen.' The next was: 'The other fellow with me was Angel, the Polack.' See why I say you're yellow, Snell? You want me to tie up with you, but you're too cowardly to say 'I did it'; you're afraid to let a woman have something on you that'll give her a break if you try to cross her."

"I—I—" Snell stammered.

"You can go now, Snell," Gail said. "I won't be seeing you again."

"Aw, lissen—" Snell began, his face purple with the tangled emotions fighting in his mind. "Lemme talk to youse, Gail; gee, kid—I don't mind you knowin' anything."

"No—not after you find I know. There isn't anything now, Snell, for you to tell me. You did the shooting; it was Angel who stood back."

"That's a damn lie!" He blurted the words, passed to a torrent of explanations.

"Angel did the shootin'," he continued. "The reason I wasn't tellin' youse was that I don't stool even on a enemy. Angel worked th' rod; him and me was to split up the terr'tory, him takin' beer 'n alky; me the rest of the rackets."

"But you didn't make the split."

"No—we was waitin'. They was too big a rumble 'n Angel was foxy enough not to seem to profit by Emmett's killin'. 'Keep on like it is,' he says to me, 'I'll stay under cover.'

"Then I got to figgerin'. All Angel had to do was to cross me off 'n he'd be the Top Guy. So I went after him. If anybody was to get some good outta Emmett's croakin' I figgered it ought to be me."

"You didn't do so good getting Angel—" Gail began, stopped at the sound of a heavy fall outside the door. "Did you, Snell?" she continued.

He was listening, his hand under his coat lapel, clutching at the butt of his rod.

"What was that?" he demanded in a whisper.

"That noise? Oh—probably the man in 9G; he's a lush, falls all over when he comes home tanked. Anyway, your men are out there, aren't they?"

"Oh, yeah?" Snell heaved a sigh of relief. "Guess I'm gettin' jumpy," he continued, grinning wryly. "Be that way until I put that damn Angel under ground. But lissen, baby; now I come clean aintcha gonna figger me into your plans?"

Gail shook her head meditatively.

"I'm not sure, Snell. You run along home now; call me tomorrow. I'm all mixed up too. If you had come clean when I asked the question first, the answer would have been 'yes.' "

She backed to the outer door, fumbled at the handle. Snell did not notice that the latch clicked three times. Intoxicated with her charm he moved forward to her side, slid an arm about her shoulders.

Gail moved as though to release herself; swung Snell with his back to the door. At the same instant it began swinging slowly inward; the muzzle of a rod appeared, the muzzle covering Snell's back.

"Up with 'em, louse!" Angel's voice demanded. He edged through the doorway, moved aside to close the door.

Snell's arm tightened about Gail's shoulders. Before she could resist, he had lifted her; thrown her as a living screen between himself and Angel's gat.

Gail felt Snell's hand fumbling behind her back for the rod in his shoulder holster.

"Shoot—punk!" Snell gritted. "—If you've got the guts, but be sure to shoot me through this stinkin' twist 'at framed me intuh your trap."

Suddenly, faster than the movement of light, he brought his right hand up heavily against Gail's temple in a crushing blow. With the other he threw her heavily against Angel, disappeared into the living room about the jut of the reception hall archway.

The roar and pound of rods spitting death over her head, the acrid fumes

Snell thrust his gun hand
out; waited for a shot.

of cordite which filled her nostrils, stirred Gail's numbed brain.

She stumbled on hands and knees to a nearby divan; crouched there in safety. Gradually the scene before her took on form.

Snell Mahaley was entrenched in the bathroom, throwing lead around the corner of the door-jamb. Angel, with the piano for a screen, was chipping splinters from the woodwork with shots directed at Snell's gun arm as it came into view.

One of Snell's slugs had creased the side of Angel's face; somehow had wrought havoc. Blood streamed from a long bullet burn across the left cheek. Shock or some long-inactive nerve center brought back to life had twisted the muscles into a maniac leer of hate.

But the right side was not affected. As Angel flashed a glance in her direction, Gail had to cover her lips to stifle the scream of horror which bubbled there unbidden. The right side of the killer's face still was a beautiful, impassive mask, making a contrast in expression horrible to see.

As she watched, Gail heard a rush of footsteps in the hallway; saw Angel turn and flash four shots into the reception hall. Then, even as a body fell heavily to the floor, Angel swung back and took up his bombardment against Snell, firing coldly, deliberately.

There was a click as Snell discarded an empty clip; slid a new one into his rod. Angel, too, held his fire. Suddenly he spoke.

"No hope, you dumb ox," he snarled. "I just croaked your outside guy. That was him you heard getting four holes in his guts."

Snell roared something inarticulate; pumped three slugs in Angel's direction.

Angel gasped, swept a heavy plaque from the top of the piano. It struck the floor with a crash like a falling body. He crouched back of the swell of the piano, hardly breathing.

There was silence while the clock ticked thrice. Then Angel groaned hollowly, shuffled his feet like one in the grip of death.

Gail, breathless, kept her eyes on his steady gun muzzle.

Snell thrust his gun hand out; waited for a shot. Then the arm followed. For a moment he showed the side of his head as he leaned forward for a quick glimpse of the outer room.

Crassshhhh!

Angel's rod spoke once, roaring through the silence like the boom from a bass drum.

Snell's rod clattered to the floor. A second later his gross body caromed off the door-jamb; fell prostrate into the living room.

Angel's last slug had entered under his eye, tearing its way through the evil brain and out again at the back of the skull.

Gail, white as death, came from behind the divan.

"You got him, Angel," she said in a tense whisper.

"Yes—the rat! And now I'm King!" Angel husked. "The town's mine—ours, Gail."

He turned his strangely twisted, blood smeared face toward her triumphantly, started at the sight of the rod in her hand.

Gail's first slug smashed its way through his throat. The second and third were above and below the heart. Angel fell forward on his face.

Gail turned, donned her hat and a light wrap; came back to snatch at his shoulder and shake him back into reality. His eyes opened dully.

"Take your time dying, Angel," she rasped. "And when you see Emmett in hell—tell him his wife gave you your tickets."

Understudy From Hell

No red-blooded, gun-totin' killer likes to be bossed by a dame—not even a hard one—and when Eddie Burns went out on the hot end of a slug and left his twist in charge, the mob did a little crabbing. So the dame used her head, took it on the lam—and when she had left all hell broke loose!

I

THE BLACK MOLL

"TAC-TAC-TAC-TAC-TAC-TAC-TAC!"

The "typewriter" in the street outside wrote its lethal message in seven stuttering blasts—with dead silence for the final period. Then came the roar of a powerful motor; the whine of big tires slipping on wet pavement.

Lota Remsden, the Black Moll, alone in her quarters adjoining the hangout, snapped erect with the first explosion. In a second she was uncoiling the wires of a head-set, plugging the tips into a series of connections under the edge of her desk.

Concealed at various points in the adjoining bar and lounge room of the hangout were several microphones. Through them Lota kept watch over the secret activities of the gang she had ruled since Eddie Burns went down in a burst of slugs during a clash with the Link Ellis mob.

The first sounds she heard were of rushing feet, the creak of poorly oiled hinges. Then followed long seconds broken only by cursing, by half finished sentences.

When the door creaked again, Lota heard a voice shout:

"Cripes! They got Aleck!"

Lota stiffened in her chair. A frown marred the beauty of her high, smooth forehead.

Aleck! The one she had known she could trust implicitly. Aleck! The always reliable. Eddie had told her dozens of times that he never would cross a pal.

The next words dispelled her thoughts of mourning, of an irreparable loss. Out of the welter of cursing and exclamation a heavy voice boomed:

"Aleck, hey? Well, who'd expect anything else from a mob run by a knot-headed broad? Youse guys all know 'at Link got him: got him just like he got Eddie—like he'll get th' rest of us, one at a time, so long's we listen to that damn twist."

"You're tootin'," a whining voice rejoined. "She's phony—mebbe a stool. Nobody don't know nothin' about her, on'y 'at she crashed Link's smoke car w'en he was tryin' for Eddie a year ago. Everybody knows Eddie was nuts about her. Hell! He took her into the mob like she was Capone himself."

Lota tensed, listened eagerly. A moment later she nodded in satisfaction when dead silence came instead of growls of approval.

"A canary—that's what us fellers think," another voice rumbled. "She oughta be rubbed out. Link'll take us—"

Lota's feet hit the floor with a bang.

She snatched the head set from her bobbed hair, tossed the receivers into a drawer; hurried to a dressing room set into the south wall.

A split-second later the concealed door in the wall of the main hangout opened and the girl stood outlined there. She was a picture of beauty in her black evening gown, brown eyes flashing; her blonde hair lying in tight waves about a face perfect in contour,

"What's the shooting?" she demanded as she slammed the door behind her.

Dead silence had greeted her entrance. Now each seemed to wait for the other to reply.

"You—Murphy!" the girl said, pointing at a heavy set, sullen visaged man near the door. There was a crackle of authority in her voice; something of cold menace.

"They burned Aleck down," Murphy growled deep in his throat. "Somebody's snitchin', Lota. Aleck ain't been in town two hours—and now he's mutton."

The outer door slammed open; three of the gang struggled in breathing heavily. Between them they bore the form of a tall man attired in a suit that once had been gray; now was a soggy, gruesome red.

"Put two tables together; lay him there!" Lota Remsden barked the command, laid her hand between the shoulders of a scrawny gunman and thrust him forward. "I mean you, Jimmy Shaw; move!" she gritted.

The little heat-man, face convulsed with anger, mumbled something under his breath, but obeyed.

The others laid Aleck's still form on the table. Lota stooped, raised an eyelid; felt for the pulse that had been stilled forever.

"They got him," she said in a warm contralto.

Then she took a square of fine linen from her corsage, spread it over the dead face. She stepped back to the bar, thrust a quick hand under her skirt and brought up a .38 automatic from a leg holster.

The men at either side moved away, drifted slowly back to their pals along the north wall.

The Black Moll flipped the rod in the air, caught it by the butt; let the muzzle point toward the floor.

"Showdown!" Lota said at last. She settled herself more firmly against the bar front, motioned the bartender out with the others.

Watching closely, she saw Murphy and Jimmy Shaw glance knowingly at one another. The rest stood silent, giving her glare for glare, deadly suspicious.

"Aleck got in from Chi at six tonight," Lota began crisply. "You all know why I sent him there; to have a slug dug out of his back muscles near the spine. Nobody—except the gang—knew he was back. Yet Link Ellis knew it—and Link's red-hots just burned him down. What's the answer?"

"A rat, Lota!" One of the gang gave it a name. Lota nodded her approval.

"Right!" she said. "*And the rat's in this room now!*"

The words brought a shuffling of feet. Suddenly each man felt the urge to stand clear of his neighbor; to make sure no one was behind him. The shifting brought the gang into a tenuous line. Jimmy and Murphy were in the middle, their backs to the door.

Lota smiled thinly; cuddled the stock of her gat more firmly in her hand.

"There's been a lot of popping off the last few days," she began coldly. "Too much talk about you boys being bossed by a woman; a lot of poison about me being a crosser. First it was just one of you. Then a pal chucked in his two cents' worth. A third got his hammer out—"

She stopped; let her gaze wander back and forth, up and down the line. The eyes which met hers were hard with anger and suspicion.

"One of them," Lota continued, and now her voice was heavy with menace, "is the rat who tipped Aleck off. His pal's in on the play too. The third's a lousy fool who's getting out tonight."

"Name 'em, Lota!" One of the men near the end of the line stepped out, reached for his rod. Lota's wrist swung over, brought the muzzle up to cover the volunteer.

"Dean!" Her tone sent the gunman scurrying back into line. "I'm the one they've framed on; I'm finishing it—and I'll do as much for any other rat who tries to cross the gang." She turned her gaze back to the pair in the center.

"Shaw!" The single word caused the little gangster to stiffen in his tracks. He looked furtively about, whispered a word out of the corner of his mouth to Murphy.

"Speak up, Jimmy!" Lota said satirically. "If you're telling Murphy to get ready to go for his gat, do it like a man. I'll even give you a break."

She tossed the rod casually to the bar top, bent her elbows, and held her hands tense before her.

For a moment Jimmy stood the burning glare of her eyes. Then his gaze shifted.

"Jeez!" he whined. "I ain't said nothin'—youse can't burn me down like a lousy dog—"

"You're not as good as a lousy dog," Lota interrupted sharply. "You're a filthy, yellow, doormat thief, you snitching punk—and when I've burned you down I'm going to throw my rod away. Now go for your gat!"

Jimmy, staring at her in utter disbelief, at last sensed the truth in Lota's eyes. He was cornered, fingered—and like many another rat in like case, he found a certain snarling bravery at the end of the trail.

"Awright!" Jimmy said, his high pitched voice rising to a shrill scream. "But I wisht Link was here; he'd send you to hell, you rotten—"

The epithet was hardly out of his lips before Lota's feet shifted tensely.

"Go for your gat, punk!"

Lota's voice was a hoarse growl now as her hands formed into steely, snatching claws.

But she waited until Jimmy's hand was on the butt of his gun, waited until she saw Murphy duplicate the motion before her hand went out like a striking reptile, brought the muzzle of her own rod up.

Two coughing blasts from its bore merged with a third from Jimmy's gun.

A purple hole bloomed in the center of Jimmy's upper lip as the heavy slug tore through, smashed the neck joint behind; buried itself in the door panel.

The impact thrust Jimmy's body backward, to collapse in a heap a moment later.

Murphy's body fell sidewise across it, as another slug burned its death trail through his heart.

While the bodies were falling, Lota was in the air.

One swift leap carried her down the bar, facing the third man to the right of where Murphy had stood.

"Stick 'em high, Kane!" she snarled. "You're number three!"

The burly gangster's face went white, but he refused to beg.

Lota, seemingly without sighting, sent a single bullet smashing through the base of the man's first two fingers on the right hand. It tore through the knuckles, pulverizing, splintering the bones, tearing the flesh back in soggy, gruesome strips. Lota stepped back.

"Jimmy, Murphy—and Digger Kane," she said softly. "Two rats and a lousy fool. Jimmy tipped off Aleck's return. Murphy was in on the play with him. Digger's been belching around about me being a soft-headed twist that some slick guy could talk into crossing up the gang. That's why I fixed up his rod hand; he's out of the rackets now."

As she spoke, Lota stepped in close, snatched at Digger's collar and twisted him about.

"Open!" she called to the men at the door. When they obeyed, she ran Digger through the exit; at the top of the stairs thrust him out and down.

There was a double crash, a scream, then stillness.

Lota pushed the door shut, motioned the others to come closer.

"If there's anybody else who doubts that I'm boss," she said coldly, "we'll smoke it out here and now. Speak up quick; I've got news for you. Any others?"

"No! No! No!" There was earnestness, truth in the voices.

"All right!" Lota walked to the wall, mounted to the top of a table. "I'm boss until I'm beef," she said, "and Cocky Halett takes Aleck's place. Oke?"

A roar of approval went up. Cocky, erect as an Indian and cocksure as a sparrow, was popular with the others. More, he was a tried and tested red-hot whose bravery was past question.

Lota turned to Cocky, motioned for him to follow her.

In the doorway she turned back to the gang.

"Cocky and I are going into a huddle," she said. "Out of it will come plenty jack for us all."

A roar of approval beat against the closed door for seconds afterward.

II

NEWS!

COCKY FOLLOWED HIS GIRL CHIEF into what seemed to him to be another world. As he passed through the wall, he sensed that he was entering the building adjoining the hangout, but he was not prepared for the luxury, the simple richness of the furnishings.

Without being elaborate, the furniture, draperies, and shaded lights were in excellent taste. There were no feminine fripperies, no clothing thrown helter skelter, shoes peeping out from under chairs, such as he was accustomed to in the quarters of the molls he had known.

Lota pulled a cellarette over beside the long desk, produced two of the dictagraph head sets and plugged them into the jacks on the edge.

"Listen carefully, Cocky," she said. "We'll hear some politics."

They had moved rapidly, so rapidly that the buzz of excitement over Cocky's elevation to the post of lieutenant still overshadowed all else. But presently words began to drift through the other sounds. Both, after months of close association with the others, could identify the voices.

It was Jeff, the barman, who voiced the first opinion.

"Cocky's oke with me, fellers," he said. "I hope Lota gives him his head. Me, I like a man boss—though Lota's a square shooter if I ever saw one."

"We get a lotta kiddin' over the broad," another voice grumbled, "but I'm not yelpin'—when Lota drove her car into Link's and busted up his smoke-party that time when he was after Eddie, she made a hit with me."

"And with Eddie," another replied. "Cripes, when you stop to figger it, we don't know a damn thing about her—except that she went strong for Eddie—and she sure showed real guts tonight."

"And how!" someone else interrupted fervently—then added: "But I'm all for askin' her to make Eddie the chief. Hell, fellers, I don't feel right takin' orders from a woman."

Lota put down her head set, motioned for Cocky to do likewise.

"You get the slant?" she asked.

Cocky nodded.

"I've got a plan," she continued. "But it'll take nineteen senators and an orphan boy to put it over."

Cocky grinned. "Shoot!" he demanded.

Lota leaned forward. For two minutes she whispered in his ear, the words tumbling over themselves in her eagerness to convince her lieutenant.

"But—" Cocky began. She tugged at his sleeve, pulled him closer. Her lips moved; spoke three words.

Cocky came to his feet, gasping with surprise.

"Hell!" he almost shouted, "You don't mean it! Well, for the luvva Pete!"

Lota put her finger to his lips; nodded.

"Surely," she answered. "And I've got the papers to prove it."

She went to a wall-safe in her bedroom, returned with a leather-bound file. This she handed to Cocky.

"There it is," she said. "Get it all in your mind—and remember you'll go out on the hot end of a slug if you ever open your yap."

Cocky's bulging eyes skimmed over the documents, one by one, stopped to rest on a photograph—leaped to a group of newspaper clippings.

Finally he closed the leather covers, drew a long breath.

"Well, I'm a dirty name!" he breathed. "And I thought I was a wise guy. Did Eddie know?"

Lota nodded smilingly.

"Yes," she said. "We were getting ready for the big stunt when somebody snitched and started Link burning our boys down. I always suspected Jimmy; that's why I made Eddie have the dictaphone put in."

"Ye-ah?" Cocky rejoined. "I was wonderin' how you had the dope on 'em like you did. What's the big plan now? What you after?"

"Link Ellis!" Lota's voice was hard again, deep and resonant.

"I want Link Ellis' head worse than I want to live myself. I'd croak willingly if I knew I'd sent him ahead of me. I want his neck, his gang, his territory, and when he's out of the way, then—"

"Yeah!" Cocky said when she paused. "I thought you was after somebody else higher up. Well, shoot the works. My jack's down on you to win."

Lota rose. "We'll go back to the boys now," she said, "but first I want to show you something you didn't suspect."

She preceded him to the bathroom, stepped to the edge of the tub and chinned herself, manlike, up to the coaming of the ceiling scuttle.

Cocky, watching her lithe, silken clad legs, and the flash of silken underthings as she pulled herself upward into the darkness, shook his head bewilderedly:

"Hell's elbows," he said to himself. "Am I gettin' kidded, or what?"

"Come on—hurry!" Lota's voice summoned him out of his daze. In a second he was beside her. "Come," she said, and led him along a rough-board floor almost to the farther wall.

Presently she stooped, caught at a ring sunk in another scuttle, and lifted it.

Instantly lights sprang into being below them.

Lota thrust her feet through the opening, hung by her hands, then dropped.

Cocky followed, found himself in a bathroom, the counterpart of the one he had just visited.

"What the—" he mumbled.

Lota drew him along and into the living-room.

"Nobody knows about this," she explained. "When Eddie leased the hangout he took the upper floors on both sides. The roof's wired with alarms and there's a charged picket fence around the whole three places that will keep anybody off from above.

"This is my own place. You're the only living soul that knows of it. It's the perfect hideout; the one thing needed to make my plan work. Do you get it, now?"

Cocky grinned.

"Turn me loose among them hyenas downstairs," he replied. "I'll sell 'em the idea if I have to hammer it into their skulls with me rod—even if I don't believe it myself."

When Lota and Cocky returned to the hangout there was a stir of excitement among the loungers. Five poker players at a table in the rear crowded forward, abandoning cards and chips.

"News for youse birds," Cocky bellowed. "Things is gonna be doin'."

He swung himself to a sitting position on the end of the bar. Lota went behind him, put her elbows on the scratched, stained surface.

"Here's the dope," Cocky began. "Lota stays boss as long's I can crook a trigger finger—but she figgers mebbe it'd be better if a man was at the head of things. So from now on she's the boss—and I'm front-guy. Anybody bellyachin'?"

A roar of approval went up.

Jeff, the barman, put it into words.

"Jeez, but I'm glad!" he said excitedly. "It's been damn tough on the boys—havin' to take the kiddin'—" He stopped, looked over at Lota apologetically.

"Don't be a fish, Jeff," Lota answered. "I know it's been tough; that's why we're making the change. All I'm asking of any of you is to stand at Cocky's back till his belly caves in."

She nodded to Jeff. "Drinks," she ordered, "with me."

When all had lined up, glasses in hand, the girl moved to the middle of the floor, held her drink aloft.

"I'm taking a run-out powder for awhile," she announced, "as soon as I finish something I'm doing now."

Cocky wiped foam from his lips with the back of his hand.

"They's more to it, youse guys," he said. "We're gonna get Link Ellis—the lousy rat."

Another approving roar came from the others. Cocky held up his hand for silence.

"But first we gotta recruit some new red-hots—we're four men shy right now. I know one good guy; any of you know any more that's on the loose?"

Dean stepped forward.

"I got one I can swear by," he said simply, "—my brother. He's just finishing a rap in Lansing, Michigan. They broke him when they sent him up. He'll hold up his end anywhere."

"Send for him, eh Lota?" Cocky asked.

"For him—and your buddy too," Lota answered.

"Four more!" Cocky said insistently. "We gotta bring the mob up to twenty to do what we're fixin' for."

It was Jeff who solved what seemed like a serious problem.

"How about the Frink boys?" he demanded. "They ain't tied up with nobody—but they worked with Eddie a coupla times when he needed help with a hijackin'—an' what them babies don't know about bein' hard just ain't been done yet."

Cocky turned to Lota. "What say?" he asked.

"Right with me," she answered. "They're five of the toughest birds I ever saw—all except Rube. I think he's got rabbit in him."

Jeff hurried to the defense.

"You got him wrong, Lota," he urged. "The kid's got the bugs 'n' the others won't let him in on mixups—but he's the best getaway driver I ever saw. He'll stick—all the way to the slab in the morgue."

"Get them!" Lota said decisively. "When'll your boy be in town from Chi?"

"Two-three days," Cocky answered absently. "He's stoppin' at Albany for some'pin'."

"Right!" Lota answered. "Let's all get set by the end of the week. We're going to get Link Ellis, run his hooligans off and take over his territory. He's been in our way too long. When that's done, I'll be under cover for awhile. Cocky'll carry on."

She gave them a tight, hard-bitten smile; turned and disappeared into her own quarters. When she had gone Jeff said appraisingly:

"Cripes, guys—'n' Murph thought she was a soft-headed broad! Hell, he had me more'n half believin' it myself."

Cocky leered at him sarcastically.

"You don't know the half of it, dearie," he answered. "She's got more surprises in that dome of hers 'n'll patch hell a mile.'

III

STAN MEETS THE GANG

SATURDAY NIGHT FOUND THE MOB READJUSTING ITSELF to a number of new conditions in the hangout.

The Frink brothers, as Jeff had predicted, had joined up and already had paired off with others of the mob instead of flocking by themselves.

Further, without putting it into words, they had let it be known that the younger brother, Rube, was not to be called on for rough-house service. Rube was hollow-chested and wan. His lungs were gone from the ravages of tuberculosis following mustard gas burns.

Despite his condition, though, the young mobster was quick-moving, alert. The underworld knew him for a getaway driver second to none.

Rube's first sight of Lota had been enough to make him her devoted slave. On the rare occasions when she entered the hangout, he lost no opportunity to be at her side.

Later, when she tried to refuse the gift of a diamond bar-pin he had bought with the proceeds of the brothers' most recent hijacking, Rube was heartbroken.

"You're a prince, Rube," Lota told him, "but you're trying to make me break one of the mob rules. I'm just one of the boys along with you and the rest. This way, you're putting me in the moll class."

"Aw hell, Lota," Rube answered. "Figger it's just something one good guy gives another, wontcha? I wisht you'd take it. Wen I go out, it'll make me happy to think you're wearing something 'at belonged to me once."

The incident served to increase Lota's popularity with the other brothers.

Steve, the elder, gave it a name.

"You're square," he said, extending his hand. "We knowed what th' kid was doin', 'n' me an' the other boys agreed we'd set back an' see how it went over. If you'd grabbed it, we'd have figgered you for a 'gimme' broad—and we'd a' crossed you up first chanst we got."

Lota's fine eyes glistened at the speech.

"See!" she answered. "This pal of Cocky's who's coming on from Chi is a top-hand rod. Maybe I'll be away when he comes, but I'll tell Cocky that he's to run with you boys when anything's doing—and be responsible to me for Rube's safety."

"Jeez, Lota—you're a honey," Steve answered. "Don't need my right arm or something, mebbe a eye? You can damn well have 'em any time you want."

Inwardly Lota congratulated herself on the early issue which had insured the loyalty of the newcomers. The Frinks, Missouri bred, had come to New York five years before with a shipment of horses. They had, like others of an adventurous nature, seen fit to remain, making friends slowly but surely in the underworld.

Necessity, the love of adventure, had taken them into the tanks of the hijackers; taken them so successfully that the name Frink was sufficient to cause many an alky baron to shudder. Their agreement to join up with Lota's gang was brought about by a deal whereby they would get an extra cut when the gang's operations embraced their specialty.

Now Lota gave another proof of her liking for the newcomers. Just before she left on the mysterious mission she had told the gang about, she drew Steve aside.

"Do something for me, will you, Steve?" she asked. When he assured her that he'd get her the moon if she wanted it, Lota continued:

"This new guy Cocky's vouching for"—she looked about to see that no one could overhear. "His name's Stanley, and I'm sure that Cocky knows what he's talking about when he says he's regular. But I want you, Steve, and the other boys to check him out; make sure."

"Damn right we will, Lota. If that guy's got yellow in him, he'll show it before he's been here an hour."

She smiled at him gratefully, dragged him toward the bar.

"Up, everybody," she called merrily. "I'm going under cover for a few days and you're going to drink with me to a successful trip."

The gang gathered around her, bellowing their assurance of good wishes, importuning her to take at least one of them with her for a guard.

"It isn't that sort of a party," she told them, and now her eyes and voice were grave, troubled. "It's part of the big plan. When I've finished what I have to do, we'll have Link and his rods ready to pack away on slabs."

Rube Frink followed her to the hidden doorway, thrust between her and Cocky, for his final goodbye.

"Gimme a yelp on the 'phone if you need somebody quick," he whispered. "Jeez, Lota! I'd like to crash out doin' some'thin' for youse."

Lota slapped his shoulder in comradely fashion.

"Stay in there and pitch, big boy," she answered. "When I come back maybe I'll bring you a Tommy-gun to wear on your watch chain."

The door closed behind her.

Two short rings; pause, a long one, shorter on the last. The signal that one of the mob was at the door.

Jeff touched a button under the bar. The lock on the outer door clicked. Instantly all eyes turned on the doorway. It was time for Cocky and the new guy from Chi to arrive.

But it was Cocky, alone, who dashed through the door.

"Everybody out," he snapped. "Link's got a smoke car cruisin' the block. I spotted it. The new guy's planted down there layin' for 'em."

Out of the resultant scurrying about came quick order. "Gats and pineapples," Cocky called, and in the space of seconds the stairway was packed with a deadly crew ready for reprisal.

"Watch out for a dude-lookin' bird in a gray suit an' hat," Cocky warned. "That's the new guy."

He stepped to the peephole in the outer door, motioned behind him for silence. After an interval, he turned back to the others.

"They just blew past again," he said. "Spread out along this side of the street; give 'em hell when I crack the first ca'tridge."

He thrust the door open and the others melted into the shadows, finding hiding places in stairways, dark store entrances, behind waste cans stacked along the sidewalk. Street warfare was no new thing to the Black Moll's mob. Each knew his part; was ready for burning powder.

Presently two dimmed headlights came into view at the corner. The street light disclosed a long, black touring car, its curtains flapping in the breeze.

Cocky whistled a soft note of warning to the red-hots nearest him. His trigger finger tightened, sent a clip of slugs battering and screaming through the curtained sides of the car.

A howl of anguish answered, mingling with a veritable hail of lead as the others went into action. The raid car's driver gunned his motor in an effort to get out of the death hail but slumped forward on the wheel as a slug sought him out.

The front wheels wavered, then straightened as the injured driver pushed himself erect and bent to his task again. At the same instant a blunt muzzle thrust through the side curtains, belched a stream of red-and-yellow flame as the Tommy went into action.

Cocky threw himself flat in a darkened doorway; jammed another clip into his rod. The slugs intended for him drew a line of holes across a plate-glass window; sent it crashing into splinters.

The car leaped forward toward the middle of the block. Now it was in the center of a perfect hell of fire. The Black Moll's mobsters were closing in from the rear; those farther along the street were centering fresh clips of bullets on it.

Suddenly the Tommy-gun started its lethal chatter again. There was a scurry as those in the line of fire ducked to safety. Then a wiry, gray-clad figure bounded forth from the shadows. The newcomer's feet were spurning the ground like those of a sprinter. The right hand was drawn back, the left extended for balance.

The running feet halted. The right hand came over in a strange sweeping motion. There was a second of waiting which seemed an age. Then a red hell tore loose beneath the speeding gangster car.

The pineapple, thrown with expert aim, had struck in the street and was rolling forward when the explosion came. The rear of the car lifted like the hind quarters of a bucking mule. When it settled back it was a mass of wreckage. The Tommy-gun was silent.

Smoke and the shower of splinters from the blast concealed the wreck from those behind it, but running feet from the other direction testified to the speed with which the rest of the gang had gotten into action.

"Attaboy, Stan!" Cocky shouted, dashing into the street and catching up with the figure of the volunteer bombardier. Together they ran forward. One of the Frinks was dragging the injured driver to the pavement.

"Others gone to hell," he bellowed. "Better get that Tommy."

"Hell with the typewriter," Cocky snapped. "Back to the hangout before the bulls get here. Gotta guy here I want you to meet, anyhow."

Jubilant, unwounded, they trooped back up the stairs. Jeff was standing at the door, grinning.

"Get yourself some white meat?" he demanded.

Cocky grinned, pushed past him. "All there was," he grunted. He walked to the end of the bar with the stranger, waited until the rest were inside.

"My pal, Stanley," he said by way of introduction. "He chucks a mean pineapple."

The others crowded about, insistent in their welcome. All except the Frinks. They stood aloof grouped about Steve. He was scowling at the nattily attired stranger whose gray garments were of the latest cut, the finest of material.

Cocky caught Stanley's arm, drew him over to the brothers.

"This is Steve Frink, Stan," he said. "You two birds'll be eatin' outta the same trough pretty soon."

Steve looked Stanley over coldly.

"I doubt it like hell," he growled. "What's his first name? Clarence?" Nevertheless he took the extended hand, winced as it shut down slowly, inexorably, grinding his knuckles together painfully.

"Stan's good enough," the newcomer said affably. "You used to be in the cavalry, didn't you?"

"Cavalry, hell!" Steve exploded. "I never wasn't in no man's army. Whatcha mean?"

"Nothing especially," Stan answered. "They say cavalrymen never wash behind their ears."

Steve spat out an oath, then went strangely quiet. Stanley was shaking hands with the other Frinks and Steve had opportunity to note the strength of the newcomer's jaw and throat, an indefinable something that told of a reserve of deadly power. Steve shook his aching hand angrily, fell to studying Stanley critically.

On the surface he saw a too-comely face for a gangster. Brown eyes under a high forehead, an unscarred, unlined face. It was the countenance of a motion picture actor rather than that of a red-hot. The man's figure was slender, athletic. He moved with the grace of a trained boxer.

Steve moved aside, mingled with the others, whispered a few words of suspicion. Soon Stanley found himself involved in a cross fire of questioning about Chicago racketeers. Stan's answers were concise, to the point. Trick names, invented for the purpose of testing him, brought a derisive smile to his face.

At the third attempt of the kind, he swung about heatedly.

"Listen, you birds," he snapped. "I didn't send for you; Cocky sent for *me*. I'm right—or wrong. You can find out damn quick, and any way you want to. I'm no punk that you can make a fool of. If you don't like that—somebody drag a rod."

Steve Frink pushed through the mob; towered over the shorter, slighter man.

"What was that about my ears bein' dirty?" he snarled.

"Yours—and your whole family," Stan replied. "You givin' a party?"

For answer Steve pivoted on his left toe; launched a murderous kick at Stan's groin. The other shifted slightly, weaved in and planted a stiff uppercut on Steve's jaw as the larger man came erect.

A grunt of surprise came up from the others. They had fallen back, forming a ring about the two fighters. It was a man to man clash, a sure war of testing the newcomer.

Steve roared and charged in, pawing at Stan in an effort to get him into a clinch; smash him within his bear-like clasp. Stan sidestepped, shot a punishing smash to Steve's kidneys as the other charged past him.

The pain brought a roar of anger from the heavier man's lips. He twisted about, threw himself through the air in a flying tackle. Stan set himself, timed the blow beautifully. The hard side of his hand caught Steve's throat just under the ear, cracked like the rending of hard wood.

Steve went to the floor, caught at the edge of the bar and tried to draw himself erect. He could not stand. He was conscious, without pain—but his legs refused to support him.

Cocky ran over, helped Steve to a chair.

"Be a good guy, Steve. Give him your mitt," he ordered. "They don't make 'em any better 'n Stan."

Steve nodded owlishly, shook Stan's hand limply.

"New punch on me," he said curiously.

"It's a sneak-wallop," Stan answered casually. "You're pretty big across the pants for me." He turned to Cocky. "Where can I wash?" he said, exhibiting two grimy palms.

While he was in the washroom Cocky called the others to him.

"Listen, you punks," he snapped meaningly. "I've seen 'em hard in my time, but this bird Stan's the hardest gun I ever met up with.

"He's hell with a rod; draws like a streak of lightning—and if you'll remember, he heaves a pineapple like nobody's business. Choose him if you like, but my advice to you is to get friendly—all of you. It's safest."

"Oke with me," Steve growled. "But the sucker looked just too damn slick to be real."

IV

AN IRON VEST

"LINK'S MOB'S TAKEN OVER THE OLD GRISWOLD HANGOUT."

Dean burst into headquarters with the news at midnight on the second day following Stanley's arrival. He was out of breath, puffing heavily with excitement and the speed with which he had mounted from the street.

Cocky held up his hand to still the astonished yells which greeted the news.

"Wait a minute!" he called over the din. "That means he's made a deal with Deathcell Jake—they're getting ready to mop us up and split the East Side between 'em."

Stanley, across the room, stopped polishing his nails on the palms of his hand to inquire:

"Who's 'Deathcell,' Cocky?"

"Twenty minute egg, Stan. He killed a guy comin' back from the Big Fuss. He was sentenced to death, but they got a new trial for him an' the star witness got bumped off. So he went free. Last year he beat another murder rap when it looked like they had it on him plenty.

"That's why they give him the moniker. He's got a alky mob in midtown, and him an' Link's been scrappin' more'n a year. Now it looks like a tie-up with Link, for Deathcell knocked Griswold off and took his red-hots into his own gang. He grabbed the Griswold dump at that time, so if Link's goin' in there, it means they've made a deal."

Stanley nodded thoughtfully.

"Anybody here know the dump?" he asked casually.

Obie Frink stepped forward.

"I do!" he said. He looked around at Steve; grinned sourly. "Me and Steve had a row over cuttin' up some jack," he continued, "so I cut loose and did a couple jobs for Griswold's mob. Then I got into a jam an' hadda blow for awhile. When I come back, me'n the boys teamed up again. Yeh, I know that dump."

"Tell me about it, Obie," Stan said. "It's still empty?"

"Yeh. It's a old-fashioned joint—three stories. The stairs run up inside next to the wall. The second floor's cut up into small rooms; the top's three big rooms. The stairs turn up there an' you come smash up against a steel door. Inside that's a iron run-around like they have at ball parks—"

"Turnstile," Stan suggested.

"Turn hell!" Obie growled. "It's fixed so only one man can get through at a time. That's why nobody ever did any business with the Griswold mob until Deathcell framed 'em into a brew'ry raid and burned 'em down comin' out."

"Sounds like a tight joint," Cocky said, "eh, Stan?"

"You ain't heard nothin' yet," Obie went on. "She's got a flat roof and there's trip wires all over it. Right in the middle, over the trap, there's a sheet steel square big enough for three men, and it's roofed over with rounded steel plates welded onto the sides. They's firin' slits all over it so they can shoot every way. Wanta try to crack that one, guy?"

Stan grinned amiably. "Let's go and take a peek at it before they take over," he suggested. He turned and called to Dean:

"When's Link and his mob movin' in?"

"They just made the deal tonight. Prob'ly tomorrow 'r next day."

Cocky gestured to Dean and Steve Frink. "You boys go with Obie and Stan," he directed. "Stan wants to do some scoutin'."

Rube crashed his chair over backward, came hurrying over.

"Lemme drive 'em, Cocky," he urged. "Mebbe they'll have to lam. Link's liable to have the place guarded by now."

"Good idea, kid," Stan answered for Cocky. "I'll feel better with you doing lookout while we're inside."

Cocky nodded approvingly. Rube, the two pink flags in his sallow cheeks flaming, flipped a cap from his pocket and dashed out through the door.

Three seconds later, the buzzer sounded as the downstairs door opened. With it came the stuttering of a Tommy-gun, a crashing burst of ten shots rising over the ordinary street sounds. Then the firing ceased.

Still the buzzer kept up its insistent clatter. Something was holding the outer door open. Steve, Ben and Obie Frink snatched out their rods, charged for the inner door at the head of the stairs.

As they moved the buzzer went mute. For a split second quiet fell in the hangout. Heavy feet were thumping, dragging their way slowly up the stairway.

Steve Frink, poised on his toes, opened the door and ran out. In a moment he was back, supporting Rube. The boy's face was white with pain. His half-closed eyes seemed cavernous in the deathly gray surrounding them.

"They get you, Rube?" Steve demanded anxiously. He ran his hands rapidly over his brother's body, held them out; inspected them unbelievingly. There were no bloody smears though Rube was breathing heavily and seemingly in great pain.

"No." Rube half whispered the word, swallowed heavily before he went on. "Lota—sent me—iron vest," he said. "Took 'em all in the—guts. Knocked—hell outta me."

Steve, cursing viciously under his breath, guided Rube to a chair. Stan aided in making the boy comfortable, opened Rube's bullet riddled coat and exposed the bullet-proof vest underneath.

It was scarred and splotched with bits of hot metal. Steve fell to cursing again as he saw how nearly the assailants had come to cutting Rube in two.

Rube grinned weakly.

"Lota saved my life that time," he whispered. "God but what a lamming I took!"

Stan undid the vest carefully, let exploring fingers touch the bony body underneath. A moment later he caught at the clothing and literally tore it back from Rube's stomach.

Already the white flesh was marred with flaming patches, the centers blue, the surrounding area a brilliant carmine.

"One, two, three, four, five, six!" Stan counted. "Hell, kid, you took enough knockout punches to ruin three men."

"Yeh, feller? You tellin' me news?"

With the last word Rube leaned forward, retched miserably.

Stan supported him with an arm about his shoulders.

"You're the best Frink in the crowd," he said softly. "Your brothers may be bigger—but they're no gamer."

When the mob's doctor had made Rube comfortable in bed, Cocky, Stan, Steve and Obie held a council of war. For the second time in a period of days, Link Ellis had struck at the mob. There could be no further ignoring of the attacks. It was war. One or the other must be wiped out—and that quickly.

Such was the result of the conference. Cocky put the finishing touch on the situation when he called the others around him and said:

"Tomorrow night—Tuesday at the latest, we'll give Link hell. It's them or us—and youse guys know the answer."

A ragged chorus of cheers and growls of approval answered him. He turned back to Stan. "Get goin'," he growled. "You know the dope."

Steve, Ben, Obie and Stan left the hangout by the rear, picked up a cruising taxi and were whirled up Second Avenue to a corner in the high Forties a half block distant from the old Griswold quarters.

They approached it from the back, watching narrowly for evidences that the cagey Link had posted guards in or about the hangout.

The building, in the middle of the block, stood dark and silent, but across the street the watchers saw the pink glow of a cigarette in the darkness of a second floor room. The window stood open. Someone was sitting there, watching across the street.

"That cooks it from the front," Stan said in a whisper. "Let's scout the rear and see if we can get in."

Ben and Obie circled the block and came down the alleyway from the west. Stan and Steve entered singly from the east, stealing from shadow to shadow; making certain there were no enemies lurking there.

Five minutes later they were inside the place, with only a splintered windowpane to prove their method of ingress. Stan went back to the yard, found a ragged section of brick and took it back into the house with him.

"Some damn kid heaved a lump through the window," he whispered, dropping the missile on the floor just beneath the windowsill.

The downstairs floor had nothing to interest them. There was dust, the musty smell of a place long closed; scurrying feet of rats inside the partitions. The furniture, old and dust covered, was of the cheapest variety.

On the second floor they found a similar condition. Apparently no one had entered the place since the Griswold gang checked out. Stan turned a flashlight beam on the stairway leading to the third floor, motioned for the others to follow him.

Halfway up, a stair-tread creaked and at the same instant a bell tinkled higher up. It rattled weakly, stopped. "Battery gone," Stan whispered over his shoulder.

Six feet below the head of the stairway it turned at right angles. Stan went ahead, turned his flash on the heavy door before him. It was of the sliding variety, its plates flush with the metal facing around the jamb.

Obie came up beside Stan, pointed.

"They's some way to open it from outside, but I don't know it," he whispered. "See! They's no way to get a pry-bar to work on it—sides, top or bottom."

Stan went over the door and its casing with his flash. Nowhere was there evidence of a concealed lever or push button. He began going over it inch by inch with his sensitive finger tips. Steve moved back to give him room.

Instantly there was a creaking sound and the door, long closed, rolled slowly back on its supports. Steve turned his flash downward, marking the position of his feet.

"It's under one of these boards," he said. "I felt it give when I stepped back."

Stan let the door roll to again, motioned for Steve to put his weight first on one foot then the other. It proved to be the right, for again the door moved back a few inches. Stan motioned the others forward; let the door roll shut behind them.

Now they found themselves in a narrow, box-like passageway, four feet wide and not more than six feet in length. At the further end was the turnstile Obie had mentioned. The walls curved inward to meet it in such a manner that anyone using the gate had to turn sidewise to get past the corner of the wall.

"Slick," Stan said under his breath and pressed forward. He uttered another exclamation of surprise a second later as he saw that the uprights of the gate had been carried upward in such a manner that even an agile enemy could not hurl himself over the barrier.

With Stan leading, the, intruders made their way into the anteroom. The gate turned readily enough, but at the end of each half revolution there was a click and it became immovable for a matter of seconds.

"Safe'n a jailhouse," Obie said. "Now here's the rest of the layout."

His flash screened by several folds of his handkerchief, he led them through to the front of the house, then through two other rooms to the back. The windows were heavily barred with iron set into steel frames. There also was a metal bound door leading to the roof.

"Cripes! What a fort she is," Steve exclaimed. "Any business we do with Link'd better be done before he hives up here."

Stan looked about him speculatively. "What I want's downstairs," he said. "Come on."

They trooped back to the ground floor, followed Stan back to the kitchen. For long minutes he circled the room, his light stabbing here and there. Finally it came to rest on a trap under the sink. Stan grunted in satisfaction.

He threw it back, leaned down into the hole and inspected the area within the reach of his eyes. The building was on stone supports, with a brick foundation under the four sides. Underneath was a muddy stretch of ground with service pipes stretching here and there. One, a water pipe, was leaking on the street side of the meter. A fetid smell of sour earth floated upward.

Stan lay flat on the floor, thrust his head and shoulder through the opening. Presently he came to his feet, eyes shining with satisfaction.

"Here's the dope," he told the others, motioning them to him. He talked for a full minute, giving some definite, detailed instruction.

For half an hour thereafter the empty house came alive with sounds of hushed footsteps, doors opening and closing; clank of metal on metal. Once Stan returned to the kitchen and thrust half way through the kitchen trap again, throwing the beam of his light before him.

When he came to his feet, he dusted his hands, put the flash into his coat pocket.

"All right, Billie," he said softly. "It won't be long now."

V

THE HOUSE ON FORTY-NINTH STREET

"CRIPES! I WISH'T LOTA WAS HERE."

Rube Frink, stomach, back and sides heavily bandaged to permit him to move about without pain, voiced the words as the score of others of the mob bustled about, their hands filled with clips for automatics, extra cases for the Tommys, saw-off shotguns and two suitcases over which Stan stood guard jealously.

It was the second night after the four had scouted the new hangout of the Ellis mob. Early in the darkness of the morning hours Link and his mob had moved into the Griswold hangout.

To make certain that it was not a plant, Cocky had sent his lookouts to follow the hard-boiled caravan; had checked out the former headquarters and found the rooms denuded of all physical possessions.

Rube crossed the room to Stan's side, again mourned the absence of Lota.

"What do you want her for, kid?" Stan growled. "We don't want any soft-headed twists along with us tonight."

Rube went white with anger.

"Damn you!" he gritted. "I'd burn my own brother down for that."

Stan grinned. "She's pretty good, huh?" he asked.

Rube's tenseness left him. "Good?" he repeated. "Say listen, guy! That dame's got everything that's needed—and more waitin' at home. She's got guts, I mean—g-u-double t-x—guts. And I'm gamblin' if she was a man she'd make you holler 'suey hog' an' you're claimin' to be the best there is."

"Sure would like to meet her," Stan answered. "I like 'em hard."

"She's so damn hard, she'd chip a diamond," Rube declared proudly. "But the reason I want her here to-night is so she can see me doin' my stuff. This is one time I turn on the heat along with my buds; no layin' out in a car like usual."

Stan's face became grave.

"Oh see here, kid!" he flamed. "You won't do any such a damn thing. You're one jump off being cut in two night before last and now you're trying to get some more of the same. Hell, guy! Cocky told me Lota left word me'n him was to look out for you while she was gone. Ain't that enough?"

Rube glared at him angrily, the color in his cheeks deepening as his excitement grew.

"Be damn if it is," he snarled. "I'm not askin' you or any other would-be tough guy to look out for me. I'm a Frink, me—and us Frinks does our own smokin'. I'm goin' out anyways pretty soon, 'n' I might's well ride to hell on a hot slug as to have a bunch of bugs take me."

For the first time since his association with the mob, Stan's eyes softened.

"You're a right kid, Rube," he said, "one of the best. You and I'll stick together tonight—and I'll put in a good word with Lota for you when I meet her."

Rube's fever-spotted cheeks glowed suddenly.

"You're white, Stan," he said. "Jeez, I wouldn't mind cashin' in if Lota'd say the word. What's the dope for tonight?"

Stan turned, surveyed him appraisingly.

"I can't tell you, Rube," he said in friendly fashion, "but it's something Lota wants done more than she ever wanted anything else in her life."

"Then you *do* know her," Rube snapped accusingly.

"No." Stan shook his head decisively. "So far as I know she never came into a room where I was—or the other way about."

"No? Then how'd you know what she wants?"

"Cocky told me; he has her confidence," Stan shrugged. "Nuts on that," he growled. "You 'n' me'll stick together tonight. I'll show you plenty hell when things get to smoking."

Rube's reply was lost in a bellow from Cocky.

"Snap out of it," he shouted. "Up and at 'em, youse guys. And remember, we want Link Ellis alive. Them's orders."

That was the night when hell moved in on East Forty-ninth Street.

VI

TEAR GAS

LINK ELLIS AND HIS MOB, BUSY GETTING SETTLED in their new hangout, failed to take note of a series of events in the late afternoon and evening which, occurring on their former street, would have awakened suspicion immediately.

For instance, there was a sudden upturn in transient rooming house trade, the rush centering on two old houses facing the one-time Griswold joint. In the early evening two "permanents" moved in, each bringing a heavy, landlady-satisfying trunk with him.

Midnight brought a cable-welding crew to set up its oxy-acetylene apparatus behind a screen over a manhole a few feet distant from Link's front entrance. East of the house was parked another truck, apparently dark and deserted.

Patrolman Denny Shea stopped to inspect this, found it securely padlocked and laboriously wrote out a summons for dark-parking on a midtown street.

Then he continued around the block, stopping once to chat with the foreman in charge of the welding crew. His chances of promotion went back to nil when he failed to learn the contents of the truck, or to recognize any of the five men, their eyes hidden with safety glasses in the flickering light of the welding outfit.

But it was Shea—and Steve Frink—who precipitated the first clash of the raid; who nearly brought it to disaster.

Stan and Rube already had topped the alleyway fence. Steve, Obie and Dean were preparing to follow when Steve trod on the tail of a leather-lunged tomcat. A sudden, anguished feline howl slashed through the air. Yowling and spitting the tomcat started for the Battery, arriving at the mouth of the alley just in time to be trodden on again by Patrolman Shea.

The cat, emitting another banshee wail, let out another link of speed and vanished across the street.

"Divvle fly away wit' youse," Shea barked after the animal. He stopped, stared suspiciously about. "Now what," he asked himself, "what is ut that'd start a tough old alley-bir-r-rd batin' out av an alley like that?"

He turned into the alleyway, canny eyes alert for fugitives. Dean and Obie froze into shadows behind a jut in the fence. Steve, caught flat-footed, hissed a warning. Then he fell flat on his back and lay still.

Shea's eyes led him to the tumbled heap on the cobbles. He sprayed the beam of his flash over Steve's face, then over the torso and legs.

" 'Tis not hurted yez are," he mused. Bending forward, he sniffed.

"Aha! Stinko! Soused to th' dandruff," he diagnosed.

When he bent forward again to shake the supposed drunk into wakefulness, Steve's powerful left arm settled about his neck in the dread strangle-hold. Shea braced himself, tried to pull away. Steve utilized the pull to lift himself to his feet, link his right hand into the left and increase the pressure.

Shea, gargling horribly deep in his throat, braced for a last effort. Steve clamped his hold tighter, held through, then twisted and sent the copper flying over his hip. Shea's body described a circle through the air; hit the cobbles with a breathtaking crash. He gasped once and lay still.

A hiss cut through the darkness. Stan had heard the struggle.

"Oke, Steve?" he asked. "What've you got?"

"Harness bull," Steve grunted. "He's out—cold."

Stan slipped back over the fence; looked curiously at the still form.

Stan touched Obie's arm.

"Strip him—put on the uniform," he said.

"Like hell," Obie growled. "Me—a cop!"

"Damn that," Stan snapped. "Put it on and walk the beat. You can keep butt-ins away from the boys in the manhole."

Obie growled new objections until Steve stole over and added his vote for the plan. Minutes later the copper, stripped to his underwear, bound and gagged, was boosted over the fence and hidden safely away in the shadows.

Stan and Rube, lugging the two suit-cases they had brought from the hangout, stole silently to the west side of the house at the rear and felt along the brickwork for the tiny door in the foundation which gave access to the service meters.

As it swung open, Stan grimaced with disgust at the fetid odor which came rushing forth. Despite this, he wriggled inside, held his fingers over the end of his flashlight and looked about him.

Already his legs from the knees down were soaked with the yellow, clayey mud. The stench was almost overpowering. He motioned with his torch for Rube to pass the cases through. When the hollow-chested youth started to follow, Stan hissed a warning, motioned him back.

"Keep out," he whispered. "Just keep 'em off my back."

Pulling the foundation trap shut behind him he squirmed his way forward under the house until he came to the uprights to which gas, electric and water meters were attached. It was the first to which he turned his attention, grunting in satisfaction when he saw that his wish had been realized.

The gas still was turned off at the meter, while electricity and water both were turned on.

On this one point depended the entire success of his plan. He had reasoned that Link's mob would have no use for gas; that a nearby delicatessen would be the source of food supply.

Opening first one, then the other of the two cases, he exposed to view a number of implements, among them a large sized drill, a circular collar with a nipple protruding through the band, and two tanks of metal construction.

Stan wiped his hands on the sides of his coat, took up the breast drill and bored two quarter-inch holes through and through the piping. Deftly then he inserted the two nipples, chose a small screw driver and forced the clamps together. This done, he set the tanks on end and attached flexible screw connections to the threaded butts of the nipples.

These he tightened with pliers, tested them again to make sure they were immovable. Then, his hands working like lightning, he released the wheel valves in the ends of the tanks.

Instantly a hissing sounded in the piping. Stan turned the wheel valves back, knelt there a few seconds until the hissing ceased as the pipes filled with the contents of the tanks.

Then he slowly, deliberately, turned the valves on full, thrust the suitcases and small tools aside; crawled on hands and knees back to the foundation. He knocked twice on the inside of the door, thrust it open and dragged himself out into the clean night air as an answering knock sounded.

"All set?" Rube asked the question anxiously.

"Yes," Stan breathed. "Come on now—get set." He rose to his feet, threw something he drew from his pocket out toward the street. There was the sound of splintering glass in the street—the agreed signal that all was in readiness.

"What'd you do in there?" Rube whispered the question as he and Stan stole silently back toward the fence.

Stan pulled him back to a position behind some barrels piled next to the property line fence.

"When we were here the other night," he answered, "we took all the gas cocks off the lines in every room. I figured they wouldn't be having the gas connected."

"Ye-ah—but why—?" Rube began.

Stanley chuckled evilly.

"To smoke a stinking rat out of his burrow," he answered. "I just turned loose two tanks of tear gas through the piping. There'll be plenty of lice to shoot at in another minute or so."

VII

"THEY PLUGGED ME, LOTA!"

"CRIPES, STAN! I'D GIVE MY FRONT TEETH to see Obie parading around in that cop suit."

Rube, rod in hand, awaited Stan behind some barrels piled next to the community fence when the other returned from disposing his back-yard guard advantageously. Steve and Dean were behind a pile of old brick and mortar.

Stan chuckled. "It's a damn game thing to do," he said, "but it's the one protection I hadn't counted on. A real cop might cover the boys, force 'em into the manhole and slam the cover on. I'm damned if I see how I forgot that one point. Anyway Obie'll take care of it now."

A sudden chorus of yells from within the house prevented further conversation. With the first sound, Stan ran forward and set up three flashlights in such a position that their beams fell directly on the rear door.

"Don't forget," he said to Rube as he ran back, "wing Link if you have to—but we've got to deliver him alive. He's a cinch to come out the back way when he hears the typewriters going out front."

Suddenly, as though actuated by a single spring, the entire house came to life. Lights flashed on in all of the windows. A crescendo of yells and hoarse coughing sounded as the choking gas flowed out through the open gas cocks and flooded into the rooms.

Someone threw a chair through a rear window; hung half over the sill, retching and choking.

Stan raised his rod, sent a slug burning into the sufferer's brain. The impact thrust the body to one side, sent it toppling to the ground a moment later.

"That was for their try at burning you down the other night," Stan said grimly. Rube, a-quiver with excitement answered fiercely: "Lemme get a few of 'em for myself."

The first shot found its echo ten seconds later in a perfect barrage of sound from the front. Evidently the gangsters from the second floor were pouring out into the street, meeting thudding slugs as they left the safety of the doorway.

Stan listened intently. The tac-tac-tac of the Tommys in the houses across the street was an overtone, a rhythmic accompaniment to the ragged bursts of firing from rods and the bass growl of sawed-off shotguns.

Cocky and his killers, with the exception of Obie, all were under cover. Part were in the dark truck below the house; others in the repair truck; the remainder in rooms across the street with an outpost of rod-men in the manhole, firing from behind a steel shield.

It was a beautifully conceived and executed attack of a handful of deadly killers on at least two score of enemies known to be waiting only for the chance to wipe out the Eddie Burns group and consolidate the East Side territory.

Presently, as Stan congratulated himself on the perfection of his arrangements, a new sound of firing burst forth. It was at the front of the house, but high above the street level. The defenders were firing at the flashes from outside, making a desperate effort to pick off their assailants.

Unworried, Stan turned for a last glance about the yard behind him. Well he knew that the tear gas was filling the top floor slowly but surely; that the defenders would be driven out in a space of minutes.

As the thought came to him, he heard the clatter of running feet on an inside stairway, a sound mingled with tortured coughing and bellowed curses.

"Ready, Rube," he said quietly. "The door."

A split second later the lock clicked and four men, eyes streaming with the agonizing gas, blinded in the concentrated rays of the flashlights, stood huddled in the doorway.

"Give it to 'em," Stan called.

Suiting the word to action, he cut down on the huddle and emptied a clip at the cowering wretches so near to freedom and clean air. At the same time he heard Rube's rod chattering; saw the flashes from the guns of Steve and Dean.

It was all over in a second. Four limp bodies lay on the floor, their blood mingling in a gruesome stream which already was running over the top step.

"Hold it!" Stan called, slipping another clip into his gat.

As he spoke he sensed movement in the shadows back of the grisly pile of dead. Instinct told him that there was Link Ellis waiting, watching craftily for his chance at freedom.

He dropped to the ground and buzzed a slug low through the doorway; rolled quickly back of the barrels. Three red-and-yellow flashes flicked from the doorway. Slugs tore up the grass where he had lain a moment before.

Stan knocked Rube's rod aside, took careful aim and whipped a bullet back at the doorway. This too was low—and this time it was effective. A howl of pain mingled with the roar of the shot. Then a man toppled head first onto the porch; wriggled to safety behind the screen of dead bodies.

"Steve!" Stan called. "Recognize him?"

"Yeh—Link!" Steve growled.

"Hold it then. I'm going after him. I got him through the leg."

Stan felt about on the ground. His hand encountered a short length of light wood. This he threw ahead of him and to the right. It fell with a thud. The sound was like a human body tripping over a hidden obstacle.

Instantly Link Ellis lifted himself on an elbow and fired three more shots at the sound. Stan held his fire; crept along the fence to get to the shelter of the porch end.

His movements were quiet, catlike, but reflected light from the bunched flashlights outlined the side of his face for a brief moment.

Link's rod spoke instantly. A slug tore into the ground an inch from Stan's head; two others spatted into the boards above him as he burrowed into the grass.

Suddenly it came to him that Link had fired three times, throwing three slugs each time. Three threes—nine. There was one slug left in the other's clip—and Stan still was seven feet from the porch!

Gathering his feet under him, Stan bunched his muscles, leaped erect and in the same motion threw himself forward and down.

The strategy worked. While he still was falling back to the ground, Link's rod bellowed once and was stilled. Stan thought he heard the click-click of a second and third attempt to fire, but already he was in motion.

His leap and fall had carried him well toward the steps. Now he bent low, elbows bent, hands crooked before his face, and charged sidewise into the circle of light. A leap took him to the foot of the steps; another into the horrid circle of the dead. Then something heavy struck the side of his head, sent him to his knees in the river of blood that now covered the top step.

Dazed, realizing that Link had caught him in the air with his clubbed gun, Stan drove himself onward. Actually, though it seemed that he knelt there centuries, he hardly paused before diving forward and grappling with the moving form he saw dimly before him.

Somehow he managed to catch Link's gun arm between his own left arm and his side. The right hand he brought to Link's throat; ducked his head just in time to defeat a slash of the other's gouging thumb.

Then their bodies locked. Link, taller and heavier than Stan, and an experienced street fighter, brought his knee up into Stan's groin. A great wave of purple pain swept the younger man's body but he gritted his teeth and fought down the agony.

Quickly, like the sweep of a cat's paw, he broke his hold on the sides of Link's throat, cupped thumb and first two fingers like the jaws of pincers and

Quickly, he broke his hold on the sides of Link's throat and clamped a tearing hold on the other's windpipe.

clamped a burrowing, tearing hold on the other's windpipe.

Link countered with a series of battering, blinding blows that slashed across Stan's eyes, battered fiercely across the bridge of his nose, dizzied him with the sudden reeling nausea of the first blow on his head.

At the same instant a gun flamed in the passageway back of them. The slug sung along, a hairbreadth from his head. Link cursed, chokingly, went into a frenzy of twisting jerks in an effort to break loose.

Stan, hampered by the insecure footing, clinched with an antagonist too near his own strength to handle easily, decided to win or lose in one supreme effort.

Suddenly, moving with the speed of light, he broke loose his clutch on Link's gun hand, caught a solid grip on the other's shoulder and fell backward.

In the act of falling, he bent his left knee, buried his head in the curve of Link's throat.

Almost instantly he felt his shoulders strike on the yielding body of one of the dead men. Then Link's weight came down on the up-thrust knee, tearing a great groan of anguish from the victim as the breath was driven from his lungs.

Stan heaved mightily, dragging Link with him. They rolled over the edge of the porch, struck heavily on the ground. For a moment the shock numbed Stan's faculties, though he realized that guns were flaring in the yard again; that answering shots came from the hallway.

Then there were thuds of running feet. He felt himself lifted, set upright on his feet. Dean and Rube had him by the shoulders; Steve was sitting astride Link's limp form.

Rube was shouting something in his ear. They were sounds, not words. Stan shook his head to clear it, suddenly realized that the boy was shouting the word "Police"; that sirens were screaming their way along nearby streets.

Life, and the will to do, flowed back into Stan's muscles. He leaped to Steve's side, called to him to get Link up and into the street. Somehow they accomplished it, Dean and Steve carrying the unconscious gang leader.

With Stan in the lead they made their way between the two houses and were almost at the repair truck when a police prowl car whizzed around the corner and picked the group up in its lights.

As the car grated to a stop and one of the officers came to his feet, rod in hand, a blue-coated, burly figure materialized out of the darkness, light glinting back from the shield on its breast.

It all happened in a second. Obie, in Shea's uniform, slid out of the darkness; leaped on the right running board of the car. He called to the real copper to hold his fire.

Bewildered, both occupants of the auto turned to stare at their supposed mate. He was covering them with a .45 automatic.

"Pile out; hands over your skulls," Obie thundered.

To show his willingness to burn them down, he loosed a slug that screamed between them. Stan ran forward, relieved them of their rods.

This done, he snatched the handcuffs from their belts, swung them back to back and manacled them in that position. Obie leaped forward and shoved them heavily toward the curb. One stumbled, fell; dragged the other down with him.

While they tried to untangle themselves Obie asked:

"Get Link, Stan?"

"Yes. Over there with Rube and Steve." Stan ceased talking, looked about apprehensively. "Tell you what," he went on. "Take Rube and Link in the cop's car and beat it out of here. Cops're coming from everywhere."

Steve, Rube and Dean came up, carrying Link. Obie slid under the wheel, jazzed the engine. Stan helped stow Link beside Obie, motioned for Rube to follow.

"Nix, I'm stickin'," Rube demurred. "You said you'd show me some gun-smoke."

"Dean, then," Stan gritted. "Hurry, dammit!"

It seemed that every police car in the city was centering on the block, the eerie shrieks of the sirens forming a ring of sound about them.

Obie fed gas to the cylinders, started the car in second. In a moment it was half way down the block, picking up speed with every revolution of the wheels.

"Jeez, Stan—look!" Rube shouted the words; grasped Stan's arm and started dragging him forward. The police car was slowing, twin streaks of light were turning into the street at the intersection ahead of them, the whine of sirens identifying them as police cars.

"The truck!" Rube screamed, pelting forward with Stan at his side.

Now Obie had brought the cop's car to a halt, was in reverse and backing madly back up the block. At the same instant the two police cars turned in from north and south, their drivers intent for the moment on preventing a collision.

Stan fell behind Rube, called, "Behind the truck, Obie," and ran forward. He was in the seat, with Rube at the wheel, as the underworld's best getaway driver meshed his gears and sent the truck engine whirring.

As the lights of the truck flashed on, the police drivers slowed their cars, side by side. Then each turned diagonally so as to close the street against traffic from either direction.

"Watch—burn 'em!" Rube grated.

It was his moment. The slender, delicate hands were like steel talons on the wheel. Stan found time for a glance at the youth; time to marvel at the courage, the dare-deviltry that shone from his eyes.

Then the truck moved ahead with a jerk. It was a five-ton standard make with a big steel bumper and a grated radiator guard. The gangster cargo and their Tommy-guns had disappeared.

Almost as the wheels made their first turn, Rube shifted to second gear and shot the foot throttle to the floor. It seemed to Stan that the big truck leaped through the air. There was a double crash, the sound of splintering woodwork and tortured metal. Then the overturned police cars were thrown aside and the road was clear before the truck.

Rube sent it screaming down the street while Stan leaned far out and looked to the rear. Obie was running dangerously close to the rear of the larger vehicle, stealing every second of advantage in the getaway.

Now shots sounded behind them and the lights of a pursuing car became increasingly bright. Rube turned south at the first corner, slowed instantly and shouted in Stan's ear.

"High-sign Obie to beat it. We'll stop 'em."

Stan saw the strategy instantly. As Rube swung the truck about in a tight circle, he leaned out and shouted:

"Take him to the hangout—beat it!"

Rube completed the turn, had the truck in second gear again before the pursuing police spun around the corner on two wheels. As Rube cut his wheels to run down the lighter car, one of the occupants sensed the danger and poured a rain of slugs upward at the driver's seat.

He was too late. Rube's foot went down hard on the throttle. A second later there was another splintering crash, the shouts of men mortally injured. Rube pulled the wheel straight, swung clear of the wreck.

Then he fell sidewise against Stan's shoulder. He tried to speak but a torrent of bright blood dammed his lips.

Stan pulled on the emergency brake to slow the rush of the truck. Then, with one heave of his muscles, he lifted Rube out from under the wheel to his lap. Thence he shifted him to the seat, slid under the wheel himself and began the most thrilling one-handed drive of his career.

The truck bounded and rolled southward, at times almost tearing the wheel from Stan's left hand. The right he kept clenched tightly on Rube's shoulder.

In after days he tried to reconstruct the story of that nightmare drive, but it remained always like a dope fiend's dream.

At last the entrance of the hangout came in sight. There was danger in approaching it directly, a greater danger to Rube in failure to attend to his wound immediately.

Stan decided to take the chance. In a moment the truck ground to a halt and with the screech of the brakes, dark figures materialized out of the darkness.

"Rube's hurt, boys," Stan called. "Get him into the place quick. Get Doc Raines."

"He's here now," somebody answered. "Couple more hurt."

Rube groaned as they lifted him down from the high seat.

"They plugged me—Lota," he said. "But I was in there, pitchin'."

VIII

STAN'S STORY

COCKY MET THEM AT THE HEAD OF THE STAIRS, nodded quickly in answer to Stan's questioning look.

"Obie and Dean brought him in O.K.," he said. "And Link'd rather be in hell right now than here. What happened to Rube?"

Stan frowned, cleared his throat.

"Poor devil," he said thickly, "he crashed two cop cars to clear the way for the getaway with Link, but another one took up the chase. We highballed Obie to go on and Rube swung around and smashed the third car. They got him just before we came together."

"Through the right lung," Cocky answered. "And him wit' the bugs, too."

With Cocky in the lead, they pushed through the mob and into the rooms formerly occupied by Lota.

Rube, white and still, lay on Cocky's bed. Doc Raines, a cokie but still a superb surgeon, looked up as they came in. He shook his head soberly.

"An hour or two at the most," he said. "Lost too much blood."

Stan put his hand on the white forehead. All of the hatred, the hardness, were gone from his eyes.

"Suffering?" he asked.

Doc Raines shook his head. "He won't," he answered. "Lungs are gone anyway. He'll come to after awhile. I'll keep him easy until the end."

"Do that," Stan snapped. "Now where's Link Ellis?"

"In the closet with the brooms," Cocky answered. "Ready for him?"

"I've been ready for him for a year."

Cocky swung about, stared hard at Stan. "Whatcha goin' to do with him?" he demanded.

Stan caught up a plaster figurine from a nearby table, broke it with a twist of his powerful hands; beat the pieces together until there remained only a pile of fragments on the rug.

"Like that!" he said. He whirled and rushed through the door into the hangout.

Cocky was at his elbow as they entered the bar.

"Perfect job!" Stan said appreciatively. "There's a grand for every man for tonight's work. How many hurt?"

"Six!" Steve answered him, named them; told of their whereabouts in safe hiding places.

"Cripes, Cocky!" he went on. "We musta got the whole mob."

"Yeh! and there'll be plenty hell when—"

A scream of agony interrupted him. Cocky turned, saw Stan dragging Link out of the broom closet. Link's head was in the crotch of his captor's arm. His face was purple from the throttling hold.

Stan set his muscles, cast Link's bulky form half the length of the room. The gangster came to his knees, drew himself up, one hand clutching the edge of the bar. His eyes widened incredulously as he recognized Stan.

"Yahr-r-r, pretty boy!" he husked defiantly. "You're in on this too, hey? Sore because I made your twist, that it?"

Stan leaped forward like a streak of light. His hooked thumbs caught in the corners of Link's mouth; fingers clamping down behind the ears. Link screamed with the pain as twin jets of blood leaped from deep splits in upper and lower lips.

Stan thrust backward, sent Link reeling back into the crowd.

"Now, you lousy yegg," he growled. "Do your popping off—your mouth's bigger."

He looked at his blood-smeared hands, wiped them absently on the sides of his coat. Link, one hand over his torn lips, was mumbling curses. Someone crashed a heavy blow to his stomach; sent him reeling back against the door.

Steve, his face tense with grief, slouched over to Stan.

"Th' kid—goin' out?" he demanded.

Stan nodded. "Go on in there, you Frink boys," he said. "I'll come when I've finished with this rat."

A grave-like silence had descended on the room. It was broken only by Link's agonized mumbling. Stan turned to him.

"Come and get it!" he snarled. "I promised Billie."

Link shuddered.

"Don't know—know no—Billie," he muttered.

Stan leaped in, crushed Link's lips with a chopping, overhand blow.

"Billie Wilbur—my wife. Don't lie to me," he gritted. "You kidnapped her while I was in the hospital, made her into a dope-slave. You killed her, Ellis—"

"No! No!" Link howled the words. "She—she croaked—herself."

Link's hands went up too late. Stan had him by the throat, his hands constricting with every atom of their strength.

"You—killed—her—when you—made her—a cokie!"

His voice was cold, deadly. The words dragged with chilling menace.

Link struggled against the clutching hands.

"Wait!" he gurgled painfully. "You're—wrong."

Stan loosened his grip. "Talk!" he commanded.

Link swallowed hard, let his eyes rove the circle of drawn faces about him. He saw only hatred; nowhere was there hope.

"She—was a dope—when I got her," he muttered. "I wasn't—first. She told me she'd been—actress—a doctor got her—on the stuff."

Stan turned and motioned Cocky forward.

"Watch him," he said, pointing to Link. "I'm going to let you guys say what I'm to do with the rat."

He walked to the end of the bar, stood facing the mob. Seconds passed before he began to speak.

"We're hard-boiled," he said at last, "and we don't care a damn for human life—but we do our croaking among our own kind. Link Ellis didn't.

"I used to be a big-time vaudeville actor. My partner was my pal—Little Billie, we called her. She wasn't a moll; just a sweet, decent kid with a lot of talent.

"We were on the square—married. I got cracked up in a train wreck and laid in a cast in a hospital for four months. Billie had stopped coming to see me. They told me she'd gone back to the road but there were no letters.

"When I was well again, they said she'd disappeared. All of her clothes were in our rooms, except a blue outfit she liked best.

"They told me she'd gone away in a taxicab with a tough looking redheaded man. I looked for her for months, but there wasn't a trace.

"One day I got a call to Bellevue. They took me in to see a hollow-eyed dying girl—the shadow of Billie. I won't try to tell you much of her story, except that the man's name was Link, and that he'd kept her a prisoner—drugged—for weeks until she had to have coke to keep life in her body.

"She didn't even know the man's last name. The only identification she could give me was that the first joint of the middle finger of his right hand was gone.

"The place where they'd kept her was way down on the East Side and she knew from the sounds she'd heard that it was the hangout for a gang.

"She got away at last—no matter how, then fainted in the street. Billie died in my arms that night—but before she checked out I promised her that I'd deal a worse death to the man who'd stolen her from me."

He stopped, cleared his throat. Cocky handed him a shot of liquor. "Go on pal," he said. "We're with you."

"I found weeks later that there was a racketeer named Link Ellis who was short part of one finger. I found a way to horn in with this mob—known enemies of the Ellis outfit—and now—*there's the rat!* You birds tell me what to do with him."

A yell of anger went up from the others, punctuated with: "Burn him down!" "Hang him—out the window!"

Stan nodded. "Right!" he said. "I'm going to get him my way. Any of you guys that want him can put the pieces together when I'm through—if you can."

He shrugged out of his coat, twitched back the sleeves of his shirt. The long, tapering hands twisted into talon-like claws as he swung toward his victim.

Cocky stood in the way, watching Link. One hand was in his coat pocket; the other rested on his hip.

Then Link made his final, desperate play.

With a bellow of fear he leaped forward, wound his arms about Cocky's waist; seemingly trying to use him for a shield.

In an instant he came erect. In his left hand was the rod he had snatched from Cocky's hip holster. A twitch of his right hand sent the gangster spinning down the room.

The muzzle of the rod flipped up, flamed continuously as Link's finger brought the trigger back. To the onlookers it seemed that half a dozen slugs must have found lodgment in Stan's brain.

But they sped past harmlessly, brought ruin to the mirror back of the bar. Stan had moved at the same instant that Link went into action. While the gun began roaring, Stan was diving low, arms outstretched in a flying tackle.

His shoulder caught Link in the stomach, jammed him against the panels of the door with terrific force. The rod thudded to the floor with Stan on top of it. He had miscalculated, had suffered a heavy, stupefying blow as the impact carried the top of his head against the door jamb.

Link, quick to see his opportunity, whirled and jerked the door open. It struck against Stan's shoulder; jammed. Link tugged desperately, pulled the barrier back a few inches; leaped over the body of his enemy.

Suddenly Stan flamed back into action. A brawny hand shot out, settled about Link's ankle. Howling curses, the fugitive threw himself forward. Stan was on his knees now, lurching to his feet, the hold on the other's ankle unbroken.

Again Link lurched forward. Stan, off balance, was dragged into the hall. The automatic spring sent the door crashing to behind them.

Confused sounds of struggling came from the stairway. Feet slithered and stamped on the floor. One of the gangsters put out a hand to draw the door back. Cocky growled sharply, motioned him away.

"Stan's party," he said. "Lay off."

The sounds of struggling continued, stilled suddenly. The gangster at the door leaned nearer to listen.

Suddenly a scream of mortal agony cut through the silence, a sound so bestial as to bring shudders to even the hardened mobsters within.

"Gaw—!" The word never was finished.

Jeff pressed the door button at a signal from Cocky. The portal swung open. Stan, breathing heavily but with a fiendish grin on his lips, staggered into the room.

The fingers of one hand were twisted into Link's collar. He dragged the limp form clear of the door, loosed his hold.

The shoulders came heavily to the planks. The head, horribly twisted out of line, came to rest with the cheek resting against the right shoulder. The eyes were open, staring; seemingly about to leap from their sockets.

Stan looked about him, eyes probing the others intently.

"Oke?" he demanded tensely.

"Helyes," "Too good for him!" It was a chorus.

The door in the wall opened. Steve thrust head and shoulders into the room.

"Stan," he called. "The kid wants you."

IX

THE FADEOUT

RUBE'S EYES WERE OPEN, BRILLIANT. The fever spots were gone now from his waxen cheeks. Stan hurried over to the bed.

"Sorry, kid!" He whispered the words, leaned over to take Rube's hand.

The other grinned weakly.

"Be sorry—for me'n you—both," he replied in a low, surprisingly clear voice. "I'm damn sure I ain't bothered."

Steve touched Stan's shoulder.

"Frink guts!" he said proudly. "Told you he had 'em."

Ben and Obie, the latter still in the cop's uniform, stood at the other side of the bed. They nodded when Stan's eyes met theirs.

"Rube's all jake," Obie said. "It suits him to go out tryin' to do something Lota wanted finished."

Stan gripped the boy's hand tighter.

"I'll say he did—and how. Only for Rube's guts and quick thinking we'd never have landed Link down here."

He leaned forward.

"I just croaked him out there in the stairway—with my hands," he told Rube. "That was the rest of it."

Rube closed his eyes for a moment.

"Jeez! Wish't it hadda been me," he said dreamily. He opened his eyes, stared into Stan's.

"I'm nuts about Lota; she's regular," he said. For a moment he was quiet, then went on: "I'd go out—easy—if I could—see her."

Stan turned to the doctor, eyed him inquiringly. The medico nodded, dribbled a spoonful of restorative into Rube's lips.

Stan turned back to Rube.

"Hold everything, pal," he said decisively. "I'm going after Lota!"

Rube's eyes opened wide, flickered his disbelief.

"Don't bull me, guy," he whispered. "She ain't nowheres near."

"I'll get her," Stan said reassuringly. "Take it easy, kid."

Followed by Cocky he passed into the next room; closed the door. Cocky stared at him bewildered.

"You mean it?" he demanded. "It's the blowoff, you know that."

"Who the hell gives a damn?" Stan snapped. "That kid gets what he wants. Get me?"

"But you've got the world by the tail—"

Stan scowled, held up his hand for silence.

"I'm through after tonight," he said wearily. "My job's done. An hour from now, the mob's yours."

"Jeez!" Cocky whispered the word, awed. "An' youse ain't comin' back?" he demanded.

"To what?" Stan's tone was scornful. Suddenly Cocky realized the gulf that lay between them; the future that waited for this other outside of the rackets.

Stan was unlocking drawers in a wardrobe trunk, choosing this, discarding that. He called to Cocky over his shoulder:

"Go out and tell Rube I blew the back way," he ordered. "Say I'll be right back with Lota."

Cocky slipped back into the other room, pulled the door to.

Rube lay quietly on his pillows. The hammering pulse in his temples showed that the cordial was having its effect. He tried to say something when he heard Cocky's message, but the doctor's finger on his lips silenced him.

Minutes, a quarter of an hour—went by. Steve looked a question at the doctor. The other opened and closed his hand twice. Another ten minutes of life remained.

Two more minutes had slipped past when the bedroom door opened softly.

Lota stood poised there, more radiantly beautiful than ever. A gasp of pleased surprise went up from the gunmen about the bed.

The sound penetrated to Rube's lagging mind. His eyes opened, burned with joyous surprise.

"Lota!" he whispered. "Jeez! You *did* come, didn't you?"

The girl ran quickly to his side, knelt. She took the wasted form in her arms, held it close.

"Don't go, Rube!" she whispered. "I won't let you. You're the bravest—"

The sentence never was finished.

Rube's head fell on her shoulder. The lips formed a single whispered syllable:

"Bye."

Lota rose, laid the still form back on the pillow; spread a handkerchief over the face.

Steve touched her arm.

"Thanks, Lota—" he began.

"Lota!" she interrupted. "Sorry, Steve. There isn't a Lota—never was."

Her hands went to her head, removed the yellow, bobbed wig; dabbed makeup from cheeks, eyes and lips.

"Stan!" they chorused in amazement. "What th' hell?"

"I've made my living on the stage for years as an impersonator," he answered. "I had to do my act once more to get Link. That's all. I'm out now. Cocky'll take over. All I'm worrying about is poor Rube—"

Steve Frink spoke for the brothers.

"Nuts on that!" he growled. "He was croakin' anyway. Prob'ly he's the only Frink that'll ever check out happy. G'bye, feller; you give us a damn good show."

Twisted Vengeance

Beulah Allen had the goods on Monk Diller's White Slave racket but when she was found dead in the street the department had to start all over again.

GIMPY THE BUM, TEETERING UNSTEADILY on his twisted, bullet-torn left leg, dragged himself up three low steps to a doorway, that he might see over the heads of the crowd already gathering like magpies about the still form on the pavement.

There were others already there in the entryway, but they moved aside grudgingly to make way for Gimpy. He was one of them, Gimpy of Wop Alley, the one-time flaming, bullet-headed urchin who had gone down before a spray of slugs when Monk Diller and his mob had choppered their way to control of the district ten years before.

Gimpy stretched his neck, tried to see over the shoulders of the milling crowd. Already police whistles were blowing. The distant sound of an ambulance gong merged with the shriek of sirens on police motorcycles.

Gimpy half turned his head, spoke over his shoulder.

"Who was it got the works?" he demanded.

A woman's voice answered. "Some jane—fast car knocked her for a loop. I was standin' by the window; heard her yelp. She was still rollin' when I looked out."

There was a sudden stir in the crowd. A young girl screamed. A moment later she broke free, came running toward Gimpy's lookout post.

A squat, broad-shouldered hoodlum barred her path. One hand shot out; iron-hard fingers sank into her arm above the elbow.

"What'd you see, twist?" he snarled. When she stared back at him, uncomprehending, he shook her, repeated the question.

The girl continued to stare at him, her face a frozen mask of horror. The tough flashed a glance over his shoulder, spun her along toward the group on the steps.

"Not a yip outta you!" he warned. "Here comes the bulls!"

Then the woman who had answered Gimpy thrust past him. She was screaming: "Rosie! Rosie! What—what—"

The girl put her hands before her eyes as though to shut out a gruesome picture, staggered haltingly toward the woman.

"It's—it's Miss Allen; Monk Diller croaked her!"

She spoke in the tone of one under hypnotic influence, lifelessly, without expression. A man back of Gimpy cursed, thrust the woman down the steps.

"Cripes!" he roared. "Get her into the house! Shut her up!"

The gorilla, still at the girl's heels, leered evilly.

"Ya-aah! And you'll twist her neck if you know what's good for you. She gets the works if she opens her yap again!"

There was a quick stir as the girl was dragged through the entryway. She was screaming hysterically, but Gimpy paid no attention. Slowly, moving like an automaton, he dragged himself forward and down the stairs.

A lumbering policeman thudded past him, bawling for the crowd to stand back. Unwittingly he opened a way for the cripple to stumble through and kneel beside the broken body on the muddy pavement.

The body was that of a mature woman. There were slight streaks of gray in the trimly bobbed hair, a well remembered star-shaped birthmark in the white skin back of the right ear.

Here, to Gimpy, was stark tragedy. Beulah Allen had dedicated her life to settlement work. Hers had been the hands which comforted him; hers the hands which cared for him after they had sent him back from Bellevue, his leg torn and withered from the acid bite of chopper slugs.

And hers, during the intervening ten years, had been the kindly influence which had sustained him in his fight to earn a decent living independent of the mobs. Once he had looked forward to reaching man's estate that he might become a Big Shot. But since the night of the battle of Wop Alley he had come to know that the mobs were not for him.

Now as he knelt beside the still form a great, unreasoning anger took him in its grip, shook him. The hysterical words of the girl, Rosie, rang again in his ears:

"*Monk Diller croaked her!*"

Unconsciously he had touched the dead woman's hand. Now he took it between both of his as though to impart life from his own body.

The policeman turned, touched his shoulder, then shook him when he did not answer.

"Leave her alone: she's gone, Gimpy. You see it? See who was driving the car?"

Gimpy took a deep breath.

"It's Miss Allen, the settlement worker. No—I saw the crowd and came over."

Patrolman Meagher leaned closer, playing a hunch.

"Don't lie to me, Gimpy," he said raspingly. "You know something. Now, who *did* see it?"

Gimpy struggled erect, faced him frowningly.

"I told you I just got here, Meagher. I didn't see anything—didn't hear anything!"

That was the code of Wop Alley—and down there they trusted Gimpy the Bum.

He started to turn away, encountered the vicious eyes of the tough who had questioned Rosie. They were at once taunting and threatening. Without moving, his lips said:

"Better stay smart, Step-and-a-Half; don't never blab!"

Gimpy made a vulgar sound with his lips, pivoted on his good leg to push again through the crowd. Something fell against his knee, struck his foot, rolled to the pavement. It was a woman's envelope purse, the zipper-pull half open.

Gimpy flashed a quick glance at the hoodlum, found him stowing a handful of papers in an inside pocket. The man looked from Gimpy to the purse, put his foot over it, thrust hard against the cripple's shoulder.

"Scram, monkey!" he snarled. "And remember to stay smart!"

Gimpy stumbled away as the crowd opened in kindly fashion for him. Half a dozen motorcycle coppers were converging on the death spot. An ambulance clanged up, stopped for a moment; roared away again.

The motorcycle men cleared a ring about the dead form, stood guard until the morgue wagon came. Burly plain-clothes men sifted through the crowd, asked stereotyped questions, heard the customary denials out of the corners of twisted mouths.

Gimpy flashed a glance about, saw a little girl in whispered conversation with a detective at the curb; saw the child point across the street to Rosie's home. Presently the man rose, caught the eye of another precinct man, jerked his head for the other to follow.

Gimpy crossed to the opposite side of the street, leaned against a lamp post. Five minutes, ten passed. Then a police squad car turned into the street, screamed to a stop at Rosie's house.

Two detectives got out to stand guard at each side of the steps. Minutes later the others came out, dragging Rosie and her mother between them.

A short scuffle ensued on the sidewalk before the police managed to shove the two women into the car. The crowd roared ominously, swept on a quick wave toward them. Instantly the two detectives at the steps flashed their guns. They leaped forward shouting to the driver to get going.

The engine roared. Tires screamed on the slippery pavement, then sent the car straight at the oncoming attackers. At the same instant, the driver cut in the siren. The crowd opened, formed a lane for the car.

But one man kept straight on. It was the squat hoodlum. The mudguard caught him at the level of the right hip, threw him rolling into the gutter. His face struck the rough pavement. As he came to hands and knees, blood was dripping from a deep abrasion on his cheek.

Gimpy had to turn aside to hide his approving grin. He crossed to the mouth of Wop Alley, stumbled ahead to the door which let him into the dark, poorly-furnished basement room which he called home.

He dropped into the easy chair Beulah Allen had given him—the sole item of comfort in the bare room—and for fifteen minutes gave himself over to deep thought.

He knew why the social worker had been struck down. But he had thought that he alone had been aware that she had been gathering proofs, patiently, successfully, that Monk Diller headed the White Slave ring; that the Vice Squad and the Night Court were his tools in framing girls into his clutches.

Presently he arose, took from a cleverly hinged flap in the door jamb a flat automatic and spare clips.

The afternoon papers had extras on the street when he went underground at a nearby subway station. *The Journal's* headlines shrieked:

Vice King Sought for Death of Slum Worker

Monk Diller was named in the secondary headline. A two-column cut of his features centered the first page. The caption read: "$5000 Reward," while below it was an accurate police description.

Gimpy pursed his lips, whistled soundlessly as his eyes flashed over the lead paragraph of the story. It read:

> Beulah Allen, 36, ostensibly a social worker, but actually a secret investigator of the Vice Racket, under direction of Police Commissioner Millikan, was ground to death today under the wheels of a roaring speed car in the lower East Side.
>
> The man at the wheel, eye-witnesses say, was Monk Diller, one-time racketeer boss, but now reputed to be the head of the White Slave ring. Commissioner Millikan at once authorized a general alarm for Diller, offering a $5,000 reward for his capture. Important proofs, known to be in Miss Allen's possession at the time of her death, were missing from her purse when it was discovered near her dead body.

Gimpy rode north to Forty-Seventh Street, crossed to a white-tile chain restaurant; dawdled over his food until tables near the telephone booths had been cleared of patrons.

Finally, when all was to his liking, he slipped into one of the sound-proof cubicles, dialed a number, talked long and earnestly with the person who answered his call.

His face was grim, lips taut, as he emerged. At the curb he signaled for a taxi, entered and rode uptown to Central Park, where he dismissed the cab. Thence he made his way along a footpath to a ridge, where there were seats under clumps of bushes near the crest.

He waited there, reading and smoking, for twenty minutes. A tall, red-faced man strolled past, went to the top of the ridge. In a few moments he was back.

"Which way to Central Park West?" he asked casually.

Gimpy grinned. "You turn west at Wop Alley!"

The other dropped to a seat beside him, eying him narrowly.

"So, you're the man!" he said. There was a tinge of disappointment in his tone.

Gimpy grunted. "Seven-eighths of him!" He put out a hand, set hard fingers about the other's wrist. Slowly, inexorably he twisted the arm up and back. He seemed to do it without effort, though the other set his muscles and brought every shred of his strength into play.

"To show you I can take care of myself," Gimpy said mildly. He let his fingers slip free of the bruised wrist.

The newcomer tensed and flexed his numbed fingers. "You'll do," he said gruffly. "Now tell me what you told—" He let his voice trail off, gestured toward downtown with a quick jerk of his thumb.

Gimpy moved closer, began talking in a low monotone. As his tale progressed, the other manifested intense interest. Occasionally he stopped

Gimpy to ask incisive questions. With each answer, he nodded his satisfaction, motioned for Gimpy to proceed.

At the end he said, "Okay!" crisply; handed Gimpy an envelope and a small, flat package. "Everything you need is there," he said. He added, "Good luck to you!"

Gimpy opened the unsealed envelope, read the enclosure, handed it back to the stranger.

"Mind mailing that to me at general delivery, main office?" he asked. "You've got to remember I was one of those who heard Rosie speak her piece, and already I've been warned to stay smart!"

Though detectives looped the dragnet widely over Manhattan Island, though ferries, subway stations, depots, airports and piers were watched night and day, Monk Diller remained at liberty.

Admission by the Police Commissioner that Beulah Allen was an undercover operative from his office, that she had been assigned to the task of running down the head of the White Slavers, instantly had given the case top prominence in the crime news. And, spurred on by the $5,000 reward, all of the private detectives and stool pigeons joined in the search.

But Monk Diller had gone to earth; had disappeared completely from his usual haunts. And with him had gone Silk Reagan, the one man in all of New York who had Diller's complete confidence.

Three, four days sped by. The newspapers were ragging the police, calling on them, editorially, for immediate capture of the fugitive. They were caustic in their comments, hinting at shakeups.

Gimpy, too, was missing from Wop Alley, his absence unmarked by any but the squat gorilla. He still haunted the district to make sure that the cripple's testimony might not be added to that of Rosie and her mother if Diller ever faced a jury. Under his armpit he carried a .38 automatic, each slug notched with an X across the tip. Ergo, it was well for Gimpy that he was elsewhere.

He alone, of all those seeking Diller had turned toward the French police maxim, "*cherchez la femme.*"

He reasoned that Flo Barry, blackmail queen and the light of love of Silk Reagan, was the one person who eventually would put him on the fugitives' track. Just as Diller trusted only Silk, so Silk put his faith in Flo Barry. Gimpy, knowing this, decided to let her lead him to their hideout.

So, while police raided joint after joint, while hundreds of crooks and near crooks went through the police mill, Gimpy centered on Flo.

He found it surprisingly easy, first to win the sympathy of Nels Swenson, Swedish janitor of the second-rate uptown apartment building where the woman lived; later to buy his cooperation with greenbacks from the packet the stranger had given him in the park.

"Listen, Nels," he explained craftily. "I'm in one helluva fix with this bum leg. I been savin' for years for an operation. Now I got a job that'll pay me enough to have it done and at the same time bring you in some jack too. That's why I'm diggin' into my own kick for startin' expenses."

"Ay skol have notting to do vit crooks," Nels answered virtuously. "Ef you bane goin' to steal, ay gotta give you da bum-rush!"

"I'm not goin' to steal," Gimpy reassured him. "I'm workin' for a goof 'at wants to get a line on a crook. You help me an' I'll split the jack wit' you."

At last Nels accepted Gimpy—and his double-sawbuck bills—at face value. It followed, therefore, that Gimpy had no difficulty in "bugging" Flo Barry's telephone line through the distributor box in the basement.

He led a pair of fine wires back to a dark corner, attached them to a head-set; spent most of his waking hours thereafter listening in on the girl's line.

Her calls were few, all seemingly innocent of connection with Silk and Diller. There were calls for drugs, cosmetics, cigarettes, calls for groceries from a near-by store; several short conversations with a girl Flo called "Lil." The latter talked of the search for the fugitives. Gimpy's mouth drew down at the corners when Flo answered:

"Diller's a dumb louse, but I guess he's smart enough to do a big lam. If it wasn't for somebody else I'd call in the gang and give a dance if they grabbed him and fried him until daylight."

It was early evening of the third day when Flo first left the apartment. Then Gimpy intercepted a call for a cab. Hurrying to the sidewalk, he lounged near the entrance until Flo emerged, gowned as though for a dinner engagement. As she entered the cab she gave the address of a café in the Roaring Forties loud enough for the listener to hear.

Satisfied she would be gone through the early evening, Gimpy circled the building and called Swenson out of his living quarters. Another twenty changed hands as Gimpy said:

"Go up to the superintendent's office; tell him you want the pass key so you can stop a leak in 632. Say you met Miss Barry outside just now and she asked you to fix it."

"Ay bet you bane get me fired from das gude yob yet," Swenson muttered dolefully. But he accepted the bill, turned and started for the office.

Gimpy slipped out of the main basement, took the freight elevator to the sixth floor. He was lurking in a side hall when Swenson came along, jingling the keys on a big ring.

Gimpy whistled softly through his teeth, motioned for the janitor to wait. When the other came up, he whispered:

"Give me the right key—then stand back. There may be some shooting—and I don't want you to get in the way of a slug."

Nels backed away nervously. "Vot skol ay say if tough guys is in dere?"

Gimpy told him, "Beat it like hell; say somebody shot at you when you opened the door. If they get me, I'm just a strange geek you tried to help."

With the words he stepped close, inserted the key in the lock. He got his gun into his right hand, twisted the key with his left, keeping his body flat against the wall beside the door.

There was a soft click as the door swung inward. Still hidden from possible ambushers, Gimpy stood listening through three long seconds. The cloying odor of some heady perfume drifted out. A window-shade clattered as the opened door set up a draft. Otherwise there was no sound of movement.

Gimpy pivoted on his game leg. He was inside in a split second, the door latched behind him. He stood in a small reception hall. Before him an archway led into a living room, dimly lighted by a soft glare from an adjacent room.

Again he stood silent; listening, sniffing at the air, every sense alert for the proof of the nearness of other humans. Presently the telephone shrilled. Under cover of the intermittent ringing he moved closer to the archway. A cheval glass in a corner gave him a view of a dimly lighted room and the foot of a bed. His eyes swept the living room, found it vacant.

Silently he moved ahead, flicking wary glances about. There were two switches beside the door, one black, the other red. He touched the second, and lights flashed on in every room. Rapidly he moved from opening to opening, satisfied himself that he was alone.

Not only were Diller and Silk not there, but there was nothing to show that they ever had been there.

He passed to the bedroom, searching all drawers, closets, the floor under throw rugs, even between the mattresses. Nowhere could he find the tiniest scrap of evidence, pointing to the fugitives' hideout.

In turn he examined the kitchen, a tiny guest bedroom, dining room, and lastly the kitchen with its built-in breakfast nook and electric gadgets. It was immaculate, not at all the sort of thing one would associate with Flo Barry.

Frowning sulkily he stood in the middle of the floor. After a bit he stirred uneasily. A hunch of some sort was knocking at the door of his subconscious mind; a hunch having to do with that room!

The Frigidaire! He snapped open all of the doors, peered within. It held only a small bottle of cream, some fruit, a quarter-pound of butter and some delicatessen sandwich cold-cuts.

There was hardly sufficient food in the place for one meal for a light eater—*yet he had heard Flo ordering an unbelievable quantity of groceries that afternoon*. More, he had been lurking in the shadows of the basement when they had been sent up the dumb waiter shaft!

Now he hurried back to the Martha Washington desk in the living room. In a corner lay the receipted bill for the order—a total of more than five dollars!

He thrust the bill into a pocket, glanced about to make sure he had left no traces of his visit; rejoined Nels in the hall.

"Huh! No tough guys, hey?" Nels jubilated.

Gimpy told him no absently, added, "Do you think you can find out from the superintendent if there's somebody on this side of the house—two men—who never go out; never have callers?"

Swenson shrugged. "Ay tank not. Das super don't like yanitors vat asks qvestions."

Gimpy, already on the way to the freight elevator, hardly heard the reply. Back in the basement again, he went to his dark corner. There was a triumphant grin on his face.

"They're here!" he whispered happily. "And Flo's their supply base!"

All was coming clear in his mind now. Diller and Flash had holed up in an apartment either above or below that occupied by Flo—but on the same dumb-waiter line. She ordered and received all supplies. Then, when all was quiet, she reloaded the elevator and transferred food and notes to them!

He moved closer to a light, scanned the stolen grocery bill for a clue. At first it eluded him. Then, when he went back to the top, he found listed as first choice spaghetti, onions, tomatoes, garlic and chopped meat.

These were the essentials for an Italian dinner. Topping the list as they did, they might well mean the menu for that night's dinner.

He got to his feet, went to the freight elevator and to the top floor—the eleventh. He made no secret of his movements thus far, for Nels already had accounted for him as a part-time helper with the lighter tasks.

It was not until he actually was within the hallway with the elevator door shut that his movements became furtive. But none could deny now that his acts were mysterious.

He crossed directly to the door of 1132, emptied his lungs, put his nose close to the door-jamb, inhaling once, twice, three times. Nothing but cigarette smoke filtered through, so he retreated to the built-in fire escape well and went to the tenth floor.

No odor of any sort came to his nostrils at the door of 1032.

He grinned whimsically. "A helluva garlic hound I turned out to be!" he muttered. But he pursued his sniffing way to the ninth, eighth and seventh floors.

Still disappointed, he skipped the sixth—Flo's floor. At the fifth he had to wait while two feminine tenants aired their views of the rents, the place and the management.

When the voices ceased and a distant door had slammed, he stepped out into the hall—*and into a veritable fog of garlic!*

Straight as a pointer, he moved to the door of 532, hardly needing the growing stench of the flavoring to prove he had found the hideout! It all checked down to the smallest item. They were in the apartment *below* Flo, situated so they even could talk briefly through the shaft without being overheard.

Exultant, he moved closer to the door panels, for one final, triumphant sniff of the telltale odor. He set his hands against the jamb at each side of the door, held his nose within inches of the crack.

From somewhere in the distance there came the muted warning of a buzzer. But it meant nothing to his excited brain.

Then suddenly, without the slightest warning click, the door was jerked wide open.

There was a flash of distant light. Something swished through the air; thudded against his skull. His world exploded into a vast, roaring pin-wheel of deep red light that turned to intense blackness.

After that he felt himself falling, falling into measureless depths.

A thousand hammers seemed to be clacking against as many anvils within his head as Gimpy swam back to consciousness. Near at hand was a hum of voices, but in his dazed state he sensed none of the words.

As he tried to turn his head, a bubbling groan sprang unbidden from his lips. He tried to raise one hand to his head, found that both moved in unison; that his wrists pained frightfully. At last it came to him that they were bound together.

"Watch him!" a voice said close to his ear. "He's comin' out of it!" After a pause it continued, "Make him talk while he's still fuzzy!"

There was menace in the tone, deadliness. With an effort Gimpy got his eyes open, closed them again as bright light seared the nerves.

A rough hand caught at his chin, swung his head viciously. The throbbing din started up again in his brain. Great waves of nausea swept him.

"Snap out of it, louse! Can the stallin'." It was another voice, rougher, coarser.

Gimpy drew a deep breath, opened his eyes again.

Monk Diller was bending over him, garlic-tainted breath hot in his nostrils. Gimpy grinned feebly, pretending an ease he did not feel.

"What—what happened?" he stammered. "I—I musta had one of my spells."

"Damn if you didn't, rat; damn if you didn't!" a voice snarled at his side. Gimpy glanced sidewise, saw Silk Reagan close beside him. In his hand was a half-raised slungshot, on his lips a jeering grin.

Diller jerked again at Gimpy's chin.

"Never mind him, ape: tell me what you was doin' snoopin' there at my door!"

When Gimpy didn't answer quickly enough, Silk rasped, "Start canaryin', bozo—or you get socked again. And the next one's the big one."

Gimpy pretended sudden fright, whined:

"I wasn't doin' nothin', guy. I was jus' comin' down th' hall 'n one of my dizzy fits hits me. That's all I remember."

Diller slapped first the right, then the left side of Gimpy's face with his open hands.

"Don't lie to me, punk!" he roared. "Who are you? What was you doin' in this buildin'? On this floor? Hey?"

"I was lookin' for a feller—Ed Varney," Gimpy replied fearfully. "He owes me some jack."

He had noticed the name in the tenants' rack. Now it came to him subconsciously.

Diller whirled about to Silk, jerked a thumb toward the 'phone.

"Call th' office; see if such a guy lives here," he ordered. While Silk was gone, Monk went over Gimpy's bonds at ankles and wrists.

Silk came back, said "Next floor" in an undertone.

Monk shook his head, puzzled.

"Suppose," he said slowly, watching Gimpy's face narrowly, "suppose we get your friend to come down an' say you're okay. That suit you?"

Gimpy told him "Sure!"; tried to seem eager about it to cover his sudden sense of defeat. But Silk saved him.

"Oh, yeah?" he growled. "Who's goin' after him? You? Me? And tip off—"

Diller roared, "Shut your yap, saphead!" Then he turned back to Gimpy. Grunting, he searched his pockets, found keys, a knife, cigarettes, but no identifying papers.

He straightened. "Where d'ye live, louse? I gotta know about you. See?"

Gimpy grinned. "I gotcha, chief, seven ways from the jack. Me an' my buddy handles hot radios. I was doin' a little prowl when you birds handed me the bat."

Diller looked relieved, turned back to Silk. "Stinkin' prowler!" he said.

Silk growled, "Wait!" He ran his hands expertly over Gimpy's body, found the holstered rod under his arm. Snapping it from the spring clip he held it before Diller's astonished eyes.

"Prowler, hell!" he said. "I think he's a dick."

Gimpy groaned, raised his hands as though to touch his aching head. It gave him a chance to inspect the lashings. As he had hoped, the knot was on the back of the right wrist. The rope was sash cord.

"Listen!" he whined. "You birds has got me all wrong. Sure I pack a gat. For cripes' sake, you think I prowl with a teaspoon?"

Diller eyed him speculatively. "Maybe you're all right—maybe not—"

"Sure I am!" Gimpy urged. "I ain't got no more use for coppers 'n you have. Turn me loose and I'll forget I ever saw you."

Silk cursed at the words. "Nuts on that!" he rasped. "Just one more sock with the bat and you'll never remember anything."

Diller shook his head nervously. "Cut it!" he commanded. "We gotta do some figgerin'."

For answer, Silk kicked a straight chair over beside the davenport.

"All right, we'll tie him into this and put him in the closet. But somethin' hunches me that this egg's poison!"

Together they tied Gimpy's legs to the rounds of the chair. He kept his hands up to his aching head until they had carried the lashings twice about his chest and had made the rope secure to the back of the chair. He heaved a sigh of relief when they lifted him into the closet and went out, locking the door.

After a long wait Gimpy began moving about, wriggling, twisting to get his hands up to his mouth. The rope was dusty, gritty, but he tore at it with his teeth as though it was some savory morsel.

Again and again his teeth slipped, clicking together with a snap that sent new waves of pain roaring through his aching head. Finally he felt the knot slip, hold, then slip again, then come free.

Blood flowed back into the congested veins. For long moments the pain was too severe to permit of movement. When strength came back to his fingers he finished the task of freeing himself.

After another rest he tiptoed to the door. There was no movement, no murmur of voices. He felt about for the chair, mounted it, found the ceiling fixture with questing fingers.

The light pull had snapped off at the collar. Patiently he dug into the tiny orifice with finger and thumbnails until they caught the end of the chain.

Pulling gently he snapped on a sixteen-candlepower globe and looked about him curiously. Three suits of men's ready-made clothing hung on stretchers. The suit boxes lay on the top shelf, empty. He moved them idly, gasped.

Hidden behind them was an assembled Tommy-gun and three extra drums of shells. He took the weapon in his hands, slipped one extra drum in his pocket, climbed down and went back to the door.

Still there was no sound. Sudden anger shook him as he sensed what had happened. Diller and Silk, afraid to chance a kill, had left him to starve in the closet; had lammed to a new hideout.

Pivoting on his good leg, he let his shoulder and hip crash against the door. It groaned, but held. Again and again he threw his body against the barrier. At last there was a splintering crash and the lock tore from the jamb.

Watchful, he stood in the doorway for a moment, fingering the trigger of the chopper. His hat lay on the floor where it had fallen, but of Diller and Silk there was no trace.

Crossing the room, he looked out into the hall, found it empty. Silently he stepped back inside, shut the door, threw the night latch.

Now his eyes were shining with new purpose. He crossed the room, dropped into a chair, took a scrap of folded paper from the cuff of his trousers. After that he dialed a number.

There was a brief wait, then he began speaking eagerly, his voice low, tense. Once he said "No!" explosively; ended the talk with, "I'll do it!"

From the telephone he proceeded straight to the kitchen, where he drew the dumb waiter down cautiously until its top was level with the lower molding of the doorway.

That done, he moved a kitchen table to the opening, put the Tommy on it crosswise, perched a moment precariously on the sill and caught both the dumb-waiter ropes in one hand. Then, scooping up the gun, he laid it carefully on top of the elevator, took the pull rope in both of his hands; put his full weight on the boxlike platform.

As he stood thus, he was in perfect balance. The enormous strength of his arms and shoulders made it childishly easy for him to support his own weight. At last, careful to make no move that would cause the elevator to creak in its wooden guides, he moved his right hand high, exerting a slow, steady pull on the ropes.

At the same time he flexed his knees slowly. Gradually his weight shifted from his feet to his hands and the elevator lifted more than a foot. Quickly he straightened his legs, caught a new grip on the rope and drew the elevator upward.

Again and again he repeated the maneuver. Dust floated in the dry, stagnant air. Some of it got into his nostrils and throat, choked him; for a moment it seemed that he must sneeze.

Presently he came to a cross-piece of two-by-four, a brace from the side of the shaft to the upright guides. He edged closer, balanced on the bracing with one foot and rested. Also he had time for a quick glance upward.

A thin pencil of light shone through the dumb-waiter door from Flo's kitchen. When he left, he had turned out all of the lights, and it was highly improbable that the girl had returned.

Excitedly, his breath coming in quick gasps, he started the upward climb again. Inch by inch he drew himself upward until the lower edge of the opening into Flo's apartment was level with his eyes.

Another three feet would bring him level with the opening. But it was the vital three feet. The slightest sound now would warn the fugitives and bring a searing hail of slugs into the shaft.

Somehow he managed it; how he never quite knew. But suddenly he found himself balanced across the sill, the released elevator clattering down the shaft, bright lights shining down on him from a ceiling fixture.

Without stopping to think, he cast himself forward with a great sweep of his elbows against the casing. He alighted on his knees and left hand, the right holding the Tommy-gun clear of the floor.

The impact hurt his wrist, bruised his knees, sent sharp pains skittering through his bruised head—but now there was no time for sprains or bruises.

Already feet were clattering across the hardwood floor of the living room. Even as he came erect, the muzzle of a heavy rod slithered around the door-jamb. Then a hand, the side of a head, a single, glittering eye, came into sight.

Gimpy crouched, twisted aside, brought the muzzle of the chopper up, then let a stream of slugs run up and down the woodwork at the side of the door.

The rattle of the chopper sounded like thunder in the small, enclosed space. But above it rose a single, high-pitched wail of human agony. Gimpy took his finger from the trigger, stood tense, watchful.

Another groan followed. Silk Reagan, rod in hand, slumped into sight. Blood welled from his throat. Another crimson stream bubbled down the front of his white silk shirt.

Gimpy moved closer, stooped to snatch the gun from the lax fingers. Just in time he sensed danger. For Silk, gargling his hatred, jerked to his knees and fired once at point-blank range.

Instinct twisted Gimpy's body half about. The bullet intended for his heart struck a rib, glanced, emerged at the breast bone and tore its way out through his vest.

As Silk's finger tensed for the second shot, Gimpy thrust forward with the chopper. The blunt muzzle caught Silk just above the nose. His hand jerked, sent the gun flying over his shoulder. It skidded, came to rest under the piano.

Again Silk collapsed. For a moment his knuckles beat a faint tattoo on the floor. Then a crimson tide leaped from his lips—and he was dead.

From somewhere near at hand there came a confused sound of shouting. Already, too, some one was battering heavily at the hall door. And Diller still was unaccounted for!

Gimpy, holding the gun in both hands in firing position, balanced for a moment against the doorway. Then he tensed his good right knee and threw himself forward in a curving leap into the next room.

The waxed, hardwood floor offered him no foothold. His feet went from under him and threw him heavily. The bellowing roar of a heavy gun sounded from the left side of the room.

What seemed like a flying hand twitched avidly at the collar of his coat. For a moment stinging pains numbed the back of his neck.

He twisted about, lay prone. More slugs whizzed through the air from behind a davenport.

Gimpy pushed the chopper forward, loosed a burst of ten slugs at the lower edge of the back upholstery. Then he took his finger from the trigger, listened. Dust hung in a light cloud over the line of holes through the padding.

When the echoes of the shots had died away, he heard hoarse breathing, then a familiar click. Diller was driving home a fresh clip into the butt of his automatic.

Gimpy shifted the muzzle of the chopper low, started a screaming burst from left to right in hope that he might cut Monk's legs from under him.

The weapon leaped in his hands, stuttered, "Tut-tut-tut-tut!"

Then it fell silent. Gimpy cursed, growled "Jammed!" and threw the weapon from him.

In the same split second he started rolling rapidly to the left—toward Silk's automatic there on the floor under the piano.

Monk Diller, blood streaming down his face from a bullet graze, came to his feet, loosed three screaming slugs at Gimpy's fast moving body. One struck the counter of his left shoe, tore away the heel, sent fierce pain careening up his withered leg.

Gimpy halted his roll behind a sleepy hollow chair, set his hands tight around the rear legs. Then he shoved, sent it careening across the floor as a momentary shield.

The ruse worked. Before Diller sensed its meaning, Gimpy had rolled to Silk's gun; had sent two slugs speeding at his antagonist.

Diller's left shoulder jerked and spouted blood. The second slug dug plaster from the wall, sent a fine white powder scattering over Monk's head.

After that the hall door went down with a crash. There was a babble of voices, the sound of running feet.

Frantic at thought of his interrupted vengeance, Gimpy thrust free of the piano, started a stumbling charge across the room, straight in the face of Diller's frantic firing.

Steel slugs screamed about his head. One cut through his left forearm between wrist and elbow, numbing it like an electric shock. A stinging pain, like a stab from a red-hot knife, tortured the thigh muscles of his good leg. The limb gave under him, dropped him to his knees.

Then, and then only, did Gimpy fire.

Grimly he centered the muzzle on Diller's chest. The weapon leaped in his hard fingers, four, five, six times. Then the firing pin clicked on an empty chamber.

Monk Diller's thin lips twitched, grimaced. The rod fell from his hand, bounced from the upholstery, thudded to the floor.

Blood was turning his shirt front crimson as it welled from two chest wounds. What seemed a purple blister just above his chin suddenly became a bubbling red fountain.

He toppled forward slowly. At the last his body bent at the waist until his head hung down against the cushions of the davenport.

Gimpy straightened, drew a deep, sobbing breath of content. Suddenly it all seemed very distant, a disordered dream from which he would awake to find himself in his room in Wop Alley.

Instead, rough hands were shaking him, voices were roaring in his ears. He flashed a quick glance sidewise. Two detectives were tugging at his shoulders. A tall, gray-haired man he recognized as Inspector Kane of headquarters, jerked the hot rod from his hand.

"What th' hell's the idea of the knock-off?" one of the detectives roared. "Who's them guys you croaked? What'd you do it for?"

Gimpy drew a deep breath.

"Uh-uh!" he grunted. "*You* guys got 'em. That's Monk Diller and Silk Reagan!"

The detectives gasped, ran to straighten Diller's body. Gimpy caught the inspector's eye, jerked his head for the other to come closer.

"Something private—for you alone," he whispered.

Kane approached, bent forward warily. His fingers were bent into claws for quick defense if Gimpy contemplated treachery. Gimpy felt in his vest pocket, brought out the folded scrap of paper.

" 'Phone that guy," he husked. "And ask if it wasn't them fly-bulls that knocked off Monk and Silk. Ask him if it wasn't you 'at found their hide-out and raided it."

Inspector Kane took the paper, stared at it curiously, cursed in amazement. It was the Police Commissioner's private number—one known only to officers of the grade of captain or better.

He leaned over, whispered guardedly.

"You mean you're his personal undercover man? That it?"

Gimpy nodded wearily. Suddenly it seemed that each of his gunshots and bruises was trying to outdo the other in renewed pain. He found it difficult to make sound in his throat, drew Kane closer.

"Yeah," he whispered weakly. "Temporary-like. I been—subbin' fer Beulah—Beulah Allen."

The End

OFF-TRAIL PUBLICATIONS
Specializing in the era of American pulp fiction

THE WEIRD DETECTIVE ADVENTURES OF WADE HAMMOND
By Paul Chadwick
Volume 1: 10 stories, 180 pages, $18
Volume 2: 10 stories, 172 pages, $18
Volume 3: 10 stories, 202 pages, $18
Volume 4: 9 stories, 232 pages, $18

> *The Wade Hammond stories complete in four volumes. In these chilling adventures, all from the classic 1930's pulps,* Detective-Dragnet *and* Ten Detective Aces, *freelance investigator Wade Hammond battles a series of weird enemies. Some of the best of '30s pulp fiction.*

DOCTOR COFFIN: The Living Dead Man
By Perley Poore Sheehan • Introduction by John Wooley
8 novelettes, 178 pages, $16

> *Weird stories from* Thrilling Detective, *1932-33. A former character actor who faked his own death, Doctor Coffin runs a string of mortuaries by night and fights crime at night. One of the strangest detective series.*

SUPER-DETECTIVE FLIP BOOK: Two Complete Novels
From the pulp *Super-Detective*:
"Legion of Robots" (November 1940) by Victor Rousseau • Introduction by John McMahan •• "Murder's Migrants" (March 1943) by Robert Leslie Bellem and W.T. Ballard • Introduction by John Wooley
2 short novels, 174 pages, $18

> Super-Detective *started as a Doc Savage-like adventure pulp, then changed format to hardboiled detective. The* Flip Book *features a novel from each of the two phases with intros exploring the historical background. Exciting!*

PULPWOOD DAYS: Volume 1: Editors You Want To Know
Edited by John Locke • 180 pages, $16

*Numerous articles from the writers' magazines by and about pulp editors, with ample biographical profiles. Editors include: Frank E. Blackwell (*Detective Story, Western Story*), Ray Palmer (*Amazing Stories, Fantastic Adventures*), Edwin Baird (*Weird Tales, Detective Tales*), and many more.*

GANG PULP
Edited by John Locke • 19 stories, 294 pages, $24

Hardboiled stories of the criminal underworld from the first year (1929-30) of the gang pulps: Gangster Stories, Racketeer Stories, *etc. These violent tales came under immediate censorship pressure; the history is explored in an in-depth essay. "A remarkable work of popular-culture scholarship"*—MYSTERY SCENE, *Fall 2008.*

THE GANGLAND SAGAS OF BIG NOSE SERRANO
Volume 1: Dames, Dice and the Devil
Volume 2: Horses, Hoboes and Heroes
Volume 3: Hell's Gangster
By Anatole Feldman • Introductions by Will Murray
Each: 4 novels • **Volumes 1-2**: 266 pages, $20 • **Volume 3**: 224 pages, $18

The complete Big Nose Serrano novels from Gangster Stories, Greater Gangster Stories, *and* The Gang Magazine, *1930-35. Feldman was the best of the gang pulp authors, and Big Nose was his most inspired creation, the berserking king of Chicago gangsters.*

THE CITY OF BAAL
By Charles Beadle • Introduction by John Locke
7 stories, 240 pages, $20

Authentic stories of African adventure from an author who had traveled the lands he wrote about. Lost cities, strange tribes, jungle magic. Six stories from Adventure *(1918-22) and one from* The Frontier *(1925).*

CULT OF THE CORPSES
By Maxwell Hawkins • Introduction by John Locke
2 novelettes, 150 pages, $13.95

Two weird detective stories from Detective-Dragnet *(1931) by a forgotten master. Introduction discusses the weird-detective trend of the early '30s, and the career of Maxwell Hawkins.*

THE OCEAN: 100th Anniversary Collection
Edited by John Locke
20 stories, 234 pages, $18

Munsey's The Ocean *(1907-08) was one of the first specialized pulps, a sea-story magazine. The best adventure stories are included here, along with 30+ pages of nonfiction material: a history of the pulp, and extensive author profiles.*

FROM GHOULS TO GANGSTERS: The Career Of Arthur B. Reeve
Edited by John Locke
Vol 1 (fiction): 21 stories, 264 pages, $20 • **Vol 2 (nonfic)**: 260 pages, $20

*Reeve was the leading American detective-story writer of the early 20th Century, with his scientific detective, Craig Kennedy. The astonishing breadth of his career is explored for the first time here. Vol 1 includes a cross-sction of fiction from all phases of career, including many never-before-reprinted pulp stories. Vol 2 provides a 40-page biography; an extensive Art Gallery of cover repros, interior illos, ads, etc; a 75-page guide to Reeve's work in all media; and more. An "excellent piece of scholarship"—*MYSTERY SCENE, *Spring 2008.*

AMAZON STORIES
Volume 1: Pedro & Lourenço
Volume 2: Pedro & Lourenço
By Arthur O. Friel • Introductions by John Locke
Vol 1: 10 stories, 222 pages, $18 • **Vol 2**: 10 stories, 286 pages, $20

Collects Friel's first twenty stories from Adventure *(1919-21), following the strange experiences of two Amazon Basin rubber workers as they explore the jungle. The best of pulp adventure fiction.*

GROTTOS OF CHINATOWN: The Dorus Noel Stories
By Arthur J. Burks • Introduction by John Locke
11 stories, 194 pages, $16

The complete adventures of Dorus Noel from All Detective Magazine *(1933-34). Burks' Manhattan Chinatown is a place of dark mystery, riddled with secret passageways, menaced by hatchetmen. Introduction discusses the history of* All Detective *and the career of the Speed-King of the Pulps, Arthur J. Burks.*

THE GOLDEN ANACONDA: And Other Strange Tales of Adventure
By Elmer Brown Mason • Introduction by John Locke
10 stories, 260 pages, $20

Fantastic and horror-laden stories set in the exotic corners of the world known to their globe-trotting entomologist author. Includes all five Wandering Smith stories from The Popular Magazine; *and five tales from* All-Story Weekly. *All published, 1915-16.*

CITY OF NUMBERED MEN: The Best of Prison Stories
Introduction by John Locke
12 stories, 278 pages, $20

During Prohibition, famed publisher Harold Hersey turned America's disintegrating prison system into the hardboiled Prison Stories *(1930-31). Included are stories from all issues of this rare pulp, the startling history of* Prison Stories, *cover gallery, and the first comprehensive biography of pulp publishing's most colorful character, Harold Hersey.*

THE MAGICIAN DETECTIVE: And Other Weird Mysteries
By Fulton Oursler
Introduction by John Locke
7 stories, 210 pages, $18

Fulton Oursler was one of the great editors of his time, ruling over the Macfadden publishing empire for two decades. But stage magic was his first love. In this collection of early fiction, Oursler's bewitching imagination takes flight in tales of magic, murder and mystery. Featured is an exploration of the astonishing career of Fulton Oursler.

GHOST STORIES: The Magazine and Its Makers
Edited by John Locke
Vol 1: 19 stories, 256 pages, $24 • **Vol 2**: 15 stories, 272 pages, $24

Macfadden's Ghost Stories *(1926-31) presented haunted tales in every exciting arena: the Western Front, gangland, aviation, the Klondike, the circus, etc. The personnel behind* Ghost Stories *were a fascinating group: poets and scholars, war heroes and war correspondents, adventurers and Bohemians; a few became prolific pulpsters; a few became bestselling authors. And a few led haunted lives. Vol 1 includes the history of* Ghost Stories, *bios of every editor, and every Vol 1 author. Vol 2 includes bios of every Vol 2 author, every cover artist, and a gallery of all 64* Ghost Stories *covers.*

HOBO STORIES
By Patrick & Terence Casey • Introduction by John Locke
6 stories, 332 pages, $20

The Caseys were two brothers from San Francisco who broke into the pulps while still teenagers. Within a few years, they had conned their way into the prestigious pages of Adventure. Hobo Stories *reprints their series of exploits of a teenage hobo and his dog from* The Saturday Evening Post *(1914) and* Adventure *(1916-21). Included is their story of a teenage pulp writer from* Romance *(1920); and a lengthy introduction which explores the lives of the Caseys and the origins of their hobo stories.*

www.ingramcontent.com/pod-product-compliance
Lightning Source LLC
Chambersburg PA
CBHW030329030726
47499CB00003B/699